SACRAMENTO PUBLIC LIBRARY
828 "I" STREET
SACRAMENTO, CA 95814

08/2017

From bestselling aut
in an explosive nev
world....

Her past is a blank, her future uncertain....

Recovering from a shooting,
Ross leaves her job and trav
answers about her childhoc
Daoine Sidhe knight of the
entangled in an ancient hatred b ... two arcane forces.

He has given his body and soul to fight for his people....

Barred from his homeland along with his surviving brother knights, Nikolas Sevigny is embroiled in a conflict that threatens everything he holds dear. Only by uniting their resources can his people hope to prevail against Isabeau, the deadly Queen of the Light Court. He will do anything and use anyone to return home to Lyonesse.

When Nikolas encounters Sophie, he sees a tool to be used. The insouciant witch might be the key to unlocking every passageway that has been barred to the knights of the Dark Court, even as a fascination for her takes root in what's left of his soul.

Sophie has no intention of becoming anyone's pawn, yet the fierce Nikolas is so compelling, she can't deny the temptation that endangers her guarded heart.

As magic threatens Lyonesse, Queen Isabeau unleashes her merciless Hounds, and Nikolas and Sophie become embroiled in a race for survival. Meanwhile, the passion that ignites between them burns too hot to be denied and quickly turns into obsession.

Thank goodness they both know better than to fall in love...

Praise for Moonshadow

"*Moonshadow* is exactly what I expect of a Thea Harrison story, a stay-up-all-night read. Marvelous characters, lots of action and romance, and just the right touch of humor. This one goes on my keeper shelf. I loved this book."

~ Patricia Briggs—#1 *New York Times* bestselling author of the Mercy Thompson series

"*Moonshadow* hits all the right checkmarks on my must-have paranormal romance list: an Alpha hero, a heroine who kicks butt, worldbuilding that just keeps getting better, and a steamy plot that pulls me in from the first page!"

~ Carrie Ann Ryan—*NYT* Bestselling Author of *Wolf Betrayed*

"I loved this book. *Moonshadow* is Thea Harrison at her finest. I haven't been this excited since *Dragon Bound!*"

~ Kristen Callihan—*USA Today* bestselling author

"A brilliant new chapter in an enthralling saga! *Moonshadow* kicks off a new trilogy in Thea Harrison's fantastic *Elder Races* series. With a compelling heroine entering this world, this is a perfect place for readers to step into the ongoing story. The hero is intense, the heroine clever, and the sexual tension sizzling. Can't wait to find out what happens next!"

~ Jeffe Kennedy, Award Winning Author of *The Twelve Kingdoms* and *The Uncharted Realms*

"I'm already addicted to Thea Harrison's new world of Arthurian alpha warriors—especially after an American kick-ass heroine with serious magic powers teaches them a lesson about 21st century women!"

~ Eloisa James, *New York Times* bestselling author of *When Beauty Tamed the Beast*

"Scorching chemistry, perfect pacing & memorable characters sent me on a roller coaster ride of emotions! I want to live in the Moonshadow world."

~ Katie Reus, New York Times bestselling author of
Breaking Her Rules

"*Moonshadow* is a beautiful book and exactly what I needed—hot romance, wild sex and a happy ending. Please don't miss anything written by Thea Harrison. She is a wonder."

~ Ann Aguirre, New York Times bestselling author

"Thrilling and deliciously sexy, *Moonshadow* is a smart, action-packed introduction to a new adventure in Harrison's complex and compelling Elder Races world. Intrigue goes hand-in-hand with an addictive romance that will please new and established readers alike. I can't wait to see what comes next."

~ Elizabeth Hunter, bestselling author of
the Elemental Mysteries series

"A breathless, rollercoaster ride of a tale, complete with a fierce, capable heroine and a powerful hero worthy of her in every way. The bonds of love, trust, and friendship are stretched and sometimes snapped in a war of attrition that crosses time and worlds. Thea Harrison blows the doors off with some rollicking good storytelling in *Moonshadow*."

~ Grace Draven – USA Today bestselling author of
Radiance

Moonshadow

Thea Harrison

Moonshadow
Copyright © 2016 by Teddy Harrison LLC
ISBN 13: 978-0-9971201-8-9
Print Edition

Cover Photo-illustration © Gene Mollica Studio, LLC

This book is a work of fiction. The names, characters, places, and incidents are products of the writer's imagination or have been used fictitiously and are not to be construed as real. Any resemblance to persons, living or dead, actual events, locale or organizations is entirely coincidental.

All rights reserved. No part of this book may be used or reproduced, scanned or distributed in any manner whatsoever without written permission, except in the case of brief quotations embodied in critical articles and reviews.

I owe a huge debt of gratitude to Eloisa James, for the worldbuilding emails, her enthusiasm, and for truly terrific last minute advice. Any mistakes are entirely my own.

Also, many thanks to Patty, Carrie Ann, Kristen, Jeffe, Katie, Ann, Elizabeth, and Grace. I'm so honored to know all of you.

And last but certainly not least, I owe a big thank you to my assistant, Charlotte, and to beta reader extraordinaire, Andrea. I don't know how I got to be so lucky, but I'm glad you both came into my life.

Chapter One

A FTER ANOTHER NIGHT filled with nightmares, Sophie overslept. When she finally woke and looked blearily around her bedroom, she could tell by the angle of the light along the edges of the blinds that the day was no longer new.

The day had, in fact, not been new for some time. Her stomach took a nosedive as she snatched up her alarm clock. Damn it. Her technology curse had struck again. Resorting to an old-fashioned windup clock hadn't helped in the slightest, and the clock's hands had stopped at 4:26.

Ignoring the flare of aches in her shoulder, abdomen, and right thigh, she shoved upright and limped into the living room to check her cell phone. The screen confirmed what she already knew. She was horribly late.

Now she was faced with a choice that no coffee-drinking witch ever wanted to face. She could either fix coffee or throw her runes for a quick reading before she showered and left for her meeting.

A good night's sleep had become a thing of the

past, and she really needed that caffeine. But leaving her apartment without doing a reading had become unthinkable. Not since the shooting. She never missed throwing the runes in the morning for whatever message, good or bad, the reading might be able to tell her about the day.

She could cancel the meeting, and for a moment temptation tugged at her. Part of her wanted to drink coffee in the dark with the curtains shut while listening to the distant sounds of LA traffic, but that was how she had spent most of her time since being released from the hospital.

She needed a new game plan for how to approach life, and she wasn't going to find one in the shadows of her apartment. The only things lurking here were memories, second-guessing past actions, and regrets.

Getting out in the fresh air and talking to someone she didn't know might not solve any of her problems, but it would be a step outside her door. A step somewhere else. Maybe even a step in the right direction.

So. Coffee or reading.

Choosing was painful, but after leaping into the shower, dressing, and taking five precious minutes to put on makeup and capture her long, curling hair in a loose knot at the nape of her neck, she sat at the small kitchen table with a folded, embroidered tablecloth and the worn velvet bag that held her rune stones.

She paused only for a moment to glare at the stupid, time-consuming percolator sitting on her stove.

She had bought the pot to replace the stupid Keurig that had stopped working a few months back.

Turning to the business at hand, she unfolded the small tablecloth. She had stitched the gold thread embroidery on the royal blue cloth herself. The project had taken her weeks. As she didn't embroider as a regular hobby, the symbols didn't look professional or even, but the detail was meticulous, and every stitch was imbued with the invocations she had whispered as she worked on the cloth.

She used the small tablecloth for only one thing. As she carefully spread it flat, magic unfurled, changing the air above it where it lay. Holding the bag of runes in her right hand, she placed her left palm at the center of the cloth and centered herself.

Before the shooting, she would have just left the apartment without throwing the runes. The thought caused her to hesitate. It was not the best idea to rush through a reading, and she was going to be late as it was.

But no. Sometimes things change irrevocably. You turn a corner, hear a new song, read a book, fall in or out of love, or look at a painting in a different light.

Or you get shot several times.

Then no matter how you try, you can't unsee or unexperience something to make life what it used to be. The river always flowed downstream.

She poured the runes into her hand, concentrated on her near future, and tossed them gently onto the cloth. They were pretty, made of polished rose quartz with the runes etched into the stone and painted gold, and they showed brilliantly against the rich blue cloth.

She preferred Nordic rune stones over divination cards with painted pictures because the stones opened the right mental pathways for her. The images that came were true divination, not images created by some unknown commercial artist.

Concepts tumbled and shifted in her mind as she watched the stones roll to a stop. Raidho, for travel. Thurisaz, destruction and defense. Hagalaz, destructive, uncontrollable forces. Dagaz, the stone for breakthrough. Then she let her gaze go unfocused as she stared at the pattern they made.

That was when the visions came, when her attention to the rune patterns created windows into fate.

Silence in her small apartment. Distantly she heard the dead clock begin to tick again.

She listened to the breath she took. Let her eyelids fall in a blink.

As she opened her eyes, she caught a glimpse of a strange landscape. A new wind blew through the apartment, ruffling her hair and bringing with it a faint, acrid scent like smoke.

The scent meant violence and danger. Like other messages the wind brought to her from time to time, it wasn't a physical scent but intuitive and all too familiar.

Adrenaline spiked, causing a ghost of fiery pain to ripple through her body, localized in three places—her left shoulder, right thigh, and just under her ribs on the right side. As she pressed her hand to her abdomen, the figure of a man appeared.

He was turned away so that she looked at dark hair, the long, strong line of his neck, and broad shoulders.

He stood so close she felt like she could reach out to touch him and, oh my gods, all that Power he carried. How could one physical body contain it all? It was as if his skin thinly veiled a lightning bolt. He wasn't human. He couldn't be. He had to be one of the Elder Races.

The man was so vivid he made everything else around her pale by comparison. Even though she knew better, she lifted one of her hands and reached toward him. He was only a vision. He wasn't really here in her apartment.

Then he turned his head, and *he looked straight at her.*

No. That had to be an illusion. He couldn't be looking at her, not in her vision, stimulated by a spell of her own casting.

She received the impression of a strikingly handsome face, the planes and angles so sharp they appeared as if cut from an immortal blade. His glittering dark eyes held an indomitable will and a chilling ferocity.

Power shifted as he brought his body around to face her. So smoothly he moved, with a killer's grace that was purely inhuman. It caused the tiny hairs at the nape of her neck to rise. He held a sword clenched in one fist, and the long, wicked blade dripped with crimson blood. The gold of a heavy signet ring winked on his ring finger.

The sight slammed into her along with a realization.

He turned to face her.

He saw her and turned to face her.

Shock rocked her back in her seat. She parted her lips to say something. Whoops, or maybe Hi there. Or, I'm sorry.

The kind of thing you would say if you accidentally dialed a wrong number, or stepped on someone's foot, or got your psychic wires crossed.

Or interrupted a deadly immortal creature in the middle of a killing…

While she stared, the male's fine-cut nostrils flared. He flung a hand out toward her, fingers outspread, his own cruelly beautiful mouth shifting as he spat out a word. A lightning bolt of Power shot toward her. She felt it coming, a spear of pure, sizzling malice.

That wasn't supposed to happen in a vision either. What if it hit her?

Before she had fully formed the intention, she grabbed the edge of the magic cloth and yanked. Stones flew around the kitchen, breaking the pattern.

The vision shattered so hard it left her head aching, or maybe that was an echo from the psychic attack the man had flung at her. He vanished, along with the landscape. The lightning bolt never landed, although the image remained burned into her retina.

Her heartbeat galloped like a runaway horse while adrenaline pounded through her veins. As her vision cleared, she pressed shaking fingers against equally unsteady lips and looked around the familiar landscape of her apartment, taking in each detail in an effort to ground herself.

What the royal fuck was that? She had *never* experienced anything like that, and she had been practicing magic for as long as she could remember. Had the vision been so vivid it simply overwhelmed her sense of her immediate physical reality?

It couldn't have been real.

Could it?

Her head said no, but her gut said yes. He had behaved exactly as though he had seen her. She had sensed his Power, felt the attack flare toward her like a thrown spear. Her gut had no doubt that if that spear had hit, it would have injured her, perhaps severely.

What did it mean?

It took several breaths for her to regain her composure enough to leave. A dull throbbing took up residence behind her eyes. She strode into her bedroom, opened the small closet safe, pulled out her gun, and tucked it into the concealed-carry pocket of her purse. As she left the bedroom, she glanced one last time at her percolator with a deep sense of bitterness.

Man, she chose wrong.

She should have had that cup of coffee.

✧　✧　✧

CHANGE, THE WIND whispered. *New information is coming.*

No duh. Message received, loud and clear.

Sophie's heels clicked on the hot city pavement. With one hand, she traced the outline of the Glock tucked into the concealed-carry pocket. As she paused, she studied the nearby shops and traffic.

The surrounding scene looked placid and normal, a prosperous neighborhood basking in the southern California sun. There was no immediate, impending violence, nor any danger.

But both were close somehow, like a mass of dark clouds towering on the horizon, and they felt... complex. The warning on the wind wasn't about some random drive-by shooting or liquor-store holdup. It carried too much weight, too much history.

Settling her psychic barriers firmly into place, she continued down the sidewalk until she arrived at her destination. As she pushed through the glass door, she took in the details of the restaurant.

The place was upscale. Located a few blocks from Rodeo Drive in Beverly Hills, the interior was decorated with polished natural wood, gleaming metal, and large pieces of strategically placed, high-end art. It looked too good to be true, an elegant façade that hid something rotten underneath.

But she was just being cranky. The rune reading had left her unsettled and on edge. When she thought of the psychic attack that had been directed at her, her palms grew clammy and her heart started racing again. If that lightning bolt had hit, it could have killed her.

The image of the man haunted her, like Death shadowing a dying woman's footsteps—that glimpse of the hard male face, with dark, predatory eyes and a shock of black hair falling onto a strong forehead. His face had been handsome with an inhuman beauty but entirely ruthless, his mouth hard as if cut from stone, his expression chiseled with something that looked like an ancient, settled hatred.

Or hunger.

She still felt the tremendous shock of connection from when their eyes had met. It had jarred her out of herself so that she felt displaced and ungrounded. The normal irritations of navigating through LA traffic didn't touch her. Her feet did not seem to quite make contact with the pavement. She was not sure she was entirely housed in her own body. Even her caffeine headache felt as if it belonged to someone else.

Because of the unknown male's attack, she had broken the vision off too early. She hadn't had the chance to harvest enough information. Since the reading turned out to be incomplete and unsatisfactory, she had no idea if it was attached to her lunch meeting, to the imminent change she sensed on the wind, or the hint of impending danger.

Everything might very well be related, but it might not. So far, all she had were fragments of messages, and she didn't know how or even if they fit together. As a result, tension knotted the muscles between her shoulders and she studied everything with wary eyes.

For the meeting, she had slipped on a flowing, sleeveless linen pantsuit, undyed, the cuffs of the slacks ending above the ankle and showing off her slender feet in strappy-looking sandals that were, nevertheless, still sturdy enough to sprint in.

She had accessorized with chunky teal-colored jewelry layered over a few magic-sensitive silver pieces that she had spelled with protections and charms. The magic tinkled pleasantly to her inner ear, the jewelry shifting along her skin.

As she paused by the hostess stand, a beautiful woman dressed in a chic outfit walked up. The woman carried a pile of menus and looked bored.

"Do you have a reservation?" the woman asked, looking down Sophie's figure in frank assessment.

The hostess's expression was cool and calculating. Sophie wasn't quite sure if she had passed muster.

Fuck you. I put on makeup. I look like a million bucks.

"I don't know." She glanced over the crowded tables. "I'm meeting someone."

"What is the name?"

"Kathryn Shaw."

The hostess checked the computer screen, and her expression changed. In a much friendlier voice, she said, "Very good. Please follow me."

Kathryn Shaw's name had clearly pushed Sophie over some invisible line into acceptability. Mouth tilting in a sour slant, she followed the hostess to a quiet booth located in a corner where a woman waited.

As Sophie and the hostess approached, the woman slid to her feet with cool, liquid grace. Smiling, she held out her hand. "Sophie Ross? How nice to meet you."

"Dr. Shaw." As they shook hands, Sophie sized up the other woman quickly and without being as obvious as the hostess had been.

Kathryn Shaw was not quite what she had expected. The other woman was lightly tanned and had a tall, fine-boned figure, golden-brown hair that streamed in an elegant straight fall to her shoulders, large intelligent eyes, and the kind of poise that came from education, money, and knowing her worth in the world. She had good, sensitive hands, a firm grip, and immaculately tended fingernails. A hint of Power, well contained and as honed as a scalpel, clung to her figure like an expensive perfume.

Kathryn's cool, sleek sophistication was almost the antithesis of Sophie, who stood several inches shorter. Sophie's pale skin never tanned, her body tended to curve at breasts and hips, and her thick black hair had a mind of its own.

After trying one short, disastrous haircut that made her look like a twelve-year-old with cowlicks, she had learned to keep her hair long enough so the weight straightened out some of the unruliness. That way she could at least braid or pin it out of the way.

At the moment, the knot at the nape of her neck

had loosened as she had walked from the car to the restaurant, and it now fell in loose waves down her back. Her fingernails were no-nonsense and not nearly as well tended as the other woman's. She had clipped them herself yesterday.

At first glance, it wasn't obvious that Kathryn Shaw was Wyr, but then the muted lighting in the restaurant hit her just right, and her eyes flared with a golden reflection. Sophie guessed the other woman was not just Wyr but possibly some kind of avian. It would fit, with her narrow bone structure and build.

"Please, have a seat," Kathryn said.

Sophie slid into the opposite side of the booth.

The hostess took their drinks order and left them with menus. Sophie ordered coffee. Coffee coffee coffee. After everything that had happened, she wanted to fall into a cup and bathe in it.

Kathryn set her menu aside without looking at it and folded her beautiful hands on the table. "Thank you for coming. I half expected you to not show up."

"I thought about it," Sophie admitted. "But then curiosity got the better of me."

A serious flaw, curiosity. It had gotten her into trouble before. She devoutly hoped the flaw wouldn't turn fatal.

Violent images threatened to surface. This time the images were not divination but memory, and her body reacted in response, the ghost of pain pulsing in three spots again.

She thrust it aside. No vital organs had been damaged, and the pain was getting better every day. Focusing on the present, she added, "After all, you were tenacious enough."

Kathryn grinned. "Tenacity is a bad habit of mine."

Sophie's grin turned wry. "I was just thinking the same thing about me and curiosity."

The other woman laughed, her fine-boned face opening like a flower. "And so here we are."

"Yes." Despite keeping her barriers up, Sophie found she liked Dr. Kathryn Shaw. Out of sight, she laced her hands together in her lap and clenched her fingers tight.

Their waitress came, brought their drinks, and introduced herself. After a short discussion about the day's specials, they ordered lunch.

Gripped by nerves and wariness, she ordered the first thing she saw when she opened the menu, a simple chicken-and-mango salad. When the waitress left again, she cradled her coffee cup and took her first sip of the fragrant, dark liquid. It was excellent, with a smooth, roasted flavor.

She cleared her throat. "Perhaps now you can tell me what brought you all the way from New York. Especially since I threw away your letter and never responded to your first two phone calls."

She had, in fact, been convinced that Kathryn's letter had been a scam until the other woman had left a third message at the LA precinct where Sophie did consulting work.

Angry and disturbed at the intrusion into her life, Sophie had one of her department buddies, Rodrigo, run a background check on the caller, which was when she discovered that Kathryn Shaw really was a prominent, respected New York surgeon.

Only then did she return Kathryn's phone call. As guarded as Sophie had tried to be, Kathryn had dropped too many lures in front of her, offering at least one or two answers about her past. It proved impossible to resist. After talking for several minutes, Sophie had finally agreed to meet her in person.

Sophie had been adopted into a family of witches, and her past was a blank slate before she was five. She had no early childhood memories and no knowledge of where she had come from.

The details of her adoption had offered no clue either—after she had turned eighteen and accessed her records, she had done some cursory research on the names in her file, but the research had led nowhere. Either her parents had long since vanished, or the names given when she had been surrendered to the authorities had been false.

Kathryn hesitated, her calm, intelligent expression assessing. Then she reached into her large leather purse and drew out a few manila files. "First I need to put everything I'm about to say into context with a little history. My late father was the Earl of Weston, Francis Shaw."

Sophie's attention lingered on the files while her old pal curiosity reared its head again. "An earl—an English earl?"

"Yes."

"Does that make you titled as well?" Her knowledge of English titles was almost nonexistent.

Kathryn shrugged. "It does. I'm a countess, but I've lived in the States for so long I never use it. I've become very American. The most important title to me is doctor because that's the one I earned." She set the manila folders on the table. "My father was a unique man and very dedicated to certain causes. Some time ago—decades, really—I came to the States to attend medical school, and I chose to settle in New York. One of the causes my father was dedicated to was the British government. We did not see eye to eye on my choice of domicile." One corner of Kathryn's mouth lifted briefly, a bittersweet, affectionate expression.

Fascinated and somewhat envious of the other woman's obvious sense of loss, Sophie looked down at the table. Clearly Kathryn had loved her father deeply. What would it be like to have family you loved that deeply? And who loved you just as deeply in return?

Carefully she adjusted her coffee cup in its saucer. "He's deceased?"

"Yes, he died in the London bombing in 1995. Twenty Parliament members were killed that day."

Sophie only knew the bare bones about the terrorist bombing, just sound bites from media articles. This was the first time she had met anybody personally connected to such an event.

Even more mystified than ever about what any of this had to do with her, she said, "I'm sorry."

"Thank you. It happened a long time ago." Kathryn paused. Then in a brisker tone she continued. "He was dedicated to another cause that he began in the early eighteenth century, when he rescued his first group of children. It was something he felt passionate about, so he continued with rescues throughout the years. His efforts were sporadic and situational. Whenever he heard of trafficking or of children being abused, he would investigate, and if the situation called for it, he would take action. Sometimes the rescues involved children of the Elder Races, and sometimes they involved humans."

While she listened, Sophie realized she was gripping her hands so tightly her fingers had gone numb. Loosening her grip, she whispered, "Interesting."

Kathryn picked at the edge of her rolled linen napkin. "If he couldn't return the rescued children to their families, he would work with agencies all over the world to place them in appropriate homes. Security was a consideration for those placements. He always took care to make sure nothing could be traced back to the children's homes of origin so they never ran the danger of being found and exploited again."

Sophie took a deep, unsteady breath. Certainty settled into her bones.

She said, "I was one of those children, wasn't I?"

Kathryn cleared her throat, a quiet, delicate sound. "Yes, you were one of his last rescues."

"Does that mean I'm British?" She blinked, her perspective undergoing a massive shift. The searching she had done, both through traditional means and magical ones, had all been based in the United States. It had never occurred to her to search outside the States.

"I'm sorry, I don't know. I don't have any information on the details of your rescue either."

Exploited, Kathryn had said. Trafficking. Sophie had been five years old—or younger, when he had found her. God, she had been a baby. A sudden wave of revulsion chilled her skin, and her blood pounded in her ears.

Her voice a harsh, uncertain scrape in her throat, she said bluntly, "I was a virgin when I first had sex."

She was also an asshole magnet, and every jerk she had ever dated had been a loser or worse. But that was neither here nor there at the moment.

The other woman's expression lightened with a gentle smile. "It sounds like my father rescued you in time."

Their waitress came with their lunches. Sophie's salad looked exquisite, and Kathryn had ordered steak. For the next few minutes, they ate in silence, which gave Sophie a chance to recover her poise.

After she had eaten enough to placate the empty hole in her stomach, she said, "The names of my birth parents in my records. Are they fake?"

Kathryn picked up the top manila folder. "I think so. This is the file my father kept on you. I'm sorry, there isn't much in it."

Sophie had been eyeing the files while she ate. As Kathryn offered it to her, she snatched at it and flipped it open.

Like Kathryn had warned, there wasn't much information. Just a few pages of notes, along with a photograph of a small, serious-looking girl with a mop of unruly black hair, pale skin, a light dusting of freckles, and a delicate pixie face.

Somewhere in the conversation, Sophie had lost most of her capacity for skepticism, and the photograph laid the last of it to rest. As she had matured into adulthood, the delicate pixie face had lost its youthful roundedness and turned more angular, but the girl was clearly, indisputably her.

She scanned the contents quickly, taking in key words.

Precocious. Highly magical. Mostly human child, approximately four years old.

Mostly human. Yeah, that about summed it up.

Parents, unknown. Domicile, unknown. Nonverbal, possibly trauma induced.

There were more notes, along with a few handwritten numbers—the number of digits and the way they had been written made them look like American phone numbers—then the name of an adoption agency in

Kentucky. The adoption agency that had handled her case. She flipped over the last page, but there was nothing more.

"That's it," she muttered as her stomach sank. "That's everything."

Everything about her early childhood, jotted down on a few yellowing pages. It felt unreal, like something out of a Dickens novel or a Spanish soap opera. But it wasn't a story. This was her life.

She hadn't verbalized it as a question, but Kathryn responded as if she had. "I'm sorry. I wish there was more I could tell you."

The back of Sophie's eyes burned, but she had stopped shedding tears over ancient history a long time ago. Snapping the file shut, she forced herself to think.

"You tracked me through the adoption agency in Kentucky," she said. "When I turned eighteen, I accessed my records and left contact information."

"Yes." Kathryn set her empty plate to one side.

The waitress stopped by. Kathryn ordered coffee, and when the waitress returned, she refilled Sophie's cup as well.

"Well, this has been fascinating," Sophie said when they were alone again. She met the other woman's eyes. "Even if there isn't much information, I'm grateful to have the file. The most important thing is that it shifts the geography of where I need to search if I want to try to find out anything more about my past—which is something I might decide to do. But I still don't understand why you've gone to the expense and trouble to meet with me. So far, we haven't talked about anything that couldn't have been said over the phone or FedExed to me."

"That's true." Kathryn smiled. "But everything we've discussed was just the prelude to what comes next. You see, I'm the executor of my father's specific, detailed, and quixotic will."

Sophie bit her lip as a bolt of quick, unexpected laughter shook through her body. She thought, if Kathryn says I've inherited something, I might lose it. Because it really would be just like an email scam.

She said, "Your father died over twenty years ago, and you're still not done executing the terms of his will?"

"Unfortunately, no, I'm not." Kathryn's smile turned dry. She picked up the second manila folder and offered it to Sophie. "Almost everything was settled years ago, but there is one last task yet to be completed. There's an old property that—really, I don't know how else to put it—remains stubborn. The estate has been in the family for hundreds of years. The last time my father was in the house was when he was a young man, which was a very long time ago."

The two-natured Wyr could be extremely long-lived. Some rare breeds were among the first generation of Elder Races and considered to be immortal. They could be killed, but they would never die of old age.

"You've never been there yourself?" Sophie asked.

She opened up the file to scan the contents.

Photographs of a massive medieval house lay inside. Part stone fortress, part monstrous architectural folly, it brooded against a backdrop of ancient, tangled forest. The land fell away behind the house, and in one corner a lake or the edge of a river glimmered. She looked through each of the photos, studying the different angles. The palms of her hands tingled as she handled the pictures.

The photos themselves weren't magic, not exactly. But something about the house was, or the land, and the camera had managed to capture a hint of it.

Kathryn told her, "Oh, I've been there several times, but I've not been inside the house. Nobody has since the last time my father went in. It... stopped letting people in."

Sophie rested her left palm on one of the photographs and searched for that elusive hint of magic. When she connected with it, her palm tingled again. She sensed a distant breeze blowing through the trees in the scene. The house had five gables.

A subtle, almost indefinable shift rippled under her palm. She leaned forward, her attention sharpening.

No, not five gables. There were seven.

What the hell.

Belatedly, what Kathryn had said sank in, and she looked up at the other woman. She raised an eyebrow. "What do you mean, the house won't let anybody in?"

Kathryn let out a soft laugh. "I know how that

sounds. I'm anthropomorphizing a building, but I don't know how else to say it. It's a strange place. You would have to experience it to believe it."

Sophie glanced down again at the photograph that lay underneath her palm. "Tell me more."

"The Weston family seat is in the West Marches, the land that borders England and Wales. The West Marches is a witchy place and intensely magical, with more crossover passageways per acre than anywhere else in the world. Many wars have been fought all over that land. Once upon a time, or so the story goes, there had been a crossover passage on this very spot." Kathryn reached over to tap one of the photographs.

"You mean there isn't one there now?"

As Sophie asked the question, her mind started working on the concept. What could destroy a crossover passageway? Crossover passageways had been around since the Earth was formed, when time and space had buckled. They led to Other lands, where modern technology didn't work, time flowed differently than it did on Earth, and the sun shone with a different light.

Sophie chewed on her lip as she thought.

Sometimes explosives were used to close small passageways if they were unstable and only led to tiny pockets of land, like caves. To destroy a major crossover passageway, a natural disaster like an earthquake could be powerful enough. Land crumbling, tectonic plates shifting, that sort of thing.

Or magic.

Lots and lots of magic. An almost inconceivable amount of very destructive magic. A shiver rippled through her at the thought.

"No, there isn't a passageway now, at least not a functioning one," Kathryn replied. "War happened. There was a battle on that spot, and the crossover passage shattered. Some bright ancestor of mine decided it would be a good idea to build a house there in order to seal his conquest of the land, but the land still had all that broken crossover magic. It still does, in fact. Family legend says from the very beginning when the first timbers were raised, the house was always strange, and it got stranger as time went on."

"You have an ancestor who built on a broken crossover passageway?" Sophie snorted.

"Boggles the mind, doesn't it?" Kathryn gave her a speaking look.

Sophie grinned. "I can just imagine how odd the house must be."

"The stories get pretty entertaining. Entire wings disappeared and reappeared, and the scenery outside the windows changed. People got lost inside, and they couldn't find their way out again. One pair of children disappeared for weeks before they reappeared again, dirty and starved, and babbling of strange adventures."

She leaned forward. "Do you have written records of what they saw?"

Kathryn shook her head. "There are hardly any

written records other than land ownership, just legends passed down by word of mouth. After a couple of generations, the family couldn't cope with the strangeness any longer. They built another house and moved and left this place abandoned. Every few years, someone would go to check on the property to see if it was still standing. My father said the last time he went, he could turn the key in the lock, but he couldn't get the door to open. The last time I checked the property, I couldn't even get the key in the lock."

Sophie looked down at the photograph she still touched, drawn there by the frisson she felt underneath her palm. Gabled and oddly shadowed, the house looked like something out of *Dark Shadows*, a cult show that ran on classic TV networks and had both delighted and terrified her as a child. "Did anybody try to break a window?"

"My father said he tried, but the window wouldn't break." Kathryn smiled. "The place is like a Rubik's cube. The pieces are all there—I think—but none of the colors line up. We took to calling it the family albatross. It's been hanging around our necks all this time."

Sophie raised her eyebrow again. "Did you hire experts to try to get in?"

"Of course, but no one managed it. I don't think anyone has walked through those halls since before the sixteenth century and only then intermittently, as the house had been abandoned some time before. The gods only know what might have been left inside. There aren't any written records of that either."

"How mysterious," Sophie murmured.

Kathryn turned brisk. "Now we come to the crux of the matter. The terms of my father's will state that I am to seek out the children he rescued, one by one, and extend an offer. Each person may have ninety days to find a way to get inside the house. If anyone does figure out a way in, they may take ownership of the house, any contents that may still be in it, and the grounds, which includes five acres, a small lake, and a small, four-room house that used to be the gatekeeper's cottage. They also receive a trust that is entailed to the property. Both the property and the entailment can be passed on to their beneficiaries."

Sophie blinked. And blinked again.

Grounds. House. Two houses.

Kathryn really was offering her an inheritance.

The incredulous laughter threatened to come back. She repeated, "A trust. You mean actual money?"

"Yes," Kathryn said. "The trust is tied up in investments, so the annual income is self-perpetuating. It isn't an outrageous fortune, but it's enough to pay the property taxes, cover the cost of grounds upkeep, and there's perhaps twenty-five thousand pounds a year over that. Depending on fluctuations in the exchange rate, that's roughly around thirty-seven thousand dollars a year. Let's face it, after so long, the interior of the manor house must be unlivable, but I've actually stayed in the gatekeeper's cottage, and while the furnishings are dated, it's cozy enough. If you buy a Pocket Wi-Fi, you can even get Internet service inside the cottage itself, although there's too much land magic in the countryside to get reliable connectivity every-where."

"Thirty-seven thousand dollars," Sophie repeated flatly. "A year. Just for breaking into a house."

Kathryn laughed. "Keep in mind, nobody has man-aged to do it so far. And yes, we will pay to get rid of the family albatross."

"A trust that can generate thirty-seven thousand dollars a year is a hell of a generous payment." Sophie traced the edge of the photograph with a forefinger.

"It's only a portion of the family estate, and Eng-land is an expensive place to live," Kathryn warned. "That kind of annual income wouldn't go nearly as far as it would in, say, the American Midwest. Although the cost of living is much cheaper outside of London. If somebody were interested and wanted to make a go of it, I think they could live well enough if their needs were modest and they were frugal. There would be no rent or mortgage to worry about. That would already be taken care of, which would make the money stretch a lot further. But in order to receive the inheritance, you—or someone—would have to prove that they had actually gotten inside the house."

"What kind of proof would you require?"

"Photos would be sufficient, if a camera would

work inside the house, but the broken crossover magic might prevent that. If a camera would work, given the position of the buildings, you should be able to get a clear photo of the gatekeeper's cottage as you look out the front windows. Or if you could get someone to take a photo of you standing inside the house, that would also work. Failing that, a signed affidavit from reliable witnesses would be acceptable."

Sophie touched the edge of the roofline to feel the tingle of magic again. "Ninety days is a long time," she said slowly. "For a lot of people, taking a two-week vacation overseas is stretching their resources, let alone taking that much time away from their jobs."

Kathryn nodded. "I'm afraid I can't help with the issue of taking time off work, but as far as the rest of the trip goes, the estate would provide a temporary living stipend along with travel expenses." One corner of her mouth tilted up. "Honestly, I think most people have taken the challenge just to get a three-month paid vacation. They either had no interest or any ability in trying to get into the main house itself."

Instead of looking angry at the possibility of exploitation, the other woman still looked amused. Since the same thought had occurred to Sophie, she asked carefully, "That doesn't bother you?"

Kathryn shrugged. "The money comes out of the trust that was set up specifically for this property. Since it's entailed, I couldn't access those funds for myself even if I wanted to. If somebody could just break into the house, I can stop hunting down people my father rescued and making the same offer over and over again, but other than that, it doesn't particularly bother me one way or another."

"You have been doing this for over twenty years," Sophie murmured reflectively. She was almost unaware of how her fingers stroked the photograph. Almost. "You must be very tired of it."

"Actually, it's become something of a hobby." Kathryn sipped coffee and set her cup carefully back on its saucer. "My career is stressful and demanding. If I'm not careful, it can suck the life out of me. This takes me outside of that, and it even gives me a reason to travel. Finding people whom my father rescued when they were children has become rewarding and even comforting in a way. It has been heartwarming to see how far his influence spread. He saved a lot of lives, and I'm really proud of that. Of him."

Sophie rearranged the photos in front of her, watching her hands. "I'm sure not everybody would have welcomed it. Until I had a friend at the LAPD trace the phone number you left in your message and run a background check on you, I was certain you were running some kind of scam."

"True." Kathryn nodded. "And sometimes it's hard to discover that not everybody has thrived after being rescued. One died in a car accident, and someone else joined the army and was killed in battle. But more often than not, people are like yourself."

I never said I was thriving, Sophie thought. Her body throbbed again, the three points of fire in her thigh, shoulder, and abdomen.

But then wasn't that exactly the kind of impression her good linen suit and chunky jewelry was supposed to convey?

Kathryn studied her curiously. "The notes in your file said my father couldn't discover what your inhuman side was, so he chose to place you with magical humans. Your adoptive family in the witches' demesne—were they a good match for you?"

Sophie's hand fisted where it rested on the photograph.

Oh, they were a great match. Mom baked homemade cherry pies and sprinkled them with sugar laced with magic wishes. Dad came home from work every day at 4:30 P.M. They let me pick out the family dog, Snuggles, and every year, it took me until midafternoon to open all my presents under the Christmas tree.

She couldn't voice such sarcasm in the face of Kathryn's kindness. Instead, she said somewhat huskily, "Yeah. They were great."

So great she left the moment she could when she was eighteen. After a brief attempt to find out who her birth parents were, she had struck out on her own, and she'd been blowing like a tumbleweed ever since.

Kathryn smiled. "I'm glad to hear it. And now you're a consultant for the LAPD."

"That's right," Sophie replied. "I was until about a

month ago."

One month ago, when good people I knew and cared about died. When I almost died.

But she didn't say that either. None of that was any of Kathryn's business.

"That says something about the quality of your work. They don't hire just anybody." Kathryn asked, "What are you doing now?"

Trying to recover, to figure out what to do next with her life. Slowly panicking as the medical bills roll in and the money runs out. Consulting jobs didn't come with paid sick leave.

To give herself time to reply, Sophie reached for her coffee and let the dark, roasted flavor roll over her tongue.

She said, "As it happens, I'm between contracts. I took a leave of absence from my consulting job. The LAPD wants me back, but I haven't decided yet if I'm going to return."

Kathryn leaned forward. "So you're actually in a good position to consider taking this offer. Are you interested?"

Sophie glanced down at the pictures of the house again, and she wanted to go so badly she could taste the desire.

The house fascinated her. But more than that, she could have ninety more days to fully recuperate while she decided what to do next. She could put her things in storage so she wouldn't have to pay rent while she was gone, which would stretch her current resources further.

If she wanted, she could even renew the search to see if she could discover anything more about her family and her past, although she wasn't under any illusion about that. The Earl of Weston would have had significant contacts and resources to use in his searches, and she probably wouldn't find anything more about her birth family than he had.

Old habit made her school her features in order to hide how much the offer meant to her.

"I don't know," she lied. "I need a few days to think it over."

Even as she said it, she knew she was going to take the offer. Hell, she might even escape from whatever dark menace haunted her rune readings lately, along with the owner of that predatory, handsome face.

Or if she went, she could be running right toward it. Toward him.

Ah, well. You can't fix stupid. And you can't heal crazy.

Knowing that she might be running toward trouble wouldn't stop her from going or confronting whatever fate awaited her. But it would at least make her somewhat more cautious than usual.

Hopefully.

From Kathryn's pleased expression, Sophie could

tell her prevarication hadn't fooled the other woman in the slightest.

Kathryn told her smoothly, "Of course you should think it over. Take all the time you need."

Chapter Two

A S QUICKLY AS the image of the strange woman had appeared, it vanished again, dissipating on a curling breath of fog-filled air.

Nikolas spun on one heel as he looked sharply around the clearing, sword at the ready, but there was no further sign of attack. Heavy, aged oak trees surrounded an emerald lawn, interspersed with park benches. Not twenty meters away, the waist-high fieldstone fence that bordered the small park seemed as insubstantial as a shadow, as heavy fog pressed all around, blocking out the sun, limiting sight and muffling noise.

On the other side of the fence, traffic sounded heavy and distant. A male called out, and he tensed, but the voice sounded normal, cheerful. Oblivious.

"Came on bloody quick, that did!"

Another man shouted back, "Never seen a fog roll in so fast!"

"All this astonishment has given me a thirst. Meet you at the pub in fifteen?"

The second voice called out, "Aye!"

Dismissing the exchange as harmless, Nikolas turned his attention to the carnage he had wrought.

Four slain Hounds lay scattered around the small clearing, and killing them had not been neat or simple. On edge, muscles still leaping with the aftermath of combat, he studied their massive, fur-covered bodies. Each weighed eighteen, twenty stone easily. They looked like a cross between wolf and mastiff, and something else that was entirely monstrous.

Despite their size and weight, he knew from dark experience that they could run tirelessly for kilometers, track with relentless tenacity, and rend a body to pieces with long, knifelike claws and razored teeth.

Instinct urged him to leave the scene quickly while the unnatural fog still lingered and could mask his presence, but he held himself in check. As he waited, he bent to wipe his sword clean on the grass and slipped it back into the sheath he carried on a harness between his shoulders. When the blade slid home, he felt the spell on the sheath activate, cloaking both sword and sheath from sight.

His wait did not go unrewarded.

As he watched, the body of the nearest slain Hound shimmered and began to change. Bones realigned, fur disappeared, and the long, wicked muzzle shrank back until the monster had disappeared and a dead man lay in its place.

Once they had been killed, the Hounds always shifted back to their human forms.

With the toe of one boot, Nikolas flipped the body over and took in the dead man's features. It was nobody he recognized. He searched the man's clothes, pulling out everything and stuffing the contents into his pockets to examine later. As the bodies of the other Hounds shimmered and changed, he did the same to them.

None of the slain men were Morgan, but Nikolas already knew that. Morgan was infinitely more dangerous than these creatures and would be so much more difficult to kill.

Nikolas lived for the chance to be the one who accomplished that feat. If Morgan were killed, his death would be a massive blow to the Queen and her Hounds. His death could change the course of the war between the Light and the Dark Courts.

Magic sparked here and there in the items Nikolas took—a ring on one male's finger, a medallion worn on a necklace on another. He took those items carefully, using a handkerchief to keep from touching them until he got a chance to examine them more closely.

When he was finished, he gave the bodies one last, frowning glance. How had they found him? Had he somehow given away his location, or had the encounter been sheer bad luck? And who had called the fog down to cloak what had obviously been intended to be his murder?

Morgan would have had more than enough magic to conjure the fog, but Nikolas didn't sense his presence anywhere nearby, and if Morgan had been near, he would have been present for the attack. Nikolas would give Morgan credit for one thing—he was not the type of man to stand back and let others fight his battles for him.

Had it been the unknown woman Nikolas had seen?

He had felt her first, a cool breath of presence entirely different from the red-hot killing rage that had ruled him only moments previously.

When he had turned to confront this new threat, he had seen her—dark, curling hair, pale skin and a scattering of freckles across a thin, angular face. Black Irish coloring, with high cheekbones pressing against the delicate skin that stretched over them. Lips, plush and pink. Eyes a light, indeterminate color, possibly gray or hazel. Height, irrelevant.

His first reaction had been irrelevant as well. She looked tired, possibly ill, he thought, and her face was too thin, almost gaunt.

Then their gazes had collided, and those pale, uninteresting eyes of hers had widened. She looked stunned that he had seen her, and as she opened her mouth, he moved to forestall whatever she might have said. It might have been a spell or a curse, or a simple how do you do. He didn't give a shit.

After he had lashed out at her, the vision had splintered. Now he couldn't sense her anywhere.

But he knew what she looked like. He knew what

her Power felt like. If she had been working in collusion with Isabeau's Hounds, she had just signed her own death warrant. Didn't matter when or how long it took. If Nikolas ever ran into her, he would make sure she regretted her collusion before she died.

The fog was beginning to disperse, the veil on the carnage in the clearing growing thin. His clothes were wet with the slain men's blood. It was time for him to leave, but first he had to cleanse the scene.

Kneeling, he placed his flattened hands on the ground and sank his awareness deep into the land. When he connected with the land magic that was so rich and abundant, he asked it to take the bodies. After a few moments, the land responded. The ground shifted, and the slain Hounds sank below the grass.

Once he had rid the clearing of the evidence of the battle, his attention turned to the Sainsbury bag on the ground. He had almost forgotten why he had stopped in this village in the first place. Gathering it up, he strode rapidly along the path to the nearby car park.

At least he had bought petrol before he had gone in search of a supper he could eat on the road. He didn't take time to change out of his blood-soaked clothes. Several moments later, as the fog dispersed completely and the late afternoon sun came out in full force, he pulled onto the motorway and sped north.

✧   ✧   ✧

LATER THAT NIGHT, Nikolas's black Porsche flowed

along the hairpin curves in the forest road. Dense, heavy foliage pressed in from all angles, drenching the air with the sense of an immense, green life that carpeted the land for miles around, while an early harvest moon hung low over the horizon.

He kept his windows down to let the fresh air stream in, on high alert for the slightest hint of anything out of the ordinary. Gatherings were a calculated but necessary risk, and they always put him on edge. After the Hounds' attack, he was even more on edge than usual.

Once he had put several kilometers between him and the scene of the attack, he'd pulled over to change out of his bloody clothes and examine the contents he'd stripped from the bodies. The magic items had been relatively uninteresting—either amulets of protection or strength enhancement. There were four mobile phones, all with passcodes that he didn't have time to try to break at the moment.

He tucked those away to examine more closely later, then he rifled through wallets, pocketed the men's IDs and cash, and tossed the wallets away. He found nothing to indicate how the Hounds had located him and nothing that seemed to connect them to the unknown woman in the vision.

After examining everything, he continued on his journey, and he'd had several hours to think about what had happened.

Earlier, when the questing, feminine Power had

brushed against him, he had bristled and whirled to attack, but now that the heat of battle had died down, he was fairly certain that the woman's psychic signature had felt distinctly different from both the magical fog and the Hounds.

And the woman he had seen—at first she hadn't looked afraid or guilty as if she had been caught doing something underhanded. Instead, she had simply looked amazed. He had received the impression of black, curling hair falling into wide, startled eyes. Then she began to reach out to him as if to see if he were real. It had been a gesture of wonder, not aggression.

Perhaps the psychic connection had been an accident. The thought was outlandish, but it wasn't impossible, in which case, no harm, no foul.

Or perhaps his impressions were wrong and he had indeed disrupted a spy, and the only accident had been that he had caught the other magic user before she could throw another spell. That was the possibility that kept him poised like a weapon, ready to go on the offensive at the first sign of trouble.

While he was lost in thought, the road he traveled narrowed to one paved lane, then the pavement turned to gravel. The steady purr of the car's turbo engine never faltered. After driving some distance farther, he finally came to a large open clearing. One end was covered with gravel along the edge of a crumbling fieldstone fence.

A variety of vehicles and motorcycles clustered on

the graveled end. He pulled the Porsche up beside a large Harley-Davidson. As he cut the engine, opened his door, and climbed out, quiet settled over the area. The cool, damp air smelled like woodsmoke. He reached into the car for his jacket, settled his sword harness into place over it, and slung a heavy canvas bag over one wide shoulder.

Several meters away, the shadowed figure of a large man slipped into view like a knife pulled from a sheath. The figure moved with a leashed aggression, and for a moment an answering aggression flared in Nikolas in response. He controlled an impulse to reach for his sword.

"Nikolas." The man's voice was deep, rough, and familiar. Nikolas's flare of aggression subsided as he realized the approaching figure was Rhys. "When you weren't here to greet us, we got worried."

"I ran into a pack of Hounds," Nikolas replied tersely.

Rhys hesitated. "Is everything okay?"

"They're dead. I'm not. Situation handled."

As the other man drew closer, Nikolas took note of the lines of tiredness on Rhys's face. While they stood close to the same height, that was where the similarity between the two men ended. Nikolas had black hair, dark eyes, and a dark nature, and had a slim, rangy build filled with whipcord strength, whereas Rhys was a wide, solid mass of muscle.

Rhys looked hard and drawn, and a new scar

slashed across his cheekbone.

Noticing the direction of his attention, Rhys told him with a tight smile, "You should see the other guy. Oh wait, you can't. He's dead and buried too."

"I expected nothing less." When the other man reached him, Nikolas hauled him in for a hard hug.

For the briefest of moments, Rhys's body remained stiff and unresponsive in his embrace. Then the other man relaxed and returned the hug.

When Rhys pulled back, he gave Nikolas a narrow look. "You think running into a pack of Hounds was an accident? Or do you think they somehow found you?"

Nikolas didn't want to waste time talking about the unknown woman. They had other things they needed to focus on. "When I find out, I'll let you know."

"Well, you're here now, and that's all that counts, right? Come on." Rhys slapped his back as he stepped back. "I know we don't have long, but we can take a few moments before we start. Gareth brought food."

Nikolas followed him down a narrow, overgrown path toward another clearing and the light of a small campfire. Across the clearing lay a shadowed, ancient ring of standing stones. Nikolas glanced at it before turning his full attention to the group of talking men standing or squatting around the fire.

The sight was like taking a sword thrust to the gut. He took grim note of their total.

He had known their number had diminished before

he had come, but seeing was quite a different thing from knowing. Only eight men had answered Nikolas's summons. Only eight, when they had once been a hundred warriors strong.

Quickly he searched the faces of those who were present. Rhys, Ashe, Thorne, Gareth, Cael, Rowan, Braden, and gods, it was so good to see Gawain again.

Each one stepped forward to greet him with a tight clench. Gawain was the last, most fierce embrace.

"Good to see you," he said roughly.

"And you." Gawain clapped his back. The other male had a fist like iron. Nikolas bore the blow gladly. "We made it to another solstice."

"That we did." Nikolas took a deep breath as he and Gawain shared a sober glance.

He could see the dark knowledge in Gawain's expression although neither man said a word.

If their circumstances didn't change drastically, and soon, their group might not see another solstice. The last cash withdrawal Nikolas had made on the bank accounts meant they were low on funds, although that in itself wouldn't pull them under. Nikolas could always find or make plenty of money.

No, the real killer was that they were isolated from one another. They had no sanctuary where they could gather to rely on one another and get true rest and refreshment in safety.

For decades now, they had been searching and fighting, and dying, and despair might be the worst, deadliest killer of all. Ferociously he shoved that thought out of his head. Despair had no place here. It had been a long, dark battle, in the darkest of wars, but they would hold. They would all hold.

"Come on," he said to Gawain as he handed over the canvas bag. "Distribute this so we can do what we came to do."

They strode to the fire ring, where the others made room for them. Gareth shoved a rough sandwich into Nikolas's hand, made of grilled sausage wrapped in bread. After rummaging in a Tesco bag, Ashe pulled out a pint of Guinness, popped the tab of the can, and offered it.

As Nikolas took the can, Ashe said, "What took you so long?"

"I got sidetracked." He took a long swallow.

The other man frowned. "I thought you said you were going to take the M6 north."

"Not that kind of sidetracked," he said drily, looking around the group. "But I'm here now."

Even though he had already eaten, he gladly tucked into the simple food, more to soak in the companionship than for need of the sustenance itself. As he ate, Gawain dug into the canvas bag Nikolas had brought and handed out thick packets of cash to everyone.

The passing of time pressed down on them, but it was good to take a few minutes to just be together. The food was hot and filling, useful since the group would be expending a great deal of energy in tonight's work, and there would be no time to linger when they had finished.

Nikolas listened to the other men talk, their quiet, tired voices filling the clearing. For all too brief a time, the arid wasteland that had taken over his soul eased into something that felt suspiciously like warmth and comfort.

Something that felt like home.

While the men talked of their adventures over the recent months, Nikolas remained silent, watching their faces. Living isolated and constantly on the run had marked them. Once quick to laugh and joke, Cael's profile had turned severe and closed to scrutiny. Ashe's demeanor had turned hard and sardonic, like a sword perpetually half-pulled. And just as he had when Nikolas had hugged him, Rhys held himself back, standing slightly apart from the rest, unable to relax and join in the camaraderie.

They were worn to the bone, like lean, starved wolves caught in an endless winter, caught perpetually in a long, savage fight for survival.

I need to find a safe haven for all of us before it's too late, Nikolas thought. Somewhere we can defend and claim as our own, at least for now, until we can find a way to break through to home. They need a place to rest and recuperate.

His thoughts were nothing new. He had been preoccupied with them for some time. It was challenging to try to find a safe, defensible haven that couldn't be detected or breached by their enemy. Right now the longer the group remained together, the greater the danger became. That danger cut away at the most fundamental aspect of the ties of friendship and common purpose that bound them all together.

When he finished the sandwich and swallowed down the last of the Guinness, the wasteland took over his soul again, and he was filled with nothing again but purpose and strength of will.

Nikolas said, "Time's up. Let's go."

Chewing the last of their food and gulping down their drinks, the others stood and strode across the clearing.

The stranded Daoine Sidhe knights of the Dark Court gathered at the ring of ancient standing stones under the pale light of the harvest moon.

Whenever the Daoine Sidhe gathered, they raised the natural energies of the world around them. It occurred involuntarily as each knight's Power came in contact with another's. A few knights working actively together could knock out the power grid in a large town or small city.

As a group, they couldn't remain together for long before the Light Fae Queen Isabeau and her deadly Hounds fixed on their location and launched an attack. They were too few and the Hounds too many. No matter how many Hounds they killed, Isabeau and Morgan could create more, whereas every time one of their group died, they suffered an irreplaceable loss.

Blocked from sanctuary in their own land, they had no recourse but to live on the run and occasionally stand and fight. And, eventually, no matter how well they fought, they died.

For that reason, Nikolas had chosen the night's gathering place at a stone circle located outside a remote village in Northumberland, more than two hundred kilometers away from any of their true concerns. Even so, they would only be able to take a precious few hours together at most before they would have to go their separate ways again. Isolation might be eating away at their souls, but it was also their most important means of survival.

From where Nikolas stood at the center of the stone circle, he watched the other knights step into their positions. Wherever the moon's shadow touched them, something of their true nature appeared. Moonshadow always revealed truth to those who knew how to see it.

Gawain walked through the shadow of one tall standing stone, and briefly, Nikolas saw a vision of his real nature.

Gargoyle blood ran in Gawain's veins. While he stood in the moonshadow, Gawain's face came straight from a nightmare, and gigantic wings flared behind him. He wore chain mail armor, and a sheathed sword marked with magic runes was strapped to his back.

The next moment, the other man stepped away from the standing stone and out of the shadow. The vision faded, and his physical form appeared once again, a large, somewhat rough-looking man with strong, human features, wearing biking leathers.

Demons, the Dark Court of the Daoine Sidhe had been called, although they were not Demonkind.

Changelings. Impure.

Gods' monsters.

If they were monsters, Nikolas thought, why then so be it. These were the most fierce, loyal warriors he had ever known. He would always choose his great-hearted monsters over life, luxury, and always, always over the corrupt purebloods of Isabeau's Light Court.

Ashe and Rowan were dhampyres, the strange, rare creature born of a union between a half-breed Fae or Elf and a human undergoing the transformation to Vampyre. Several of the men, Nikolas included, had Wyr blood flowing through their veins. Some had stronger animal natures than others. In the moonshadow's magic, Cael's Fae features were covered with the light green skin of a medusa, the pupils of his eyes vertical slits, and Nikolas knew all too well what would be revealed in his features.

The face of a feline beast, part man and part leopard.

They were all Fae yet not fully Fae. They were among the rarest of all the Elder Races. In modern-day slang, they were "triple threats," creatures with the blood of three different races flowing through their veins. The strongest, most magical—the most tainted.

The Fae of the Light Court called them *abomination*.

Nikolas called them brothers.

Letting his hands rest at his sides, he turned them so the palms faced the middle of the circle. He began to chant an ancient invocation, calling in a deep voice upon the balanced energies of sun and moon.

Power rose from the earth and the standing stones. One by one, the others joined in. The combined magic in their voices cut through the fabric of this land, reaching out to another.

The figure of a woman appeared. Her transparent form was less distinct than they had achieved through previous callings, but they had so few numbers now available to cast the spell.

The woman was beautiful in the way of the Fae, with angular features and elegantly pointed ears, but instead of having the pale skin and black hair of the Dark Fae, or the golden skin and tawny hair of the Light Fae, she was spotted like a cheetah, her skin speckled with golden freckles.

Large green eyes and high cheekbones contributed to the effect. Her hair was a deep russet color, with streaks of gray at her temples. Laugh lines kissed the skin at the corners of her eyes and mouth, although currently there was no smile on her face. Instead, like the men who called upon her, the woman's expression was grim and tight.

As the others held the spell strong and steady, Nikolas eased out of the casting. He said, "Annwyn."

She turned, searching until she caught sight of him. Nikolas knew from experience she wouldn't be able to see or hear the others in the circle, only him as he stood in the center.

Her expression lit with gladness. "Nikolas. It's so good to see you."

"And you," he told her. "Have you made any more progress in waking Oberon?"

She shook her head, frustration evident. "Not since he fell under the enchantment. I don't have the healing skills needed. None of our healers know what to do for Oberon. His body is cold as ice. I would think he was dead if it weren't for the fact that I can feel a spark of his life force buried deep in his body, or the fact that his Power is raging out of control."

His mouth tightened. Oberon was the strongest of the Dark Court, a weather mage, and their King. If his Power was left to rampage unchecked without his iron will to control it, it wouldn't matter how hard his knights fought to break through the barriers that blocked the crossover passageways leading back to their lands.

Soon they might not have a home to return to.

"How bad is it?" he asked, dreading to hear the answer.

"The city is completely underwater," she told him grimly. "And the sea keeps rising. We have evacuated to the highest point on the peninsula at Raven's Craig, but I don't know if it will be enough, and we've lost critical tracts of farmland. Even if the sea level stops rising, we'll be facing starvation as our food supplies run out."

They had lost Lyonesse? The news rippled through the group like a physical blow.

Braden had family in the Other land. His chanting faltered, causing the spell to waver. Nikolas shot him a warning look, and the other knight's voice steadied.

"Annwyn, how long has it been since we last contacted you?" Nikolas asked.

He always asked when they talked. She replied readily, "A fortnight. And you?"

"Winter solstice," he told her. "Six months ago."

She sucked in a breath. "So the time slippage between the two lands remains significant."

"That is working in our favor right now," Nikolas said. "Have faith and stay strong. We're fighting to get home to you."

He didn't mention how few of them were left to fight their way home. That, at least, was one blow he could spare her.

She shook her head. "You know my strength lies in combat spells, but I'm doing what I can. We all are."

"It will be enough. Hold strong." As he pushed conviction into every word, the spell was beginning to fray around the edges. He told her, "We'll see you soon."

Her slanted, green eyes turned fierce. She said, "When you get here, you'd better bring a talented healer with you, or we'll have to abandon this land and Oberon with it."

They would lose their home and their King, and Isabeau, Queen of the Light Court, would have won.

Nikolas's determination hardened anew.

He would *never* let go of his home and King.

"That will never happen," he said between his teeth. "I swear it. Not as long as I draw breath."

Annwyn gave him a curt nod. "Good to hear."

Her face began to break apart. Quickly before the spell frayed away completely, he said, "Until next time."

As her image faded, she told him, "Fare well, old friend. Gods be with you."

Silence fell over the clearing. The nine males regarded one another in grim silence.

They needed a healer but not just any healer. They needed a superb one proficient in both physical and magical arts.

They were low on funds, which meant they were low on supplies.

They needed sanctuary, real rest, and a way to break through whatever magic was blocking the crossover passageways.

And they needed Oberon to wake the fuck up. Maybe then they could rally enough to vanquish the bitch Queen once and for all.

Chapter Three

TWO WEEKS AFTER meeting Kathryn Shaw in LA, Sophie came to the last stage of her journey, and the engine in her rental car stopped.

As in flat out quit. No coughing, wheezing, or knocking to give her any warning. No puff of oily smoke. *Click*, off.

She almost pulled right. At the last moment, she remembered she was driving in England, not in the United States, and she yanked her wheel left. Not that it mattered since the area was deserted anyway.

Still, better to get off the road if she could instead of leaving the car stranded in the middle of the lane. The Mini coasted gently onto the shoulder and rolled to a stop with its snub nose resting in tall green weeds.

She turned the key in the engine. Nothing. The starter didn't even turn over.

Silence pressed against her senses, green and heavy with the rich sense of a profligate summer. The sound of her tense breathing filled the interior.

She tapped a fingernail against the brand-new GPS mounted on the dashboard. It was dead as a doornail.

The only thing she knew for certain was that she was several miles south of Shrewsbury, either near or over the border of Shropshire, and a few miles away from her destination, the village of Westmarch.

Just for shits and giggles, she checked her new cell phone and Pocket Wi-Fi. While it was supposed to be fully charged, the phone was also dead.

Naturally.

Climbing out of the car, she looked north and south. There wasn't a soul to be seen. The rolling countryside was intersected with lines of green—hedges, bushes, and dense, tangled copses of trees.

It seemed like as good a time as any to cut loose. After several weeks of deep physical trauma and emotional stress, a switch flipped in her head, and she melted down. Swearing at the car, she kicked the tires and slapped the windshield like a bitch while she counted up all the *what the fucks* in her life.

Of which there were oh, so many.

The most relevant *what the fuck* at the moment was how her technology curse seemed to have grown exponentially overnight. Up to this point, it had been limited to small electronics. Alarm clocks, the stupid Keurig. Her computers constantly went on the fritz, and she burned through an average of three iPads a year. Phones came and went with depressing frequency—although usually, she managed to get five or six months out of them if she left them to recharge in places other than her bedroom. She glared at her current phone.

She ought to be grateful the curse hadn't caused her 747 to fall randomly out of the sky. That thought sent a chill running over her skin, and she slapped the car again.

A spark of awareness began to insinuate itself into her exhausted brain.

Snap out of it, Sophie, she scolded herself. You're pounding on an inanimate object like it knows or cares. Get your act together. You're acting like a whack job.

As quickly as her meltdown had come, it faded. Mostly, if she were to be honest, because she was too jet-lagged to sustain it, not because of any self-control on her part. Her partially healed injuries throbbed, and the major muscles in her thigh ached. The journey had taxed her body's resources to the limit.

Sucking in a deep breath, she took a step back and considered her choices.

She could sit in the car and feel sorry for herself, and she was tempted. Even more tempting—she could climb back into the car, flip the locks, and take a nap.

But she really couldn't see anybody. No person, piece of farm equipment, power line, or any kind of building was in sight—not even a pile of ancient ruins, which were sprinkled throughout this area of the world like so many Starbucks in Manhattan.

Last time she had checked, it had been close to 6:00 P.M. Summertime in England meant she had a good three and a half hours of sunlight left.

She could watch and wait, but it was entirely possible that nobody would be traveling on this road until tomorrow.

And she was so hungry. It hit with an urgency that felt like a spike piercing through her middle. Her confused body didn't know if it was supposed to be day or night. The lunch she had eaten before she met with the solicitor in Shrewsbury had been hefty, but that had been several hours ago.

She had a couple of packages of sweet nuts and crisps from the plane flight, but at the thought of eating more of them, she got a queasy feeling. Her body needed real nourishment, not empty calories.

So, walking it was. The village of Westmarch had to be just a few miles away, maybe as many as five. Normally that kind of hike wasn't an issue. Now she had to brace her tired spine at the thought.

All she had to do was reach the village. Paul, the solicitor in charge of overseeing the old entailed estate, had said Westmarch had a pub with rooms for rent, where she could get a hot meal and spend the night before she bought supplies and headed to the gatekeeper's cottage in the morning.

That idea had appealed, so he had called ahead to reserve a room for her. Once she reached the village, someone could come back for the car and the rest of her things in the morning.

She still wore the skirt and blouse that she had worn to the solicitor's office. Moving quickly, she opened the boot, rummaged through one of her suitcases, and pulled out jeans, a black T-shirt, a jean jacket, and black Doc Martens boots, which would be comfortable and sturdy for walking. Or running, if need be.

Last, she fingercombed her dark, curling hair back and snapped a band around it. Instinctively she reached to check for her Glock before she remembered she didn't have it with her.

She'd had no problem leaving her apartment or notifying the precinct she would be taking an extended break. The most difficulty she'd had in leaving was when she had said good-bye to Rodrigo. When she had told him the news, she had reached out to hug him in the same moment he had reached for her.

Somehow the good-bye hug had turned into a tight clench, and they clung to each other for a long moment before letting go. They'd always worked well together and over the last couple of years had become good friends. Now they were the only two survivors of a confrontation nobody had expected to turn fatal.

After that, she had left LA without a backward glance, but she missed her gun with a passionate intensity that some felt over losing a best friend or a lover. Despite the array of offensive and defensive spells in her repertoire, she felt naked without her gun.

The Glock was streamlined and understated, and unlike her taste in the guys she'd dated or her curse with electronics, the gun was utterly reliable. It had saved her ass more times than she could count.

She would fucking marry that gun if she could.

Instead, she'd had to pack it away with the rest of her possessions in order to make this trip. Her California concealed-carry permit meant nothing in the UK, where handguns, semiautomatics, and pump-action rifles were prohibited for most citizens. Sophie had a better chance of contracting malaria here than obtaining a firearm certificate.

As she changed, she kept a wary eye on the secluded Shropshire countryside, but nobody showed up to offer her a ride.

Naturally.

Because if they had, it would have made this too fucking easy. *Fuck.*

Finally she settled her bag across her body, messenger-style, grabbed a water bottle from the front passenger seat, and forced herself to put two of the small packages of nuts and crisps into the pocket of her jacket.

After she took a long pull of water from the bottle, she wiped her mouth with the back of one hand, then locked the car. Then she swung into a walk that would eat through the miles at an easy pace that her body could handle, heading down the road.

The tight ache in her right thigh eased as tired muscles loosened. Soon her stride turned loose and flowing, and the surrounding quiet began to sink in. The heat of the day had fled, leaving behind the growing chill of a cool summer evening. She felt almost as if she were swimming in pure, ageless golden sunlight.

She began to understand why Kathryn had said the Welsh Marches, or the area that bordered Wales and England, was some of the most mystical land in the world. Land magic wrapped around her, archaic and untamed. Crossover passages to Other lands existed somewhere nearby. Maybe several of them. Maybe even a lot of them.

Soaking it in, walking steadily, Sophie fell into a trance until what looked like the head of a dark mop trundled onto the road several yards ahead.

It just so happened, her trajectory along the edge of the road brought her closer to the wandering object. At first she thought it might be a badger, but when she drew closer, she discovered that wasn't the case.

Huh. It really did look like the head of a dark mop, sort of all poufy and puffy, and roughly the same size.

It meandered down the middle of the road at a slow enough pace that she caught up with it without really wanting to or trying.

She wanted to ignore it and pass on by. She didn't want to pay attention. That ambulatory mophead was a *what the fuck* she didn't need to jot onto her list.

Angling out her jaw, she paused to look, first down the road in one direction, then behind her. Still no vehicle in sight—but that didn't mean it would stay that way. This was deep country, and there weren't any streetlamps. The road would get very dark after sunset.

The mophead was dark too. It wouldn't show up well in a vehicle's headlights. Her imagination did the rest.

"Shoo," she told it. "Get off the road."

One end of the mop appeared to lift up and turn in her direction. It approached unhurriedly.

Crossing her arms, she waited. When it got close enough, the starch in her knees gave out. In spite of herself, she squatted.

A small, bizarre face like a miniature Ewok's blinked up at her from a mane of dirty, tangled hair. It had huge, bulbous eyes, one decidedly off-kilter, and a small, black button nose.

It was a walleyed Ewok.

It was... Was it a dog? Maybe it was a Pekinese or a Shih Tzu mix. It had dreadlocks embedded in hair that fell down to the ground. The matting was so pronounced she ground her teeth.

She held out her hand to it. "Don't bite me," she warned. "Or I'll walk away from you without a second glance."

The Ewok ambled closer. It sniffed at her, then nosed her fingers, the gentle touch so fleeting it was over before she knew it.

Aw, hell.

Her squat turned into a kneeling position. Carefully she patted the creature. When it drew closer and put a paw on her knee, she gently deepened the inspection.

Opposite the round head, a curly tail was embedded in the tangled filth, and yes, four legs were buried in that mess. The shape of the body felt like a dog's. When she sank her fingers into the hair, she could feel the small curve of protruding ribs.

Fingering the matted hair around that ridiculous little face, she found two delicate flaps of ears. Maybe it wore a collar with a name and address, but at the thought of finding its owner, anger shook through her.

The dog was too small to survive long on its own in this kind of deserted countryside. The protruding ribs and the dreadlocks in its hair spoke of long-term neglect, even abuse.

As she pulled the dreadlocks apart to look for a collar, she found a knot of silvery rope, tied too tightly around the dog's neck and broken at one trailing end. When she touched the rope, magic seared her fingers.

Muttering a curse, she recoiled. There was real, magic-sensitive silver wound into the rope, and it was bound with some kind of broken incantation that still held enough cruel Power to raise reddened welts on the ends of her fingers.

If it did that to her skin, what was it doing to the dog's neck?

Suddenly this *what the fuck* shot to the top of her long list. Her anger turned into a deep, fierce rage.

"Okay, little guy." She kept her rage out of her quiet voice. "You haven't bitten me yet. Hold still. I'm going to get this off you."

The dog sat on the pavement, blinking up at her, almost as if it knew what she was saying.

Digging into her bag, she pulled out her pair of nail clippers and set to work. Although she knew she had to be hurting it, the dog never moved, nor did it appear to flinch.

Despite the broken incantation, the knot in the rope seemed to twist and slide away from her efforts like a live creature while cold pain seared her fingers. She spat out a null spell to negate the magic.

For a brief moment the Power in the broken silver rope dissipated. When she felt it begin to coalesce again, she worked faster, digging the pointed end of the nail file into the knot until she finally yanked it loose.

When she pulled the rope away, the dog rounded on her with a snarl. It moved so fast she didn't have time to pull back. Sharp-looking white fangs flashed as it snatched the length of silver rope from her hands and flung it over its shoulder.

She had gotten too used to the dog's docile cooperation. Sitting back on her heels, she stared, but the brief display of savagery was already over. The Ewok face turned up to her, its large, filmy eyes blinking mildly.

A few feet away, the length of silvery rope dissolved with an acidic hiss until all that was left on the pavement was a darkened smear that stank like rotten eggs and left a faint shadow of psychic malice. What would the rope have done if she'd still held it? Would it have burned through her fingers?

Sophie looked around at the peaceful-seeming countryside, then back down at the dog.

Sighing, it put its chin on her knee.

"Oh, for God's sake," she muttered. "You did not just do that, did you?"

But it had, indeed, just done that.

She inspected her fingers. The reddened welts had turned into raised blisters in places. She wanted to check the dog's neck to see if it was blistered too, but there was too much matted hair in the way. Also, it was wretchedly filthy.

She needed to cut the dreadlocks off and give the dog a bath with a mild soap, then check for blisters.

But first things first.

Pulling out her water bottle, she poured water into the palm of one cupped hand and offered it. There was no telling how long ago it'd had a chance to drink, let alone eat.

Sniffing at her hand, it opened an oddly hinged mouth, wide as a frog's, and sucked at the water in her palm. Sucked, not lapped, making small, audible sounds as it swallowed. Tilting her head, she watched it drink.

When it finished the water, she poured more into her palm until it stopped drinking. Only then did she take a drink herself. Afterward, she capped the mostly empty bottle and stuck it back inside her bag.

"All right, kiddo," she said to the dog. "I saw those toofers of yours. I know you could do real damage if you tried. Don't you bite me."

With that admonition, she picked it up gently. As she did, it climbed up her torso and stuck its face in her neck with a deep sigh.

Automatically her arms closed around the small body. She knelt there frozen, holding a strange, stinky dog in her arms. It probably had heartworm and fleas.

Oh, no. Oh, no.

This wasn't going to happen. She had an agenda for the foreseeable future, and it didn't include adopting a pet, let alone adopting a special-needs pet.

She was going to carry it to the village and hand it over to somebody else. Surely, there had to be a country vet somewhere that could give it medical care.

But there was the abuse, the neglect. The cruel magic rope that had dissolved into nothing. Her jaw clenched on another surge of rage. She didn't know who would do such a thing to an animal, but whoever they were, they had to either live in the area or to have passed through recently.

Sophie, she said to herself, you're not here five minutes, and you've already started a shit list. Some people don't know how to take a vacation.

Aloud, she told the dog, "I just want you to know, this conversation isn't over."

As she climbed to her feet, she sensed Power. Not the kind of magic that radiated from the ancient land. Not the kind of Power she'd sensed in the length of rope.

This was a strong concentration of personal Power.

It traveled toward her with the speed of a bullet. At the same moment, she heard the deep mechanical growl of an approaching engine.

Instinct caused her to leap to her feet. Maybe that approaching Power was benevolent or at the very least indifferent.

Maybe it wasn't.

She was in no shape for a possible confrontation with an unknown entity that held that kind of strength here, in an unknown land, especially without her Glock as backup. Striding off the pavement, she plunged into the thicket of brush bordering the road.

As branches of green foliage closed around her, she *pulled* the shadows around her like a cloak. Only then did she glance back at the way she had come.

The road curved gently with the land and was still visible where it followed the rise over the horizon. She could see her Mini, small in the distance, parked on the shoulder.

A figure on a motorcycle came over the rise. The sense of approaching Power grew stronger. Her muscles tightened as she watched it, straining for every detail.

The bike was a big one. Still too far away for her to say for sure, from the bulk and general shape, she guessed it was a Harley. The figure wore black jeans, boots, a black leather jacket, and a helmet with a faceless, featureless black front.

Tiny hairs at the back of her neck raised. It was

clearly a masculine figure, with a large frame strong enough to control that massive bike, and the sulfurous Power it carried felt like a thunderclap.

It didn't slow down or pause as it passed the Mini. Within moments it came to the area where she hid, still clutching the dog.

Then it slowed.

The deep roar of the motorcycle throttled down to a quiet growl as it slowly passed the spot where the magic rope had melted. As the figure on the bike came to where she had stepped off the road, that featureless black helmet turned left, then right. He looked as if he was searching for something.

The air felt compressed and sizzled with energy. If his Power had seemed like a thunderclap before, this close, the force of his presence bent the air around him.

Why had he slowed down? Was he looking for the dog?

Could he be Wyr? He couldn't smell them, could he?

Sophie's hands shook, and her heart plunged into a crazy race. She wasn't ready to face combat again, not so soon and so unexpectedly.

Maybe he was not as he appeared. She whispered the null spell again, and for a brief moment the figure shimmered and changed.

She clocked details fast. The butt of a gun protruded from a holster aligned to the male's long thigh. It could have been either a sawed-off shotgun, or maybe it was a semiautomatic. She didn't know all the details of England's license-to-carry laws, but this guy looked about as legal as a saber-toothed tiger.

And he had a sword strapped to his wide, powerful-looking back. The hilt lay positioned at one wide shoulder so he could reach behind his head and unsheathe it with a single hand.

A sword. The male she had seen in her vision had been carrying a bloodied sword. Was this the same guy? She couldn't tell—he had virtually no identifying features visible—but the very thought made her break into a light sweat.

After a brief glimpse, his cloaking spell returned. Both gun and sword disappeared from sight.

What was he?

She couldn't connect him to the man in her vision from the feel of his Power alone. Too much time had passed since she had made that first contact. She also didn't find any similarity between his Power and the cruel enchantment that had laced the silvery rope, but she was on overload. All her internal systems flashed an emergency red, the primitive reaction blasting out of her hindbrain.

The motorcycle rider didn't stop. Several yards on, his speed picked up again, and the dangerous, quiet purr turned into a mechanical roar once again. Within moments, he shot out of her sight.

She gave him a few minutes, to be sure he didn't change his mind and turn around. Only then did she let go of the shadows she had *pulled* around her and stepped out of the brush.

An invisible fuselage of the rider's presence hung in the air. Obeying an impulse, she gently set the dog on the ground and walked through that lingering trail of Power. For a fleeting moment, an intense, alien masculinity surrounded her, and she opened her senses wide to try to pull any information she could from it. Then it dissipated on a mild evening breeze.

Frustrated, she rubbed her tired face. As she looked over the ends of her fingers, the dog ambled up and vomited at her feet.

Together, they regarded the foamy puddle on the asphalt. When the dog looked up, she murmured, "I gave you too much water, too fast, didn't I? Sorry, kiddo."

She knelt, and he climbed back into her arms.

Within the space of a few moments, the dog was sound asleep. Stifling a groan, she hoisted her tired, aching body upright.

As she walked, she hugged him and whispered, "I'm going to make sure everything's okay."

And she only made promises she intended on keeping.

Although it did appear that her *what the fuck* list was growing at an exponential rate.

Chapter Four

E ARLY IN THE evening, Nikolas's mobile rang. When he checked the screen and saw Gawain's name, he frowned. Phone calls were traceable by magical means, so they rarely talked, and when they did, they kept conversations brief.

Texts were safer. If Gawain was calling, it had to be important.

He answered. "What is it?"

Gawain said, "I caught the puck's scent, along with a hint of the Queen's magic."

Like a blade being pulled for battle, Nikolas's attention sharpened. Once a favorite of Oberon's, the puck Robin had been missing for a very long time. No one knew if he had been caught Earth-side when the last of the crossover passageways had been blocked, or if he was still in Lyonesse—but if he was in Lyonesse, he had chosen to disappear, because no one had seen or heard from him in quite a long time. Nikolas had wondered if Robin's talent for mischief might have turned out to be an ill thing for the knights of the Dark Court.

If Robin was Earth-side, and his allegiance had truly shifted to Isabeau, there was no telling what evil the sprite might indulge in.

He might have even been responsible for the unnatural fog that had rolled over the village park where Nikolas had been attacked. His magic was related to nature, and it fit. Nikolas didn't want it to, but it did fit.

He said, "Tell me exactly where you caught his scent."

"It was a few miles north of Westmarch on Old Friars Lane." Gawain paused, and Nikolas heard the sound of a passing lorry in the background. "I've been combing through the town's streets, but so far I haven't picked up a hint of either the puck or the Queen—or the scent of any Hounds, for that matter."

Old Friars Lane was what the road had been called centuries ago. As the years unfolded, often the ancient pathways had been renamed and modernized, but the Daoine Sidhe still kept to the old names, and Nicholas knew exactly where Gawain meant.

Old Friars Lane and the town of Westmarch bordered the site where the Dark Court had suffered one of the most bitter defeats in their history, in a battle that had lasted for five days and nights and had long since faded from the memories of most people.

The end had come when, with a surge of Power that had cracked the world, Morgan had shattered the crossover passageway that led to Lyonesse. Cut off from their homeland at that crucial access point, denied reinforcements and outnumbered, the Dark Court forces had fled.

That had been one of the first crossover passageways to Lyonesse that Morgan had either broken or blocked. Once many passageways had covered the border between England and Wales, and the people of the Dark Court had journeyed freely back and forth from their homeland.

Now those passageways that still existed were shrouded in webs of magic so dense and impenetrable Nikolas and his men could no longer find them. More disturbing, he knew from scrying with Annwyn that the people in Lyonesse couldn't find the passageways either. The two lands were virtually cut off from each other.

What business did the puck have for being in that area, or the Queen, for that matter? What fresh mischief was Isabeau up to?

"I want to check out the stretch of road for myself," he told Gawain. "I'm only forty minutes away, so I'll be there shortly."

The chance to capture the puck and possibly discover information on the Queen's movements superseded any risk of banding together and possibly attracting a pack of Hounds. Besides, if a confrontation did occur, there was no one Nicholas trusted more to have at his back in a battle than Gawain.

The other male grunted an assent. "I found the spot about a hundred meters south of a broken-down

Mini, but the car might have been towed by now. Look for a cluster of three white oaks on the west side of the road, and you'll find it. I'll wait for you in town."

After disconnecting, Nicholas moved quickly through the flat he had sublet for the month, gathering weapons and his black leather go-bag. He paused only to send out a group text.

`Possible lead on the puck's whereabouts. Watch for updates, and prepare to mobilize.`

Rhys was the first to respond. `Where did you find him?`

`We haven't yet. Gawain caught his scent on Old Friars Lane. More news when I have it.` After sending the quick reply, Nikolas pocketed his phone and left.

As he sped to the area, Nikolas thought of what he had gleaned from the mobile phones of the dead Hounds. On the day he had been attacked, one of the Hounds had received a call from a public call box. Then much as Nikolas had just done, that Hound had sent out a group text to three people, and they had responded quickly.

Each mobile Nikolas had collected had the same corresponding texts on it. He had killed all the participants involved in the attack.

Like terrorists, Hounds tended to operate in cells or, more accurately, in packs. The alpha had received a phone call, mobilized his pack, and they had converged on the village where Nikolas had been.

Someone had known where Nikolas was going to be that afternoon, and they had informed a pack of Hounds. Could Robin have done such a thing? Had he been tracking the knights of the Dark Court, only to betray them one at a time? Was he the reason why their numbers had diminished so drastically over the last six months?

Nikolas hadn't shared Oberon's good opinion of the sprite. He'd never been overly fond of Robin, finding him capricious and unpredictable, but he also would have never believed Robin to be capable of such treachery.

Now he was no longer so sure. None of them were quite who they once were, when Oberon had been a strong, vital leader ruling over a thriving, prosperous court.

The Porsche ate the miles with a languid purr, and in the evening's fading light, Nikolas came over a rise and looked out over the land. Patches of farmland traced a different pattern than they once had, but the dip and curve of the land itself hadn't changed.

Ancient memories drifted through his mind. The thunder of Fae horses' hooves pounding the ground and the clash of swords. The screams of pain, and the flares of deadly magic so bright and beautiful, warriors stopped to stare in awe as they died.

And then that final unsurpassable roar of Power, as Morgan unleashed what he had been holding in reserve.

The earth shook and *cracked* with a force that had thrown horses to the ground and brought everyone— the most Powerful nobles and foot soldiers of two kingdoms, the Light Court and the Dark, and the humans allied to either side, both friend and foe alike— to their knees.

As long as Nikolas lived, he would never forget that sound.

A human had done that. A human had brought some of the oldest and most Powerful of the Elder Races to their knees.

Or, at least, a creature that had once been human.

Nikolas didn't see any sign of a Mini, but when he drew close to the cluster of white oak trees, he pulled to the side of the road, stepped out of the Porsche, and walked.

The sun's light waned and shadows lengthened, and insects played a seesaw symphony in the underbrush. The gloaming was near, the time that was neither day nor night, when shadows left their anchors to mingle and whisper together before the moon's pale light sent them scurrying home again.

As Nikolas strolled alongside the underbrush, the symphony fell silent, and it only began to play again when he had passed.

At first he didn't pick up Robin's scent, but he did sense a smear of darkness on the road that drew him. He reached the spot where a hiss of dark magic had expired and knelt on one knee to examine it. The darkness was both psychic and physical. The magic had burned into the asphalt.

Isabeau's Power signature was quite distinct. When he passed his hand over the shadow, it bit his skin, the last toxic sting before the last of the magic dissipated completely. Glancing at his palm where a reddened welt raised, he dismissed the tiny injury and took a deep breath.

With the exception of Oberon, none of the Dark Court who had Wyr in their ancestry could change into their animal forms, but their Wyr blood did give them enhanced abilities. Gawain was the better tracker, and it must have been several hours since Robin passed this way, but once Nikolas had knelt down, he could finally scent the puck, along with the faint scent of a strange woman.

What was she? Clearly she wasn't Isabeau herself, and she didn't smell like Light Fae.

He laid his hand on the asphalt road and asked it to tell him what it knew of her. The oldest roads in this in-between land that bordered England and Wales, and Other lands and Earth, were more sentient than most realized.

The road woke and gave him the impression of dichotomies. Strength and fragility. Exhaustion and determination. And magic. So much magic.

And something else. There was something about her. Something distinct, perhaps even familiar. He strained to glean more information, but the road had ceased talking to him and had fallen asleep again.

"I wish to know what you are doing here," he whispered to the unknown woman, drumming his fingers on the road. "And what you might have to do with a stray puck and an enemy Queen."

Now that he had located Robin's fading scent, he stood and followed it a few meters farther until it disappeared. Then there was only the woman's scent for many meters. Unless Robin had managed to take flight somehow—and the puck could change his shape into many creatures, but he could not fly—the woman must have picked him up.

Nikolas tracked Robin's scent backward to the place where it left the road and disappeared into a hole in the bordering hedge. Robin had cut across the land until he reached the road. Then Nikolas turned to trace the woman's scent back along the road and came to a place where tire tracks disturbed the tall grasses on the narrow shoulder.

There had been a Mini, Gawain had said, and the woman must have been driving it. When it broke down, she walked into town.

And she had encountered a wandering puck along the way.

The rest of the tale would not be told here. He walked back to the Porsche and drove into Westmarch.

The town was younger than that ancient, cataclysmic battle but older than most. Worn cobblestone streets cut across one another in a crooked pattern. The shops had closed some time earlier, all except for a single newsagent's, a liquor store at one end of the high street, and a large, sprawling pub nestled in the center of the town, named Dark Knight.

The pub's wooden sign had a painting of a knight, bearing a shield with Oberon's crest—a white lion rampant against crimson crossed swords on a black background. Some people had long memories in these places.

When Nikolas came to the pub's parking lot, he saw Gawain's Harley-Davidson parked between other vehicles. A Mini was tucked out of the way at the back of the lot. He pulled in and switched off the engine.

Briefly he checked his phone. Gawain had texted him fifteen minutes ago. `Waiting for you in the pub. Robin's been here. I can smell him.`

So as he had suspected, the puck and the woman had indeed come into town together. That was a tale Nikolas quite wanted to hear.

And if the Mini was any indication, at least the woman was still here.

He texted Gawain, `Guard the front door. I'm going to test a theory and come in the back way.`

`You got it,` Gawain replied.

SOPHIE COULDN'T MAKE it until the evening.

No matter how she fought to stay awake, an inexorable black tide washed over her, and she fell into a deep pit of unconsciousness.

She dreamed she lived in a cage.

She stared between the bars at a woman who was both beautiful and terrible to look at, with long, shining golden hair and wide, cornflower blue eyes, and a lovely, young face that was a cross between a flower and a nightmare.

The woman's gigantic face came closer, and the nightmare was the rage in the woman's eyes.

I warned you to watch your tongue, Imp, the woman said. *So. You will watch your tongue.*

Then others came and put their giant, hurting hands on her. No matter how she struggled, she couldn't break free of their grip. They had too much strength, too much magic. They forced her mouth open, took hold of her tongue in iron tongs, and ripped it out. She screamed and screamed, a wordless wail of bloody agony. As she watched, they threw the piece of her flesh into a fire.

With an appetizing smell of roasting meat, the tongue turned black as it burned.

Sophie woke with a muffled shout. Heart pounding, she stared around the shadowed, unfamiliar room. For a moment she felt completely displaced. Where were the bars of her cage?

Then a snore beside her on the bed snapped her fully back into reality.

She was in her room at the pub, lying fully clothed on top of the covers. The newly shorn and washed dog lay sleeping at her side.

When she had arrived, Arran, the owner of the pub, had sent his son, who owned a rusted Land Rover with a tow bar, to retrieve the Mini. According to the son, when he had turned the keys in the engine, the Mini had started perfectly.

Of course it had, the fucking fucker.

Arran's son had towed it into town and parked it at the back of the pub. When she had tried to apologize for the inconvenience and pay for the tow, neither Arran nor his son would accept her money.

Arran had told her good-naturedly enough, "Not to worry. Odd things happen around here sometimes. Living here, ye get used to it."

"Good to know," she muttered. The Mini inspired her with hope. Maybe her cell phone wasn't as dead as she had thought. Pulling it out of her pocket, she checked the power. Sure enough, the screen lit up.

So she had settled into her room, borrowed sewing scissors from Arran's wife, Maggie, who had clucked sympathetically over the dog's condition, and had cut away all the matted hair. Underneath, he looked as starved as she had suspected, with protruding ribs, a concave belly, and hip bones visible under his skin. The area around his neck was thick with deep, half-healed blisters that were half her thumb's length in size.

Clenching down on a rage that wouldn't ease, she

had washed him gently and wrapped him in a towel, and together they had shared the snack of boiled eggs Maggie had offered to tide them over until the pub started serving supper.

At least he didn't have fleas. Sophie had been surprised at that.

He had gulped down without chewing the pieces of egg she had fed him and growled at her when she stopped. "You quit that," she said in a firm voice. "It's not okay to growl at me. I don't want you to throw up again. You can have more food soon, I promise."

At that, he had stopped growling, almost as if he understood her, and curled into a tight ball on the old narrow bed. Intense weariness dragged her down beside him. Unable to fight off the black tide that took her, she closed her eyes.

She had only meant to rest for a few minutes, not fall asleep. Now jet lag would keep her up through the night.

The horrific dream still clung to her, like sticky black cobwebs in her face and hair, and her heart raced. Just another thing to add to her *what the fuck* list. Rubbing her face, she sat, turned on the bedside light, and looked down at her unexpected companion. She didn't know how to cut a dog's hair, and he looked pretty bad, a small bundle of ragged hair and bones. At least the mats were gone.

She washed her face and hands at the small basin in one corner of the room, then walked over to gently touch the dog's shoulder. "Time to wake up, kiddo."

He growled without opening his eyes.

"Hey!" she said sharply. "No growling! Do you want supper or not?"

At that, he snapped upright and looked at her alertly. Again, almost as if he understood her.

She frowned at him. What the hell, maybe the dog did understand her. She had seen a lot of strange things in her life, both inhuman creatures and events that logic alone couldn't fully explain.

"And you need to go outside so you don't have an accident in this nice place," she told him, then sighed. "And tomorrow we'll start looking for a good home for you, with someone who will love and take care of you."

At that, the dog let out the cutest little whimper and, tail wagging, came across the bed to stand his forelegs against her hip as he nudged her hand.

Stroking his round head and thin, silken ears, she scowled against the sneaky melting in her heart and muttered, "Suck-up."

Scooping him under one arm, she left her room, locked the door, and pocketed the key in the back of her jeans. As she headed down the narrow, steep staircase, she told him, "I'll look after you, and I promise, I'll make sure you're okay. But you've got to understand something—I don't live the kind of lifestyle that's good for a dog. Do you hear me? I'm not good for you. I'm too mobile, and I'm not just an asshole magnet. I'm a weirdo magnet. Weird things happen to me all the time."

Kind of like the dog itself. And that rope tied around his neck. That rope hadn't just been weird. It had been evil.

As she told the dog all the reasons why she couldn't keep him, she reached the ground floor. The pub had several public rooms, and the staircase let out into the game room toward the back, where a dwarf and a human male were smoking, drinking pints, and throwing darts.

She raised her eyebrows at the smoke, pretty sure the two were breaking the law from the articles she had read about the UK in preparation for her trip, while the two males watched her with unbridled curiosity.

Giving them a nod, she strode to the front room. She was starving again, and a classic pub supper of fish and chips or shepherd's pie sounded heavenly. It probably wasn't the healthiest thing to feed the dog, but any calories right now had to be good calories for him. A diet of proper dog food could start tomorrow.

As she stepped across the threshold into the front room, the dog started making noise, a cross between a growl and a high whine. Staring down at it in puzzlement, at first she didn't take in the details of who populated the room.

Then she felt a male presence so heavy with Power it felt like a thunderclap.

Lifting her head, she found the male sitting by the large picture window near the front door. He wore biker's leathers and was as big as she remembered, this saber-toothed tiger of a man, only now his face wasn't obscured by the blank, featureless helmet.

She took in the sharp eyes that were at odds with his relaxed demeanor, and the strong features that carried a rough sort of handsomeness. While she was usually good at spotting and identifying those of the Elder Races, she couldn't place his heritage. But whatever he was, he wasn't human.

He was looking right at her or, more accurately, at the dog under her arm. He recognized the dog, and clearly, the dog recognized him.

Leisurely the male came to his feet.

A heavy dose of adrenaline dumped into her veins. Bitching under her breath for letting herself get caught unawares—like the magic fucking rope didn't give you enough of a massive fucking clue to make sure you had your shit together, Sophie—she backed out of the doorway, turned and strode rapidly toward the back.

Her limbs shook. There was too much fight or flight going on for her system to absorb.

Just as it had been when she'd watched the gun swing toward her, and she looked down the wrong end of the barrel as the shooter had taken aim.

She'd reached for the shadows to pull *them around her, but she'd been too late for that trick to work. He had already laid eyes on her... and she'd heard a flat tat-tat-tat and felt the individual blows to her body, but by then Rodrigo had dived into the room, his own gun firing.*

As her body went into a slow spiral downward, she watched red dots explode across the shooter's forehead, arm, and chest, and they both fell together....

A part of her still lived in that space, always falling. She was in no shape for a possible confrontation, either mentally or physically. It was too soon. She was still healing. And she didn't have her Glock or any offensive spells prepared.

But she had the dog, and she'd made it a promise that she would make everything okay. She wasn't going to give it up to more abuse, not without a fight. Sometimes confrontations came whether you were goddamn ready or not, so somehow she was going to have to suck it up and make something good come out of this.

Her mind sped like a race car hurtling down an open highway. The shadow trick wouldn't work, not indoors. Not now that he knew she and the dog were here. The best defense she had was the other people in the pub... hopefully... and the best offensive spell she had on the fly, if it came to it, was a raw, inelegant curse she'd learned in the backwoods of Kentucky that would knock her down as much as it would flatten the other guy.

Not an optimal choice.

But hopefully it wouldn't come to that if she could only get outside first, and under the trees, then she was confident she could *pull* enough shadows around them to hide them from the most intensive scrutiny, if only the damn dog would stop that high, wacky sort of growly-whiny thing it was doing.

She hissed at it. "Shush!"

Ahead of her, the door to the kitchen opened, and a bolt of lightning came toward her.

Lightning, she saw as she blinked rapidly to clear her overloaded vision, which was just barely contained in a lethal male form that moved toward her like Death shadowing a dying woman...

His face. His face.

She knew his face.

The planes and angles so sharp they appeared as if they had been cut from an immortal blade. The indomitable will in those dark, chilling eyes and the ferocity.

The killer's grace that was purely inhuman, sleek muscles sliding underneath his skin like a python swimming underwater, and oh my gods, he carried so much Power, even more Power than the other male did. He wore all black, the uncompromising clothes outlining every lethal line of his lean body. Once, Sophie had helped the LAPD catch an infamous gang leader who had always worn black, the better to hide all the blood.

The male newcomer recognized her too. She saw the moment it happened.

His eyes narrowed, and that incredible face of his sharpened—really, she wouldn't have thought he could have looked any sharper or harder, but he did, he did—and he reached up and behind his head, and she knew what he was doing then too.

He was pulling his sword. The one that had dripped crimson with blood in her vision.

Everything crescendoed inside, the terror and the shakes and the sense of doom connected to the realization that she was trapped, with Lightning headed straight at her and Thunder coming up behind, and all that nightmarish PTSD she had bottled up inside her, and the damn dog hadn't shut up at all. Now it was yodeling.

And she was full up. Full up and overloaded until she shot into a completely different mind space.

Ah, well.

There really was no fixing stupid or healing crazy.

"*You!*" she spat. Rage blinded her. She hated things that scared her. They made her so *angry*. She strode toward the terrifying male and shoved him in the chest as hard as she could with her free hand. "You bastard! You attacked me for no reason! Are you nuts—what is wrong with you? Who does that?! Crazy people? Serial killers?"

He raised his hand, and the hilt appeared.

Oh dear, here comes the sword. Better get ready with that curse.

If she could put enough strength into it, they would all go down together. But it was going to take a hell of a lot of strength to bring down these two males. Chances were good she would just piss them off while she knocked herself out.

As Lightning finished drawing his sword, he grabbed her wrist. A liquid, foreign language spilled out of his cruelly beautiful mouth, and she tensed, but it didn't seem to be a magic spell. He had turned those ferocious eyes onto the dog, and he was...

Telling it off?

The dog bared its teeth at him, and it had a surprising number of teeth. For such a small creature, those fangs looked surprisingly wicked, long and sharp.

Part of her sensed the moment Thunder stepped into the room. Even though her attention was on Lightning, she couldn't help but know it. Between the two males, there was so much Power in the room, together they could blow out the walls of the building if they wanted to. Hell, they could probably blow out the town.

She tugged at her wrist and struggled to free herself from his hold, but Lightning's long, bruising fingers were like a manacle.

His hard, deadly eyes lifted to hers. When their eyes met, the shock of connection almost sent her to her knees. In slightly accented English, he ordered, "Drop him."

"Drop him?" she repeated blankly. "Drop who, the dog? While you're standing there with your goddamn sword pulled out, so you can, what—chop him in half? Fuck you."

Both men stared at her. She didn't let any hint of her intention cross her face when she stepped into his body, quick and smooth, and hauled up her knee.

It was an awesome move. She had practiced it countless times and used it more than once. She was good at it, confident in using it, and she didn't hesitate. And she was very motivated to land that blow. Maybe it would loosen his grip on her wrist.

But she had used her right knee, on her bad side, and she hadn't started back to training and conditioning after her hospital stay. The move pulled weakened muscles in her abdomen, so that she groaned in pain as she tried to knee him.

With a swift move as balletic as a dancer's, he shifted lean hips to avoid the hit, and her knee grazed along his lean, hard thigh. Then he leveraged her around, shoved her against the wall, and pinned her in place with his body.

"Nikolas," Thunder said, frowning. He placed a big hand on the other man's shoulder.

Lightning—apparently named Nikolas—shrugged angrily at Thunder's hold. Another quick stream of the Gaelic-sounding language spilled out of his mouth.

He was breathing hard, still staring at her, and while his assault wasn't sexual in any way, still there was something about the way he looked at her. A pivotal awareness of his maleness and her femininity. She recognized it because she carried the same awareness of him. She couldn't stop watching his lips.

The dog snarled and snapped, biting at their attacker's shirt. Thunder stood just at Lightning's shoulder.

Behind them, the customers in the pub had gathered, along with Arran and his white-faced wife.

All of them existed on the other side of an invisible wall, along with decency, right and wrong, social mores, and normal behavior. Inside the wall, she and Lightning stared at each other.

Male. Female.

A connection so sizzling it whited out every other consideration in her head. If she'd had a free hand, she would have reached up to trace the line of his cruel, beautiful mouth. She was dying to know what it felt like….

"Nikolas, *hold*." The strength in Thunder's voice finally broke through to both of them.

Almost imperceptibly, Nikolas eased his weight off her, although the bruising hold on her wrist never loosened.

Shaken at her own impulses, Sophie reached deep into her personal well of strength, stiffened her spine, and mentally readied herself to throw the curse. Man, this was going to suck if she had to use it.

She said between gritted teeth, "I don't care who you are or what you are. This dog has suffered more abuse than most prisoners of war do. I'm not putting him down or giving him over to you. So if you want him, you're going to have to come through me to get him. And for Christ's sake, what's the matter with you? Who wants a dog this badly anyway?"

It was sheer, stupid bravado. She was outclassed

and outgunned, and the only thing she had going for her at the moment was a curse that was more likely to kill her than cause them anything more than a few moments' discomfort. They were so much stronger. Damn it. She might be stupid and crazy, but she wasn't suicidal.

A tiny silence fell as they stared at her again.

Then Thunder said, "Lady. That's not a dog."

"What?" she uttered. She glanced down at the ridiculous Ewok face tucked under her arm. Huge, walleyed, filmy eyes blinked up at her. Whatever it was, it looked aged and sad. Her voice hardened. "I don't care what it is. It's been hurt and used badly, and I won't stand for any more of it."

If, that is, she had any choice about the matter. As far as strength went, they could easily wrestle it away from her.

Unpredictability shimmered in the air. She held firm in the face of it. She had dealt many times with those of the Elder Races, and despite the vastly different personalities and situations, invariably, they all respected a show of strength.

Nikolas's attention shifted down to the creature she held. After a long moment, he lifted his sword behind his head and sheathed it. She watched him warily. In fact, she couldn't look away.

He didn't need to feel for the sheath with his second hand or fumble to get the sword in. He knew precisely how long his sword was and exactly where the sheath rode between his shoulder blades, like both items were extensions of his body. This was not a man to engage in a sword fight.

Then he released her wrist and took a step back. She felt, rather than heard, their witnesses let out a collective sigh. If she were honest with herself, she would admit to losing her own breath as well.

"You're American." His voice was clipped and cold. "I want to hear what you were doing two weeks ago when your magic accosted me. And I want to hear everything about how you and the puck met."

The puck. The puck?

The only puck Sophie knew of was a hockey puck. And this guy might be able to carry off every ounce of his monumental arrogance, but after he'd bared his weapon and assaulted her, she was still too full of anger and adrenaline to give in to it.

She told him in an insolent, indifferent voice. "Do you? I want a million bucks and a villa in Capri. Thanks for asking, asshole."

The lightning of his Power flared, whiting out her mental senses until all she could see was the masculine outline of his body. He looked—felt—like an avenging angel.

He snarled, "*Do not push me, human.*"

But when Sophie reached this level of overload, she truly had no concept of sense or limits. She lifted her face to his and hissed. "*I'll push you every bit as much as you've pushed me.*"

Out of the corner of her eye, she saw Thunder's fingers clench on Nikolas's shoulder, and suddenly Arran was on his other side as well.

Arran said in a conciliatory tone, "Tempers have run very high on both sides, my lord. Perhaps if everyone could take a moment, I'm sure this unfortunate misunderstanding can be cleared up. I would be honored to offer you all a drink, on the house as it were, and you can sit down to discuss your differences all civil-like. And I can get the miss a bite of supper. I know she was looking forward to a hot meal, seeing as she just arrived in England today."

My lord. Arran talked as if this guy was a prince of his people. Sophie tried to sneer at the thought, but actually, given his utterly atrocious behavior, she could well believe it.

On the other side, Thunder muttered, "Damn it, man, listen to him. Do it."

The rage in Nikolas's face eased somewhat as he listened to the others speak, but Sophie's didn't. She wanted to *push* him, and *push* him, and see what he might do then, because like the part of her that had needed to melt down earlier, the part of her that had no sense, had the bit between its teeth and wanted to run amok.

Then she caught another glimpse of Arran's wife, back against the wall. Maggie wiped her face with a visibly trembling hand, and Sophie's uncontrollable rage died. This confrontation was not just frightening for her. It was frightening other people.

Sliding away from Nikolas's taut body, she said directly to Maggie, "I'm sorry we've caused such a fuss. If we have any more arguing to do, we'll take it outside, well away from here."

She put an extra glare in her glance at Nikolas as she said that. He looked supremely, utterly indifferent to it. In a calm voice, as if he had never lost his temper, he said to Arran, "Thank you for your offer, but there's no need for you to bear the financial brunt of our conflict. Please see that everyone gets a drink, whatever they want, and put it on my tab. We'll be at the corner table when you're done."

Relief flooded Arran's weathered features. He nodded and smiled. "Yes, sir. Thank you, sir."

With a long, inscrutable look at her and another one at the dog... the doglike creature... she still clutched, Nikolas turned away.

Her capacity to glare after him was disrupted as Thunder stepped in front of her, blocked her view of Nikolas's back, and offered his hand. In a low voice, he said, "I'm Gawain. My apologies for what just happened. We've been too involved for too long in combat situations. Our first reaction to any kind of conflict or inexplicable event tends to be, well, less than peaceful."

That gave her pause. She had known men like that, men who had been at war for so long their response to any kind of conflict was violent. Often they were unable to assimilate back into normal society, and they re-upped and went back into the army, or they became police officers. Occasionally they turned a gun on themselves.

Her eyes narrowed as she studied Thunder's rough features. He appeared to be sincere enough, and the dog (doglike creature) wasn't yapping or yodeling any longer or acting fearful.

Taking her cue from that, cautiously she took Gawain's hand and shook it. "Sophie Ross. Maybe there's no harm done this time, but there's no trust won either. If one of you draws your weapon or manhandles me again, I'll slap you with a curse so fast it will make your head spin. That's a promise, Gawain."

"I understand, and I respect it." Gently his fingers squeezed hers, and then he released her. "Please, come join us at the table and tell us your story. It's important."

She hesitated, looking from one male to the other, but as deadly as Gawain was, she sensed no danger coming from him.

Nikolas though. She gave him a narrow look, which he returned with more than a hint of banked malice.

As far as Nikolas went, whether he was a prince of his people or not, she wouldn't trust him as far as she could throw him.

Chapter Five

THE ROUND, WOODEN table in the corner of the front room was stained dark and scarred from many years of use. Nikolas chose a worn velvet chair tucked in the corner so he could look out over the rest of the room and watch the door.

From that vantage point, he watched Gawain talk with the American woman and listened easily to their low-voiced exchange. Nikolas filed her name away for future reference as he took in the details of her appearance.

She wasn't short for a female, but she appeared short and slight next to Gawain, whose brawny height emphasized the femininity of her slender figure. Many of the details Nikolas had gleaned from the vision two weeks ago held true.

Her hair was long, black, and curling. She kept it pulled back from her pale, angular face by looping it into a short braid. It exploded from the end of the braid in an extravagant cloud of curls. Like the vision, her creamy skin was sprinkled with freckles, her lips were plush and pink, and she looked tired and too thin, almost gaunt. Dark circles ringed her eyes.

There was one arresting change from what he had seen before.

Those eyes. In the vision, her eyes had been pale and uninteresting. In reality, they were spectacular. They might be called pale gray or even light blue—it was hard to tell across the room—but mere descriptive words were inadequate and didn't do them justice.

Her eyes were brilliant, and not just with the force of her personality and the magic she carried. They seemed to draw from every light around her and sparkled with luminosity, almost like diamonds.

He drew in a deep breath, filtering out the other scents in the pub to bring her feminine scent into his lungs. There was something different about her. She wasn't quite fully human, and she held a significant amount of personal Power. It would be a mistake to underestimate her.

Gawain persuaded her to join them, and still carrying Robin under her arm, she followed him reluctantly to the corner table where she gave Nikolas one sour, brief glance before choosing a seat to his right, which kept her from having her back to the room as well.

Gawain took the seat to Nikolas's left, settling his large, powerful body with care into the chair, leaving Nikolas's view of the room unobstructed.

He completed his study of the female and turned his attention to Robin, who looked strangely small and frail. The puck's Power felt nonexistent, and there was something wrong with his eyes as well. One of them was off-center, appearing to look off to the side. Frowning, Nikolas cupped his chin in one hand, resting the elbow on the other arm, which he crossed over his chest as he studied the puck.

In a low voice, Gawain said to him, "How long do you think we have?"

"Not long," he responded. "A half an hour at most. We should not take any longer than that. This isn't an isolated area, like our gathering was up north."

"I can leave, while you two talk."

"Oh no. No, no." Sophie threw up her free hand in a universal "stop" gesture. She said to Gawain, "If you leave, I'm leaving too. I'm not going to stay here and talk to *him* alone."

The emphasis she put on that was most distinctly not a positive one. Nikolas's eyes narrowed. While he couldn't care less about what the female thought of him, one way or another, she *would* talk with him.

He told her, "I am not leaving, and neither are you. You and I have things to say to each other."

When she finally looked at him, her face was drawn tight with anger and distaste. "What are you going to do to keep me here? This again?" She held up her free hand, showing a pale slender wrist that was swollen and red with his fingermarks.

At the sight, Nikolas's mouth tightened. The ghost of the man he used to be turned uneasily in its grave.

He had no illusions about himself. Once he would

have been filled with remorse at bruising a female, but long ago he had turned cold and hard.

A female had killed so very many of his people. His friends. That female was hell-bent on annihilating an entire demesne, and Nikolas was capable of doing things now that he had never dreamed possible.

He said in a soft, warning voice, "I would do that and so much more if it meant we get answers we need."

Robin growled while the woman leaned forward.

Forward, toward Nikolas, not away from him in fear. Meeting aggression with aggression. He raised his eyebrows. Usually people didn't respond to him in such a manner.

She whispered, "You touch me again without my permission, and I will damage you."

That face. Those mesmerizing eyes. She showed absolutely no fear even though he could detect traces of it in her scent. Surprised, he almost smiled before he remembered she was not someone he felt any inclination to smile at.

Gawain leaned forward too. "We don't have time for this." Looking at Sophie, he explained, "When Nikolas and I are together, we raise a discernible amount of energy between us. It is the same when we are with our comrades. The more of us who gather, the stronger the effect. We don't do anything to generate it. It occurs naturally, although the effect also grows in intensity whenever we use magic."

As Gawain spoke, Nikolas kept his attention trained on her. He found himself reluctant to look away. The miniscule changes in her expression were fascinating.

Her eyelids lowered briefly. "I think I understand what you're saying. I can feel it just sitting here with you."

"Our enemies use that to hunt us. As we are not a strong enough force to defeat them, it keeps us from banding together for any length of time."

Her attention turned sharp and piercing. She looked interested in their problem almost in spite of herself. "What if you throw a null spell? Won't that dissipate the energy?"

Nikolas didn't like how she focused solely on Gawain. He said abruptly, "Yes, but the effect only lasts for a few minutes."

"Usually, my null spells don't last long either." She hesitated, then said slowly, almost reluctantly, "What if I told you I might have a way to hold the null spell in place for longer than a few minutes. Would you be interested?"

"Do you mean like an amulet?" Nikolas didn't like the sound of that.

No magic user liked null spells in amulets or jewelry. Typically, only nonmagical creatures liked to use null spell jewelry for protection, and prisons used null spells in cells and handcuffs to contain dangerous, Powerful prisoners.

Null spell amulets also worked counter to the Da-oine Sidhe purpose when they gathered to cast the invocation to contact Lyonesse. Handling null amulets hampered their ability to cast defensive and offensive spells and to detect dangers around them.

"No," Sophie replied. "What I can do is not that permanent, and it's easily negated. Would you be interested?"

Nikolas met Gawain's eyes. He could see the other man was as intrigued as he was. Gawain said, "Even if you could, it would have limited application. Dampening our Power also means crippling our abilities and dulling our senses. It's a dangerous proposition to consider."

"True," Sophie agreed. "It would really only achieve one thing—it would give you the ability to be together for longer than a few minutes without being detected."

He glanced at Gawain again. They could have a real conversation, maybe share a meal together. The lure was so strong Nikolas pulled back emotionally from it. In a harsh voice, he said, "What's the catch to this?"

Sophie's slender black eyebrows rose. "As far as I can tell, there are two catches. You already know the first. It would hamper your ability to cast spells, at least until you rinsed the spell off, which is easy to do. The second is—you haven't convinced me yet that I should do a goddamn thing for you."

She held Robin on her lap protectively as she

spoke, while she glared first at Nikolas then at Gawain, who replied with quiet courtesy, "You have every right to feel the way you do, after what just happened. What can we do to convince you?"

She compressed those luscious, sensual lips of hers. Then in a tight voice, she asked, "Did either of you have anything to do with a nasty spell I encountered while I was walking into town?" She looked at Gawain. "You know what I'm talking about. I saw you slow down on your bike and study the area where it landed."

Gawain's expression changed. "You were there when I was?"

"Yes." She looked down at the creature in her lap. "Both—what is his name, Robin?—and I were."

"I had no idea," he murmured as if to himself. "I didn't sense you at all."

Her mouth quirked. "That's because I didn't want you to."

She was cocky, Nikolas would give her that. Absently he twisted the signet ring on his ring finger while he listened to their exchange. Sophie's attention dropped to the movement.

He told her abruptly, "The woman who created that spell is our mortal enemy. She's the one who is trying to destroy us."

For the first time, Sophie regarded him without anger or distaste. Gently she pulled one of the dog's ears to the side, revealing its bony, blistered neck. She said, "That spell was woven into a broken silver rope tied around Robin's neck."

"Is that what happened?" Nikolas asked the puck. "Did the Queen imprison you?" The puck remained silent. "Robin? Why aren't you speaking?"

The dog opened its mouth and showed him. In the recess where a tongue should be, there was only a stump.

Nikolas clenched his teeth. Gawain swore under his breath. Sophie blanched visibly while horror darkened her eyes. She whispered, "Earlier when I fell asleep, I dreamed about being in a cage while they tore out my tongue and threw it on a fire."

Nikolas tried telepathy. *Robin. Tell me what happened to you.*

The puck gave no indication that he heard. Tilting his head back, he watched Sophie's face unwaveringly, like the dog he appeared to be.

Aloud, Nikolas said, "He's not talking telepathically either. I'm not even sure I connected with him."

An odd expression crossed Sophie's face, and a small, bitter smile twisted her lips. She murmured, "He's nonverbal, possibly trauma induced. Hopefully he'll recover his language as he heals. I've known it to happen."

As they talked, Arran walked up to their table, carrying a tray. He looked at Nikolas. "Everyone else has been served, my lord, just as you requested. What can I bring you? Drinks and supper?"

Nikolas glanced at Gawain, who said, "A half hour

is almost up. Either we need to split up, or we can see what this young lady might be able to do for us." Gawain turned to Sophie. "I don't want to be forced to leave before we've finished this conversation. I'll volunteer for your spell if you would be so kind to cast it."

Every muscle in Nikolas's body tensed. It went against all his instincts to trust a stranger to put a spell on one of them, especially when he had clashed with her before, and even now, she held a creature he had never entirely trusted on her lap as they talked.

Then he looked at Robin again, at the protruding bones underneath the thin skin, and the filmy look in eyes had that once snapped with dark sparks of intelligence and mischief. The puck looked ruined, and Nikolas did not think Robin would sit so trustingly on the lap of someone who had been involved in what had happened to him.

He also noticed the gentle protectiveness in the way Sophie curled her hand around the dog's shoulder, and he remembered how she had stood up to both him and Gawain in defense of what she had thought was an abused pet.

That took courage and decency.

Sophie had noticed his tension and hesitation. "While I appreciate that I frighten you deeply, you can relax," she said in a sour aside to him. "It's just a spell drawn with magic-sensitive colloidal silver. It'll rinse off with water, or you can spit on it and rub it off on your jeans in a pinch. You don't have to carry an amulet, and there's no damage done. And it will last for hours, if you want it to, as long as you don't work up a sweat."

At her sarcasm, antagonism flared, hot and bright, but he held himself in a clench because Gawain had been right. They had been too long at war, and all his responses to conflict were violent and deadly.

She must have seen it in his eyes, along the dangerous way his body was coiled as if to strike, because her expression flickered and she edged away from him. She hadn't blinked or flinched before that moment.

Nikolas dismissed her before he did something he couldn't take back and turned his attention to Arran, who was still waiting. He told the pub keeper, "Bring us Guinness and supper. Whatever your special is for the evening will do."

"Very good, my lord." The pub keeper slipped away.

"I don't know if I like Guinness," Sophie said. "I've never had it before. And I'm not sure I want to sit here and try to choke down food with you two watching me. Thanks for asking, asshole."

"For the love of all the gods, you stupid woman," Nikolas said between his teeth. "Is that petty point really what you want to focus on right now?"

He didn't realize he had spoken in the old tongue until he saw the incomprehension in her face. Gawain coughed quietly into one hand and nudged him under the table with one foot.

Sophie lifted one shoulder. "I'm not sure what you said there, but I have a feeling it was not complimentary. Let's clear up a few things for you old-timey folks—not that this is likely to come up again anytime soon. Don't touch me without my permission. Don't order anything for me again. Don't speak for me when I can speak for myself. Don't open doors for me, and don't take that patronizing, lord-of-all-you-survey tone with me. Not if you want me to do a goddamn thing for you. You still owe me for the attack from two weeks ago—and for this." She indicated the bruises appearing on her wrist. "Understood?"

Nikolas curled a nostril and didn't deign to reply. Gawain coughed again. "I, for one, understood that perfectly."

She gave Gawain a tight smile. "I'll go get my vial. Be right back."

Gawain nodded. "Thank you."

As she stood, she tried to put Robin down in her seat, but the dog let out a sudden *ki-yi* that was so loud all conversation paused as everybody looked at them.

"Oh fine," she snapped. She tucked him under her arm, and together they left.

When they were alone again, Nikolas and Gawain looked at each other. Gawain said, "What is the matter with you? You grabbed her and shoved her into the wall, and all because she stopped to help an injured creature?"

The edged note in the other man's quiet voice rankled. Nikolas snapped, "There's more going on than that."

"Well, I've never seen you act this way." The other man studied him keenly. "What did she mean when she said you attacked her?"

"You remember when I killed four Hounds a fortnight ago, just before the summer solstice gathering?"

Gawain frowned. "Yes."

"The fog rolled over the park within seconds, and the Hounds attacked. Just as I killed the last one, I felt a presence. When I turned around, she was there. Not physically. It was more like a vision. I thought she was part of the ambush, possibly responsible for the fog, and I threw a morningstar at her." Nikolas set his teeth. "And we still don't know if she was involved or not. All we really know is that Robin seems attached to her, so it's unlikely she was involved in torturing him."

Gawain's frown deepened as he considered that. "The pub keeper said she just arrived in England."

"He said she just arrived in England *today*." Nikolas stressed the last word. "That has nothing to do with where she was two weeks ago. She could have been here, left, and come back again. Or she could have been involved while in a different location. We never connected physically. It was all psychic, all magical."

"Damn. Okay." Gawain blew out a breath as he rubbed the back of his neck. "If she was involved in the attack, she might try to make a run for it."

"We'll know if she tries to leave," Nikolas said.

"And I'm sure she has figured that out."

A pause, as they both listened to the normal sounds in the pub, and Nikolas listened with more than just his ears. He could sense her presence above them, on the second floor, and hear her light, decisive footsteps.

"I don't think she's going to try to leave," Gawain said suddenly. "She's become too immersed in what's happening. And she wouldn't let go of the dog when she thought we might want to hurt it. That doesn't sound like someone who would cast a blanket of fog to cover up a murder."

"No, it doesn't, does it?" Nikolas murmured. He tilted his head. "She wouldn't even put Robin down just now when he didn't want her to leave him."

He still didn't like how she had shown up at the same time Robin had reappeared, but that could have been a coincidence. What had happened a fortnight ago could have been a coincidence too—but that was a hell of a lot of coincidence. It made him uneasy.

In any case, he had to give credit where credit was due. She might be irritating and mouthy, and she seemed to embody more than one contradiction, but she also appeared to have a streak of genuine kindness.

The woman might end up having more soul than he did.

"WHAT I WOULDN'T give for my Glock," Sophie said under her breath to the dog who wasn't a dog riding in the curve of her arm. To the puck. Whatever a puck was. "You have no idea. I know a gun isn't the answer to everything. I know I have many other skills I can rely upon, but a gun is ready, you see, when spells might not be. It can lie under your pillow while you sleep, standing sentinel as you dream, all the bullets nicely nested and just waiting to be fired."

Robin blinked up at her, looking as if he was trying to comprehend what she was saying. Really, he was playing the dog very well.

She muttered, "I know it's not attractive to constantly complain about something you can do nothing about, but as long as you're riding with me, I guess you're going to have to put up with it."

While she talked, she unlocked the door to her room, opened her bigger suitcase, and rummaged through the contents until she found the correct royal blue, stoppered bottle along with the small, thin brush she had attached to it with a rubber band. After locking her room again, she loped down the stairs.

Ignoring the sidelong looks from the patrons they'd not yet managed to scare off, she crossed the front room quickly to slide back into her seat. The two men had been conversing in low voices. As she joined them, they sat back and turned their attention to her.

Gawain was the one she trusted so far, at least to some extent. He was the one who made an effort to be decent, whereas Nikolas might have sheathed his physical weapon, but he had never fully put away his blade.

Nikolas watched her now, his dark eyes cold and assessing. He had an utterly beautiful, completely mesmerizing face that was ruined with the edge of malice that was never far from his expression.

At least it wasn't very far whenever he looked at her. When he turned his attention to Gawain, something much warmer and truer appeared, like the glimpse of a golden city concealed behind a midnight curtain.

It made her heart heavy in a way she didn't understand, that the one part of the man could be so filled with rancor, while the other part, the barely glimpsed part, was so... so...

So fine. There was a fineness to him, or there could be, if the chilling ferocity eased up and gave the other side of him a chance to breathe.

Well. What she felt or thought about this deadly stranger didn't matter in the slightest to anyone except for her. Shoving her ruminations aside, she smiled at Gawain. It said something about a man when a saber-toothed tiger was the safer, kinder bet.

Noting the fascinated look on Gawain's face, she held out the bottle for him to inspect. "Colloidal silver. You know what that is, right?"

Shaking his head, Gawain opened the bottle and pulled out the stopper to sniff at it. He squeezed a few drops onto the tip of one blunt finger, then stopped the bottle and handed it over to Nikolas, who inspected it just as thoroughly.

While they ascertained for themselves that the liquid in the bottle was essentially harmless—at least in its inert state—she said, "Colloidal silver is a simple concoction of silver particles in demineralized water. Some people take it as a supplement for health reasons. I have no idea if it does them any good. A lot of sites, like the National Institutes of Health, have a list of serious side effects that can occur if you take it regularly as an oral supplement. At least for humans."

Just as Gawain had, Nikolas took a few drops on his finger and tasted it cautiously. "You said this is made with magic-sensitive silver."

"That's right. At the moment, the liquid is neutral, like a blank page." She smiled at Gawain. "Ready?"

"Ready when you are."

"Give me your hand."

Obligingly, he held his hand across the table. Settling Robin in her lap, she urged Gawain to turn his hand over so that the broad back was upright.

"I'll go slowly," she told him. "If you're uncomfortable and you want me to stop at any time, all you have to do is say so. And remember, the only thing you have to do to get rid of this particular spell is splash it with some kind of liquid and rub it off. Okay?"

"Okay," he told her in a steady voice.

He watched her calmly as she took the stopper out and dipped her thin paintbrush in the liquid. Then, lightly, she began to stroke a rune onto his skin while she whispered the null spell that would sink into the pattern the silver made. Gawain remained calm and interested, which was not at all how Nikolas reacted.

Thank gods the spell was a technically simple one that she could cast in her sleep, because the nuclear warhead watching her work had an expression filled with such terrible promises of retribution if she did anything to hurt his friend, it was enough to give her nightmares for weeks.

Like she needed any more fodder for nightmares.

She was used to handling a certain amount of pressure, but still her fingers were shaking slightly by the time she finished. Once the spell had been solidly cast, she could feel the energy in the room ease down. Now only Nikolas still shone like a pillar of flame against her mind's eye.

She looked up into Gawain's eyes. "You good?"

He nodded. "I'm good. You have a light touch with your magic."

Capping the vial, she murmured, "Why use a sledgehammer when a butterfly net will suffice?"

She most emphatically didn't look to her left where the sledgehammer sat.

Either the sledgehammer was not aware it was being discussed, or it was not amused. It emitted a chilly silence while Gawain coughed into his hand again. Sophie could see a corner of his mouth turn up in brief amusement.

He said, "I can feel the spell lying on my skin, but

it's not irritating. It's a little like a temporary tattoo, isn't it?"

"In a way."

"Where did you learn this skill?" He flattened his hand and tilted it back and forth. There was a faint shimmer where the rune lay against his skin. "Can you buy this liquid?"

"When I left home, I came across an old Native American woman in Nevada who showed me how to work with magic-sensitive silver. She taught me how to make the colloidal silver and cast spells with it. I've never heard of anybody else with the skill, and I've never seen magic-sensitive colloidal silver for sale." She shook the vial before pocketing it. "I made this myself."

"Fascinating."

After giving Gawain a smile, she turned to look into Nikolas's dark, cold eyes. "You have questions. I have questions. Since I just helped you and your friend eat supper together, I'll go first. What is a puck?"

She braced herself for some sort of retaliation for all the snark she'd been feeding him, but he surprised her by giving her a straightforward answer.

"Some people call them lesser Fae, but they aren't strictly Fae," he said. "They are like sprites or brownies. In his normal state, Robin looks almost like a boy. He has an affinity with nature, he can shapeshift into a variety of forms, and he's intensely magical. Usually."

All three of them looked at Robin, sitting quietly in

her lap. The puck seemed to be watching shadows move on the wall, appearing to pay no attention to them.

"My turn," Nikolas said. The intensity in his expression sharpened. "Where were you a fortnight ago, and what were you doing?"

For some reason she felt a flush warm her cheeks as if she had been caught spying on him, when she had done no such thing. "I was in Los Angeles, where I've been living, and I was casting runes for a reading. I focused on my near future, threw the stones, and a vision of you appeared. You were holding a bloody sword, you saw me, and you threw something at me. I could feel it coming, and it didn't feel good, so I scattered the stones and broke the connection. End of story."

She paused. Both men were listening to her intently and watching every move she made. She had no doubt that they had highly developed truthsense and were using it. "My turn," she said. "What were *you* doing two weeks ago? Why was your sword bloody? And why did you attack me?"

"I had just been attacked myself, and I thought you were part of the ambush. I was defending myself." His eyes narrowed. "Were you a part of it?"

"*No*," she said emphatically. "Absolutely not. I'm going to say this as clearly as possible so you can hear the truth in my voice. I have never met you before. I've never heard of either one of you before. I have no idea what you're up to, or who you are fighting, and I did not have anything to do with what happened to you. In fact, I don't know why my reading didn't behave normally. You should never have been able to see me, and I wasn't scrying—I was working divination. They're two totally different magics."

"Of course they are," Gawain muttered, rubbing his jaw thoughtfully.

"Then how did we collide like that?" Sophie asked. She was eager for some explanation, because she never wanted to have it happen again.

Ever since that morning two weeks ago, she hadn't felt easy about casting the runes. She had still done it a few times anyway, but she was always on highest alert for any danger, and she had never felt that way before about her rune readings. They used to be a source of comfort and information, and she missed the familiar ease with which she had done them.

"There was other magic that day." Nikolas leaned back and crossed his arms. The corner wall light threw part of his face into shadow while emphasizing the inhuman beauty in his bone structure. His black shirt fell open at the collar, revealing the strong, pure line of his throat. He regarded the puck narrowly. "Something else was in play. I'm still working to discover what. I thought it was part of the ambush too, but now I'm not so certain. Maybe it was, maybe it wasn't."

Their conversation was interrupted as Arran walked up with a tray of food and drink.

Sophie used the time to regroup as she considered everything they had discussed.

She did not have the highly developed truthsense that many of the Elder Races acquired with experience and age, but she still didn't believe they had lied to her. They had a dangerous enemy, who was also the one responsible for abusing Robin.

Nikolas had believed she'd helped to attack him. It explained why he had responded the way he had, both two weeks ago and just earlier. It didn't make him likeable or friendly, and it certainly didn't make him any less dangerous, but knowing that did ease her tension.

Suddenly the plate of beef stew and homemade bread that Arran set in front of her smelled appetizing, and she thought she might be able to eat at the same table with the two males after all.

When the food arrived, Robin began to tremble so violently he almost slid off her lap.

She offered him a piece of the fragrant bread. He nearly bit her fingers as he snatched at it. "I'm going to put some stew in a dish for you," she told him gently. "Since you're in the form of a dog, you'll be more comfortable eating on the floor."

As he worked at gulping down the bread, she lifted him onto the floor. When she straightened, she caught Nikolas watching her, his expression inscrutable. His close attention made her uncomfortable. She decided the best thing to do was to ignore it.

Ladling stew onto her bread plate, she picked out

the choicest pieces of beef and potatoes as she said to Nikolas, "One thing rang true out of this. I asked for a vision of my near future, and you were in it. And now we've done it. We've met. So that bit is over. We can all move on and go our separate ways."

She set the filled bread plate on the floor, and Robin attacked it. It was hard to watch him bolt the food while his body still trembled. Her eyes prickled with a flood of moisture, and after a moment, she had to look away—back at Nikolas, as it happened, who had not stopped watching her.

"Why are you in England?" he asked. "What are you doing here?"

Blinking away the wetness, she focused on her food. "That's a long story. The short version is, I'm on vacation for three months. I'm here to see if I can somehow get into the old Weston manor. If I can, then I'll inherit it and the grounds, along with an annuity. Kind of kooky, huh?"

While Nikolas hadn't picked up a utensil yet, Gawain ate with a kind of single-minded attention that said he thoroughly appreciated a hot, filling meal. Gawain asked, "What do you do in LA?"

"I was a witch consultant for the LAPD," she told him as she slipped another piece of bread to Robin. She hesitated. She should make herself talk about it. It's just a thing that happened in her past. Say it. Be done with it. Move on. "There was a shooting. I was involved. I needed a break, so when this opportunity came, I leaped at it."

Nikolas said, "You were shot?"

How had he known to ask that question? She glanced at him. She didn't mean to meet his eyes, but she did, and the shock of connection was there again, jolting her down to her shoes. Clearing her throat, she said in a husky voice, "Yeah, I was. I got over it."

Even to her own ears, she could hear the lie in that. Of course they heard it too. Plunging onward, she said, "You never told me who your enemy was."

"Some names you don't speak in public," Nikolas said quietly.

Her fork paused in midair as she absorbed the implications of that. She reached out with telepathy. *How about telepathically?*

Some names shouldn't be spoken telepathically either. His mental voice was a deep, true baritone. *Not if all of us are going our separate ways. The wisest thing, by far the safest thing, would be for you to give Robin over to us and go back to your own agenda.*

But she wasn't exactly talented at picking the wisest or the safest thing. She looked down at the puck. Robin had finished eating, and he moved to lean against her ankle. Bending down, she looked into his filmy eyes and said softly, "Robin, I made you a promise that I would make everything okay. That hasn't changed just because I know you're not a dog. Do you want to go with Nikolas or Gawain, or would you rather stay with me until you're feeling better?"

He didn't answer her in words. Instead, he stood against her leg, begging for her to pick him up. As she gathered him into her arms, she felt his belly, which was visibly rounded after his meal.

Straightening, she looked at Nikolas and Gawain. They were both watching her with troubled frowns. She told them, "He's staying with me for now."

Nikolas's frown turned fierce. "You're making a mistake."

Her voice turned cool. "I'm making a decision to honor a promise I made. That's never a mistake."

"No, but you weren't in the possession of all the facts when you made it." Nikolas nodded at Robin. "He's been involved in our war in some way, and that could be very bad, for both you and for him."

She didn't waver. "I knew about the rope when I took it off his neck. I knew I had a major problem with whoever had created it, and I made the promise to him then. You're choosing to withhold information from me that could be useful, but that doesn't actually change a thing."

Gawain rubbed his face. "We're not telling you anything, lass, because we're trying to protect you."

"I should have added one more thing to my list." She gave them a cold, thin smile. "Don't try to protect me in spite of myself."

Quick anger burned in Nikolas's dark eyes. "You don't know what you're getting yourself into."

"Yeah, well, whose fault is that?" They looked at

each other but remained silent, so she stood and hoisted Robin under her arm. "Glad we got a chance to clear the air. Thanks for supper. Good-bye."

When she walked away, neither of them tried to stop her. She wasn't surprised. She hadn't expected them to. They might have cleared the air, but that was all they had achieved.

Because they knew as well as she did: the enemy of her enemy was not necessarily her friend.

Chapter Six

B ACK IN HER room, Sophie set Robin on the bed and paced. They might have cleared the air, but the aftermath of the confrontation with Nikolas still leaped in her muscles. She was wound too tightly, and after that horrible nap, she was never going to get to sleep.

She almost scooped up her purse and keys to leave, but running into Nikolas had been a strong wake-up call. Instead, she sat at the old, worn armchair tucked into one corner of the room and pulled out her colloidal silver. Not the water-based colloidal silver that she had used on Gawain. This time she pulled out another vial from her suitcase.

Robin had curled up on the bed, but when she uncapped the vial, he sat up to watch her. His eyes seemed brighter and more focused.

After giving him an assessing look, she turned to her work. Fifteen minutes later, after whispering spells that she painted onto her hands and forearms, she finally felt ready to leave her room. When the last spell was dry, she capped the vial, stood, and scooped up her purse.

Robin leaped off the bed. She told him, "There's no reason for you to come along just because I've got insomnia. You should stay and rest."

Instead of taking her up on her suggestion, he went over to stand by the door. He was moving better too, she saw, so she shrugged and opened the door for him. Together they went quietly down the stairs.

Business in the pub was winding down. She found Maggie washing glasses. The other woman greeted her with more reserve than she had earlier. Sophie regretted that, but she didn't blame her. She said, "I'm going for a drive. How would you like for me to come back in?"

Maggie told her, "We lock up the front of the building where the liquor is, but you can come in the back entrance. We'll be up late for a private gathering." She eyed Sophie curiously. "You won't find anything open. Town's all closed up this time of night."

"That's all right. The countryside is beautiful, and I'm never going to sleep anyway."

Besides, curiosity was eating her alive. Sophie turned to go, Robin at her heels. She let the puck leap into the Mini first, then she climbed into the driver's seat.

"Here goes nothing," she muttered, reaching for the ignition.

The car started perfectly. The GPS worked as well, the fucking fucker. Annoyed but not surprised, she smacked it with the back of her hand, double-checked her directions, then pulled out of the lot.

Within a few moments, she had left the streetlights of Westmarch behind and plunged into deep countryside. Overhead, the moon was full and gorgeous in a midnight blue, clear sky, and the stars were so bright and seemed so close Sophie felt like she could pluck them out of the sky.

The roads she drove were narrow and winding, and clusters of trees and hedges threw deep, almost impenetrable shadows, so she drove slowly. The land was alive with such aged magic, after a few moments she felt drunk on it. She rolled down the windows to let a fitful breeze gust into the car. Beside her in the passenger seat, Robin sat still, his eyes glistening in the dim dashboard lights.

As they drew closer, she could feel it, the broken crossover passageway. Then stone pillars emerged from the darkness, outlined by the car's headlights. They had once supported iron gates that blocked the drive to the house, but as she turned gently onto the gravel drive, she saw that the gates now leaned against the pillars, overgrown with ivy.

The sound of tires crunching on the gravel seemed very loud in the dense quiet. The grass on either side of the driveway looked freshly mowed, while a deep, unkempt forest bordered the green lawn. After she had turned into the drive, a small cottage came into view. That would be the gatekeeper's house, her home for the next three months.

She could explore that tomorrow. She went farther, about a hundred yards or so, and as she drove around a bend past a clump of trees, the house came into view.

The house. The family albatross.

In the full moonlight, the massive manor house was a hulking, shadowed mystery. She let the car drift to a stop, then turned off the engine and stepped out, holding the door for Robin to follow. To her senses, the house felt steeped with all the magnificent, shattered magic of the crossover passageway.

Studying the roof, she counted. There seemed to be five gables at first, but then, just as it had when she had studied the photograph, her vision shifted and there were seven. She laughed softly, as she felt herself doing the most foolish thing she had done in years.

She fell in love with the albatross. Right there, in the moonlight, she fell in love with what had to be the most useless piece of real estate in the United Kingdom.

One of the things she had packed for her trip was a compact Maglite that fit easily into her purse. She pulled it out now to shine light on the ground as she picked her way along the broken flagstone path to the wide front doors. They were thick and sturdy, made of oak and bound with iron. Surprised that the flashlight worked so close to the building, she wondered if that meant she would be able to take photos from inside.

She had brought the keys to both the gatekeeper's house and the manor, but she didn't bother to pull out the manor house's ancient key. Instead, she clicked off the Maglite, tucked it into the back pocket of her jeans, and placed both flattened hands on the oak doors to see what the house had to say for itself.

Intense darkness settled around her as she stood in the house's shadow. For long moments she lost herself, tracing the shards of the crossover magic. So much magic. She could immerse herself completely in it, like plunging into the deep part of a pool.

There it was, the part she had been searching for that was slightly off. When she had seen the photos, she had wondered, but now she knew for a certainty.

"You're going to be mine," she whispered to the house.

But even she had her limits. Trying to enter this place was not something to be done in the middle of the night. She would wait until tomorrow to see if she was right.

As she mentally hugged herself with glee, a voice spoke behind her. A deep, slightly accented, unfortunately familiar voice.

Nikolas said, "It's not wise to wander this countryside during a full moon."

Her heart knocked against her ribs like a wild creature trying to break free of a cage. Whirling, she put the oak and iron doors to her back as she stared at the tall, imposing figure standing a few yards away. He was a shadow within a shadow, an intense, midnight star of magic more Powerful than all the magic of the land around her.

She clenched her hands, grateful she had prepared both defensive and offensive spells this time instead of feeling naked and defenseless as the day she was born. "What are you doing here?"

Her cold furious intent came out breathless and shaken.

"Following you." The black shadow strode toward her. "What in hell possessed you to come out to this gods forsaken place in the middle of the night?"

I was too curious. I have such a burning need to feel a part of something, to own my own space of ground even if it's a haunted and hollow place, that I couldn't wait for tomorrow.

All the truthful words were tangled and too revealing. She swallowed hard and snapped, "What I do or don't do is none of your damn business. Stop walking."

"You make no sense. Why on earth should I stop walking?" The black shadow still moved toward her with some unknown purposeful intent.

It unsettled her so much she dug out the Maglite, clicked it on and aimed it at his face.

What she saw startled her so badly she dropped the flashlight. "Jesus Christ."

As Nikolas reached her, he bent to pick up the flashlight. He said coldly, "I assume that means you have the ability to see what the moonshadow reveals."

"I've no idea what you're talking about," she whispered, staring at him.

For a moment when she had first laid eyes on him, she had seen the predatory eyes of a leopard looking back at her. Then the leopard was gone, and in its place stood a tall knight in chain mail, his black cloak falling to the ankles of tall boots.

It was Nikolas, and yet not Nikolas. He had the same terrible, immortal beauty, the same eyes, the same mouth, but his hair wasn't cut short. It fell to his broad shoulders, and his expression was stamped with clear, implacable determination.

Then that image was gone too, and the real Nikolas stood before her, leaner, harder and darker. He was dressed in the same black pants and shirt he had worn at the pub. The folds of the dark cloth shifted as he moved, catching the strong streak of illumination from the flashlight in the intense shadows and hinting at the powerful body it sheathed.

"No?" In the slanted light that he pointed away from them, his expression was stony, while his dark eyes glittered like onyx. "Then tell me, what did you see that frightened you so?"

"I wasn't frightened," she said frankly, knocked out of her outrage at finding him here. She paused, for some reason reluctant to describe the knight that she had seen. "I was startled. I think I saw a flash of a leopard. Are you part Wyr?"

"Yes. And Elven. And Dark Fae." His voice was icy, bored. "Why, do you find me monstrous now?"

"Of course not!" she snapped. "Why would you say

such a thing?"

"Because many do. The enemy we fight wants to exterminate us for our mixed race."

"Then they're stupid. I'm not stupid." She held out her hand for the flashlight. "What did the—what did you call it?—the moonshadow have to do with my seeing that?"

"This land is steeped in so much magic that you don't understand, history that you don't know, and dangers you don't comprehend."

"Just because I don't know something doesn't mean I can't learn it," she pointed out acerbically. "Bigotry and racism are flaws. Withholding information because you think you know better is a flaw. Ignorance isn't a flaw."

He handed the flashlight to her, and she turned it off, plunging them both into deep darkness. After a moment, he said, "Standing in a shadow cast by the moon reveals a person's true nature to those with the ability to see it."

His true nature, leopard, knight, and prince. She was still shaken and awed in spite of herself. Busily she ran around inside her head, stamping out all the sneaky pieces of awe she could find.

"So what exactly does that mean?" she asked. "What do you see when you look at me?"

"Just as you see the Wyr in me, I see the Djinn in you."

✧　✧　✧

EARLIER IN THE pub, Nikolas had been glad when Sophie had walked off in a huff. It meant he could concentrate on eating the rest of his meal in peace and enjoy the rare chance of relaxing with Gawain.

The beef stew was excellent. He finished his meal in a few bites. As he wiped the corners of his mouth, Gawain muttered, "I know we can't be responsible for everybody we run into, but sometimes that sits ill in my belly. That girl is going to get herself killed."

"She's not a girl," Nikolas said. "As she pointed out earlier, she's a woman fully capable of making her own decisions, no matter how imbecilic they may be. And let's be accurate. Robin is the one who will get her killed. He should have stayed with us instead of going with her. If we're right, and the Queen had been holding him prisoner, she'll be looking for him. And he will lead her right to Sophie."

"*Agh.*" Gawain ran big hands through his hair. "I want to strangle her with my bare hands."

Nikolas knew Gawain wasn't referring to Sophie. He finished his Guinness. "As good as it's been to sit with you for a while, we need to split up."

"Aye, I know." Gawain looked down at the back of his hand. He said softly, "It's a good spell, a good technique."

"Yes, it is. I'll give her that." After a moment's hesitation, Nikolas told him, "You go on. I'm going to stay."

A look of relief crossed the other man's face.

"You'll watch over her?"

"I'm certainly going to watch her, at least for a while." His tone was dry as he rephrased what Gawain had said in a small but important way. "Maybe I can talk to her again and convince her to send the puck with me. Or maybe I can talk to Robin again and convince him to leave her."

Gawain blew out a breath. "If you want, I can be the one to stay and watch over them."

"No." His response was so swift and decisive the other man paused to stare at him. "I'll be the one to do it."

If Gawain stayed to do the job, he would be too nice about it. He might hesitate if he had to make a difficult decision, whereas Nikolas had lost the nice part of himself a long time ago.

Besides, he didn't want the other man around Sophie, watching her, possibly even spending time with her. That was his to do, no one else's. He frowned, caught by the unusual thought.

"I don't know, man. She didn't react so well to you," Gawain pointed out. "And to be honest, you didn't react so well to her either. She responded better to me."

"We're worried about her feelings now?" Nikolas narrowed his eyes and gave the other man a hard look. "I don't think so. I'm the one who needs to stay. She saw a vision with me in it, and there's something that connected us together strongly enough so that I saw her too. Some other kind of magic. She said her vision was complete now that we'd met, but I don't know that I believe her. Besides, she might have more skills that would be useful to us." He paused. "It would also come in handy if she would teach one of us the technique she used to cast the temporary null spell she painted on your hand."

"I'm not going to argue with that," Gawain said. He stood, and Nikolas followed suit to haul him into a hard hug. "You want me to update the others?"

"You can if you want. There's not much to tell them yet."

Gawain squeezed his arm. "Look after yourself, Nik."

"You do the same."

As he watched, Gawain spat on the back of his hand and rubbed it on his napkin. Within seconds, the null spell evaporated. The witch had been true to her word.

Gawain strode out, and Nikolas stayed just long enough to pay the bill, then he too left and studied the outside of the building until he found the window of Sophie's room. Settling his back against the trunk of a tree, he watched until her light went dark. A few moments later, she left the pub.

Now, facing her in the shadow of the cursed house, he was glad she had turned off the flashlight. His night vision adjusted quickly until he could see almost as well as if it were daylight.

Except it wasn't daylight. The moon's magic spilled all around them, and in the privacy of the relative darkness, he was able to stare his full at the female who stood in front of him.

She was magnificent. In the truth revealed by the moonshadow, her eyes gleamed brilliant like diamonds, and an unseen wind played in her dark hair. The angles of her face blended harmoniously into a strong, feminine whole. The effect was softened by the generous curves of her mouth. Silver runes shone on her hands and arms, gleaming with magic spells overlaid upon spells.

She was an enchantress, dangerous and Powerful, and for the first time since they had met in the flesh, he fully acknowledged she was her own force to be reckoned with.

When he named her as part Djinn, she stared at him. "No one has ever been able to tell me what I was before. I had to find it out for myself."

"Did you?" He found that he was intrigued, while his attention lingered on the shining spells on her arms. They made her look both elegant and barbaric at once. "How did you discover your nature, if no one was able to tell you? Didn't your family know?"

"When I was five, I was adopted into a family of witches. It wasn't a good experience, and I left home when I was eighteen. But I had plenty of training while I lived with them, and I already knew there was something odd about me when I left. Something not quite human."

"Did that bother your adopted family?"

She snorted. "When I was younger, I liked to blame how they treated me on that unknown part of me, but the truth was, they were just predatory jerks. They trained their children in witchcraft to work in the family business. I was very magical and not quite theirs, so I was expected to work harder than everyone else to justify my place. They made their affection conditional on how well I did, and I never quite measured up. I was never quite good enough, so I always had to keep working harder and harder. They made a good profit off me for a while until I was old enough to understand what they were doing and choose a better life for myself."

He raised his eyebrows. "That is a subtle kind of cruelty, especially to a child who doesn't have the defenses and filters that an adult has."

"Yes." She turned away from the house and picked her way carefully along the flagstone path back to the Mini, and he strode along beside her. "Anyway, I left home as soon as I could, and I traveled from demesne to demesne and talked to the most knowledgeable people I could find in each place. When I reached the Demonkind demesne in Houston, I found my answer with the Djinn. I stayed with them for a while and learned what I could, then I made my way west and spent a few years with my teacher in Nevada before getting the consultant job in LA. So there you have it—

twenty-nine years encapsulated in a few sentences."

"For you to carry Djinn magic, the Djinn in your past must have fallen into flesh and mated with your human ancestor."

"That's my understanding."

From what little Nikolas knew, the rare Djinn who fell into flesh were typically not fertile or able to bear children. He murmured, "You are a very rare occurrence, Sophie Ross."

"I've been called less flattering things. 'Anomaly,' 'abnormality.' Personally, I like 'statistical outlier' the best." Several yards from the car, she swung around to confront him. "I don't like being followed. What are you doing here?"

He smiled to himself. She had drawn him out of the shadow of the house, into the open clearing where she could see more clearly. If he wasn't careful, he might end up liking this almost-human female.

"Earlier you said that now we've met, we're done. I don't believe you," he told her. Then he switched to telepathy. *And Robin is going to get you killed. If he escaped from the one who was holding him prisoner, she's going to come after him.*

Isabeau, you mean? she said. *The Fae Queen of the Light Court is going to come here, to me?*

He clenched his teeth and gave her a dark look.

She laughed, and the wind picked up the sound, carrying it across the open space. The wind loved her, Nikolas noted. He barely felt the breeze in passing, but it played with her hair constantly.

She told him, *Did you think I wouldn't notice when you said "Queen" earlier, or I wouldn't put two and two together? I read a few things before I came, so I'm not quite as ignorant as you might think. Your enemy is the Light Court. I'm guessing that makes you a member of the Dark Court, and probably one of high standing, but I'm not going to make any assumptions— from what I've heard and read about her, I'm guessing Isabeau has a talent for making enemies.*

He did not like how much he enjoyed the sound of her laughter. He did not like the casual way she stated her assumptions, even if she was right.

"And the more I see of you, the more I'm convinced you're going to die badly of your own stupidity," he growled aloud.

That caused her to laugh harder. "Well, that could certainly be true."

Some angry impulse propelled him forward into her personal space. She turned her face up to him, and her eyes sparkled like precious jewels while the moonlight on her skin was unutterably lovely.

She looked too calm for his peace of mind, too unruffled, and far too beautiful, and his wayward thoughts had turned too poetic.

He snapped in a low tone, "You do not take this nearly seriously enough. You might be talented at your own magic. I believe you. I see that message written clearly in the runes you bear on your skin. But if you try to stand against her, *she will obliterate you.* She has more

Power at her command than you can possibly imagine, and she has killed many of us—strong, mature warriors who were just as talented and as experienced as you are. She caused *this* to happen."

With a sweeping, violent gesture, he indicated the landscape around them.

She looked around, her expression finally sobering. "She's the one who broke the crossover passageway?"

"Not her personally." The bloody memories caused him to clench his fists while a muscle leaped in his jaw. "That was Morgan, the Captain of her Hounds."

"Morgan le Fae," she whispered.

"You've heard of him," Nikolas said, turning to watch her expression closely.

"I think almost everyone with some kind of tie to the magical has heard of the most famous bard and sorcerer of the Middle Ages. I can't imagine how a human has managed to live so long, let alone have the Power that could cause this kind of destruction." A shudder seemed to pass through her body, and she rubbed her arms. She glanced at him. "Were you here when it happened?"

"Yes," he replied shortly. "It was one of the most terrible things I've ever seen, and I have seen many terrible things and lived a very long time. Much longer than your twenty-nine years."

"Where did the crossover lead to?"

"My home, Lyonesse." Turning away, he looked over the shadowed land. "It was the longest, bloodiest battle I've ever been in. Our armies covered the whole valley, and we fought for days. We were holding our own, and we even had some hope of winning, as we waited for Oberon to bring reinforcements through the passageway. Then Morgan broke the passageway. He stood on that rise, over there, looking down at the battle. It sounded like the earth had cracked in half."

"How did he do it?" she whispered. "Was it a spell or some kind of magic item?"

"I'm not sure. After that, the battle became a rout, and half our troops were killed." With an effort, Nikolas dragged himself out of the past and looked at the woman standing beside him. "It took Morgan centuries to either break or obscure all the passageways that led to Lyonesse. Now our land is completely cut off from Earth, and we can't get home."

"And they can't get to you," she murmured. "How horrible."

"Now maybe you begin to understand the danger and the stakes involved in what plays out here." On impulse, he hooked his fingers under her chin and turned her face toward him. He could feel her start as he touched her, but she didn't flinch away, not even after what had occurred between them earlier at the pub. Her skin looked like marble in the moonlight, but it was soft and warm. "Give Robin over to us. It is the safest thing for you to do. You can enjoy your vacation and then go safely home again."

"I don't own Robin," she said. "As you were very

quick to point out, he's not a dog, and he's not mine to keep or give away. I made him a promise, and promises matter to me. If he wants to stay with me, he can." Only then did she ease her chin away from his fingers as she nodded to the dark, silent hulk of a building nearby. "And if I have anything to say about it—and I think I do—I'm going to get inside that house and claim this property for my own. This isn't just a vacation for me. I'm planning to stay."

She was incomprehensible. He growled. "Why would you want to claim such a cursed place?"

Giving him a wry look, she lifted a shoulder. "Maybe I'm crazy. Maybe I need a place to call my own, and maybe I feel an affinity for broken things. I'm sorry your people struggled so terribly here, but maybe this place is actually more beautiful than your memories allow you to see."

"How do you think you're going to defend yourself—with these?" He reached out to touch one of the runes on her forearm.

This time she jerked away from his fingers. "You don't want to touch that one."

"Why not?" He gave her a narrow look.

"Because that one will burn you to the bone, and it will keep burning until eventually it consumes your entire body." She tilted her own forearm to look down at it. "It's kind of a magic napalm, I guess. Trust me, it's a nasty way to die."

"How does it not burn you or anything else it

touches?"

"You mean, like my purse?" She tapped her purse to the silver rune on her skin. "It's a defensive spell, so it lies inert when something neutral touches it. You're not neutral. After our confrontation earlier in the pub, I'm not exactly sure what the spell would do if you came in contact with it. It's best we don't find out."

He cocked his head, growing more fascinated as she talked. "A defensive spell... You aren't worried about it melting off if you sweat or get wet?"

"These runes are stronger and a bit more permanent than the one I painted on Gawain." She gave him a crooked grin. "I used tiny magic-sensitive silver shavings in clear nail polish for these. They won't come off for a couple of days, unless I scratch or peel them off or take them off with nail polish remover."

Nail polish. Polish remover. He let the foreign, feminine words wash over him as he watched the hint of mischief that played across her expression while she spoke.

"What do the other runes do?"

"Some are defensive, and others are offensive." She held up one palm. "This one is telekinetic. It's strong enough to knock a troll on its ass." She held up her other palm. "This other one creates confusion. If I slapped your face with this one, you wouldn't be able to find your car keys for hours even if they were in your pocket. I used it once on a drunk guy who tried to grope me. By the time the spell wore off, he was sober enough to drive home. They're all one-use-only spells, and they all require contact. I don't have much in the way of long-range weapons, which is why I miss my gun so much."

He knew how to cast webs of confusion so that the unwary might wander for hours lost in the spell. He also knew how to cast a glamour that could snare one into believing every word he said, and how to make ancient sleeping roads speak, but he was surprised that she had learned such proficiency so young.

He said slowly, "You created all these, yourself?"

"No, not really." She let her hands fall to her side. "My teacher taught me the basics and how to make the colloidal silver, and I have an affinity for runes, so I put the one thing together with the other and got creative. I think there might be some interesting applications with permanent tattooing, if you could stand to have the silver tattooed into your skin and knew how to renew the spells when they had been used, but I'm too human, and that much silver would be toxic for my system, so I haven't pursued it."

She was clever and inventive. He liked that too. He liked her, which was the biggest surprise to come out of the whole evening.

He felt the impulse to reach out and trace one of the runes and had to restrain himself. "Teach me how to cast the null spell the way you do," he said. "And sell me a vial of your colloidal silver."

"Why?" Now it was her turn to give him a narrow

look.

"Because with your technique, I can call the eight men who remain to spend the evening together, or even a night or two. We could set one of us apart to stand as guard and even set up shifts, while the rest can talk and rest." He paused. "It's been a long time since we've been able to do that."

She looked shaken, as she had when he had talked of Morgan breaking the crossover passageway. "That's all you have left, eight people?"

He felt his expression turn stony, as it always did when he focused on bearing the unbearable. "Of the Dark Court warriors on this side of the passageways, yes, just eight men—nine, including myself. Others of the Dark Court who are not warriors and have been barred from returning home are either spending their lives in hiding, or they have emigrated to other countries."

"I'm sorry." Reaching out, she brushed the tips of her fingers across the back of his fist.

The fleeting touch made him clench his fist tighter to keep from grasping her hand, an odd, unwelcome urge. "As our numbers have dwindled, so too have our options. Once, we would have been able to gather in strength and hold our own against any attack. Now we need to be much more wary. And like you, we need to find a place to call our own. But until we do, being able to disguise our whereabouts when we meet would be the next best thing."

"I'll help you," she said abruptly. "I'll show you how to make magic-sensitive colloidal silver for yourself, and I'll teach you how to infuse it with the null spell. There's no need for payment."

He gave her a long, dark look. A better man would have insisted upon paying her, but he didn't.

A better man would have pointed out that the more she became involved with him, the more danger she was putting herself in, but he didn't do that either.

Sophie Ross was proving that she could be very useful to him. If his people needed what she could teach him, he would take everything from her that he could get. Never mind what his old, damaged conscience might have to say about it.

His conscience wasn't useful in helping his men or Lyonesse, so he told it to shut the hell up. He had warned her, and she had already made it clear she was capable of making her own decisions.

She didn't have any magic runes painted in her dark hair. Obeying a wordless impulse, he reached for a stray curl and tucked it behind her ear, while her eyes went wide and she stared at him. She didn't pull away from him either, and as he dropped his hand, his fingers stroked down the side of her face, marveling at the marble paleness of her skin and the fragile warmth of life beating underneath it.

Even knowing he could bring her death, he told her, "I'll take you up on that offer."

Chapter Seven

WHY DID HE touch her?

That's what Sophie wanted to know.

Why did he touch her, and why did she let him? The whole thing was inexplicable, but he did, and she did, and when his fingers trailed down the side of her face, the muscles in her thighs shook in a fine tremor.

He was a man with a killer's face, living through a tragedy with his people dwindling away, and he was fighting for existence any way he knew how. He was using her, and she knew it, and she was going to let him.

At least for teaching him how to cast the silver rune.

That was *all*. Just the rune.

Because she had grown a little over the years, and she had learned a lot about herself. She knew she was an asshole magnet, and if there ever was an asshole, this guy was it.

So. She would help him with *just the rune*.

That was more than enough, and she was being more than generous after the way he had behaved. She understood what had happened and why he had acted the way he had. She could let bygones be bygones, but they weren't going to magically turn around and become besties during the course of a single evening.

"I'm done talking," she said. It was raw and awkward, but he didn't seem to mind in the least. She paused. "By the way, how did you get here without me hearing you?"

He stepped back. "I parked at the road and walked up the drive."

"Oh. Well, we can talk sometime soon about when I'll teach you how to make the colloidal silver and cast the rune, but for now, I've had enough. Good night."

Exhaustion was beginning to color the edges of her thinking. As she turned to walk to the Mini, she looked around. She really wasn't Robin's keeper, and he was free to take off whenever he felt like it, but it was going to bother her if he didn't show up by the time she started the car.

She needn't have worried. As she opened the door of the Mini, a dark streak raced across the open lawn from the shadow of the neighboring forest, tail up and wagging. She raised her eyebrows as the dog reached the open door and leaped in. The change in him from when she had found him wandering down the road was remarkable.

Sliding into the driver's seat, she murmured, "You're feeling better, I take it."

Large bright eyes blinked at her from the shadowed

darkness. For a brief moment, as she looked at Robin, she caught a flash of something else. Something that wasn't a dog. Blinking rapidly, she tried to see it again, but the vision was gone.

The moonshadow had offered its magic to her again.

"Is it wrong to pet you as if you really were a dog?" she asked, holding out her hand.

Even though she didn't live the kind of lifestyle that was good for a dog, she was going to miss the dog she had thought Robin was. He sniffed at her fingers and didn't seem to mind as she scratched him gently behind the ear.

Smiling to herself, she started the car and turned on the interior light to inspect the raised blisters that ringed his neck. They were completely healed. He was indeed feeling better.

She switched off the light and headed back down the drive. When she pulled out between the gateposts, she didn't see a car parked on the side of the road, so Nikolas must have already left.

Even driving the unfamiliar roads slowly and carefully, the drive back to the pub took less than ten minutes. As she pulled into the parking lot and opened the door, the sound of screaming split the night.

The screaming came from inside the pub. It was a woman's voice.

Maggie.

This time adrenaline hit hard, and the only imperative it gave her was *fight*.

Stupid. Crazy.

She lunged out of the car and sprinted for the pub, straining with every sense to glean information about what was happening inside.

The screaming came from the front. From the pub side. As she rounded the corner of the building, a gun went off. One shot.

A monkey leaped and ran beside her, shrieking at her.

A… a capuchin monkey… a monkey?

Her stride faltered, and she stared at it. As it yelled at her, she saw in the light of a nearby streetlamp the monkey had no tongue. "Go back to the car!" she ordered.

Instead, Robin jumped to hang on her leg. He dragged at her, clearly trying to stop her from going forward.

She tried to brush him off as she charged toward the front door. Toward what used to be the front door. The door itself was in shreds, a piece of wood still hanging from the hinges.

Ignoring the monkey hanging on her leg—at least he had stopped shrieking although his hard little monkey fingers pinched at her thigh painfully—she slowed, walked along the edge of the building quietly, and peered in.

There was blood everywhere, with furniture knocked awry, body parts and playing cards strewn everywhere, and monsters.

Huge, very werewolf-y looking monsters. One monster savaged a body. As she stared at it, Arran stood up from behind the bar and fired a hunting rifle point-blank into the face of a second monster that rushed toward him. It fell but just as quickly rolled onto its feet.

Aw, damn. It was never a good sign when bullets didn't faze a creature.

She didn't pause to think. Instead, she acted. Lunging toward the monster that was getting to its feet, she slapped the confusion spell onto its back. It faltered and looked over its shoulder at her.

For a breathless moment she looked down a massive, bloody muzzle with long, sharp teeth meant for rending. The monster turned toward her, and it kept turning in a circle... and turning. Its growl changed to a puzzled whine.

Arran was dead white and shaking. "What the fuck is wrong with it?"

"Doesn't matter." She gasped. "It'll do that for hours."

She felt a rush of air. The monkey had climbed up her body and shrieked an earsplitting warning in her ear. Arran jerked the rifle up to his shoulder and fired just behind her. Whirling, she saw the first monster already climbing to its feet.

She had two confusion spells, one on each side of her hand; two telekinesis spells, again, one on each side of her hand; and the corrosive defensive spells on her forearms. Before the monster could scramble to its feet, she slapped it with the second confusion spell.

Another scream split the night.

Arran said, his voice shaking, "Maggie."

"Call for help," Sophie told him. She grabbed the puck, pulled it off her back, and flung it to the area behind the bar where it could take cover, then she raced to the back game room with the dartboard.

Pausing on the doorstep, she took in the details of the room at a glance. Dead body parts, check. Blood all over, check. One of the monsters was in the process of tearing apart a closet door while Maggie screamed from inside it.

Really bad situation, check.

Oh man. If the gunshots didn't keep one of these monsters down, would her telekinesis spells do much better?

She couldn't stand by and watch it rip Maggie to shreds. Striding forward, she delivered a roundhouse punch to the monster's broad, powerful side. The blow lifted the creature into the air and slammed it into the opposite wall. It crashed halfway through the plaster and hung suspended in the hole it had created, half in the room and half in the kitchen behind it.

Sophie turned and, ignoring the painful tearing pull in her weak side, hauled Maggie bodily out of the closet. The other woman was hysterical, sobbing and babbling. Sophie grabbed her by the shoulders.

That got the other woman's attention. With a hiccup, Maggie stopped screaming to stare at her.

Behind the other woman, Sophie could see the monster pulling itself out of the hole in the plaster. She told Maggie, "Run."

As Maggie raced out of the room, Sophie didn't wait to watch the monster finish extricating itself from the ruined wall. Her spells called for close quarters and being proactive. Striding forward, she swiped at the monster's shoulder, activating the corrosive spell and skipping back several paces.

While she watched, the spell began to eat away at the monster's shoulder. With a final yank that pulled down half the wall in a cloud of plaster dust, the monster broke free and tried to swipe at its shoulder.

At the same time, the monkey leaped on her back and shrieked in her ear again. She snapped, "Not helpful!"

The monster fixed on her. Even as the corrosive spell consumed flesh and bone, it began to stalk her from across the room.

Her mind raced. Option: run until the corrosive spell ate it up. That sounded like a great one, but for the next several moments, it could run too, and she had already seen for herself that these monsters were much faster than she was.

As she backed up, it advanced.

She had one telekinesis spell and one corrosive spell left. Both necessitated her getting within biting distance of those wicked teeth. This was going to suck so bad.

Calmly she told the monkey, "Go on, Robin."

The monkey pinched her ear painfully. *Ow!* Not helpful!

Keeping her eyes on the advancing monster, she edged toward the door. With one hand, she plucked the monkey off her shoulder and threw it through the doorway. The monster's reddened eyes tracked the movement. For a moment she thought it was going to go after Robin. Then its attention came back to fix on her. It gathered itself, and she tensed.

It was going to leap, and when it did, it wouldn't be expecting her to dive forward, because that would be Stupid and Crazy™. But if she could get underneath it, she could punch it as hard as she could with her last telekinesis spell.

After that, she didn't know what she was going to do. One step at a time.

The monster leaped, and she dove forward. The maneuver didn't turn out as well as she had hoped. She landed hard on the floor and didn't flip over fast enough to get a punch in as it sailed overhead, so when it spun around to face her again, she was lying on her back looking up at it.

Good news: she still had the telekinesis spell. Bad news: she was going to have to use it while she faced all those killer teeth head-on.

Before she could roll away, it limped forward and

landed on top of her, driving the breath out of her lungs. Gods, it was so heavy she couldn't move. The corrosive spell had eaten away one shoulder and part of its torso, and she didn't know how it was still moving, but it was.

Why didn't it go down?

It bared massive teeth and snaked its head down to her. She fought to grab hold of its neck and keep that giant muzzle at bay, at least long enough for the stupid creature to realize it was dying.

Behind it, an avenging angel appeared, lean, dark, and fast, and wearing the same chilling, ferocious expression she remembered from the first time she had seen him.

Who'da thunk it? She was actually glad to see that terrifying asshole.

He had his sword drawn, and it was dripping with blood again. His eyes blazed with dark fire as he whirled to strike. She felt the blow shudder through the monster's body as Nikolas decapitated it.

The head flew through the air, and she lost track of where it went as a fountain of blood gushed over her. She managed to get one arm over her eyes before the warm wetness drenched her, while the monster's body collapsed heavily over hers.

Shouts sounded outside, and sirens, but in the room, silence fell.

Sophie peered out from underneath her arm. Nikolas stood over her, breathing heavily, and his hard, beautiful face wore an expression she didn't know how to identify. Anger? Relief? Incredulity?

He pointed the dripping tip of his sword at her and said between his teeth, "Are you insane? You ran *into the building.*"

She wiped monster blood off her lips. "Apparently, so did you."

He glared at her, while behind him, the weight of something heavy creaked on the stairs. Before she had a chance to call out a warning, Nikolas had already whirled. He was ready when another one of the monsters rushed down into the room and attacked.

Sophie struggled to get out from under the dead weight lying on top of her. The monster lunged, and Nikolas danced to one side, the blade of his sword flashing silver and crimson. As she wriggled free and rolled to her feet, Nikolas hit a pool of blood and skidded, going down on one knee. Flawlessly he shifted position with his sword to cover his fall, as the monster bunched its muscles to leap at him.

Both Nikolas and the monster were wholly focused on each other. Taking advantage of that preoccupation, she jumped forward and slapped the monster on the haunch with the telekinesis spell. The blow spun it around and knocked it sidelong into the damaged wall, which brought a fresh rain of plaster down.

When it whirled toward her with a snarl, Nikolas had gained his feet and was standing between them. In a powerful, full-body swing, he decapitated the monster. Wincing, she watched the head spin into the air and bounce into one corner.

Silence fell again. Outside, sirens approached, and she could hear people shouting. None of it touched the room, where she and Nikolas stood staring at each other. Plaster dust floated in the air like white powdery snow, coating the sprays and pools of deep, liquid red.

Nikolas threw his sword down, strode over and grabbed her shoulders. "Are you hurt? Did you get bitten?"

"What?" She didn't understand his blazing expression, and her attention wandered back over the scene. The monster that had landed on her was gone, and in its place lay a dead, decapitated man.

What. The. Fuck.

He shook her urgently. *"Sophie, did one of them bite you?"*

"No! I'm fine!" She tried to shrug off his hold. "I know I must look like Carrie at the high school prom, but none of this is my blood. Nikolas, where did the monster go?"

He looked where she gestured, at the body of the man nearby. He told her grimly, "That is the monster."

She nodded. It was the only thing that made sense. As he bent to pick up his sword, she turned and walked through the ruined front room, out into the cool night air.

As she stepped outside, Maggie and Arran rushed at her. She fielded questions and effusive, tearful thanks as best she could, while the police arrived. Then she fielded questions from them too, answering everything patiently, sometimes multiple times. No stranger to crime scenes, she felt a tired calm settle over her as she watched them cordon off the area.

Since Sophie was a latecomer to the scene, the police focused much of their questioning on Arran and Maggie, and when Nikolas stepped outside, they focused on him too, giving her room to breathe.

Walking several yards away to get some space, she drew in deep breaths of the cool, damp air. A neighboring woman brought her a warm, wet towel, a hot cup of tea, and a blanket.

"Don't worry about the towel or the blanket, love," the woman told her when Sophie tried to refuse it. "They're old, ragged things, and it doesn't matter in the slightest if you get blood on them."

Thanking her, Sophie moved several yards to the side and used the towel to wipe off the worst of the blood from her face and hands. Then, as the night had turned damp and cool, she pulled the blanket around her shoulders and sat at the curb to drink the tea. It was hot, creamy and sweet. It wasn't how she usually drank tea, but it was utterly delicious.

When she sat at the curb, the monkey reappeared. It climbed up her body and pushed its way into the blanket, chittering at her grumpily.

"Don't you be grumpy at me," she told it as she put an arm around it. "I'm very annoyed with you right now. What was all that pinching about?"

The monkey bitched back at her wordlessly, dark eyes snapping.

She rubbed her tired face. "Stop. Just stop."

It fell silent and huddled against her side.

Why hadn't anybody remarked on the monkey? Granted, the scene in the pub was dramatic in its horror, but a monkey was quite an oddity. Couldn't they see it, or was the puck cloaking himself? She gave up questioning and focused on drinking her tea.

Black-clad legs appeared beside her, the material streaked in blood. As she looked up, Nikolas squatted beside her. Dark hair fell on the strong plane of his brow, and his expression was shuttered. He carried a mug of tea too.

She told him, "I'm surprised you stayed to talk to the police. I half expected you to disappear out the back when they arrived."

"I almost did," he said. "But too many people had seen me, and you'd given your statement before you and I had a chance to discuss it. Besides, I might come into town again. Better to be upfront. We didn't do anything wrong, and we prevented more people from getting killed."

She nodded. "So, about those werewolf-y looking monsters."

"They're werewolves," he replied.

She took a deep breath. "Is that why you said it wasn't wise to roam the countryside during full moon?"

"Yes, although London and other urban areas are worse."

"London." She set her mug down on the curb and turned to look at him. "You're saying there are werewolves, in London? Like the song—'Werewolves of London'?"

He raised one sleek eyebrow. "Of course. That's where the song came from. Didn't you know?"

A laugh barked out of her. When a nearby man frowned at her, she covered her mouth to muffle the noise. When she could speak again, she said, "No, I didn't know."

"You don't have werewolves in the States, do you?"

Lifting one shoulder, she replied, "I don't know, we might. I don't know of any. If we do, they aren't prevalent enough to reach the news. The only wolves I know of are Wyr shapeshifters, which isn't the same thing." She paused, frowning. "I guess I shouldn't take anything for granted. What do you mean when you say 'werewolf'? Are we talking about the same thing?"

"I mean lycanthropy, a virus. It was why I was so worried about your being bitten. A victim who has been bitten has only a short window of time to get treatment before the virus becomes irreversible." He shifted closer to her and said in a low voice, "Those weren't just normal werewolves that attacked the pub."

That was another unwelcome set of concepts. There was such a thing as normal werewolves? And abnormal ones?

Sophie watched his mouth as he shaped his words. Really, he had the sexiest mouth she had ever seen.

Fascinated and feeling as if she had stepped into a strange dream, she murmured, "How could you tell?"

"Werewolves by law are required to register with the National Health Service and cage themselves during the full moon. There are public cages available for those who don't have the ability to build one for themselves. Those that don't cage themselves run wild. They're undisciplined and chaotic, like rabid dogs, and they hunt down animals to feed on—rabbits, deer, unwary humans. They don't break into houses to attack people." He set his mug beside hers. "The ones that broke into the pub here did so for a reason. They were acting under orders, which means they were the Queen's Hounds."

Under the blanket, the monkey was shivering. She put her head in her hands and said telepathically, *Isabeau has a legion of werewolves?*

Yes, but her werewolves don't need the full moon in order to change. They can change at will, and they band together and strategize. Gawain believes they can telepathize even in their bestial form. He paused. *That means either her Hounds were searching for Robin, or they were searching for me. Since we killed all of them, we can hope that nobody else has become aware of your presence yet.* Switching to verbal speech, he said softly, "You still have time to back out and go home."

"LA isn't my home," she muttered. "It's just a place where I stayed for a while."

Lifting the edge of the blanket, she looked at the creature nestled inside. Large dark eyes watched her from the deep shadow. The filmy cloudiness had vanished, and he watched her with sharp intelligence. She noticed his skewed eye had straightened. If that could heal, it must have been damage he sustained in captivity.

With a gentle finger, she urged him to open his mouth, and he did so obligingly. A new bud of flesh had appeared at the stump at the base of his mouth. He was regrowing his tongue. He was still too thin, and he needed a series of meals to correct that, but he was healing. Maybe as he recovered he would begin to speak again.

Watching her, Nikolas said, "You're not going to leave, are you?"

"Nope," she said. "Although I'm going to leave here."

Setting the monkey on the ground, she pushed stiffly to her feet. Now that the battle was over, she was beginning to feel every bruise and ache. Sharp pain radiated out from her weak side, and somehow her shoulder had gotten wrenched. She wrapped her arm around her torso protectively.

The tea had given her a small boost of energy, but heavy exhaustion dragged at her, and she knew she had a limited amount of time before she had to go horizontal.

Nikolas had straightened to his full height when she

had, and he was watching her sharply. He took a step closer until she could sense his body heat along one side of her body. "You said you weren't bitten, but you were hurt, weren't you?"

"Soft tissue stuff," she said in brief reply. "I strained old injuries. I'll be okay, but I need your help. Would you carry my luggage down to the car? I can't stay here."

"Of course you can't. Let's go get your things."

The police had the front of the building cordoned off, so they walked together around to the back entrance. Maggie broke away from her husband and a cluster of neighbors to hurry over to them. "I can't thank you enough for what you did," she said to them. She looked at Sophie. "You risked your life to save mine."

Guilt gnawed at Sophie, much like the corrosive spell. If she and Robin hadn't been at the pub to begin with, the attack would never have happened. She met Nikolas's eyes and saw a dark understanding. Then she turned to Maggie. "I'm glad there was something I could do. I can't stay here tonight, so I'll get my things."

"Of course you can't, love, but where will you go at this time of night?"

"I'll go ahead and go to the cottage."

Maggie's expression creased. "It'll be cold, and the bed will be unmade, and you won't have any supplies with you. And I don't like how isolated that old moldy place is."

"It's all right," Sophie told her. "It doesn't matter. I like isolation. It'll be a roof over my head, and I can get groceries in the morning."

"I'll stay with her," Nikolas told the other woman. "She won't be alone."

He would? Sophie raised her eyebrows as she looked at him pointedly. Thanks for asking, asshole.

He looked magnificently impervious to her speaking glance. Actually, truly magnificent. His innately elegant, erect carriage and the imperious tilt of his head drew glances from everyone around them. The fact that Sophie was affected by it irritated her to no end. With an effort, she had to restrain herself from making a face at him.

"Well… all right," Maggie said reluctantly. "But at least let me gather some things together for you, love." As Sophie started to protest, the other woman insisted. "Just a small box to get you started."

Let her help you. Nikolas's deep telepathic voice sounded unexpectedly in her head. *It's a small thing, and it will make her feel better about your leaving.*

Sophie glowered at him, and when that look rolled off his broad shoulders too, she said to Maggie, "That would be wonderful. Thank you."

"I won't be just a minute." Maggie hurried into her shattered kitchen, muttering under her breath at the mess.

Silent as a wraith and just as deadly, Nikolas followed Sophie up the stairs.

There was no need for her to unlock the door to her room. Like the front entrance to the pub, there was no door. She paused in the doorway to take in the mess inside.

The furniture had been knocked askew, and the bed had been shredded.

She took in a deep breath and glanced over her shoulder. Nikolas's expression was grim. He nodded in the direction of the rest of the hall. As she looked down the hall, she realized all the other doors were still intact and closed.

Her stomach clenched. Either the Hounds had been hunting for the puck, or her, or both.

Nikolas said, "Let's hope this cell of Hounds didn't have a chance to relay information up the chain of command."

He didn't sound very hopeful, and she didn't blame him. It sounded too much like unrealistic optimism to her as well.

She limped into the destroyed room. Since she'd been planning to stay only for one night, she hadn't unpacked very much, and the pieces of her sturdy Samsonite luggage had been knocked around, but at least they were intact. Picking through the mess, she collected the rest of her things—a cell phone charger, clean set of clothes for the morning, and her travel toiletry bag.

Straightening with an effort, she pressed a hand

against her aching side and said breathlessly, "Okay, I'm ready."

Nikolas had collected her suitcases. He waited by the door, watching her with an inscrutable expression. As she reached him, he picked up the luggage and led the way down the stairs.

Maggie greeted them down below. She held a cardboard box. Sophie caught a glimpse of tea bags, a bottle of milk, and a loaf of bread tucked inside, along with other items. Maggie said, "It's not much, but it will get you started in the morning."

"It's terrific, thank you." Sophie set her toiletry bag on top of the box and accepted it. "It was kind of you to think of this with so much else going on."

"It's the least I can do in return for what you did for us." Maggie's eyes glittered with wetness. "You not only saved my life, but Arran says you saved his too." She turned to Nikolas. "Thank you, both of you."

He didn't appear to look uncomfortable at all, while Sophie was barely able to keep from blurting out the truth. She swallowed the impulse down. It wouldn't do anybody any good, and the knowledge could possibly put them in more danger.

Instead, she said, "I'm sorry for the people you lost tonight."

"It's a hard blow," Maggie said. "It'll be hard for the whole town. They were good men just enjoying a bit of an after-hours card game, you see."

"I do see," Sophie said gently.

Maggie turned back to the shambles of her pub. As Sophie and Nikolas walked to the Mini, Sophie muttered between her teeth, "I want her dead for this."

Nikolas said, "As do I, and mine."

Chapter Eight

WHEN THEY REACHED the Mini, they discovered the puck, still in the form of a monkey, waiting inside.

No doubt Robin found opposable thumbs more useful than dog paws. After setting the box and the luggage into the boot of the car, Nikolas stood back and watched Sophie drive away, then he walked down the side alley where he had parked his Porsche and followed.

He didn't like how she had looked. Underneath the thorough dousing of blood, her skin had turned chalky, the freckles standing out in stark contrast, and the shadows underneath her spectacular eyes were as dark as bruises. She didn't complain, but she moved like she was in pain, stiffly and off-balance.

He pulled into the property drive and parked beside the Mini. By the time he had switched off the engine, Sophie was already at the entrance of the cottage, unlocking the door by the light of her slim flashlight.

He pulled his go-bag out of the car and retrieved her luggage from the Mini's boot. When he stepped inside an aged but comfortable-looking kitchen, she had turned on all the lights and stuck her head into a cupboard.

"There's some way to turn on the water heater," she said, her voice muffled. "The solicitor told me how to do it, but I don't remember."

"Sit down," Nikolas ordered.

That made her emerge so she could glare at him. He could almost hear her say it: *Thanks for asking, asshole.*

"Seriously, sit," he told her impatiently. "I'll take care of the water heater."

She must be feeling even worse than he thought, because she straightened to ease into one of the four chairs at the wooden, farm-style kitchen table.

He moved quickly through the cottage, taking stock. The rest of the furnishings looked as aged and comfortable as the kitchen. There was a musty, unused smell in the place and a slightly damp feeling.

The sitting room had a gas fire, and he paused to light it so it could chase the chill and the dampness out of the place. There was a minimally furnished bedroom with a bare mattress, a halfway-decent bath with a washer/dryer unit tucked in one corner, and the kitchen, which was actually the largest room in the cottage.

The refrigerator needed to be plugged in. After doing so, he set the bottle of milk in it and checked the contents of the box that Maggie had given them. There were eggs as well as bread, an orange and an apple, a package of cheese, and sugar for the tea, along with a few packets of guest soaps.

"You don't have to stay," she said.

He glanced at her. She sat with her forehead propped in one hand, and she looked as weary as anyone he had ever seen. "Yes, I do," he told her. "There may be more Hounds on the hunt. I won't have you getting hurt or killed, not when you can be of use to me."

She laughed and immediately winced. "That's breathtakingly callous, even for you."

"So it is." He had also regretted it as soon as he had said it, but he didn't bother to apologize. Not only was it true, but he also didn't think she would believe him if he did. Rummaging through the kitchen cupboards, he found and filled a teakettle and set it to warm on the stove. "In a half an hour or so, you'll be able to take a comfortable shower, but in the meantime, there'll be warm water here in a few minutes to wash up at the kitchen sink."

"I don't care," she said as she rummaged through her toiletry bag to locate a small travel-sized bottle filled with liquid. Pushing to her feet, she moved to the sink, turned on the faucet, and stuck her head under the running water, swearing at the cold.

He laughed silently. They had only been acquainted through the course of a very long evening, but she had already surprised him in a multitude of ways. The water ran dark pink as it whirled down the drain.

"If you can stand it for long enough, I'll help you wash the blood out of your hair."

"Please," she said through gritted teeth. "But hurry."

She thrust the small bottle at him blindly, and he took it to squirt some of the liquid into the palm of one hand. Working the shampoo quickly through her hair, he massaged her scalp until there was a thick lather. The water ran cold enough to make the bones of his hands ache, and he could feel her body shaking.

"Hold on," he said. Twisting, he grabbed the full teakettle. It hadn't had a chance to get very warm, but it had to be better than sticking her head under the tap again. Carefully he rinsed the dark stream of wet hair, marveling at how the curls sprang up when he ran his fingers through the long strands. As he worked, she scrubbed at her face and hands.

The act of helping her to wash her hair seemed inappropriately intimate. It was as velvety soft as it looked. He wondered what her skin would taste like at the nape of her neck. He wondered what she would say or do if he bent to find out.

But no, he didn't have to wonder very much at that.
Thanks for asking, asshole!

Biting back another smile, he found he was reluctant to draw the task to its end, but then the kettle was empty and there was no reason to keep her hanging over the sink any longer.

"Thank you," she told him, turning her head to one side to squeeze the excess water out of her hair. "My clothes feel vile enough, but somehow it was worse having blood all over my head and in my hair."

"Stay put. I'll get you a towel." Down the short hall, he found the linen cupboard and brought back a towel for her to wrap her hair in.

When she stood, her face was no longer pale but a deep, pleasing pink, although the shadows under her eyes were still too dark. "If any more of those were-wolves crash in here, I'm not going to be much help," she said. "I'm jet-lagged and exhausted, and I pulled something deep on my bad side."

He nodded to himself. It was pretty much what he had thought. "I'm going outside to lay some aversion spells around the area. If we're lucky, the rest of the night will be quiet."

"Quiet would be good." Her face tightened. "Those things hardly paused when Arran shot them."

"He probably didn't have silver in his bullets," Nikolas told her. "Most gun owners don't. The bullets are expensive, and a lycanthrope running wild is pretty rare. Most of them are disturbed by the change, and they're all too happy to cage themselves during full moons."

Her expression lit with interest. "Silver bullets affect them?"

"Yes." He paused, reluctant to look away from her mesmerizing eyes. "They're still tough to kill, but if you put a silver bullet between their eyes, it'll kill them well enough. Also, they can't heal at a magical rate from wounds inflicted with silver bullets or weapons."

"Good to know." She clenched her hands. "I'm never going to be able to get a gun legally here, am I?"

"As you're not a UK citizen, it's highly doubtful. You would only warrant one if you needed it in some official capacity, and the government approved of that reason. Some demesne leaders and their entourages are granted firearm certificates." He cocked his head. "Why, do you want one?"

"Oh my gods, yes. Like I told you, my spells are only useful in close quarters." With an explosive sigh, she said, "The water has got to be at least bearable by now, don't you think? I'm going to finish cleaning up."

She had gone head-to-head with monsters that were over twice her size and weight, and she had done it without hesitating. He had seen her race alone toward the pub. It was one of the bravest things he had ever seen anybody do.

As she turned away from him, he caught her by the arm. "What you did back there—"

"Jesus, don't touch me there!" she cried, yanking away from his hold. They stared at each other. She whispered, "I had one active spell left."

He clenched. She grabbed his hand and turned it over, stroking his fingers and palm and turning it over. After a moment, she sagged and looked up at him again with relief brimming in her eyes.

She said, "Thank God. The spell didn't recognize you as an enemy."

He gave in to his impulse at last and cupped her chin, stepping close so that he could feel the heat from her body. It was a subtle warmth that touched him in places he didn't understand and had long denied existed. "That's because I'm not your enemy, Sophie."

As he watched, she licked her lips. Watching her tongue slide over the plush, pink curve of her lower lip caused him to harden and woke a hunger he hadn't felt for anyone in years.

Years.

What the hell was happening to him? He jerked away and stalked toward the door. He snapped, "I'm going to lay down those spells while you shower."

"Right," she said without looking at him. "I'll make it quick, so there should be some warm water left for you."

He didn't bother to answer that. Instead, he stalked out the door, breathing hard in the cool, damp night air. He had no business feeling any kind of desire for her. She was someone who was possibly of some use to him, nothing more.

She chose to stay when she shouldn't have. Earlier, she had chosen to engage with the Hounds—and she shouldn't have. She was also choosing to defend the puck, and by gods, she had already been warned multiple times she shouldn't have done that.

And he had his mission. There was nothing more

critical, more important, than making sure he did everything he possibly could to keep his men alive, to try to find a way back to Lyonesse, and to take down Isabeau and Morgan any way he could.

He had no interest, and no time, for anything else.

After a few minutes, the unwelcome tightening in his groin eased.

He got down to business and set a series of aversion spells around the property, grimly ignoring the ghosts in his head and the ancient memories of the battle that tried to resurface. Whether or not the aversion spells would be useful was anybody's guess.

The effect of an aversion spell could be directly measured against the intelligence and determination of the creature that encountered it. At least if something tripped a spell, Nikolas would feel it, so he would have advance warning before anything got too close to the cottage.

Also, there were no direct scent trails to lead any questing Hounds to this location. The only way the Hounds could possibly learn to come here would be if they spent some time in human form, questioning people in town. Nikolas and Sophie were probably safe from attack for one night. Possibly not for any longer, but he felt fairly confident about tonight.

Finally he felt like he had done what he could. Only then did he pause to text Gawain. Hounds attacked the pub. Sophie, Robin, and I have moved to a different location.

Gawain replied almost immediately. `Damn. Was anyone hurt?`

`Four casualties. We're fine.` Nikolas paused, then typed more slowly. `Sophie ran into the pub to help before I could stop her. She saved lives. She's a brave fighter.`

He paused and then, choosing not to overthink it, hit send.

Gawain's reply was a few minutes in coming. `I'm glad she's okay. I filled the others in earlier, after I left. We're all moving into position so that none of us are too far away. Call us for backup if you need to.`

`I will.`

The conversation finished, Nikolas pocketed his phone. He paused to consider the shadowed manor house sprawling over the shattered land magic. It was an ugly, useless building, sitting on a cursed location. The gods only knew what Sophie saw in it.

Turning his back on the manor house, he strode back to the cottage.

Inside, everything was quiet. Sophie's luggage had disappeared, while his go-bag still rested in the corner nearest the door. The puck was nowhere to be seen. Walking through the small place, he saw that the bedroom was darkened and the door half shut.

Gently he pushed the door open wider to look inside. As it creaked on its hinges, Sophie's weary voice said, "I don't recall inviting you in here."

Thanks for asking, asshole.

Neither of them had to say it.

She had taken a blanket from the linen cupboard and curled up on the bed wrapped in it, atop the bare mattress.

"Too tired to make the bed, I see," he said quietly.

"I'm clean, dry, warm, and horizontal. And alive. It'll do for tonight." She shifted under the blanket and grunted. "The bed can get made tomorrow."

He had spent far too many nights with much the same reduced survival list, and he almost turned to go, but that quiet sound of pain, and the memory of how stiffly she had been moving after the pub battle stopped him.

Slowly he said, "I know you're still in pain. I can help you and give you the chance to get some real rest."

For a long moment he thought she might ignore him. Then she sighed, and the curled knot under the blanket unfurled. "Come in."

He pushed the door open the rest of the way and prowled in. That was when he saw the puck. Robin had been perched on the headboard. His dark eyes glistened in the shadows. What was he thinking?

As Nikolas approached, Robin slipped down off the headboard and disappeared into another part of the cottage. With a frown, he watched the puck leave. He would never understand Robin, no matter how long either of them lived.

Then he stood by the bed, looking down at Sophie. Even in a shadowed room as dark as this, her eyes gathered every particle of light and magnified them, gleaming like stars. He could see she was uncomfortable with him standing over her, so he nudged her thigh. As she shifted, he sat on the edge of the mattress.

"Watch yourself," he said. Reaching over to shade her eyes, he turned on the bedside lamp. Underneath his palm, he saw her wince.

"Is the light really necessary?" she said grumpily.

"I don't know." He removed his hand and watched her squint.

"How did you not get splashed with blood?" she muttered, eyeing his shirt with resentment. "I almost drowned in it."

"I was moving fast, while you were on the floor. I got some splashed on my legs." He angled his head. "Show me where you hurt."

She grimaced. "Just assume if it's between the top of my head and the bottom of my feet, it hurts."

"You said you pulled something in your side. Was that the place you got shot?"

With a sigh, she replied, "One of them."

She had been shot multiple times. He took in a deep breath and let it out slowly as he absorbed the news. When he was confident that he could sound calm and steady, he urged her, "Show me."

She sighed again, this time impatiently, and flung

back one corner of the blanket. Underneath, she wore a spaghetti strap tank top and matching shorts that were very short. They showed off the long line of her slender, muscled legs. She pulled up one corner of the tank, and he saw the scar.

It was a skewed starburst of ridged, livid flesh under the right side of her rib cage, still new enough that the redness hadn't had a chance to fade. Not questioning his impulse—not thinking about anything other than reacting to the visual evidence of how her life had been in jeopardy—he touched the ridged scar lightly with the tips of his fingers.

Watching him, she said nothing, did nothing, although he could tell by her clenched tension that something about revealing the injury was difficult for her.

"Where else were you shot?" he murmured.

"Right thigh, left shoulder." She clipped out the words.

Now that she had mentioned it, he could see the edge of the scar peeking out from the tank top, in the flesh of her shoulder, just over her right breast. So her body had been strained on both sides tonight.

He could also see large bruises and contusions on her legs and arms. No doubt she had them on her back as well. She had hit the floor hard, and the Hound had landed its full, considerable weight on top of her.

This time, without asking, he took the edge of the blanket and lifted it farther to reveal the jagged slash on her leg. The scar was a violation of that beautiful, creamy cinnamon-speckled skin. She would have needed surgery on all three wounds. He had known she was still recovering somehow, but this was more, and far worse, than he had imagined.

With gentle firmness, he laid one hand flat on her abdomen, covering the scar. With his right hand, he covered the scar on her shoulder. She took hold of his wrists but didn't try to force him away.

Then in his native tongue he said the invocation for healing, and Power flowed into her until her body glowed with it. Connected to her as he was, he could sense her pain lessen. Torn, inflamed muscles eased, and the massive bruises faded. They didn't disappear totally and still showed like faint shadows of mortality darkening her skin. But the deep, livid red was gone.

When he was finished, he didn't lift his hands from her body. Instead, carefully pressing down, he leaned over her and met her wide, questioning eyes, his expression hard.

"You had no business running into that pub, Sophie Ross," he said, quietly stern. "No business, especially with serious injuries that are still so fresh."

She said in a steady voice, "Fuck you, Nikolas whatever-the-fuck your last fucking name is. I was going to say thank you, but then you ruined the fucking moment."

"Sevigny," he said.

He could see in her expression that, exhausted or

not, she had clearly meant to rip into him some more for his high-handed attitude, but at that, she paused, thrown off stride.

"It's my last fucking name," he told her. "Sevigny. And you say 'fuck' too often."

Something sparked in her eyes, and he could tell she almost—almost—smiled. "Fuck yeah, I do. And it's none of your fucking business how often I say 'fuck.' Nor is it any of your fucking business if I choose to run into a pub because people are being attacked, if I rescue a dog who's been abused, or if I decide to fucking jaywalk just because I feel like it—"

"You're actually maddening," he said on a note of discovery. "You. Madden. Me."

She rolled her eyes. "Do I look like I care? Let me lay out a few more things for you. Don't assume I give a shit what you think. Don't expect me to believe the world revolves around you—because it doesn't, bucko. It doesn't. And don't think just because you helped me to feel better—thank you, by the way, I really do feel better—that I'm going to start paying attention to anything you say to me."

"Oh dear Lord and Lady," Nikolas said. "Cease talking."

She frowned at him, and from the uncomprehending expression in her eyes, he realized he had slipped into the old tongue again.

"*Mmm-hmm*, and when you talk like that?" she said, drawing a circle with a forefinger in front of his face.

"You just sound stuck-up, because you know I don't understand a single word you're saying."

He glared at her. "Stuck-up."

She nodded. As tired as she looked, the dark shadows under her eyes had lightened, and her eyes sparkled with irate feeling. She repeated, "Stuck-up."

What an idiotic, immature thing to say. From out of nowhere, a bolt of laughter shot up. He stamped on it hard. She was being ludicrous, and what's more, he suspected she knew it and didn't care.

Underneath his hands, her skin felt luxuriously soft and warm. He could feel the rhythm of her breathing. It felt like a heartbeat. It felt alive and vital and as necessary as air or water.

She was something so foreign to how he had grown accustomed to living he didn't even have words to express it. He thought his shell of isolation had become immutable, irreversible, but with a few words and that diamond-like fire in her eyes, she shattered it.

So much hunger came roaring out from the same, deep, mysterious place the laughter had come from. So much. His fingers tightened on her soft flesh. She opened her mouth, and he could tell from the saucy spark in her expression that she wasn't done telling him off.

Instead of listening to any more of her lecture, he came down on her, torso to torso. "You're a damn mouthy broad," he said and kissed her.

Her curved, generous lips were as soft as they

looked. As his body came over hers, the sensation of her lying underneath him satisfied something deep and primal in him.

He could feel the curve of her breasts, her narrower, slighter bone structure. Her warmth burned him, and that mouth, that mouth, he had never felt before the kind of hunger he did as he conquered that soft, lush mouth.

After a moment of shocked stillness came the biggest surprise of all. She tilted her head and kissed him back, molding her lips to his, shifting as he shifted, giving way as he pressed hard for entrance and plunged his tongue deep inside her. He could feel every single one of her fingers as she threaded them through his hair in a caress that sent a shock of pleasure through his entire body.

He couldn't remember the last time he had been touched with any kind of sensuality or affection. That part of his nature had been cold and unused for so long it roared to life with the strength of a tidal wave.

Hungrily he ate at her. He ravaged her mouth as if it were the first meal he had seen in years. Another shock of awareness bolted through him as her tongue dueled with his.

She lifted her head off the pillow in order to kiss him back, following him up eagerly as he tried to ease back to take a breath, to take stock. Her fingers worked at the back of his neck, wordlessly asking him for more.

It brought him down again. Cupping her head in

both hands, he kissed her wildly while his cock stiffened into a hard, painful spike of hunger that he pressed against the curve of her hip. Her legs shifted restlessly, entwining with his.

Just like that, he was crazy to discover what she felt like naked. As he cupped her breast, he could feel the jut of her nipple through the thin material. It would be as plush as her mouth and just as pink. Maybe a darker, dusky rose.

It would taste fantastic. She had generous breasts. The curve fit beautifully into his hand. He molded the lush mound of flesh while he licked at her mouth. Her breath was coming fast, soft, urgent puffs of air against his heated skin, egging him onward.

Her fingers closed around his wrist, and she turned her face away from his kiss. "Stop," she said, her voice strangled. "This—we—I shouldn't be doing this."

Nikolas froze. His heart pounded as he tried to make sense of what she was saying.

Then her words sank in, and they leveraged a glimmer of sanity into his overheated, lust-filled brain.

Her heart was pounding as hard as his, and they were both breathing heavily, the sound ragged in the quiet room.

Her expression held a wry vulnerability he had not seen in her before. Carefully he lifted his hand from her breast and told her, "I had not intended for this to happen."

"No," she said. "Of course you hadn't. Neither had

I. You are not one of my short-term goals, and you have no part in my life plan."

"And you are certainly not in my agenda, in any way." He narrowed his eyes. "I don't even like you."

She threw open her arms and let them fall onto the bed. "Exactly! I don't like you either! In fact, you're pretty insufferable."

At that, he cocked his head and glared. "As are you."

She shrugged. "I'm blaming my part in all of this on jet lag. I haven't slept in so long everything feels unreal. Why not kiss the hot guy in my bed? It's all a dream anyway, ha-ha. You're going to have to come up with an explanation for your own behavior."

"I have no explanation," he said between his teeth. "This is inexplicable. You're a pain in the ass, you make foolhardy, dangerous decisions, and I don't think you know how to have a normal conversation."

She took a deep breath and let it out slowly while something darkened in her expression. Something that might look a little like disappointment. "Glad we cleared that up."

His eyes dropped to watch her lips form the words.

And then there was that mouth of hers, that outrageously sensual, generous, responsive mouth. He bent forward again slowly, giving her plenty of time to respond as he lowered his mouth to hers. She scowled but didn't push him away, nor did she say anything, and as his lips brushed hers, she lifted up her face to kiss him back again.

This time the kiss he gave her was gentle and fleeting, while his unruly cock throbbed with the most painful hard-on he'd ever had, and all he wanted to do was rip her clothes off and take her until she screamed with pleasure.

As he lifted his head, he told her, "Sleep now. Tomorrow you can show me how to make the colloidal silver and cast the rune."

A glint appeared in her eye, which was his warning. "Can I? Oh, thank you, thank you! I'm so glad I can do this since I had absolutely nothing else on my agenda for the day tomorrow, other than serving your needs. Asshole."

Earlier, her insouciance had made him angry, but this time he laughed. When she would have said more, he put his hand over her mouth.

Looking into her angry eyes, he said, "And when you teach me, I am going to get you a gun, along with silver bullets. It won't be legal, so you'll have to keep it hidden, but at least you'll have an effective weapon you can use if you run across another lycanthrope, and you won't have to rely on your contact spells."

Her expression changed, the anger vaporizing. As he lifted his hand away, she said, "You've got a deal."

"Get some rest." He lifted off her, and in the absence of her body in alignment with his, the air felt cold.

It wasn't cold enough.

As she curled in the blanket, he left the room, pulling the door closed but not latching it. He grabbed his bag from the kitchen and stepped into the bathroom to take a biting cold shower. Only then did his erection finally subside.

Afterward, he grabbed a blanket from the linen closet and went to the sitting room. The settee wouldn't be the worst place he had used for a bed.

Robin perched on the arm of a chair near the gas fire, his skinny, hairy arms wrapped around himself. When Nikolas entered the room, the puck glanced at him, then went back to staring at the fire.

Nonverbal, Sophie had said. Possibly trauma induced.

As Nikolas stretched out on the settee and plumped a pillow under his head, he said quietly, "Good night, Robin."

Just before he closed his eyes, the monkey slipped off the chair and loped back to the bedroom.

Chapter Nine

WHEN NIKOLAS LEFT the bedroom, Sophie half expected she would lie awake and kick herself for indulging in that stupid kiss. Instead, she fell immediately into a dark pit and slept like the dead, without dreams, until she came alert with a jerk.

The feeling was reminiscent of the first time she had laid eyes on Nikolas, in that blasted vision back in LA. She could sense the day had advanced well past early morning. *Ugh*, at this rate, she was never going to get her days and nights sorted out. At least she had slept, really slept, and not tossed and turned from nightmares all night long.

A slow, rhythmic scraping sounded from somewhere else in the cottage. It sounded metallic and grated on her nerves. Pushing out of bed, she ran her hands through her hair in a lame effort to tame it somewhat, but it sprang from her fingers in a wild, untamed mess.

She felt dull and hungover, and oh my God, had she really kissed Nikolas last night? Where was her sanity?

I'm not just blaming it on jet lag, she thought. I'm blaming it on post-battle emotions.

She knew others who experienced post-battle highs. The guys she had worked with at the precinct were often edgy and boisterous after a conflict involving violence, and those who were unattached often indulged in one-night stands.

But she never had.

She glared at the bed as if it were responsible for her own lapse in judgment, while the memory of Nikolas's mouth moving over hers sent a thrill of remembered heat through her body. He was off-the-charts sexy, damn it, and an asshole, two things that were, apparently, her kryptonite.

Sophie Ross, she told herself, you need therapy in the worst way.

Just don't kiss assholes. That's all you've got to do. You can eat anything you want, drink anything you want, you can do anything else that you want, and if you get into that house like you think you can, you'll be able to sleep in every morning all you want.

You have one job. Just don't kiss assholes.

The cottage was cool, and she shivered as she dug through her luggage for a pair of flannel pants and a long-sleeved knit shirt. Donning the clothes, she slipped her feet into flip-flop sandals and went to see what was making that irritating noise.

She found Nikolas in the kitchen. He appeared to have recently showered. He wore another pair of black pants, but he hadn't put on a shirt yet, and his hair was wet and slicked back, outlining the strong, graceful bone structure of his head, neck, and shoulders.

He had positioned his chair so that he sat in a patch of sunlight streaming in through the window, and he was running a whetstone along the edge of his sword, sharpening it with slow, steady strokes.

She glared at him. His beauty was hard and uncompromising and completely, entirely masculine. Without a shirt, she could see scars on his torso, and for all his lean height, he had the bulky muscle of a swordsman across his shoulders and down his arms and back. The slanting sunlight sliced across his face, highlighting the sharp cheekbones, the bold, straight nose and lean jaw, and it lit the flat surface of his signet ring into a blaze of fiery gold.

So he was mouthwateringly handsome. *Inhumanly handsome.* So what. Enjoy the view while you've got it.

Just don't kiss assholes. One job, Sophie. Only one.

"I don't know how you can stand to sit there without your shirt on." Her voice was too husky, and she was blaming *that* on having just gotten up. "I'm freezing."

He glanced at her, a sharp, piercing look, then went back to sharpening his sword. "It's not so bad in the sunlight. If you want to take the chill out of the kitchen, you can fire up the stove. There's not much to eat for breakfast. You can have dry toast and black tea if you want."

She gave the large, foreign stove a leery look. Paul, the solicitor, had called it an Aga, but it looked like a machine out of a 1950s sci-fi film. "Not much to eat? What happened to the box of stuff Maggie gave us last night?"

"A certain puck must have gotten into the supplies." His voice was dry as he bent his head over his sword. "When I got up, I found all the eggs had been sucked out of their shells. He also ate the butter and cheese, and drank the milk. On the upside, the cottage is sparkling clean, which was a surprise since usually brownies are the ones that like to clean house."

When she started to laugh, he gave her a speaking look.

She moved to fill the teakettle with water and set it on the stove. "I won't hold it against him. He was painfully thin when I found him. If he can eat his fill enough times, he probably won't need to clean out the kitchen."

The monkey appeared at the top of the fridge and jumped to land on her shoulder. His little fingers began to work through her hair. She tilted her head to give him a leery glance. As long as he wasn't pinching her, she supposed he wasn't doing any harm. Looking through cupboards, she found an ancient, heavy toaster and plugged it in.

"Do you want toast?" she asked Nikolas. The prosaic, domestic question sounded odd to her ears. They barely knew each other, and they had argued for most of that time.

And kissed once. Her cheeks heated, and she was glad she had her back to him.

"Yes." He paused. Maybe the exchange sounded odd to him too. "Thank you."

While the water heated for tea, she popped a couple of slices of bread into the toaster, then turned to lean against the counter to watch Nikolas work, remembering the flashes she had seen of him in the fight. He had been quick, fierce, and powerful, and her first impression had been accurate—he knew his sword like it was an extension of his own body.

Sophie didn't know much about swords, but even she could tell his was a beautiful, sleek work of art. Silver was worked into the flat of the blade in a Celtic-looking pattern. She squatted in front of it, and Nikolas paused with the whetstone as he watched her. His expression was unreadable. What did he see what he looked at her?

With light fingers, she touched the blade. "The silver. Does it help when you're fighting a lycanthrope?"

"Yes," he said. "When I cut them with this, they can't heal at an accelerated rate. They bleed, and they die."

"I should have studied swordwork." She sighed.

"You have no business engaging a lycanthrope anyway, so it doesn't matter," he told her. "They're faster, at least twice as heavy, and much stronger than you. You're lucky you lived through last night."

She glowered at him. If he hadn't spoken in such a cool, analytical way, she would have bristled more than she had, but the truth was, he was right. The kettle whistled, and she rose to make the tea. "Maybe so, but I regret nothing. Arran and Maggie are still alive."

He set aside the whetstone and sheathed the sword. "About that offer I made, to get you a gun and silver bullets. I should have asked. Can you shoot?"

"I don't have much experience with rifles or shotguns, but I'm experienced with a handgun. I prefer carrying a Glock."

As she finished putting together their Spartan breakfast, the monkey left her shoulder and climbed up to the top of the fridge. While he had been riding on her shoulder, he had done something to her hair. She wasn't sure what, but it felt like he had worked several braids through the unruly mass, and at least it kept it off her face at the moment.

"How good?" Nikolas asked.

She handed him a mug of tea and a plate of toast. "Good. I hit what I'm aiming at."

"That's the weapon you need against a lycanthrope." He bit into a piece of toast with strong, white teeth. "But if the authorities caught you with it, you'd be deported. You might possibly face jail time, unless…"

As he paused, she leaned forward. "Unless what?"

"Unless you become a member of the Dark Court, perhaps in a consulting capacity, much like the work you did in LA. If you're affiliated officially to our demesne, you would have weapons privileges." His eyelids lowered, shielding his expression. "I'm not necessarily offering the position to you. I'm just saying that would be one way to solve the problem if you were caught with the gun in your possession."

She frowned. "Okay. The pro is, it would give me some legal protection, if I ever end up needing it."

"The con is, you would become publicly associated with the Dark Court, and you would absolutely become a target for Isabeau and her Hounds. Right now you exist with some anonymity and ambiguity. There's nothing tying you to us. There's just a few accidental meetings. Robin and I could disappear, and your story could be that you helped a stray dog and gave it to its owner—me—and you don't know anything else about either of us. You don't know where we went or where we live."

She breathed deeply and nodded. "You'll get me the gun and the silver bullets."

"I promised I would, and I will. And you'll show me how to make the colloidal silver and cast the rune."

"I said I would," she told him. "And I will. If the situation comes up, and I'm caught with the gun, I'll say I'm a member of the Dark Court, and you'll back me up?"

The stern, beautiful line of his mouth twisted as if he tasted something sour. "Yes. If it comes to that."

"Well, it may not. It's not like I'm going to be walking down the town's high street waving the gun in the air. I'll keep it tucked out of sight but on hand, just in case." She smiled. "Okay, fair enough. I'll feel better having it as backup."

"Actually, I would feel better if you had it as back-up too. If it comes down to your needing to use the gun, declaring yourself a member of the Dark Court is going to be the least of your worries."

She made a face as she ate her toast. "You can sure be full of doom and gloom."

"That I can." He finished his tea. "About that colloidal silver."

She sniffed. "Not so fast, buckaroo. I have my own agenda for the day. Remember the reason why I said I came to England in the first place? I want to test my theory for getting into the manor house."

His dark brows came down again. Really, he was very talented at throwing a fierce frown when he was displeased. "And this is important, why?"

She didn't fault him for feeling the pressure of his own concerns. She might fault him for a lot of other reasons but not for that.

She replied patiently, "Because if I do manage to get in, I'll inherit five acres of this land and receive an annuity, and that means I can take my time getting back to work. I can train and condition at my own speed, build back the muscle tone and stamina I've lost from the surgeries, and I won't have to take on any new jobs until I feel like I'm ready for them. That's very important to me."

His frown eased. "I see."

She carried her tea and plate to the sink. "After I get dressed, I want to walk around the house and get a feel for things in the daylight. When I'm through with that, I'm going to send you shopping with a list of things we'll need to make the colloidal silver."

His brief expression of understanding vanished as he raised one imperious eyebrow. "Why should I be the one to go shopping?"

"Because I don't know where to buy things," she told him, exasperated. "I also want to get groceries." Tilting her head to look at the monkey still perched on top of the refrigerator, she added, "A lot of groceries."

"All right," Nikolas said. He carried his things to the kitchen sink too. "I agree. It sounds like a sensible plan."

He stood at her shoulder as he set the dish and mug in the sink. Turning, she angled her face and went to nose to nose with him as she said, "Not that I needed your approval—but good. I'm glad we're on the same page."

His eyes narrowed, and they dropped to her mouth as she shaped the words. Good Lord, when he going to put on a shirt?

She mouthed at him silently, "Stop looking at my mouth."

His eyes darkened as she saw his pupils dilate. He mouthed back, just as silently, "What if I don't want to stop looking at your mouth?"

The air sucked out of her lungs. What was the one job she had? She couldn't remember. All she could remember was repeating it to herself as she walked out of the bedroom. Licking her bottom lip, she whispered, "I'm still jet-lagged."

"And I still have no damn excuse." He snaked an arm around her waist and hauled her against his torso, angling his head to swoop down and cover her mouth with his.

His kiss was just as hot as she remembered. It was better than last night. Last night really had felt dream-like, but this felt all too real.

This felt shocking and blatantly sexual, and part of her was overcome with glee that she was crushed all up against that broad, muscled chest of his, while the other part melted down into wordless gibberish.

He took her by the back of the neck and ate at her like he was a starving man, pushing her back against the counter so that his hardened body was flush against hers. Her arms lifted of their own accord and wound around his neck while she kissed him just as hungrily.

Heated images ran through her imagination. What she wanted to do to him. What she wanted him to do to her. She dug her nails into the back of his neck. He growled, thrusting the bulge of a long, hard erection against the bowl of her pelvis, and his heart thudded, heavy and powerful, against her breasts.

Nothing else existed, just the two of them together.

Male. Female.

An electronic sound blinged in the intense silence. It sounded like the kind of noise a phone would make, but it didn't come from her phone. He paused and lifted his head. His lips were wet from her mouth, while the dark look in his eyes was so heated she knew the same images had run through his imagination too.

"You're still insufferable," she said. "Just saying."

"And you're the same mouthy broad you were last night," he growled.

"I don't even like you," she snapped.

There went that eyebrow again. He had that imperious expression down to perfection. "What does liking have to do with any of this?"

She started to laugh under her breath. "Not a damn thing, apparently."

Holding her gaze, he took hold of her hips, firmly enough so that she felt the pressure from each of his long fingers, and with slow deliberation, he pushed his hips against hers. It felt so good she let her head fall back as she watched him.

"The gods only know why," he whispered. "But I find you sexy as hell. So far, you've been nothing but trouble."

"*Ugh*, stop talking," she told him, putting the fingers of both hands over his mouth. "You ruin it when you talk. I find you sexy as hell too, as long as you stay silent."

She felt him smile against her fingers. He bit at her

forefinger lightly, then stepped back. "Get dressed. We have things to do."

Angling out her jaw, she said, "I think I'm going to choose to get dressed now, and I don't really care how you feel or think about that. I'm doing it because I want to, and I've got things I'm interested in doing today. Thanks for asking again, asshole."

As she stomped out of the room, the dark sound of his laughter followed her. It had almost the same effect as if he had licked down her naked back. Shivering from reaction, she slammed the bathroom door and stared at herself in the aged mirror over the sink.

"One job," she whispered to the wide-eyed woman staring back at her. "You had one job, and you blew it. Again."

Here was a serious consideration: She found him hot, and he found her hot, as long as they didn't talk to each other. So, what if they didn't talk to each other? What if, instead, they turned out all the lights, stripped off their clothes, and came together?

Male and female.

How amazing would that be? She almost melted into a puddle at the thought. Her body wanted sex, just sex, lots of exuberant pleasure without any emotional entanglements.

Worst of all, her body wanted sex with Nikolas. Not just any sex, with any random person. Not sex with his companion Gawain, who was pretty buff all on his own and a good-looking guy, and also, she thought he was a nice man to boot.

No, Sophie didn't want Gawain.

She wanted the asshole.

There might be a certain kind of freedom in that. He didn't like her. She didn't like him. They could have (tremendous, mind-blowing, screaming, utterly fantastic, wildly pleasurable) sex and then go their separate ways. No misunderstandings, no long-term commitment, no commitment of any kind, no friends with benefits.

Only the benefits…

How crazy and stupid was she to be considering it? She wasn't sure. She just knew she had a talent for crazy and stupid.

Her attention caught on her hair, and she tilted her head back and forth as she considered what the puck had done to it.

He had braided several smaller braids down each side, just enough to tame her hair and keep it back off her face, while leaving the rest of it to tumble crazily down her back. It actually looked pretty nice, kind of tribal.

She decided to leave it and got on with the business of washing up and brushing her teeth. Then she slipped into the bedroom to dress in jeans, the Doc Martens, and a black scoop-neck T-shirt. She glanced at her makeup bag and laughed under her breath—like anybody cared what she looked like, least of all herself—and left it tucked in the open suitcase. Then she grabbed up her own cell phone and the heavy, old keys to the manor house and walked out.

Nikolas had finished dressing, and he had strapped the sword to his back. He stood as still as a statue, arms crossed, staring out the kitchen window at the manor house.

He had absolutely none of the affectations or sense of male fashion she had seen in many other men. None. His hair was cut short. He wore simple plain black clothes and his weapon, yet there was a simple, powerful lethal quality about him that made her weak at the knees.

He looked like he could face down an army, and he was fully prepared to do so.

As she cleared her throat, the statue came alive, and he turned to face her.

"Give me your list of things to buy for the colloidal silver," he said. "I'll send Gawain after them."

She nodded. "Okay. I brought magic-sensitive silver with me, so he doesn't need to waste time looking for that. I know it's pretty rare and expensive here since most of the mines are in the States. You'll need to get some, but for now we can use mine." She thumbed the screen of her phone on. "What's your number? I'll text the list to you."

He told her, and she keyed the numbers in, copied the list she had already made for him, and sent it in a text. When he received it, he studied the items. "Interesting."

"We're going to be building a machine," she told him. "It's a very simple one, but this version won't work in an Other land because it requires batteries. There's another system you can set up that doesn't require batteries, and I can show you how to make that too. In the States, I could pick up everything I need at a local hardware store. I'm sure there's a version of something like that here, but I don't know where to look for it."

"Not a problem." He worked briefly on his phone then slipped it in his pocket. "Gawain will pick up everything we need. I also rang the local butcher and the grocer while you were dressing. They're putting packages of groceries together. The orders will be ready to be picked up in a few hours."

Not *what would you like to eat, Sophie? Do you drink coffee? Are you allergic to nuts?* Of course not.

He was *so arrogant* she was beginning to suspect he didn't even know when he was being arrogant. Was she even going to bother to point it out, yet again? Gritting her teeth, she decided not to waste the time or the energy. If she wanted to buy herself groceries, she was by God going to go into town and buy herself some fucking groceries.

Shaking her head, she stalked out of the cottage, and she didn't stop walking until she stood a few feet in front of the manor house.

Nikolas caught up with her and stalked along by her side. After a minute, he said between his teeth, "I took care of all your needs with a few phone calls, and you're acting like I committed some kind of crime. What on earth is your problem now, woman? Because clearly there's a problem."

"I'm not talking to you. Hush, and let me think."

He muttered something in his language. It sounded beautiful, and it probably had something to do with her being insufferable again. She curled a lip at him and turned her attention back to the house.

The day was gorgeous, a perfect hot summer day in England. Bees droned by. Lavish, untamed greenery spilled from underneath trees, barely held in check by the simple, crude mowing job that kept the wide lawn from turning into an overgrown pasture.

Soon her shirt began to stick to her back, and she almost wished she had put on a pair of shorts. She asked him, "How many gables do you see?"

He had crossed his arms again and stood with his chin tucked close to his chest. At her question, he gave the house an indifferent glance and shrugged. "Five."

Smiling, she shook her head at him. "There's more than five. I want to walk around the whole house."

His attention sharpened, and he gave the house a second, more thoughtful look. "How many gables do you see?"

"I'll tell you after I've gone all the way around."

They strode the circuit around the massive house in silence. For the first time since she had arrived, she caught a glimpse of the small lake behind the house.

Nikolas remained watchful, his expression grim. It must still be difficult for him to be in the place of such a painful defeat. He had lost friends and comrades here. She couldn't imagine how that must feel, actually, and since she couldn't find the right words to say in sympathy, she left him to his own thoughts.

When they finally stood in the same spot in front of the house again, she said, "How many did you see?"

"Still five," he told her. "What about you?"

"On this side of the house, I can see seven. But there's an eighth gable tucked around the back."

"I want to say that's impossible, but mostly I think it's inexplicable," Nikolas muttered. "How do you see more gables than I do?"

She held up her hands and gestured around her. "I think it's the land itself. The crossover passageway is broken, but all the pieces of that magic are still here. Kathryn, the surviving member of the Shaw family, said that when her father was young, he was able to get into the house, but that was quite some time ago. She didn't say exactly when, but she indicated it had been hundreds of years ago."

"They're not human," he said.

"No, they're Wyr. From the story she told me, I gather her ancestor fought for the Light Court. The last time her father tried to get into the house, the key turned in the lock but the door wouldn't open. Nobody can break a window, she said, or make the door budge." She turned sparkling eyes to Nikolas, who was listening to her with close attention. "I think it's because the house isn't fully here. It's *mostly* here, but it's slightly—ever so slightly—not in sync with this Earth where we stand."

He frowned. "But we can see and touch it."

"You can see some of it and touch some of it. I can see more of it." She put her two fists together, side by side and aligned the knuckles of each finger to their opposite. "Think of tectonic plates, and then the earth moves. Maybe it's a massive earthquake, or maybe it's just a small shift." She moved one fist slightly. "Then all of a sudden, the two plates don't match up the way they had before and the land isn't quite aligned as it was. I'm wondering if this is something like that, only more so. This isn't just a place shift. This is a time, place, and dimension shift."

He was wholly engaged now, listening closely to every word. He jerked his chin at the house. "Do you think you can see more of it because you're part Djinn?"

"Yeah, maybe. If I'm right." Looking back at the house, she chewed on a thumbnail. "Kathryn said the family had gotten experts to try to get into the house, but she didn't say who those experts were or what they were experts in. It had all happened so long ago, and nobody had kept decent records of what they had done. I'm guessing they didn't engage a Djinn as one of their experts. Why obligate yourself in an unnamed, possibly dangerous favor to a Djinn for something that was, to them, merely an exasperating mystery?"

"And why would they consider a Djinn for the job anyway?" He rubbed his chin thoughtfully. "They could see and touch the house, just as we can."

She nodded. "Exactly. But I noticed the anomaly in the photos Kathryn showed me. The camera had captured something of the magic in this place. I've been thinking about it ever since, and I've been dying to see it in person."

His dark eyes studied her. "And you still think you might be able to get into the house."

"Maybe. I'm not a full Djinn. I can't dematerialize—not fully—and whisk off to the other side of the world within a few moments, but I do have a certain affinity for manipulating my placement in time and space."

"You can't dematerialize fully," he repeated. Fascination gleamed in his eyes. "Are you saying you can dematerialize *partially?*"

"No, not that." She paused, frustrated with the limitations of language. "I can slightly shift things around me. Or a better way to say it is, I can shift myself in relation to everything else around me. Slightly. Not enough to really dematerialize, but enough sometimes to go unnoticed when I want to."

"Is that how you hid with Robin from Gawain?"

"Yes. In my mind, I say that I *pulled* shadows around me, but really what I'm doing is stepping into shadows that existed at some time in that specific place.

It's—it's like turning a corner. I know that sounds kind of mind-bendy, but believe me, it's nothing like listening to full Djinn carry on a conversation. They literally don't experience reality the same way we do."

He shifted his weight onto one hip and gestured to her. It was as princely a gesture as she'd ever seen him make. "Show me."

She scowled. "I'm not a trick pony to perform on your command."

"No, a trick pony doesn't know how to talk back like you do." The exasperation was heavy in his voice.

What on earth did he have to be exasperated about? It was enough to make *her* exasperated with *him*.

She rolled her eyes. "Besides, it doesn't work very well out in the open, in full sunlight. You know I'm standing here, and you'd be watching for it, so I wouldn't be able to fool you. So getting back to what is actually relevant, what if the house is ever so slightly out of alignment with this Earth? And what if I could shift slightly enough to align with it, open the door, and get inside? If I'm right, a full Djinn could do it, but again, who wants to owe an unnamed, possibly dangerous favor to a Djinn? I certainly don't want to ask one, and I don't want to suggest it to Kathryn, because if I can do it, I win the land and the annuity."

"If you're right, the house is dangerous and probably unstable," he pointed out. He turned to study it again. "According to the story Kathryn Shaw told you, it shifted even further while her father was alive. Parts of it must exist in different broken pieces of land magic."

"Kathryn called it a Rubik's cube, but all the colors don't line up. It might be more like a jigsaw puzzle, with pieces sitting on different planes. All the pieces together make up a full house, but the separate pieces themselves exist in different time-space-dimensional realities." She shrugged. "As far as it being unstable goes—it hasn't gone anywhere for several hundred years, so I'll take my chances. I mean, who knows what's still inside there? There could be anything. The family didn't keep records of what they had left behind."

"You said nobody could break a window when they tried," he said slowly. There was something dawning in his expression, an extra alertness or a comprehension.

"That's what Kathryn told me. Apparently, the house as it stands right now is pretty impregnable." It was her turn to watch him closely. What was he thinking?

He said, "Okay if I give it a try?"

Chapter Ten

SHE COCKED HER head and shrugged. "It's not my property... yet... but Kathryn's family already tried it before, so I'm going to take a chance and say sure, go ahead. Besides, if you can break a window, I can crawl through it and get inside, and then the house will be mine anyway."

This time she was the one to follow him as he stalked slowly across the lawn, looking at the ground. When he came to a broken piece of flagstone, he squatted, pried it up, and hefted it. The stone was big enough it would have been uncomfortably heavy for her to lift, but he carried it as if the weight was no big deal, a small but telling piece of evidence of how different they were.

Once he had selected a stone, he strode closer to the nearest window. Then he whirled like a discus thrower and hurled the stone at the window. He moved so impossibly fast she felt both a shock and a thrill just watching him. The stone shot like a bullet, and when it hit the window, the sound of the impact rocketed across the clearing.

But the window didn't break.

Excited, she jogged over to him and took his arm. "That's exactly what Kathryn described."

He didn't seem to mind that she touched him. Rubbing the back of his neck, he muttered, "But if it connected, why didn't the window break?"

"It hit," she said. "It just didn't hit exactly right."

He tilted his head. "But we can actually touch the house. The stone hit the house. We heard it."

She rubbed her face as she tried to formulate the right words. "You know how in a fight, you might throw a punch, but you are only able to land a glancing blow? Or if you brush against something—you're touching it lightly but not completely."

"You're saying we're not fully touching the house," he said.

"I think so." She paused. "Or maybe this is a better explanation. I've only traveled down a crossover passage a few times, so I'm no expert, but I know if you come at one from the wrong direction, you don't enter the passageway. Assuming the terrain will allow for it, you can walk right across one and never go inside. It's part of the land magic. You're touching the land—you're walking on it—but you're not in alignment with the passageway."

"The house is inside the crossover magic, so it's the alignment that matters."

"Yeah." She nodded. "Except the crossover passageway is broken. It's in pieces, so there's no smooth entryway like there is with passageways that function normally."

"I'm going to try one more time," he said. "Stand back."

She skipped back a step, watching him curiously. This time he didn't reach for anything to throw. Instead, she felt a massive surge in his Power. Suddenly light appeared in the palm of one of his hands, and he threw it. Like a bolt of lightning, the Power snapped across the space to the window and impacted it with another crack that echoed across the clearing.

A chill ran down her spine as she watched. That bolt of lightning—that had been what he had thrown at her two weeks ago.

She was a good, competent magic user. She had her bag of tricks: an affinity working with silver and with runes, a certain ability of prescience that she had honed over the years, a decent repertoire of spells, and a nice little bit of time-space-dimension woo-woo from her Djinn heritage—not a lot, just a little. She was talented enough that, so far, she had made her skills work to her advantage.

But in terms of raw strength, she had nothing to compare to this. Nikolas's Power was world-class, and he would be able to hold his own among the heaviest hitters in any of the demesnes. What else was he capable of doing?

He turned to her and caught her staring at him. For the first time, she saw real excitement in his eyes. "I threw as much Power as I could into that morningstar, and it still didn't break."

Was that what the spell was called? She glanced at the intact window, then back at him. Why was he so excited? She murmured, "That's not really a surprise at this point...."

"This building might be dangerous," he told her. "But unless you have Djinn magic, the inside has got to be one of the most secure places on Earth. Virtually a fortress."

"Sure," she said, watching him uncertainly. "Probably. That's what it looks like, anyway."

He advanced to grab her by the shoulders. His handsome features were ablaze. "And one of those pieces of the jigsaw puzzle must connect to home. That's where the old crossover passageway here used to lead. Right?"

She took hold of his wrists, gripping him as he gripped her. "I-I don't know. I guess it might be possible? But the operative word here is *might*."

He said, "Djinn can't dematerialize and travel from Earth to Other lands, and back again. They can only travel within a certain dimension. They have to use crossover passageways just like everyone else. We all knew that. None of us ever considered, in all of this time, that a Djinn might still be able to use the pieces of broken land magic to make the trip from here to Lyonesse."

She sucked in a breath. There was so much hope in

his face he looked like an entirely different man from the hard, closed-down stranger she had first laid eyes on. It was painful to look at him. In the intensity of his hope, she saw the true depth of the tragedy he had endured and the heartbreak.

Gently she said, "Oh, Nikolas, this is all just a theory. We still don't know if I'm right. Please don't let your hopes get too high."

In response, he hauled her close, kissed her hard, and then looked at the house again. "Too late."

SOPHIE LOOKED WORRIED. It was not an expression he was used to seeing on her face. Strangely, it made him want to pause long enough to pass his hand over the heavy, curling mass of her hair.

A better man than he would remind her again of the increasing danger she faced as she grew more and more entangled with the Dark Court.

But he was not a better man. He would do anything, use anyone, and use himself hardest of all, in order to break through to home, to find that safe fortress for his men, to turn the murderous tide that had all but washed the Daoine Sidhe away into memory.

And he knew what she would say if he did try to warn her. He would get another old-timey folk lecture. She was suicidally brave, he had to give her that.

Obeying an instinct he couldn't put into words, he

pressed his lips to her forehead. "Break into that house," he told her. "Claim it. Own it. And I will rent it from you for a fortune. I'll get you anything you want. Money. Jewels. A villa in Capri. I'll build you a house that is actually comfortable and safe to live in."

She lifted one shoulder and gave him a sly, mischievous smile. "I don't really want a villa in Capri. I just like to say that to assholes."

He bit back a returning smile. "And you do like to call me an asshole, don't you?"

Her eyes widened. "I *do*. In fact, it's become one of my favorite pastimes." That caused him to laugh out loud—something he couldn't remember doing for a very long time. Her eyes twinkled in response, and then she sobered to say, "I'm not the kind of person that likes to take advantage of other people's misfortunes, and I have no interest in taking a fortune from you. If I'm able to break into the house, I'll consider renting it to you for a fair price. I don't even know what that means or what a fair price would be to rent a hulking, magical, dangerous, unlivable pile of a building. Let's take it one step at a time, okay?"

She wasn't just suicidally brave. She had a good heart. Nikolas didn't believe that about many people anymore, but he was starting to believe that about her. Lightly he placed a flattened hand over the middle of her chest, covering where her heart lived and beat its strong, true, steady beat.

Her expression softened and grew puzzled, but she

didn't push his hand away. Instead, she patted it, then she turned to give the house a determined look. He turned to look at it too.

He said, "If worse comes to worst, it would be worth it to me to bargain with a full Djinn to try to break through to home."

"You don't know that it would work," she warned. "Don't waste a costly, unpredictable bargain on such a big gamble. Let me try first. I won't make you promise to do something random, like give up your firstborn son or assassinate a head of state, or make me a bowl of homemade guacamole. Djinn are weird. Trust me. I lived with them for a couple of years. I know."

It was hard to rein in his galloping thoughts, but after a moment, he nodded.

As she crossed the lawn back to the big, double front doors, he followed. Placing both hands on one of the doors, she stood for a while with her head bowed.

He would not interrupt her like some undisciplined, half-trained youth. He would not. Crossing his arms, he glared out over the clearing while he clenched down on the powerful, uncontrolled emotions coursing through his veins.

Enough time passed that he was beginning to re-think that position and ask her what she was doing.

Then something happened. Something so fine and subtle that if he hadn't already been hyperalert, he might have missed it.

He whipped his head around to stare at her. "What

was that?"

She shook her head. Now she leaned her whole body against one of the doors, and she had inserted a large, old key into the lock. "I'm trying to shift into alignment with the door," she muttered. "I got close enough to turn the key in the lock, but I can't push the door open. I might not be aligned well enough, or the door might be stuck. It hasn't been opened in a really long time."

"Here, let me help." He positioned his body behind hers, placing both flattened hands against the sturdy wood. "Let me know when to push."

"Okay." She went silent again, head turned to one side. He watched her profile, the tense, minute shifts in her expression. Her eyes were closed, the delicate muscles fluttering underneath that fine, creamy skin.

Then that subtle something happened again.

She said, "Now."

He threw all his strength and weight against the heavy oak door, all the power of his frustration, his grief and anger over the years, everything.

For a brief, heartrending moment, nothing happened. Then with a gigantic, rusty creak, the door sprang open so suddenly Sophie plunged forward to sprawl flat on dusty flagstones just inside the dim interior of the house. Caught by surprise, he fell awkwardly on top of her.

She coughed. "Fuck. *Ow.*"

The door was open.

Nikolas lifted his weight, urged her over, and when she flopped onto her back, he landed back on top of her and said into her face, "*The door's open.*"

She coughed again and laughed, threw her arms around his neck and laughed some more. Exhilaration plunged at breakneck speed through his body. He cupped her head and laughed with her, and she looked so beautiful in that moment, with those gorgeous eyes dancing and her face lit with delight, he lost himself in the desire to kiss her again.

She kissed him back, meeting his every shift and caress fiercely, tenderly, sensually, only breaking away from his mouth to suck in another gulp of air. "You're heavier than you look."

"I landed hard on top of you too," he muttered. Finally, with an effort at some self-control, he pulled away from her reclining body. "Sorry."

"Don't be sorry! We're in. I'm in! *This is my house now.*" Lying there on the flagstones, she flung her arms wide and laughed again. The exuberance in her voice was impossible to resist. He grinned. "My land. Mine. Do you know I've never owned any property before?" Suddenly she sat up and stared at him. "Wait, the property isn't really mine, not yet. I need to send proof that I got inside to Kathryn so that she can acknowledge it and transfer ownership."

"What kind of proof does she need?" Nikolas rolled to his feet and offered a hand to Sophie, who accepted it. He hauled her upright.

"She said a photo would do, but I don't think I can take a photo from inside the house. My flashlight worked outside, but the land magic feels too strong in here." She frowned.

"Give me your phone and stand in the middle of the open doorway," he told her. "I'll take a photo of you from some distance back. It'll be irrefutable. You're in."

"Good idea." She dug out her phone and handed it to him.

She had a standard smartphone with familiar apps. Loping across the lawn, he spun and thumbed through the apps to the camera and trained it on her. She stood with one hand gripping the edge of the open door, still grinning from ear-to-ear.

He snapped several photos, then checked the phone.

"Got it!" he called out.

She bolted across the lawn toward him, hands out, beaming. "Gimme."

"Hold on a moment," he said, moving his fingers rapidly over the small keyboard.

"What are you doing to my phone?"

"You didn't save my number when you texted me earlier. I programmed my number into it." He tossed the phone to her. She snatched it out of the air and checked the screen. Then as he watched, she thumbed through her contacts, chose one, and sent several photos.

When she had finished, she twisted around to stare at the open door. Then she checked her phone. "Oh man, I'm going to keep checking my phone until she responds. What is the time difference between here and New York, when it's midafternoon here?"

"It's five hours," he said as he mentally did the calculation. "It's not that early for her. She has probably started her workday, so she might not check her personal messages for a while."

"She's a physician, and she said her job is really challenging. I don't want to wait." Sophie scowled. As he watched, she pressed the call button and held the phone to her ear. Distantly, he could hear it ringing.

Then the ringing stopped, and a woman said in a calm, professional voice, "Kathryn Shaw."

"Kathryn, this is Sophie Ross." Sophie looked at him, excitement fizzing in her eyes. "Check your messages. I sent you photos as proof that I got inside the house."

"You didn't!" The woman's voice changed completely. "You did? That's amazing! Congratulations! How on earth did you do it? Wait—let me see the photos…. Oh my God, I can't believe someone finally did it!"

Sophie laughed gleefully. "I had to call you."

"I'm so glad you did! Have you had a chance to look around yet? Please be careful. After so long without any maintenance or upkeep, it's got to be a death trap. The gods only know what's in there."

"No, I haven't looked around. I wanted to contact you first."

"But how did you get inside?"

Sophie glanced at Nikolas. "That's a bit of a story. The short version is, I tested out a theory, and it worked."

"Well, I have to go into surgery in twenty minutes, so I don't have time to hear the whole thing now, but I want to hear it soon!"

"Sure." Sophie turned slightly away from him as she said, "So what does this mean legally? Where do we stand right now, today?"

"According to the terms of the will, you gained ownership of the property and the annuity the moment you stepped inside that door. But as you're no doubt well aware, it's going to take a little time to process the final documents. It'll be three to four weeks before you get the full title work and the financials. I still can't believe you did it! Are you excited?"

Sophie looked over her shoulder at Nikolas. "You have no idea."

"For several years now I've kept a letter on file ready to send to the solicitor in case someone managed to fulfill the terms in the will. All it needs is today's date, your legal name, and my signature." Kathryn's voice grew muffled and distant as she told someone else, "I'll be right there." Then her voice came back stronger. "I'm afraid I have to cut this short. In a few hours, when I'm back at my desk, I'll update and sign that letter, then send the scanned copy to both you and Paul. You won't be able to resell any of the property—if you want to—until you get the paperwork, but you'll be able to draw on the annuity within a day or two. Will that do for now?"

"Will that do?" Sophie laughed. "That's amazing! I can't thank you enough!"

"Thank the ghost of my father. He's the one who set this up."

"I know you have to go, but I have one last question, quickly. I'm having a hard time internalizing this. I actually own the property right now?"

"You own it. Right now you own five acres of land in England, which includes the manor house and the cottage. You can't sell any of the land until you get the paperwork, and—sorry, I should have said this before, but I'm distracted—you need to retain ownership of the manor house to keep the annuity. The entailment is attached to the owner of the house. I know it's a weird legality. If you need to go over that in detail, Paul can explain it better than I can. All right?"

"Yes. Thank you!"

"I'm so excited for you! Again, congratulations! Let's talk again soon!"

As Sophie ended the call, she swiveled to stare at Nikolas. "I take it you heard all of that?"

Nodding, he strode over to cup her chin in his fingers. "You can't sell any of the property until you get the papers, but you own it. If you were to sell the manor house, you'd be selling the annuity too, which makes it a very valuable piece of real estate, whether the building is useable or not."

"I don't want to sell it." She looked back at the house. "Don't ask me to explain, but I love every crumbling, creepy, unlivable inch of it."

She said that so fervently he had to grin. His attention traveled back to that open, inviting door. He said, "Why don't we see what's inside those walls?"

"I can't wait." She turned to lope back to the house, and he caught up with her and kept pace easily.

When she stepped across the threshold, he was half a step behind her. A deep silence filled the large space they entered. Sophie walked into the middle of the area and turned around, looking around her with wide eyes.

She said in a hushed voice, "It feels funny to be walking somewhere no one has been for centuries."

"Yes, it does." The interior looked very solid, with a flagstone floor and walls made of stone. There was a raised dais at the far end of the open space. He tilted his head to study the high rafters overhead, looking for any potential weaknesses, signs of rot, or water stains that might indicate a possible collapse.

When he looked at her again, she was regarding him curiously. "Even for someone of your age?"

His mouth tilted. He told her wryly, "Several hundred years is a long time for any creature."

A touch of pink washed across her cheekbones. She nodded, then looked around. "This is a very large space, and I don't know where to go from here."

"This is the great hall," he said. "It would have been used for formal occasions, to receive important visitors, and for the whole household to eat together. It looks fairly barren right now with all the stone, but there would have been tapestries hanging all along the walls to give them color and help hold in the warmth."

"They must have taken the tapestries when they left," Sophie said, staring around her.

"There might be some tapestries still hanging elsewhere," he told her. "With a manor house of this size, there will be private rooms, a family sitting area or drawing room, which was sometimes called a solar, and bedrooms, a kitchen, pantry, a buttery, smoke room, a larder, servants' quarters, possibly an inner courtyard, and the Shaw family clearly had wealth and education, so I suspect there'll be a library, a chapel, and even an armory."

She blew out a breath. "All that."

"Yes. All that. This didn't shelter just a family household. It housed an entire small community."

The hall itself looked to be in surprisingly good shape. The roof didn't appear ready to collapse. Above, a balcony ran the length of the hall, where people could gather to watch events below. He could see a hint of shadowed hallways between stone arches. If the house was like other manor houses of the time, they would lead to the private family rooms.

There was a massive stone fireplace at one end of

the great hall, big enough for a man of Nikolas's height to stand upright inside. It had been swept clean when the family had left, but a shadow from the fires stained the stone.

He stepped inside and craned his neck to try to see up the chimney, but it was too dark to see past a few feet. It was possible something could have nested in the crevice. Could there be any creatures living inside the house? How would they exist, and what would they have fed on? He could always light a fire to find out.

All in all, the hall looked plenty big enough to hold eight men who were used to living in rough conditions. It was thick with dust but dry, with no sign of stains or mold, and with modern camping gear, they could actually make it pretty comfortable. Propane stoves should work. They weren't technologically complex enough to stop working around the magic of Other lands. Basically all one did was open a valve to release the gas, light it, and set it under a grill. And the fireplace itself might be viable.

So, they could have shelter immediately and explore the rest of the house at their leisure. They could cook. They needed a clean water source and a latrine. Camping gear, firewood, and a big enough supply of food to last them through a lengthy siege, if necessary.

It was doable. The setup would be relatively primitive, but it was defensible, and eminently doable.

When he stepped out of the fireplace and looked around, Sophie was nowhere in sight. "Hey!" he called out sharply. "I thought we agreed this house wasn't safe. No disappearing! Where are you?"

Quick, light footsteps sounded in the hall off to his left, and she stepped into view. "I didn't go far," she said. Her eyes had gone wide again. "Just down the hall a little way. Nikolas, there's a shift about twenty feet down the hall."

He strode rapidly over to her, still feeling irritated that she had gone out of sight. "You didn't step into it, did you?"

"No! Oh, no." She shuddered. "I don't think anybody should go off by themselves in here. Kathryn said there was a pair of children who disappeared for weeks. When they reappeared again, they were dirty and starved and babbling about strange things."

He rested his hands on his hips as he looked down the hall. "We need to map out the house and mark off where the shifts occur."

"Yes!" When he turned his attention back to Sophie, her eyes had lit up. "We need different colored chalk or better yet, paint. The great hall can be the green zone. Down there can be the red zone." She waved her hands in the air. "The colors don't matter. I'm just being random. Then the next zone can be blue, and yellow, and orange, and so forth. When we have a floor plan, we can draw in the zones and see if we can detect any patterns."

"And because we don't know what happens when you cross from one zone to the next, nobody goes exploring alone," he told her.

She cocked her head and angled her jaw out. "Who owns this house again?"

"Sophie," he snapped. "This isn't worth arguing over. It doesn't matter if you own the house. Don't risk your life over it."

She blew out a breath. "Okay. Okay! This *one time* you happen to be right. It's the law of averages. Eventually you were going to be right at some point, but really, you shouldn't expect that to happen again now for years and years—"

There was only one way he knew of to shut her up. He grabbed her by the wrist, hauled her against his chest, and as she *oofed* at the impact and laughed, he snaked his other hand around the back of her neck and kissed her.

This time there was no surprise or uncertainty. He knew what to expect, and it happened. Like striking a match, sexuality flared to life and shot along all his nerve endings. Her plush, full lips were still trembling with laughter.

He ate it all down. He devoured her, greedily. His cock stiffened into a painful hard spike of desire, while she slipped her arms around his waist, molded her body to his, and kissed him back. She met him, greed for greed, ragged breath for breath. He had never felt so alive, so connected.

So perplexed by all of it. By her.

Lifting up his head, he glared down at her. "What

the hell is the matter with you?"

There was something vulnerable in her face, like fine, thin crystal. For a moment she looked blinded, lost, and her lower lip trembled before she sucked it between even, white teeth. The sight bothered him greatly. He wanted to tuck her face into his neck and shelter that fragile vulnerability from the rest of the world so no one else ever saw it.

As he stared, the expression vanished and she snapped back to alertness. The mischief came back slowly, but it did come back.

She laughed up at him. "I'm still jet-lagged. It's going to take me three or four days to get over it. But there's still no excuse for you."

Lightly he touched the dark smudge of shadow underneath one of her eyes. All joking aside, she did need more rest.

"Sophie," he said seriously.

At his tone, her humor faded. "What is it?"

"I didn't know I was looking for you, but I was," he whispered. "You might be the key to keeping my men together and alive. You might be the key to everything."

Her eyes darkened. "Don't put that kind of burden on me. I'll do what I can to help you, and it will be what it will be. Maybe it will be enough. I hope so. That's all."

"It's more than enough." His fingers were too callused to fully sense how soft her skin was, so he stroked the back of his fingers down her cheek. "How does five thousand a month sound?"

She blinked. "For what?"

"For renting the house, of course."

"You mean, five thousand *pounds*? A month?" Her sleek dark brows pulled together. "I don't know, that doesn't sound right. That's too much."

"You're a lousy negotiator," he told her. "I would pay twice that and say thank you for the opportunity."

That sly humor slid back into her expression. "Well, I don't know. There's no central heating, no warm water—no water at all that we've found yet—no toilets, no phone or cable. And I don't think the bus stops out here."

He couldn't smile back. "This place is impregnable from most, if not all, forms of attack. With your colloidal silver and the null spell, my men can rest here in some safety and regroup. And who knows what else we might be able to achieve if we can figure out how all the puzzle pieces fit together."

Bowing her head, she smoothed her hands over his chest and patted him very gently. "I'm really afraid your hopes are much too high."

Her touch soothed him in a way he had never experienced before. He covered one of her hands with his, pressing it harder against his skin.

"Maybe they are," he said. "But I'm finding I would rather live in too much hope than exist the way I've been living these past few decades. So can we rent the house from you?"

"You can use the house," she said firmly. "I'm not at all sure about the rent though."

"Lousy at negotiating," he told her.

She made a face but didn't bother to fire back with anything. Instead, she looked around with an eager smile. "I can't wait to do more exploring."

"Let's leave it for now," he said. "I need to get in touch with my men, and we need to collect a whole new set of supplies, including the different colors of paint. When we're prepared, you and I can go through the house together. We'll map it as we go and mark the shifts. Okay?"

"You sound so boringly sensible!" She rolled her eyes. "I bet you were in middle management at some point in your life."

"Also," he added in a relentlessly even tone of voice, "if two children disappeared and came back starved after two weeks, we shouldn't go anywhere in here without backpacks filled with supplies. Right?"

Heaving a sigh, she conceded. "Right."

"Good." Keeping one arm firmly around her shoulders, he steered her in the direction of the great hall and the open door. "And Sophie?"

"Yeeeees?" she replied, drawing the word out in a tone of long suffering.

"Keep quiet about this, okay? Don't tell people in town that you got into the house. Those Hounds attacked for a reason last night, and we might see more in the guise of men, asking questions. What people don't know, they can't tell others."

Her playful attitude fell away, leaving behind a sober, alert look. She said, "Of course."

They stepped out of the house, and she pulled the door shut behind them, then pulled the key out of her pocket and considered it. As she hesitated, Nikolas said, "Let me check something."

Obligingly she stepped to one side and watched as he tried to open the door. He put his whole weight into the effort, but the door didn't budge. When he turned to face her, eyebrows up, she smirked and pocketed the key. "You're not in alignment. Nobody is getting into my house without my say-so."

He grinned. "Apparently not."

Chapter Eleven

A S THEY WALKED back to the cottage, the excitement slipped away, and suddenly Sophie was so wiped out she could barely keep her eyes open. Yawning, she said, "You mentioned something about groceries."

Nikolas gave her a thoughtful, assessing look. "I'll go into town to pick things up. Why don't you rest? You've had an eventful couple of days."

"I sure have." When they stepped into the cottage, she rummaged around in the kitchen. Suddenly her stomach felt so hollow she would settle for anything to eat. Disappointed, she said, "I thought I saw two pieces of fruit earlier."

"You did," he replied, glancing around as well. "An apple and an orange."

She threw up her hands. "Well, they're gone now." The monkey was nowhere to be seen, so she raised her voice. "You could have left me the orange!"

"I'll head into town to pick up the groceries," he told her. "Shouldn't be longer than an hour."

She paused to stare at him. That sounded odd too,

almost domestic. His offer to get groceries was like having a dragon offer to make her tea, incongruous and unsettling. "How did we become so... so... team-like?"

His dark eyes snapped with something that looked suspiciously like laughter. "You're such a pain in the neck, I haven't a clue."

Her mouth dropped open in outrage. "*I'm* the pain in the neck? Who shoots first and asks questions later? I bet you're the lousiest date on the planet. Who would want to go out with that kind of nonsense?"

"What?" His expression went blank.

"You..." Her voice trailed away as realization dawned.

He hadn't been on a date, not for decades at least, and maybe not ever, since dating was a fairly recent concept in historical terms. He had been embroiled in this conflict for so long he was barely house-trained any longer and stripped of most niceties.

The fact that he had offered to get groceries actually was kind of a big deal. The fact that he had relaxed enough to joke with her, smile, and even laugh on occasion, was nothing short of miraculous. If anybody was ripe for a protracted case of PTSD, it had to be Nikolas.

Her face softened. Reaching out, she hooked her fingers through his and gave them a quick squeeze. "Never mind. Thanks for getting the food."

"You're welcome," he said, frowning. "Lock the door when I leave."

Biting back a sigh, she told him, "I might choose to lock the door when you leave because it's a good idea, not because you ordered me to."

His eyes narrowed. "One of these days you're going to say, 'Sure, Nik. That's a good idea, I think I'm going to do that.'"

Nik. She liked that.

"Don't hold your breath." She laughed.

"Give me your car key," he said.

That wiped the smile off her face. "Why?"

"Nobody would look twice at my car in the city, but here in the countryside it's pretty noticeable. I need to store it or get rid of it, but for now, I'd like to use your car."

He had a point. She dug out the car keys and handed them to him. Silent as a shadow, he slipped out the door, and a moment later, the Mini purred down the drive.

Left alone, she slowly walked through the shadowed cottage and threw herself in a sprawl on the couch. My cottage, she thought. This is all mine now. My couch, my chair, my—my—

The monkey appeared. It had the same little stick arms and legs, but its belly was rounded. It climbed into her lap.

With a gentle hand, she petted his back. Realization dawned.

"This *is* my circus," she said. "You *are* my monkey. At least for now, huh? You know, the Porsche isn't the only thing that sticks out like a sore thumb in the English countryside. Hint, hint."

He regarded her with his sad eyes and wizened, old-man face. When she stopped stroking him, he picked up her hand and put it on his head. Smiling, she started to pet him again.

"One of these days, I'm hoping you're going to feel comfortable enough to shapeshift into your natural form," she told him as she settled back into a reclining position. "And maybe, someday not too far off, you'll feel safe enough to start talking again. What do you think of that?"

As she stretched out into a horizontal position, he curled up against her side and put his head on her shoulder, and it may or may not have been in answer to her question. She wrapped an arm around him.

Despite her best efforts to rest yet stay awake, she crashed headlong into sleep until the crunch of tires on gravel roused her. Knuckling her eyes, she sat up. Damn it! She had an eight-hour time difference to overcome from Los Angeles, but at this rate, she was never going to get her days and nights sorted out.

The light had changed, and the shadows in the cottage had lengthened. The monkey loped toward the kitchen and the door. When Nikolas carried in bags of food, she forced herself upright to join him.

He carried in a large amount of what looked like everything they could possibly need, from dish soap to laundry detergent, fruits, vegetables, cans of beans, packages of meat and fish, bread, eggs, cheeses, butter, yogurt and milk, some prepared meals, and even a few bottles of wine, a six-pack of lager, and a bottle of brandy.

Hungrily she tore open a package filled with two Scotch eggs and bit into one, which was when she discovered that a Scotch egg was sausage wrapped around a hard-boiled egg. Oh yum. She said around her mouthful, "Thank you."

One corner of Nikolas's mouth lifted. "You're welcome. I contacted my men. Gawain is going to arrive first, tomorrow morning. Then they'll all show up, one by one, staggered over the next few days. That way they won't draw attention to themselves, and when each one shows up, you can paint the null spell on them." He paused. "We might not even need the null spell when we're in the house. The land magic could mask our energies."

"It might. It certainly seems to drown out everything else. You might only need to use the null spell when more than one of you leaves the house." Finishing the egg, she rummaged through the groceries. "Oh man, you didn't buy coffee? Who doesn't buy coffee?"

"I bought more tea," he pointed out as he slipped packages into the fridge.

"Tea isn't the same. At all." She rubbed her face. "*Ugh.* This is why you ask somebody what they want when you're buying groceries. Didn't anybody train you right?"

"My training didn't involve running household errands," he said dryly. As she watched, he paused to shrug. Once he had removed the sword harness from between his shoulders, the cloaking spell eased and it came into view. He set it in one corner.

"No, I suppose it didn't," she muttered, staring at the sword in its sheath. "I'll go into town tomorrow to buy some. I promised to stop by the pub to see Maggie and Arran anyway." She glanced at him. "What was it like in town?"

"Subdued. People have started putting black ribbons in their windows. The butcher said it was to remember those who were killed."

Her appetite disappeared, and she offered the second Scotch egg to the monkey, who snatched at it. Nikolas watched her movements, but he didn't say anything. Instead, he took a bottle of cabernet sauvignon and opened it. Pouring wine into a tumbler, he handed it to her.

Instantly she forgave him the lack of coffee as she took a large swallow of the rich, ruby red liquid and sighed.

He poured more wine into another tumbler, set it on the counter, and lit the bulky, alien-looking stove. "I bought a steak and kidney pie for supper. It's already cooked, but it will taste better warmed up. Do you want a salad to go with it?"

She drank more wine as she watched him. He did everything with the same lethal, seamless grace as he fought, and it was mesmerizing. If she wasn't careful, she could fall into a trance and merely watch him, like looking at the graceful flow of a river, for hours on end.

They were drinking wine—well, at the moment, at least she was anyway. Sharing the simple chore of putting groceries away. Talking together about making supper as if they were friends. What on earth was going on here?

Realizing she had paused for too long, she said, "Sure, I'll make it."

Setting aside her glass, she gathered up lettuce and fresh vegetables to wash at the kitchen sink. Glancing out the window at the deepening evening, she looked at the darkened manor house.

Her house. The thrill at saying those words wasn't going to get old.

That reminded her. Abandoning her task, she strode quickly into the sitting room where she had left her phone and opened her email account. Scrolling through the messages, she saw an email from Rodrigo but left it unopened to read later.

She found a new message from Kathryn, with a PDF attachment, and clicked on it. It was the letter Kathryn had promised to send to Paul. Warmth spread through her, along with giddy delight.

"What is it?" Nikolas said from the doorway.

She turned, smiling. "Kathryn emailed the letter to the solicitor in Shrewsbury. It's official. This land, and everything on it, is mine."

Strolling over to her side, he angled his head to study the small screen. "Congratulations. When you go into town tomorrow, you can open a checking account, and I'll transfer your first month's rent into it." Then as she opened her mouth to argue, he told her, "Hush. The building itself might be uncomfortable and lacking in amenities, but it more than makes up for it in other ways. It's a fair exchange."

She scowled. "Here's another thing you don't seem to grasp. Seeing as I'm not five years old any longer, I'm not about to hush just because you tell me to."

His expression heated, and one corner of his mouth lifted in a smile. Sliding an arm around her, he pulled her against his torso. "Do I need to resort to the one technique I have for shutting you up?"

The intensity of his expression warmed her to her toes. Tilting her head, she focused her eyes on one of his shirt buttons. His black shirt was open at the throat, exposing the long graceful line of his tanned neck.

She fiddled with the button. "I didn't want to embarrass you, but to be honest, your technique could use some practice."

Standing flush against him, she could feel his torso shake in a silent laugh. "You're a truly dreadful woman."

She widened her eyes. "Naturally, you would think so." Waving the fingers of one hand at her own head, she told him, "It's because I have all these modern, newfangled ideas, you know. Things like, I know how to speak my own mind. I'm a perfectly capable, autonomous person in my own right. I deserve to get all the pleasure I can from someone else's technique, and I have the right to crit—*Mmph*."

He lowered his head, and her last words got mashed against his lips as he took her mouth. His hot, hardened lips moved across hers, while he slid a hand around the nape of her neck, tilting her head back.

The first time he had kissed her had been an odd, shocking pleasure. The next few times, she had grown a little more accustomed to the idea. This time her body knew what was coming and welcomed it eagerly.

The shocking pleasure hadn't lessened. If anything, it had increased as she left the doubts and disbelief behind and concentrated solely on the sensual experience of his mouth moving over hers with such wicked expertise it sent pulses of pleasure spreading throughout her body.

He knew what he was doing when he kissed someone. He knew it and clearly relished the act, as he put the full force of his considerable concentration into it. Skillfully he teased her lips apart so that he could penetrate deeper. By then, her muscles were melting and her mind had switched off.

She wound one arm around his neck and kissed him back. There was something she was supposed to remember. One thing. One job. But oh wait, that job didn't matter anymore if she was going to proposition him for (tremendous, mind-blowing, screaming, utterly fantastic, wildly pleasurable) sex.

Just the thought of it had her melting down further. Oh my God, if they did end up deciding to have sex, *he would take his clothes off.*

She had already gotten a hint of what that would be like when she had seen him without his shirt. The thought of him totally nude broke the logical part of her brain. Hunger gained control of the wheel and began to drive her actions.

Sliding her fingers through his hair, she lost herself in the sensual pleasure of his mouth. He gripped her hips, pulled her tight against him and held her stationary, pelvis to pelvis. She felt his cock harden, and a sheen of sweat broke over her skin. His entire body was hard as a rock, the muscles rigid underneath her stroking fingers, while his breathing roughened.

He broke off the kiss, ran his open mouth down the side of her neck, and muttered against her skin, "What the fuck are we doing?"

Afterward, he ran his teeth along the sensitive cord at the side of her neck and bit her lightly. Her knees threatened to buckle. She gasped. "Still can't speak for you, but I'm not over jet lag yet. Plus I'm drunk."

That brought his head up. He stared down at her, eyes narrowed. He looked like he had been thoroughly kissed. His elegant lips were darkened with color, his hair falling onto his brow.

She had made him look like that. The knowledge

sent another thrill through her body. She was hungry for him, literally, physically hungry.

"You took one swallow of your wine," he accused.

She hadn't realized he'd been watching her so closely. That was sexy too. She lied, "I'm sensitive to alcohol."

"You're so full of shit." He slid one large hand underneath her shirt, and the sensation of his callused fingers stroking over her sensitive skin sent a flash fire of sensation rippling over her. He cupped her breast.

She let him. Slipping her own hand inside his shirt, she ran her palm over the bulge and hollow of his muscular chest. "And your reasons are still inexplicable."

"I've got nothing else to do," he growled.

She burst out laughing. "You're bored? *That's* your excuse right now?"

"Why?" Lowering his head, he nipped at her lower lip. Huskily he whispered, "Do you have anything better to do?"

Her critical thinking skills had already been in trouble. Now her mind flatlined as he molded and stroked her breast with such clever, clever fingers, teasing the tip of her nipple through the thin material of her bra.

She wanted to push herself into his hand, rub herself all over him like a cat. She felt addicted, drugged. It was like he exuded some kind of pheromone that promised pure pleasure.

She murmured raggedly, "I can't think of anything."

He froze. For a moment he didn't even breathe. Standing so flush against him, she could tell, while his heart beat a rapid tattoo against her fingers.

When he withdrew his hand from underneath her shirt, she almost groaned in disappointment. He cupped her face with both hands. Stroking her lips with his thumbs, he looked into her eyes for a long moment, and she knew in that moment they had gone past all joking.

"Tell me to stop," he whispered. "Tell me, and I'll walk away and say nothing more about it."

There it was: decision time. If he said he would walk away, she believed him, because for all their differences, he kept his word too.

"I don't want you to stop," she whispered back. "We both know what this is. We have a night ahead us, the opportunity to spend some time together and give each other some pleasure—there's nothing more to it than that."

She wanted to add *we don't even like each other*, but the words stuck in her throat, and she knew, at least on her end, that it wasn't true any longer.

"There can't be anything more," he said. The line of his jaw had turned tight, and his fingers moved over her skin restlessly, as if he wanted to let go of her but couldn't. "Do you understand? I don't have anything to give a lover. No safety, no home, not even the promise of my time and attention. Everything I have, everything

I am, is wrapped up in trying to save my men and my people."

There it was, the fineness she had sensed in him the day before, the trueness of self and purpose. If he ever chose to look at someone with that same sense of commitment, Sophie knew that woman would never doubt anything about him and would never want for anything.

For now, there was even integrity in his insistence on having this conversation at this particular point in time. He risked destroying the heat of the moment in order to make sure there was no misunderstanding between them.

"I know who you are and what is at stake for you," she told him. Gently she disengaged, and his hands dropped as he let her go. Turning away, she said over her shoulder, "I'm getting my glass of wine and going to bed, and I would like for you to join me, but I understand if you feel you can't."

Behind her, all she heard was silence.

She didn't linger. Nikolas had made it clear he had his own battles to fight, and this decision was one of them.

By the time she reached the kitchen, she knew he wasn't going to join her. The burden of his own mission held him back. Disappointment weighted her limbs, and only then did she realize how much she had hoped he would take her up on her invitation.

It only went to show—her asshole curse stayed as

true as her technology curse. As soon as she found out the asshole wasn't quite as much of an asshole as she had at first thought, the magic died and any opportunity they had to be together passed on by. She reached for her wineglass to drain it dry.

A rush of air brushed against the back of her neck. Instinctively she turned as Nikolas came up behind her. His face was set, dark eyes blazing. Before she could react, he picked her up bodily and set her on the counter behind her.

Coming between her legs, he held her, one arm braced low around her hips while he gripped her by the back of the neck. The whole maneuver was so swift, so decisive she had barely enough time to gasp.

He said into her face, "I want you."

The words rippled through her body, banishing the leaden disappointment and replacing it with incredulity. Desire for him roared back to life so powerfully she began to shake.

Touching his taut face, she whispered back, "I want you."

A muscle leaped beside that beautiful mouth. "We take tonight."

She nodded. "Yes."

It was as if she had set him on fire. He kissed her so fiercely it vaporized the memory of every other kiss she had ever shared. There was only this one, this moment with this man. She made a noise at the back of her throat. It sounded needy and vulnerable and quite unlike any other noise she had ever made.

Still kissing her, he picked her up. She wrapped her arms and legs around him, utterly shaken by how much emotion came roaring up in response.

The effortless strength with which he held her, the broad curve of his shoulders, the ferocity of his kiss as his hardened lips slanted over and over hers—it all spoke to her in a language she hadn't realized she knew, and she had never known she'd needed to hear.

She drank it all down, while dimly she realized he was striding through the cottage, carrying her to the bedroom. They couldn't get there fast enough for her. He held her weight effortlessly enough; she trusted in his grip and loosened her hold around his neck long enough to drag her shirt over her head.

She let it fall to the floor as he climbed onto the bed and laid her on her back, and together they removed his shirt too. The sight of him, his scent, his expression, each piece of sensory input was like a spike driving into her, splintering preconceived notions, barriers, expectations, stripping her bare emotionally as physically he removed all her clothing.

She was not just nude; she felt exposed in a way that baffled her. She was no stranger to good sex, but this felt...

This felt raw, powerful, and unique.

There was no time to analyze why. As soon as he had helped her remove her clothes, he pulled back up to strip off his pants. *He took all his clothes off* and stood naked at the side of the bed.

He was naked.

For the first time, she saw the seamless beauty of his body without obstruction, the feline grace of his bone structure flowing from long, muscular legs up slim hips to the widening flare of his chest and shoulders. He was a dusky gold all over, with a sprinkle of dark hair across his chest that arrowed down the long muscles of his abdomen to a large, erect cock jutting over the tight, round sac underneath.

Staring at him, she forgot how exposed she felt, how odd and raw and powerful this moment felt, and lost herself in wonder. Looking up at his hard, beautiful face, the face that couldn't help but be ferocious because ferocity was an inherent part of his nature, with those dark, glittering eyes focused solely on her, she knew somehow that she stood poised on the threshold of a new reality.

He began to crawl onto the bed, and *he had no clothes on* to mask the flawless, inhuman fluidity with which he moved. She could stare at him for years and never get tired of it.

Pausing, he met her gaze. "Everything okay?"

Hell no, nothing was okay. He was taking her apart and remaking her, and he hadn't even touched her again yet.

But he waited for her reply, and she wasn't about to deny herself a moment of this singular experience, no matter what it did to her or who she became when she reached the other side of it.

Opening her arms to him, she said, "Everything is perfect."

✧   ✧   ✧

NIKOLAS WAS HARD put to describe to himself or understand exactly why Sophie affected him so powerfully.

All he truly knew was that she did. Her insane courage, the way she thought, the way she laughed, the way her incredible eyes sparkled with so much lively humor or outrage, and how either emotion could change in an instant.

Her clever use of her magic and her fierce defense of her own boundaries—stitched together, all those characteristics created a person of such wholeness and appeal that in the course of a single day, she had moved effortlessly to take center stage in his thoughts.

He loved her curves. Loved them. They were so alien to his own body, so compelling. He touched her lips, the tips of her breasts, and ran his fingers lightly over the swell of her hips and felt her shiver underneath his touch.

Aside from the three ragged scars at shoulder, abdomen, and thigh, her creamy skin was flawless. She might disagree, but he thought those scars were beautiful. Each one was a badge honoring her courage and strength.

She had said she had lost muscle tone, but he didn't

see it. Her body was sleek and toned. Only the concave hollows at her stomach, under her collarbones and cheekbones gave any hint at the weight she had lost. Her breasts were generously rounded, the plump dusky nipples erect and inviting.

Her eyes gathered all the light in the room. For a moment he had the oddest feeling that they gathered all the light inside him too, however much had managed to survive these past several years, and they magnified all of it to shine as brilliant as stars in the bedroom's muted lighting. He had always loved starlight's cool, distant magic.

He needed to touch and taste her everywhere, badly enough that his hands shook with a fine tremor as he pulled her into his arms. The sensation of her body against his, bare skin to bare skin, reverberated through both of them, creating a vibration that was neither one nor the other but a combination of both.

There was nothing else in the entire universe, nothing but the two of them together. Her curves, his angles. Her light, his darkness. Her softness, his exquisitely aching hardness.

Male. Female.

Her head fell back against his arm as she stared at him, and her plump, delectable lips parted.

It was all the invitation he needed. He gave into the internal fire that burned so hot for her, and it consumed him.

Chapter Twelve

Y ANKING HER BODY against him, he ravaged her mouth, succumbing to blind instinct as he plunged his tongue into her as deeply as he could. Her groan trembled against his lips. Unsure if she welcomed his onslaught, he paused, and in response, she gripped his shoulders and kissed him back with wild abandon.

Her transparent eagerness burned away the last of his restraint. Easing her back onto the bed, bringing the weight of his body over hers to pin her down, he ran a hand down her torso while he feasted on her mouth.

The soft, pliant responsiveness of her lips, the plump generosity of her breasts, the way her legs moved restlessly against his, every detail of the sensory input fed his hunger until he felt like his skin was nothing more than the thinnest of covers for the light and heat that roared inside him.

Ravenously he nipped and suckled at her skin as he moved down her body, her enticing lower lip, the delicate spot at the juncture of her neck and shoulder, the gorgeous round flesh of her breasts, oh gods, her breasts. He lost himself in teasing her nipples, biting gently at the turgid peaks until she cried out in incoherent pleasure, working her fingers restlessly against his scalp as she held his head to her.

He sucked harder, and she bucked underneath him, pushing off the bed as she arched into his touch. She was so perfectly, exquisitely responsive, the heavy spike of need that dangled between his legs grew even tighter, harder.

"I want to do everything to you, all at once," he muttered. "I want to stroke you, fuck you, hold you down, lift you up, pin you, take you. I want you to take me. Lord and Lady, Sophie, I don't know that I have any gentleness in me tonight."

"You talk awfully sexy in bed." She twisted to whisper unsteadily in his ear just before she bit his lobe hard enough to send a jolt of sensation all the way down to his cock. "But if you're wanting to actually communicate something to me, you're going to have to do it in English."

Lifting his head, he stared down at her. He hadn't even realized he had slipped into his native tongue. Running his hand down the slope of her stomach, he stroked along the gentle curve of her pelvis, fingering the black tuft of silken hair at the juncture between her legs.

He'd already forgotten what he had said before.

"I want to fuck you into tomorrow," he said between his teeth. Probing carefully between her legs, he fingered the soft, delectable folds of flesh that grew slick with the evidence of her desire. "I want to fuck you so hard you can't walk until next week."

"Promises," she gasped on an unsteady laugh.

As he explored her, she opened her legs and her expression twisted in a combination of pleasure and distress, and her breathing came harder and more raggedly. She pushed up with her hips, rubbing herself against his hand, while she raised her head and they both looked down at their bodies.

Their legs lay entwined. His were heavier, corded with muscle and sprinkled with dark hair, while her more delicate bone structure made her legs looked lighter and leaner. His thick, hard erection lay against her hip, the broad mushroom head exposed.

"*Mmm*," she said in throaty welcome as she reached for it with both hands. When she touched him, the bolt of pleasure was so sharp he nearly spurted into her palm. She stroked her thumb along the small, sensitive slit at the tip, and in response a drop of moisture appeared. She rubbed it into his skin.

Then in his own exploration of her most sensitive flesh, he found the stiff, delicate little pearl hidden in her private folds, and as he rubbed it, she nearly came off the bed with a strangled scream.

Oh, he loved that. He *loved* her reaction. Fiercely clamping down on his self-control, he flicked and massaged her clitoris in teasing circles until she gripped his wrist and ripples of reaction shook visibly through her body.

Unable to hold back his own hunger, he bent to fill his mouth again with one of her luscious nipples, and he suckled at her while he flicked at her clit, and the tension in her body grew and grew until a fine sweat broke over her silken skin and she vibrated like the taut string on an archer's bow.

Give it to me, he said in her head. *Come for me.*

I-I can't. She gasped for air and shook harder. *I love this, I love how it feels, but I can't climax like this. Not during our first time together.*

What was this? He lifted his head to frown down at her. "What do you mean, you cannot climax like this?"

Lifting one shoulder, she gave him a lopsided smile. "It takes me a while to grow to trust my partner enough to let go. It's just a thing; it's not a big deal. It's just who I am."

"Well, I do not accept that reasoning," he growled. "You trust me. You would not be here with me now, unclothed in your bed, if you did not."

"Well…" Her voice trailed away as she frowned.

She had nothing to say, he knew, because he was right. Stroking his hand down the shapely, slender length of her thigh, he told her, "Relax, my Sophie. Breathe deep. Enjoy yourself, and know that you are safe."

Safe. Why had he felt the need to say those specific reassuring words to her, when he, of all people, knew just how unsafe they really were? Why was that the only answer to the vulnerability he saw in her eyes?

She resurrected something inside him, the kind of man he used to be, protective of and attentive to those he cared for. He wanted to shelter her, not because she asked for it or because she even needed it, but because he needed to be the one to give it to her.

There was something dangerous in that path of reasoning, some line in himself he had been determined not to cross, but he forgot what it was when she responded, relaxing visibly as he stroked her body in long, soothing sweeps with one hand. He slid down the length of her body, urged her to part her legs again, and when she did so, he settled between them and stroked the tender folds of her skin with a thumb.

Then he split the folds apart to reveal that little, delicate nubbin. She was beautiful there, as she was beautiful everywhere, the fluted folds of her flesh rich with color and her scent, warmth, and wetness. At the sight, he made a quiet sound of pleasure and put his mouth over her clitoris, tasting her private flesh for the first time.

Her thighs shook, and she made a thin, uncertain sound. *Shh*, he whispered in her head. *Relax. Enjoy. You are the most delicious thing I have ever tasted. You're beautiful. I want to plant myself in you, right here. Fill you up. Fuck you, make love to you, give you pleasure, make you scream.*

As he talked to her, he suckled and flicked at her with his tongue, working her with a rhythm, while he slipped a single finger into her tight, wet sheath. She was so warm, so wet, so ready.

Lifting from his task, he told her, "When I was in town, I bought condoms."

Her eyebrows rose. "You were already planning this?"

There was something complex in her expression, but he did not think it was distaste or dislike. Rather, she seemed to be pleased.

"I wasn't planning on anything, but I had thoughts," he said. "And I do not believe in being careless. I may be part Wyr, but I am not Wyr enough to have their ability to prevent pregnancy."

"Nik, thank you for thinking so responsibly, but I'm part Djinn," she whispered. "I don't know how my ancestor managed to participate in a viable pregnancy, but however they did it, I don't have that ability. I've seen more than one doctor to be sure, and they were conclusive. I can't get pregnant."

"Sophie," he murmured. Placing a hand over her flat stomach, he paused to search her face for any sign of pain or sadness.

There was none. Her expression was clear, calm, and open. She smiled at him. "You don't need to look at me that way," she told him. "I love children, but I've known from an early age, I'm not cut out for mother-hood. I'm not even good dog-owner material. Since the Elder Races don't catch or transmit human diseases, we don't need to use condoms."

He smiled. "Let's not get too ahead of ourselves. I'm not finished down here."

Her breath caught as he turned his attention back to pleasuring her. Nestling his lips against the most sensitive part of her body, he soon found his rhythm again, flicking, nibbling and sucking until soon her hips bucked in response.

"That's—that's wonderful, but that's enough," she gasped. "It's too sharp, too intense—"

Is that what happened to you, my Sophie? he purred in her head. *Did your other lovers give up on you too soon? Were they greedy boys, focused only on themselves and their own needs without paying any attention to you and yours?*

Yes. No. I don't know! she gasped, her head turning restlessly on the pillow while her body shivered underneath his relentless attentions.

I am no green, foolish youth, he murmured. *I know what you need and how to give it to you. Work with me, my Sophie. Don't give up. Relax, trust, let me inside your head. You feel like wet, tight silk. You taste like sex. You are the most delicious thing I've ever tasted. My cock aches for you. My body aches for you.*

While he talked, he slipped a second finger, massaging her gently inside. Her pleasure was building higher again. He could feel it in the escalating heat in her body, the tightness of her muscles, the way her hands shook as she stroked his hair. Nothing else existed in the world, just her body, her pleasure, the sound of her ragged breathing, and the exquisite torment on her face.

She began to plead. "Nikolas—Nik—it's on the

other side of this wall, I just don't know how to get there—"

You don't have to get anywhere, he whispered. *Ease up, my Sophie. Let it come to you. I will bring it to you. I promise. Trust me. And when I bring it to you, I am going to come inside you. I'm so hard and ready for you. My skin burns with it. Feel the heat coming off my skin. I am on fire for you.*

She touched his face, and he knew she could feel it. He had never burned so hot for anyone before. She lifted her head to stare at him.

Their eyes met. Nikolas touched the cool, starlit magic in her gaze with the dark blaze in his own. There was some kind of message that passed between them, some kind of truth.

Then her head fell back onto the pillow, and she cried out as she climaxed. He felt it ripple through her inner muscles. Her tiny, delectable clit pulsed. Fierce emotion roared through him.

He had given that to her, no one else, and in giving it, her climax became *his*. He claimed her pleasure, owned her response in that moment.

Mine, he thought. Mine.

He forced himself to wait, wait, wait, until the rhythm of her pleasure began to subside. Only then did he rise up to cover her body with his and unleash his own need. Kissing her, biting at her mouth, he took his cock and rubbed it against her entrance.

Reaching down between their bodies, she welcomed him and helped to guide him in. Then he slipped in, just the tip, and as he broke through her entrance and felt her body grip his most sensitive place, a groan broke out of him. Unable to move forward, unable to pull away, he froze.

She whispered, "What is it?"

"I'm back in that place again," he said between his teeth, resting his forehead on hers. "I don't know if I can be gentle any longer."

She laughed, and it was a completely joyous sound, as she threw her arms around his neck, her legs around his hips and hugged him with her whole body. Putting her lips to his ear, she gasped, "You need to go, let's go. Do it, Nikolas, cut loose, *I want you to fuck me so hard right now.*"

She incited him to riot, and he had no brakes, no barriers left, so riot he did.

The fire in his body took over. He plunged into her, all the way, to the hilt, and she was so hot, so tight, just exactly what he needed, he had to pull out and plunge all the way back in again. She met him thrust for thrust, rocking up with her hips as he hammered down, and it was so damned perfect he didn't know how he could ever stop. Gripping her by the hip, by the breast, swearing in her ear, he fucked her while the blaze inside him built and built until it peaked in a fiery gush.

His climax roared up the base of his spine. Helpless in the grip of it, he thrust and thrust again with every new spurt. She ran her hands down his back, holding him to her, rocking with him until the rhythmic jerk of his cock began to subside.

Either he was shaking, or she was. His lungs pumped hard like bellows, while she stroked his back, his shoulders, and he buried his face in the crook of her neck until finally his climax began to subside.

For a moment he was gripped with the strangest compulsion. He wasn't done, he wasn't done. He needed more, to pin her down and claim her until there was no doubt left anywhere that she was his. His cock still felt hard as a spike and as agonized.

He tensed, frozen on some kind of precipice.

Then, as she threw her arms around his neck and hugged him, the moment passed. "This was wonderful," she whispered. "Thank you."

The words grounded him, not much but just enough. Carefully he backed away from the internal precipice as he withdrew from her even though every muscle in his body screamed at him to stop, change course, claim her until they both knew beyond a shadow of a doubt that she was his alone.

He paused long enough to kiss her lingeringly on the mouth, down her throat, and finally he pressed his lips against the scar above her left breast, where her heart beat strong and true.

"You are so beautiful," he told her in a quiet voice. "What a surprise this night has been. You've given me more pleasure than I've known in years. Good night, my Sophie."

He shouldn't say those words. She wasn't his Sophie. As she had said earlier, they both knew what this was. This was a stolen night of pleasure, nothing more, nothing else. They were little more than strangers, their lives lived on two separate trajectories.

This was not a mating. There would be no claiming her for his own even if she would have welcomed such an outlandish proposition. Yet his Wyr side didn't understand logic and reason. It pounded through his blood, urging him to take her again, to mate with her.

But Wyr mated for life, and he had no room in his life for that kind of commitment. He had already given his life to his people. The thought of taking a steady lover was laughably inappropriate. The thought of mating, utterly impossible.

He had never been gifted with such an experience. He had never felt such a driving compulsion to mate with anybody before, and he accepted the rare gift for what it was—an arrow through the heart.

As she realized he didn't intend to stay, the light in her eyes dimmed, and it was another arrow to the heart. She deserved to be held, in that moment more than ever, and she deserved to explore the new realm of pleasure he could give her as he brought her to climax over and over until she fell into exhaustion. Every instinct in his body told him to go take her in his arms and refuse to let that light in her eyes die.

Without another word, he turned his back on those instincts and on her, picked his clothes off the floor, and shut the door on his way out.

❖   ❖   ❖

WELL, IT WAS a good thing they'd had a clear understanding of what they were getting themselves into when they had sex.

Otherwise, Sophie would be feeling let down and disappointed that Nikolas chose to walk out the door rather than stay and enjoy more time together. If her vision blurred with wetness, it was because she was so tired. It didn't have anything to do with the fact that he chose not only to leave her bedroom but to leave the cottage as well.

Almost as if he couldn't get away from her fast enough.

As she heard the cottage door close, she rolled over to hug a pillow. *Gah*, she would never understand men. As far as she was concerned, they'd had a pretty spectacular time. He had been...

He had been so much more than she had expected. So much more considerate, tender, and passionate.

She closed her eyes, but she couldn't block the images that played through her mind.

His face as he moved inside her, fierce and gentle, determined and sensual. They had barely gotten started, damn it. She had things she wanted to do to him. Really cool, sexy, fun things. She had been hungry to try them, and she was still hungry. But apparently he wasn't interested enough in exploring anything further with her.

Of course he wasn't.

He was no longer the asshole she had thought he was. There was something decent, true, and fine in him, and just as she glimpsed it, it moved away.

His scent was still on her skin. She loved his scent. Loved it. She was never going to get to sleep if she kept experiencing his scent, as if he were still with her, while she fantasized about taking his cock into her mouth.

Pushing out of bed, she grabbed a nightshirt and went into the bathroom to take a shower. When she was through and fragrant with her shower soap, she padded into the kitchen to drink the tumbler of wine still left on the counter.

Sipping it, she stood at the kitchen sink, looked out the window, and saw him. The moon still looked quite full, and the scene outside was almost as bright as day.

Nikolas had dressed, and he stood with his hands on his hips near one end of the manor house, his back to the cottage as he looked out over the landscape. Instinctively Sophie glanced at the corner of the kitchen where his sword harness had been, but it was missing. She felt better knowing that he was armed even if the cloaking spell prevented her from seeing it on him.

He had so many bad memories wrapped into this place. He had so much history, period. She barely knew him, so why did the sight of him standing alone out in the night tug so hard at her emotions?

She felt a pull to go outside and join him that was so strong she almost gave in to it. But he had been the one to leave her, and with a stinging realization, she knew he would not welcome her presence.

As she finished the wine in the tumbler, the monkey came into the kitchen, jumped onto the counter, and sat looking out the window beside her. She said, "Robin, I wish I knew how to help him."

The monkey took her hand and patted her fingers.

"I know," she said. "I'm doing what I can. And he didn't ask me to do anything more anyway." Forcing herself to look away from the lone figure outside, she turned her attention to the puck. He seemed bigger, more substantial, and for the first time, she could feel a hint of his Power. Pleased, she said, "You're getting better."

He nodded.

"I'm so glad." Passing a hand gently down the back of his head, she rinsed out her glass and set it in the sink. Then she went to bed.

For the first time, she realized somebody had made the bed, and she knew it hadn't been her, and she was pretty sure it hadn't been Nikolas.

She and Nikolas had made love on top of the bedspread. Made love, huh. She meant they'd had (tremendous, mind-blowing, screaming, utterly fantastic, wildly pleasurable) sex, and it had lived up to every single one of those adjectives. Every single one and more.

Her damn eyes threatened to dampen again. She whispered to herself, "Be careful what you ask for."

Robin slipped into the room. The monkey jumped to the headboard and settled into a sitting position. Now that she knew he wasn't a monkey or a dog, it was probably weird to let him spend the night in her room, but he never invaded her privacy or tried to hang around when she was dressing or undressing, and she got comfort from the companionship. She thought he got comfort from it as well.

Climbing under the covers, she curled on her side and fell fast asleep.

This time she wasn't nearly so lucky in her rest. This time the nightmares came.

She never outran the gunman. That was not how her story had gone, and her body knew it. The gunman chased her and chased her through the dark, shadowed warehouse where they had cornered him, and she could never remember to *pull* the shadows around her before he brought his gun up to point it at her.

The *tat-tat-tat* of gunshot had grown all too familiar. And then she was falling again. Still, somewhere in her mind, she was always falling.

THE QUIET SOUND of voices woke her, but God, she didn't want to be awake. Rolling over, she stuck her head under one of the pillows and tried to go back to sleep.

Voices?

Even as she thought the question, the answer came to her. Gawain had arrived, and he and Nikolas were somewhere close by, talking. The sound of their conversation didn't come through the window, so there weren't many options—they were either in the kitchen or the sitting room.

Once awareness had come so forcefully, she knew she would never get back to sleep. Swearing under her breath, she got out of bed and dressed. There were places all over her body, intimate places, that ached with a sensitized tenderness that hadn't been present yesterday.

Her nipples felt the rasp of cloth as she donned her bra, and the muscles of her inner thighs were sore. The folds of her private flesh felt full and delicate. Even as memory flashed through her mind of his head between her legs, of the sensation of him moving inside her, a pulse of renewed hunger made her ache. Even though her mind wanted nothing more than to move on and forget the sense of abandonment she had felt the night before, her body remembered what had happened, and it wanted more.

Dressed again in her flannel pants, soft, long-sleeved shirt, and flip-flops, she left the bedroom to go in search of coffee. Oh, right. There was no coffee. This day had barely begun, and it was already a pain in the ass.

Nikolas and Gawain sat at the kitchen table. As she appeared, Gawain gave her a smile. "Hello again."

She found she was unable to snarl at the friendliness in his expression, so she raised a hand and grunted in greeting as she made a beeline for the teakettle. Cautiously she touched the side. It was hot. After checking to make sure it had water, she lit the burner underneath it. As she turned to search for a mug and a tea bag, Nikolas stepped in front of her.

"*Unh*," she said, checking so she didn't bump into him.

He frowned at her, dark eyes sharp. "What is the matter with you?"

"Huh?" She didn't have the energy to face him first thing, not after last night. Stepping around him, she muttered in a husky voice, "I don't know what you're talking about."

She found a mug and the box of tea. When she turned back to the kettle on the stove, he stood so close the sense of his nearness abraded her already raw nerves. His frown had turned fierce. He touched the delicate skin underneath her eyes.

"You look awful. The shadows under your eyes have gotten worse, not better. Are you sick?" he demanded.

She jerked back from his touch. "First, get out of my face. Second, you didn't buy coffee. Third, don't talk so loud—or better yet, don't talk at all. Fourth, I didn't sleep well. I usually don't. Mornings are not my best time. Fifth, did I mention the fact that you didn't buy coffee?"

"Multiple times," he snapped.

"Your presence offends me." She patted her chest.

"It literally hurts right here. Not you, Gawain," she said in an aside. "It's nice to see you."

"It's good to see you too, Sophie." Gawain sounded amused, but she noticed with gratitude he also kept his voice at a quiet enough level that it didn't sound abrasive. Looking pointedly at Nikolas, he said, "I thought you said you two were getting along better."

"That was apparently before I forgot to buy coffee," Nikolas replied dryly. He plucked the mug and tea bag out of her hand. "I will make you a cup."

"Make two while you're at it," she muttered. "I'm going to need a second one."

Gawain said in a diffident voice, "Lass, I hate to bother you, especially right now, but is there any way you could do your silver null spell on me so I can stay?"

"Damn it," she muttered. "Of course. I'll be right back."

She left to retrieve her vial of colloidal silver, and when she returned, Gawain held out his hand without a word. She cast the spell as she painted the rune, and after she finished, Nikolas set a hot, bracing mug of tea on the table in front of her. She latched on to it and didn't let go until she had drunk the whole thing. He had added milk and sugar too, and she decided she liked the combination.

Giving her space to wake up properly, the men resumed talking about people she didn't know, but she presumed she would probably meet in the next few days. Gawain stood and worked at the stove, and within a few minutes the smell of frying bacon and eggs filled the air.

When she had drained the first mug of tea, without a word, Nikolas took it from her and set another full mug on the table near her elbow. This time Gawain also slid a plate filled with a hot, cooked breakfast in front of her.

She stared at the plate. Bacon, sausages, beans, eggs, fried mushrooms, sliced tomatoes, and what looked like fried bread. It looked like enough food to feed someone twice her size. For a moment her stomach reacted with an uncertain queasiness, then sharp, genuine hunger set in. The last time she had eaten a proper meal had been two nights ago, in the pub.

She fell on the food and practically inhaled it while Nikolas and Gawain also ate. The talk fell away, and for a while all three existed in the quiet comfort of the sunny kitchen as they finished breakfast. To her own astonishment, she ate everything on her plate, and afterward she finished the second mug of tea too.

Finally she felt comfortably full and alert. She pushed that empty mug away too and looked up to discover both men watching her, Gawain with a slight smile, while Nikolas wore a brooding expression she didn't know how to interpret.

She knew what his mouth tasted like. She knew how his hair felt, as the short, silken strands slipped through her fingers. Scowling, she averted her face and said to Gawain, "Thank you for breakfast. That was amazing."

"You're welcome, lass." Gawain stood. "I need to get the packages in the storage compartment of my bike. Be right back."

After he walked out, Nikolas said, "Why don't you sleep well?"

"It's just a thing," she said. "It's who I am. It's not a big deal."

"You say that a lot," he told her. "I don't believe it now, any more than I did before."

She remembered the last time she had said it and how he had brought her to climax in spite of herself. A flood of warmth washed over her face. "Well, sometimes when I say it," she said between her teeth, "it's a boundary that you're not supposed to cross. This is one of those times."

She rose to slap their dirty plates together in a stack and carried them to the sink. He wasn't going to let it go, she just knew it. They were rubbing each other the wrong way this morning, and this wasn't going to end well.

But just in that moment, Gawain stepped back inside and the invisible pressure that had been simmering in the kitchen eased.

He set the packages on the table and unwrapped them while she finished clearing the table. When she started to wash the dishes, Gawain said, "Sit down, lass.

You're helping us so much you don't need to do the washing up too. I'll do those in a bit."

"You can't," she pointed out. "Not and keep the null spell active."

By the chagrin that passed over his face, she saw that he had forgotten. Nikolas stood. He told her, "Leave that for now. Come show us how to make the colloidal silver."

"And that leads us to something we'd been talking about before you came to join us," Gawain said. "The rent we'll be paying you is more than fair, but we should be also paying you for your other services—for this and for helping us to explore the possibilities in your witchy house."

She couldn't wash dishes and have this conversation with them at the same time. Turning her back to the sink, she wiped her hands on a towel while she shook her head.

"My consulting services cost the LAPD a hundred grand a year," she said. "But that's not what we agreed upon. I'm teaching you the colloidal silver and null spell combination, and in return, you're giving me a handgun with silver bullets and the legal right to use it. As far as exploring the manor house goes, I want to do that anyway. It's my house. I should know its strengths and pitfalls and if there's anything of worth inside that I might want to sell. If you want to engage me for anything else, we can talk about a consulting fee at that time. For now, the bargains we've struck are more than fair."

Nikolas said, "Actually, there is something else we would like for you to consider doing. We want you to cast your runes and do a reading for us."

She raised her eyebrows. "I guess that changes things a bit." Looking from Nikolas to Gawain, she added, "I'm all about monetizing my skill set, but just doing a reading for you is not that big of a deal."

Nikolas walked over and took the dish towel out of her hands. "It's a big deal to us," he said quietly. "We need to understand how and why I was ambushed, and what other magic had been in play that day and if it might still pose a danger. Also, after the attack on the pub, we need to try to figure out how much the Hounds may know about us, about the puck, and about you."

Frowning, she looked at him directly for the first time since having breakfast. "Knowing that would be of benefit to me too," she pointed out.

"Here's what I propose," Nikolas said. He laid his hands on her shoulders. "Instead of bargaining piece-meal over every little thing or added service, I want to pay you a blanket amount for a month of your consulting services. If you're not going to go away, *as you should*, that's a fair offer."

Why did he keep approaching her and touching her? It made her cranky and confused her. She wanted to step forward into his arms. She wanted to slap his hands away.

Most of all, she wanted to get back down to the business they had begun last night before he had so precipitously walked away.

Throwing up her hands, she shrugged out of his hold. She said, "If you want to pay me for a month of consulting work, I'd be happy to take your money, but I don't have a work visa."

"I'll add it to the amount we're paying you for rent," Nikolas told her. He turned to watch her with a sharp frown as she sidled away from him. "Fifteen thousand."

The British pound was worth more than the dollar, and adding ten thousand pounds to cover her consulting fees was more than she would have made in LA. But it wasn't so much over the top that it caused her conscience to twinge.

From a distance of six feet away, she gave Nikolas a thin, not-altogether-friendly smile. "You want to hand over your money? Fine, I'll be happy to take it."

Chapter Thirteen

HAVING COME TO that agreement, they got down to business. In short order, they had the table completely cleared and various items unwrapped from the packages Gawain had brought in. Sophie had already brought her vial of colloidal silver out to the kitchen, and she collected the rest of the things she wanted from her bedroom—pieces of magic-sensitive silver, a pen and pad of paper.

"Making your own colloidal silver generator is the easiest thing in the world," she told the two males who were focused so intently on her. "It's like learning to park a car. Once you know it, you know it. You need a power source, alligator clips, silver, distilled water, and containers. Silver colloidal enthusiasts who believe in using it for medicinal purposes might also use a regulator diode, because the theory is, as the electrical current grows, it strips larger particles of silver off. That's not good for their purposes, but that's great for ours, so we're not going to use a regulator diode. We want the larger particles because that's what makes magic-sensitive colloidal silver so viable."

As she talked, her hands moved over the various items, arranging them to her satisfaction. She connected the batteries to each other, then to the alligator clips, to two of the pieces of the magic-sensitive silver she had brought, set it all in the container, and filled it with distilled water.

"And that's it," she said. "We're done. The solution will be ready in several hours when it has a yellow tint to it. We can check it again this evening, and it will probably be viable then. Like I said before, there's a way to make a generator without batteries, just by using sunlight, but I've never used that method before. If you're interested, I can dig up some instructions."

Nikolas took several photos of the apparatus while both men asked her questions. She answered them readily enough, and when they seemed ready, she pulled out her vial of viable colloidal silver.

"You've already seen the end result to the process," she said. She took her pen and drew the rune on the paper, then flipped it for them to see. "And this is the rune I use."

"Is that Nordic?" Nikolas asked as he angled his head to study the rune.

"Yes." She paused uncertainly. "That's not an issue, is it?"

He shook his head. "No. I'm just not as familiar with the Nordic runes as I am with the Celtic."

"Once you know the technique, you can get creative with your spells and use the runes you're more familiar with," she told him. "Drawing the rune and infusing it with the magic spell is the same technique that jewelry makers use when they create magic items. If you know how to put a cloaking spell on your sword hilt, you can do this too."

"I understand. It's the silver in the solution that holds the spell."

"Exactly." She smiled. "I use the rune Algiz for this particular spell. It's a rune of protection, which might not seem to fit, but it can also be used for channeling energies a certain way or for turning something away. Together with the null spell, it combines to turn away or negate magic. It's a negation, not a destruction, so the magic can always return. Get it?"

Gawain murmured, "You are one of the cleverest women I have ever met."

Surprised by the compliment, she felt her cheeks turn warm. "Thank you. I'm not, but—thank you. Remember, I learned a lot of this from other people. I'm like a magpie. I love picking up bits and pieces of things. Then I start playing with them, and sometimes they go together in surprising ways."

"You may have learned a lot of this from other people, but you're the one who put it together," Nikolas said. "Gawain said it was almost like a temporary tattoo, and he was right. You're creating temporary magic items."

"Yeah," she said, pleased with the description. "And you know, painting magic spells on someone isn't a new technique—tribal shamans do it all the time. Painting them with magic-sensitive silver just means the spells can be stronger and more durable. There's a limited application for this, and I make magic jewelry too, amulets and such, but I like painting certain spells on my skin. You can lose a necklace or a bracelet in a fight, and rings can catch on things—I know someone who lost a finger that way—but you're much less likely to lose a spell that's glued onto you."

At Gawain's blank look, Nikolas told him, "She's referring to the spells she used against the Hounds in the attack. They were painted on her skin with…"

When he glanced at her, eyebrows raised, she grinned. "It's a different solution than this. I put tiny magic-sensitive silver shavings in clear nail polish."

"Like I said. Clever, clever woman." Gawain patted her shoulder.

Nikolas practiced working the null spell on Sophie until he cast it competently. Then it was Gawain's turn to practice on her while Nikolas wore a null spell. By the time both men felt confident in casting the spell quickly, it was almost noon.

"We owe you a gun, along with silver bullets," Nikolas said.

She straightened her shoulders from bending over the table. "Yes, you do."

He picked up the last package Gawain had brought in and pulled out a metal micro gun vault, along with boxes of ammunition. She opened the vault, saw the

Glock nestled inside, and patted her chest again. "Be still, my heart."

Gawain laughed, but Nikolas didn't. He watched her intently. "Now show me you know how to use it," he said.

She felt a brief impulse to irritation, but it faded almost immediately into a certain kind of appreciation. He was being careful, and it was one of the things she liked best about him. He didn't leave things to chance.

Not looking away from his face, she disassembled and assembled the gun by touch alone. It took her seconds. Then she loaded it while the men watched every move she made. She explained, "Because you should be able to do it in the dark, if need be."

Nikolas gave her a fierce, approving smile. "Yes, you should."

Not that she had done *any of it*, learned any of it, practiced any of it, to gain his approval, but that did cause the corner of her mouth to lift. Just a bit.

Setting the gun aside, she inspected the silver bullets. As she had suspected, they weren't made of solid silver. Silver was a hard metal, and besides, solid silver bullets would be much more expensive. The bullets were jacketed ammunition, with a metal shell and tipped with silver.

As she examined the bullet, she murmured almost to herself, "You know, I've never run into lycanthropes in the States, but I've used magic-sensitive silver to make my own bullets. Once you have the hollow metal shells, it's easy. Then I can spell those bullets any way I like. Let me tell you, a null spelled silver bullet is super useful when you're fighting a magic user who's out of his mind on LSD." She glanced up to find them staring at her. She told them, "What? I was there. I saw it happen."

Gawain breathed. "The lass makes magic bullets."

If she'd had their full attention before, now they caught fire.

Yes, she promised to make them magic bullets. Yes, she would teach them how to make magic bullets for themselves. Yes, they would need to order a good amount of magic-sensitive silver, along with all the tools she would need for silversmithing. Yes, of course she would make a list—she wrote it out for them while they watched, then Gawain took the paper and pocketed it.

At that point, she held up her hands, stood up from the table, and said, "I'm done. I'm all done today. I haven't even showered or gotten dressed properly yet—and I still need to go into town to check in on Maggie, set up a bank account, and buy coffee. You kids are going to have to go outside and play on your own."

Nikolas stood as well. "We got sidetracked by a great deal more information than we were expecting. That's not a bad thing. All of it is useful, but I was going to ask you to do a reading."

Now that she was no longer focused on something

else, her hyperawareness of him returned. Not quite looking at him, she asked, "Can it wait until this evening?"

"Yes, it can. I need to find someplace to hide the Porsche." He looked at Gawain. "We also need to show you the great hall in the manor house."

"I poked around early this morning," Gawain said. "There's a gravel access road that goes to the back of the property. It leads to a field that's lying fallow, so the road is a bit overgrown and obviously unused. You could tuck your Porsche back there, and nobody would be the wiser."

"Sounds good." Nikolas looked at Sophie. "Would you let us into the manor house before you leave for the afternoon?"

"Sure," she said. "Let's do that now."

Together they walked across the lawn to the front doors of the house. Now that Sophie had felt her way to coming into alignment with the house once, she was able to do it much quicker a second time.

Nikolas braced his hands on the oaken door. When she gave the word, he shoved it hard and it opened with a creak. He said, "We need to oil those hinges. Not only will it make the doors quieter, it'll make them easier to open."

As Gawain peered inside, Nikolas twisted to pick out another broken flagstone, which he used as a doorstop to keep the door from shutting and locking the men out of the house again.

Now that the prospect of going into town was so close, Sophie felt eager to get some space from Nikolas's intense presence and baffling behavior. As she turned to leave, Nikolas took hold of her arm. His fierce frown was back, making his handsome features intimidating.

"I don't know that I'm comfortable with your going to town by yourself," he said almost to himself.

Raising her eyebrows, she pulled away from his touch. "I don't know that I care if you're comfortable or not."

"Sophie," he said in an abrupt, clipped voice. "There may be Hounds in the town. Remember, we don't know what they might know about you, and they can change at will. And you don't know who belongs in town and who doesn't."

She squared her shoulders at the reminder, and after a moment, she nodded. "Point taken," she muttered. "I'll go armed, and I'll be careful."

He angled his jaw. "I still don't like it."

"We all have things we don't like," she replied with rather more acerbity than she had meant to. "I'm sure you'll deal with it."

As she started to turn away, he caught her hand. He tangled his long fingers through hers, and the warmth of his touch reverberated through her. She stared at him with a combination of exasperation and pain. He was the one who had walked away from her, so why did he keep touching her?

His dark, fiery eyes met hers. "Why didn't you sleep well?"

Her mouth tightened. Maybe if she told him, she could get him to back off and leave her alone for a few damn hours.

"Because I don't. I just don't," she whispered, the words exploding out of her with staccato force. "Every time I close my eyes I see that gun pointed at me. Every time I fall asleep, I try to run away from him, but I never get away, because that didn't happen. I didn't get away. He shot me, and he shot me, and I remember every single one. And my brain won't let it go, so I keep reliving it." She paused to take a breath. His expression had tightened, and she didn't want to read what was in his eyes. If it was pity, she might haul off and hit him. Pulling her hand out of his, she told him, "When I'm ready to let it go, it'll fade. Until then, I just grit my teeth."

"Sophie," he said.

"I told you I was done," she snapped. "I'm really done. Back off and let me have a couple of hours to myself."

"We're not done talking," he told her, even as he took a step back. "This is just on pause for now."

If she said another word to him, she thought she might do something horribly humiliating and burst into tears. What the fuck, Sophie. So she turned her back and stalked away.

Back in the cottage, she caught Robin eating a pie.

It looked like it might be the steak and kidney pie Nikolas had bought for supper the night before. It looked massive in his little monkey hands.

As the puck froze, she told him, "Eat it, sweetheart. Eat whatever you want. Is there anything you want from town? Just tell me, and I'll bring it back for you."

For a moment the monkey's eyes lingered on her expression, and she thought he would finally break through his silence and tell her. She held her breath, but then he tucked his wizened face down to the pie he clutched close to him, and the moment passed.

"Never mind," she said gently as she passed a hand down his small back. "You'll talk when you're ready. I'll bring you back a cake."

As the monkey's eyes flashed with interest, she knew she had struck the right chord. Smiling, she went to shower and prepare for her trip to town. Taking Nikolas's warning to heart, she painted both offensive and defensive spells on her arms.

There was so much silver in the nail polish the runes shimmered in the light, so she dug out one of her favorite pieces of clothing, a gauzy, semitransparent top with long sleeves that flared at the wrists, with a tight, black spaghetti strap camisole underneath. She paired it with a pair of stonewashed jeans and the Doc Martens, and she even took a few minutes to stroke on some makeup, enhancing her eyes with a smoky pewter color, while brushing a fire-engine red lipstick on her lips.

The makeup made her look different, sultry. Who was she trying to impress with all this?

Nikolas's dark, intense eyes came to mind.

"Fuck you for walking away," she whispered to him. "I put on makeup. I look like a million bucks."

So. It appeared she wasn't over what had happened last night, not in the slightest. Sighing, she dug out her messenger-style purse and put every piece of identification she had into it, including her passport. Last of all, she checked her new, beautiful Glock to make sure it was loaded and all was in order, and when she was satisfied—and because all her purses had a concealed-carry pocket—she slipped it into her purse.

When she tucked her cell phone into the back pocket of her jeans, she was finally ready to head into town. Her spirits lifted as she drove away from the property. The English countryside was gorgeous, and as she drove into town, for the first time since she arrived, she was able to see it in the sunlight and appreciate how picturesque it looked.

She stopped at the pub first to talk to Arran and Maggie. They were busy working on repairs, so she didn't stay long, but they both gave her hugs so tight it warmed her heart. Arran whispered in her ear, "Thank you for my wife."

She patted his back and smiled at him. "You are so welcome."

"Aren't you lonesome out there at that old place?" Maggie asked her curiously.

She laughed. Oh, if she could only get some real time to herself. "Not at all," she told the other woman with complete truth. "I'm enjoying the space."

"Well, if there's anything you need, anything at all," Maggie said. "You let us know."

"Anything *ever*," Arran broke in to emphasize.

"I promise, I will. When are you going to open again?"

They looked at each other, and a shadow fell across their faces. Arran said, "We'll have to open soon. It's tourist season, and we need the business, but we're going to hold off until a week after the funerals."

She touched Maggie's arm. "Good luck, and I'll stop by again in a few days."

"It'll be good to see you, lass," Maggie told her. "Maybe by then, this place will be looking good enough I can make you a cuppa."

"I'd like that."

As she walked out, her phone buzzed. It was a call from Paul, the solicitor, offering her congratulations. Pausing to talk with him for a few minutes, she promised to get him the information on her new bank account when she had it, and then she headed to the small Barclays Bank to open a checking account.

When that business was complete, she browsed through some of the local shops and took some time to read and respond to Rodrigo's email. He had sent a quick query, asking how her trip was going, and she got excited all over again as she wrote about becoming a landowner.

Nikolas's warning stayed with her, so she kept a wary eye out, but everything in the town seemed so peaceful and normal she relaxed her hypervigilance as she stopped at the grocers to buy coffee. There wasn't a coffeemaker at the house, so she settled for instant coffee, while she made a promise to herself to buy a percolator soon.

Then on impulse, she bought hot chocolate mix, a bunch of fresh flowers to brighten up the cottage kitchen, and Black Forest gateaux cake she thought Robin would like. As she was walking back to her car, a small shop featuring children's clothes caught her eye. There was the most darling little navy blue jacket in the window that looked like it might fit Robin. Her gaze lingered on it while she struggled with temptation.

He's not really a monkey, she scolded herself. And he's certainly not a child.

But the jacket was so cute, and maybe he got cold sometimes. He might be healing at a magical speed, but he was still so underweight. *Ugh.* She pushed through the front door. As she bought the jacket, she told the friendly shopgirl, "It's for my nephew."

"It's a lovely prezzie," the girl said as she wrapped it carefully in tissue paper. "He'll look so cute in it."

"Yes, he will. Thank you." She tucked the shopping bag into the crook of her arm, picked up the cake box, and pushed outside again.

As she slipped out the door, the bunch of flowers

tipped over and fell out of the grocery bag. Muttering a curse, she juggled packages while she squatted to reach for them.

Dark boots came into view, and a man's strong, tanned hand beat her to picking up the flowers. The man said in a pleasant Welsh accent, "Please, allow me."

"Thank you," she said.

She and the man straightened at the same time while Sophie took in details of his appearance. He was tall and broad shouldered, although not quite as tall as Gawain, and deeply tanned. He wore tailored gray slacks woven with a silver thread and a matching shirt that was open at the neck, with the sleeves rolled up to reveal muscular forearms.

The understated elegance looked good on him. She took in other details. He had chestnut hair, a strong face with good bones, and wore an intelligent, even contemplative expression, and while he appeared to be a human man in his midthirties, when she looked into his brilliant hazel gaze, she felt such a roar of Power coming from him, she staggered back a step.

Frowning, he held a hand out to her but checked himself. "Are you all right?"

"I'm fine," she said tightly, staring.

She hadn't sensed his Power until she had looked into his eyes, which meant he must have a titanic amount of control over himself in order to keep it so tightly contained. How could one person hold that much Power and still remain sane?

Giving her a pleasant smile, the man said, "Would it be all right if I carried your flowers for you to your car?"

Her options ran through her mind at supersonic speed. The gun was buried deep in her purse, not her best, first choice should he try to attack. She would have to hit him with either the confusion spell or with the telekinesis, but with his kind of Power, he might shrug off the spells. So the gun might be the only effective weapon against him.

If it came to that.

Belatedly, she realized she hadn't answered his question. "No," she told him bluntly. If he was going to try to do anything to her, she would make him do it on the high street, in front of everybody, not tucked away in a side parking lot. "It's not all right with me. Who are you, and what do you want?"

His smile never dimmed, and his body language remained open, easy. There were slight lines fanning out from the corners of his eyes. If he hadn't been setting off all the alarm bells in her head, she would have found him quite attractive.

"I want a few moments of your time, that's all," the man said. His quiet voice remained as nonthreatening as his body language. "Just a quick conversation, I promise. Are you by any chance Sophie Ross?"

"How did you learn that name?" she countered, taking another step back.

"The people in town speak highly of you," the man said. "They say you saved the lives of the pub owner and his wife during an attack from lycanthropes. That was very brave."

"You still haven't told me who you are," she said, eyeing him narrowly. She was going to have to drop the cake to get the gun, and she didn't like what that would signal.

His smile never wavered. "My name is Morgan."

Morgan.

The sound of his name was like a punch to the kidneys. The town wavered around her. Oh God, no wonder he held such Power. If he chose to do anything to her, she was toast.

She whispered, "Could there possibly be more than one Morgan in the UK who carries the amount of Power that you do?"

His smile dimmed. He said, "It was not my intention to frighten you. I apologize."

"Why are you here, talking to townspeople about me?" she asked through numb lips. "What do you really want?"

"I meant what I said, Sophie Ross," Morgan replied. "I just want to talk and to ask you a few questions, that's all. I mean you no harm. For the moment, you are safe."

"*For the moment?*" she echoed. Then because he had frightened her so badly, a wave of anger hit. She held the cake as if she might throw it at him. "What the fuck do you mean by that?"

Out of the corner of her eye, she could see the shopgirl watching them worriedly. Morgan noticed her too, and as he waved the fingers of one hand in a subtle gesture, the shopgirl appeared to lose interest and wandered into the back of the store.

Morgan turned his attention back to Sophie. The smile in his eyes had disappeared. He said in a quiet, courteous voice, "Right now, my Queen knows nothing of your existence, and I am free to act as I choose. And I choose to wish you no harm, Sophie Ross. But if my Queen does learn about you, and she orders me to do a thing, you must understand—I will do it. I must."

As reassurances went, this one basically sucked donkey balls. Still angry, she asked, "Why would your Queen learn anything about me? What am I to her?"

"She has misplaced her pet, and she wants him back," Morgan said. "She wants him back badly enough, she sent me to search for him. At the pub, the owners told me that you had brought a stray dog into town when you arrived. If I might ask, what happened to him?"

The question fanned her anger into outright fury, and she jettisoned straight into Stupid and Crazy™.

Advancing on one of the most dangerous men she had ever met, she said between her teeth, "That dog was a pathetic mess. He had been tortured and starved. What kind of man are you to serve someone who could treat a creature with such cruelty? Do you have any ethics or morality, or any sense of decency?"

His expression slammed tight as a vault, while a muscle flexed in his lean jaw. Morgan said, still with that terrible, even courtesy, "My Queen commands, and I must obey. Do you still have the dog?"

"No, I do not still have the dog," she snapped, throwing the weight of all her fury into a perfect blend of truth and misdirection, and she knew instinctively that she had hit the exact right note. "It disappeared at the time of the pub attack, and I haven't seen it since." Looking him up and down, she added contemptuously, "But if I did see that dog again, you can be sure as fuck I wouldn't tell you anything about it."

"No, I can see that you would not," Morgan said, holding his body still, his expression calm and stony. "At any rate, not by choice." He offered her the bunch of flowers. "I wish you well, Sophie Ross. Enjoy your day. Pray there's no need for us to meet again."

Breathing hard, she accepted the flowers gingerly, as if they might bite. In an archaic-seeming courtesy, Morgan inclined his head to her, then strode away.

She stood staring until he disappeared around a corner. Only then was she able to get her feet unglued from the pavement. She made it back to the car, tucked her purchases in the back, then sat in the driver's seat and shook. When she felt she was capable of driving safely, she started the Mini and pulled carefully onto the road.

Her mind was leaping around like a scalded cat. Maybe she shouldn't drive back to the property. But everybody in town knew she was staying there. Maybe it would look worse if she didn't go back.

Maybe Hounds had already been to the property to search the cottage. Maybe Nikolas and Gawain had already been attacked. By the time she parked at the cottage, she was in a clench of worry. Already familiar, the scene looked peaceful, untouched by violence, but as she knew from bitter experience, looks could be lethally deceiving.

As she turned off the engine, the cottage door opened and Nikolas strode out. "What took you so long?" he demanded. "I almost came looking for you."

She was so relieved and happy to see him whole and unharmed she forgot that normally she would be irritated with his brusque tone. She whispered, "Nik."

He took in her expression, and his manner changed. "What is it?" He took hold of her hands, and alarm flashed through his sharp gaze. "You're shaking like a leaf."

She walked forward until she bumped into his body, then she put her arms around his waist. As his arms closed around her, she told him, "I met Morgan in town. He was looking for Robin."

Chapter Fourteen

A T HER WORDS, Nikolas's arms turned into iron
bands. Bowing his head over her, he crushed her
body against him.

I met Morgan in town.

The words were worse than his worst fears, and at
the thought of her facing Morgan alone, a sense of
wrongness, like nausea, clenched his stomach.

She coughed. "Too tight. Ease up."

"I shouldn't have let you go into town by yourself,"
he growled. "I did it anyway, and I knew better."

Sighing, she rested her head on his shoulder. She
said, sounding tired, "You don't *let me do* anything. 'Let'
and 'permit' are not words we modern folk allow in our
vocabulary. Do we understand this concept yet?"

"Sophie, for God's sake," he snapped while he
stroked her hair. He couldn't seem to help himself. His
hands wanted to roam all over her body so that he
could finally insert into his overheated brain that she
had returned unmaimed.

At that, she seemed to get how genuinely upset he
was. Lifting her head, she searched his face. "I'm okay.

For the moment, everything is okay."

He took in her appearance for the first time, and his eyes narrowed. Her dark curls were glossy and defined, and they fell down her back in an extravagantly feminine mane. And she had done something to her eyes and mouth, making them dramatic and sensual. The smoky accents she had applied to her eyes had turned them even more electric than usual.

"You went into town looking like that?" he asked. He couldn't help himself and touched a forefinger to her red, ripe mouth. A soft smear of color stained his fingertip, and he licked at it. It tasted of her. His cock went from zero to sixty in a single second, rock hard and straining against the seam of his jeans.

She gave him a leery glance. "Like… what, exactly?"

The truth tore out of his gut, raw and husky. "Like something I couldn't wait to eat up."

Her pupils dilated in quick, involuntary reaction. She recoiled, pulling out of his arms. "Too late," she said harshly. "You had your chance and decided to cut it short."

As she turned back to the Mini, he gritted, "Sophie, I still want you."

"No." She stuck her head into the back and pulled out packages. When she emerged again, her cheeks were flushed with pink color and her eyes snapped with some unnamed emotion. She met his gaze, the line of her jaw tight. "You walked away last night, and you got to do that. That was your choice, so okay. I can go with it. But you don't get to push me away, only to try to pull me back in again. I don't play that kind of game."

He snapped, "I don't play any games."

Instead of responding in the lively way he had come to expect, she merely looked bruised. "Oh, no? Well, I don't know what you're doing then."

"I don't either," he whispered.

That made her pause. She searched his expression uncertainly, but when he would have reached out for her again, to touch her in any way he could, the cottage door opened and Gawain strode out.

"Hello, lass," he said. His intelligent gaze traveled from her to Nikolas, who stood with his fists clenched. "How was your trip to town?"

"She ran into Morgan," Nikolas bit out. As Gawain's expression changed, he said telepathically to Sophie, *We're not finished talking.*

She not-quite-glanced at him. The flush of pink color had fled, leaving her looking pale and strained.

Oh no, we're finished, she said. *Until you figure out what you're doing—whatever that might be—we don't have anything more to say to each other that's of a personal nature.*

"Come inside, lass," Gawain said gently while looking around sharply at their surroundings. He put a protective arm around her. "Tell us all about what happened."

As he touched Sophie, Nikolas nearly went for his throat.

His friend's throat. One of his closest, staunchest friends.

Rooted to the spot, he watched them step into the cottage together. Just before Gawain stepped inside, the other man speared him with a look that clearly said he thought Nikolas had lost his damn mind.

Nikolas couldn't blame him—or Sophie. He *had* lost his damn mind. Glancing around one last time, he clamped down on his self-control and strode into the cottage.

Inside, he found Sophie on her knees, offering a small blue jacket to Robin. Looking befuddled, the monkey blinked as he took it. She said gently, "It's okay if you don't like it. I just thought you might get cold sometimes."

From nowhere, her compassion struck Nikolas with an evil kind of accuracy, deep inside where he wore no armor. Pressing his knuckles against his mouth, he watched as the monkey *ooh-oohed* silently and turned the jacket over and over in his spidery hands. Sophie helped the puck slip into it, and he sat looking down at himself, fingering the gold buttons.

"I brought you a cake too," she whispered to Robin. "It's three times your size, and you can have all of it."

Robin's eyes were shining. *Ooh-ooh*, he mouthed and set his hand against her cheek. She covered his small hand with hers.

She brought the puck a jacket and a cake, Gawain said to

Nikolas. *And she bought flowers and hot chocolate and coffee. That's all she wanted from town. Flowers, for fuck sake. She shines with spells, and she can make magic bullets. Every single fucking one of our men is going to fall in love with her, Nik. Every single fucking one. Hell, I might even fall in love with her a little myself.*

You can't, Nikolas thought, as his hands clenched again. She's mine.

The naked aggression on his face caused Gawain to check, and comprehension dawned on the other man's face. "Oh, boyo," Gawain said softly while his gaze darkened. "Like that, is it?"

Her interaction with Robin over, Sophie stood and looked at them. She asked, "What's like what?"

"Nothing," Nikolas said harshly. He gave the other man a warning stare. "Tell us what happened with Morgan."

"Okay, but I get to have some of that brandy you bought yesterday while I do it." She pulled out a chair, sat, and put her head in her hands while Gawain broke open the bottle and poured some of the amber liquid into a glass for her. She took a deep, bracing swallow, then told them everything.

Just listening to how she confronted Morgan over Isabeau's cruelty had Nikolas heading for the brandy bottle himself. He poured a hefty amount into a glass and knocked it back. It burned all the way down. Then he pivoted to glare at her.

"What is wrong with you?" he demanded. "Are you

suicidal?"

Her beautiful, luscious mouth, that mouth he wanted to eat right up, dropped open. She glared back.
Then a kind of hilarity entered her expression.

She muttered, "You really are an asshole, aren't
you? You almost tricked me into believing otherwise,
but nope. Still an asshole. Honestly, I don't know
whether to be relieved or disappointed by that fact. My
head is turned upside down. Mostly I think I'm just
disturbed."

"You knew he was a killer, and you confronted him
anyway." Nikolas advanced on her, rage blinding him.
A belated rage born of fear that came much too late to
be of good to anybody. "While I've been congratulating
myself on being *modern* and *reasonable* by *letting* you go to
town by yourself, you could have been kidnapped,
killed, or tortured every bit as badly as Robin had been
or worse. *Do you realize what he could have done to you?*"

He was shaking from the force that raged through
his body. Out of the corner of his eye, he saw Gawain
shift away from leaning against the counter, but Sophie
beat the other man to it as she stood and advanced
quickly to Nikolas.

Toward him, not away, just as she had done that
first night in the pub. Just as she had done during the
attack. Just as she had done to Morgan. This woman,
this woman—she might be the death of him.

"Hey," Sophie said in a soft voice. She spread her
fingers over his chest, and he clamped his hands

around her wrists. "I know what a serious trigger Morgan is for you, and I'm sorry for that. He was a pretty serious trigger for me too when I found out who he was. But it's okay. For the moment, everything is okay."

Nothing was okay. His head, his thinking, his emotions, they were all in shambles. Looking into her luminous gaze, he said telepathically, *I would not be okay if you put yourself at risk and you came to harm because of it. You must take better care of yourself, my Sophie.*

Her eyes widened, and she looked as vulnerable as he had ever seen her look. She told him, *I have a terrible temper, and when I lose it, all sense flies out the window. I know it's a flaw, and I will try to do better. I promise, Nik.*

Her quiet words, along with her touch, soothed him, and the shaking fury eased. He gave her a curt nod.

She lingered, studying him, and said aloud, "Okay?"

"Okay." Touching her felt too good, and he didn't want to stop. Releasing her wrists, he stepped away, back to the counter to pour himself another brandy.

Sophie felt her way back to her seat and sank into it, while Gawain rubbed his face hard with one massive hand.

"Morgan may be a great many things, but he's also a man of his word," the other man said. "He said he meant you no harm for the moment, but he also gave you plenty of warning that will change. Are you sure he believed you when you said the dog disappeared?"

"Yeah," Sophie said. She ran her fingers through her hair, turning it into even more of a wild, unruly mane. "I'm confident of that. You know the feeling when you're sure you've gotten off a good shot or struck the right blow? I had that sense."

"Good girl," Gawain murmured. "That's a help."

She looked at the both of them. "But all he has to do is start thinking around the edges, and considering what Robin is capable of, and come up with a few more questions, and he will probably come out here to ask them. And if Isabeau finds out about me and orders him to do something like bring me to her for questioning, he made it very clear he would do it." She frowned. "In fact, he said he must do it. It was almost like he was saying he would have no choice. Do you think—do you think she might have him under some sort of compulsion?"

Nikolas shook his head, rejecting that idea. "If Oberon ordered any of us to do something, we would be honor bound to do it too. And in any case, it's beside the point whether or not Morgan is compelled or if he acts of his own volition. He will do it. He has always done it. He would tear Britain to pieces if Isabeau wanted him to. That's the relevant point."

She sighed. "In that case, I think we need to expect he will come here and sooner rather than later. He's not going to find Robin otherwise, which means he will retrace his steps and look everywhere more thoroughly."

As she spoke, the monkey climbed into her lap, and she put her arms around him, hugging him tight.

"We need to consider our choices," Nikolas said, looking at Gawain.

Gawain blew out a breath. "One choice is, we scatter more widely again. We don't converge here, like we had planned. We take Robin with us, like we had originally planned, and Sophie denies everything."

Nikolas shook his head. "Unacceptable. Our scents are all over this property, and there's no telling what Isabeau might order Morgan to do once she finds out about Sophie."

"Yeah, I didn't like that one either," Sophie muttered. She put her face in the monkey's fur while Robin slipped a skinny arm around her neck.

"Second choice," Gawain said, giving her and the puck a troubled look. "We scatter, we don't converge, and we take both Sophie and Robin with us. Lass, I'm sorry, but I think we're past the point where separating will be of any benefit to you. I think you would be in more danger if we left you alone."

"That's okay," she said. "I knew that the moment Morgan showed up and called me by name."

"Taking both Sophie and Robin is a better option," Nikolas said. "But it's still not good enough. That won't allow us to explore what the house might have to offer. If it can give us a way to access Lyonesse, we need to take that choice, no matter what the risk."

"Agreed," Gawain said.

Nikolas looked at Sophie. He told her, "I can still bargain with a Djinn, and Gawain can take you and Robin somewhere safe."

She straightened. "Not acceptable. You don't know what the Djinn might demand of you in return, whereas the worst thing that will happen with me is a bill for services, and you already agreed to pay that."

That wasn't the worst thing that could happen. She could be hurt. She could die. The better man he had used to be was trying to resurrect himself. He rubbed his eyes. "I don't like the danger for you."

She told him in a gentle, firm voice, "Nik, I'm not your pet. I'm not your property. I can assess the relative dangers for myself and make my own decisions."

He looked over his hand at her. He said, "That doesn't make it easier for us old-timey folk."

Her expression lit with smiling warmth. Was that approval? Wonders never ceased. "I have faith in you," she said. "I know you can handle it."

She had more faith in him than he had in himself, because he knew if something happened to her, he wouldn't handle it. Turning his back, he scowled at the view out the kitchen window.

That house. That ugly, monstrous, broken-down house. He was going to throw everything at it in the most insane gamble of his life. "We go in the house," he said. "And we barricade ourselves in. Morgan can't get inside, and we have reason to hope he can't damage it either."

"If he can do some damage," Gawain said, "you and the lass are going to need help. We call the others in, and we converge, like we had planned—only we don't space it out. They need to get here as quickly as possible, tonight."

"Yes." Nikolas turned back to them. He said to Sophie, "Thank you."

"It'll be the dirtiest, most unhygienic sleepover ever," she told them with a lopsided grin. "It'll be fun."

Out of nowhere, humor bubbled up. It felt good to let it out in a laugh. "When we get inside, the first order of business will be to locate the privy chambers and hope there's an internal water source, like a well. Chances are, it will have dried out long ago, so we'll have to dig to hit water again. Failing that, pray there's a courtyard. With the lake situated so close, I'm going to bet we can hit water somehow."

Gawain dug out his phone. "I'll contact the others and tell them to get here as soon as possible and prepare for a siege."

"Tell Gareth and Cael to focus on weapons," Nikolas said. "We need longbows and crossbows, and a good supply of arrows. We won't be able to fire guns from the house."

"Will do," Gawain said. "Braden was going to gather camping gear. The rest can concentrate on food and fuel. We need as many supplies as they can lay their hands on. And firewood. Stacks and stacks of firewood."

Nikolas moved to kneel by Sophie's side. He looked into the monkey's eyes. "Robin, do you think you've recovered enough that you can create a storm tonight to cover our scents?"

Braiding a long strand of Sophie's hair, the monkey nodded.

"Good."

"There's a shed behind the cottage with a riding lawn mower, wheelbarrow, gardening tools, and an axe," Gawain told them. "I'm going to start tackling that firewood issue."

"There's gardening tools and a lawn mower," Sophie breathed as Gawain strode out. "I never thought to walk all the way around the cottage."

After Gawain had left, the puck slipped off Sophie's lap to go to the kitchen counter, wrap his arms around the cake box, and leap to the floor again. He tottered toward the sitting room.

That left Nikolas and Sophie alone. He still knelt by her side, and instead of rising to his feet, he took one of her hands in his.

She shifted to face him. "You wanted me to do a reading when I got back. What is it you want to find out?"

"I don't know that it's relevant any longer." Absently he rubbed her fingers against his lips. He only grew aware of what he was doing when her hand tightened on his, and she pulled her hand down. But she didn't try to release his fingers. Instead, she held his hand in her lap. He said telepathically, *I still want to try to find out more about the Hounds that attacked me, if I can—whose magic was in play, besides yours. Someone called the fog in. Robin's a nature sprite. He could have done it. But now I believe he would have been forced.*

Could that be the reason Isabeau wants her "pet" back so much? she asked.

Maybe. He looked at her broodingly. *I'd also like to know how they knew how to find me. I've run through everything multiple times, and I don't see how I made a mistake, or left a trail, so it bothers me.*

No, you wouldn't have made a mistake like that. She gave him a lopsided smile. *You're too careful.* Aloud, she said, "For what it's worth, it wouldn't take long to cast the runes for a reading."

He nodded. "Let's do it. The men won't show up before nightfall anyway. After you're through, we can pack everything that needs to be moved into the great hall."

"I'm going to start a load of laundry, then I'll get my runes." Squeezing his fingers, she let go of his hand and stood. "If we're going to get caught in a siege, I can at least start out with clean clothes."

Nikolas rose as well and watched her leave. Then he walked back to his glass of brandy to take another hefty swallow. He held it in his mouth for a moment, focusing on the subtle, warming flavor. For good or for ill, they were throwing everything they had at this venture. Everything they had on Sophie's abilities.

As she stepped back into the kitchen, he turned. She carried a small bundle of richly colored cloth, which she set on the table while she took a seat. He joined her at the table, sitting opposite her and watching with fascination as she unfolded a dark blue, embroidered cloth. Magic unfurled in the air.

Holding his hand over the cloth to savor the cool sensation of magic, he said, "You did this. You made this."

"Yes." She looked surprised. "How can you tell?"

"It feels like you."

A tinge of color touched her cheeks. "Is that a good thing?"

"It's a very good thing," he murmured, watching her. That tinge of color was for him, only this time it wasn't from distress or anger. Surprised by how good that knowledge felt, he pressed for more. "It's one of the best things I've felt in a long time."

The pink in her cheeks turned brighter while the expression in her eyes grew vulnerable again. She asked, "What are you doing now?"

Wanting to feel the real thing, not just her Power, he reached out to stroke the petal-soft skin of her cheek. "I want you to trust me," he said steadily. "I'm going to ask you to believe that I walked away last night for good reasons, and none of those reasons had anything to do with you. None of them had anything to do with how much I wanted to stay with you. We can talk more about it later, but for now, can you trust me that much?"

Her breath came out of her on a gentle, unsteady sigh. After compressing her lips together for a brief moment, she nodded. "Okay. I do trust you that much."

"Thank you, my Sophie," he whispered.

Her attention fell to the pouch she held. Opening it, she shook a pile of polished stones into one palm. They were pretty, rose quartz with gold runes engraved into them. Her eyes went unfocused. "I'm trying to figure out how to phrase the issue. You want answers about what happened."

"I guess the key is not so much to find out if I made a mistake." He rubbed the back of his neck. "The key is to make sure that whatever it was doesn't happen again. That's why I haven't been able to let it go. Maybe it *was* a mistake I made. Maybe they have an ability to track us that we don't know about. If Robin created the fog, I can let that go, but maybe the person responsible for the fog wasn't Robin. Maybe that person was the same someone who also found me."

As she listened, she nodded. "So the question becomes, what are the vulnerabilities we have that we do not know?" Her glance darted sidelong at him, as quick as a silverfish, and then away again. She added, "Regarding this conflict. Would that be correct?"

"Yes." He sat back and folded his arms. "That's the essence of the issue."

"All right. I can use that. Now I need for you to be quiet and let me work. Don't ask questions until I'm done."

As he watched, she held the stones cupped in both hands for a long moment while her features settled into an expression of concentration. Then she tossed the rune stones gently onto the cloth.

This was what she had done when she had received the vision of him and when he had connected to the image of her. He watched her closely, fascinated by every small, minute shift in her expression. Her attention focused on things he couldn't see.

As he watched, her skin darkened. Her mouth opened as if she would speak, but no sound came out. She placed a hand to her throat, and that was when he realized she wasn't breathing.

"Sophie," he said. His heart pounded.

When she didn't respond, he stood so fast it shot his chair back against the wall. He shoved the table aside, sending cloth and stones flying, picked her up, and laid her quickly on her back, on the floor.

She still isn't breathing.

Panic fired along all his nerve endings. Gently he parted her lips and ran his forefinger through her mouth to make sure there weren't any obstructions. He hadn't seen her put anything in her mouth, but he had to make sure. Then he sealed her lips with his and blew air into her lungs. Then again. And again.

"Come on," he rasped in between breaths. What do

you say when your world has stopped? "What the fuck is the matter with you, Sophie, *come on.*"

After giving her three breaths, he felt for a pulse. Part of him couldn't believe he was doing this. She had been fine. She had just been fine.

Suddenly she broke into a spasm of coughing, and it was the most beautiful thing he had ever heard. Her eyes flared wide. She stared at him, then rolled onto her side, sucking air and coughing.

"Easy, take it easy," he said hoarsely while he rubbed her back. "You're okay."

But you almost weren't.

As she pushed herself into a sitting position, he slid an arm underneath her to help, then he kept gathering her up until he held her in his arms. She didn't appear to mind. Either she was shaking or he was. Gods damn, this day had been hell on his nerves, and he hadn't even seen any combat.

He knew how to fight and fight well. He didn't know how to deal with any of this other shit. At this point, combat would be a relief.

Rein it in, Nik. One thing at a time.

Putting his face in her hair, he forced himself to say calmly, "You stopped breathing. Are you aware that you stopped breathing?"

"I came to that conclusion," she croaked. She was still sucking in great lungsful of air. "I need a drink of water."

Immediately he rose, rinsed her brandy glass and

filled it with fresh water, and brought it to her. He knelt on one knee while she drank. She drained the glass, and he took it from her to set it aside.

As her color returned to normal, he said, again in a too-calm voice, "Why the fuck didn't you tell me that casting the runes was so dangerous? If I had known, I never would have asked that of you."

"Normally, they're not." Her voice hitched and sounded raspy. She coughed again. "Normally I just see your garden-variety type of vision. This is only the second time it's become too real. I've got to stop throwing those stones."

He agreed wholeheartedly. While he glanced around the kitchen, he opened his senses wide to check for dangerous magic. Was there a hint of something in the air that he had felt before, something on that first day when the Hounds had ambushed him? Some other Power in play...

There, low to the ground, he saw the monkey peering around the corner, watching them from the doorway to the sitting room. Even for a monkey, Robin wore an odd expression, looking somehow feral and sad all at once.

Rage detonated deep inside. Nikolas hissed, *Did you do this to her? After everything she has done for you?*

The puck whisked out of sight. Intent on going after him, Nikolas started to rise. The only thing that stopped him was Sophie reaching for his hand. She looked so distressed he abandoned going after the puck for the moment and put his arms around her.

She tucked her face into the crook of his neck and leaned against him, and it was so unlike her usual, snappy self he had no choice but to enfold her, cradling her against his chest as close as he could.

The detonation of rage didn't die. Instead, it grew stronger. He growled, "What did you see in the vision?"

"I don't want to talk about it," she whispered.

Her voice sounded hurt and small, which frankly made a part of him crazy. He hated that something had managed to get inside her and wound her like that. He cupped her head as if to shield her from the world.

As if to shield her most especially from himself, even as he said in a quiet, hard voice, "It doesn't matter whether you want to or not. You have to talk about it."

When she didn't respond, he slipped a hand underneath her chin and forced her to look up. Her eyes had filled with tears, and she looked at him with such... such compassion?... it started an entirely different alarm going off inside him.

"What?" he said.

Her face tightened. "In the vision, one of your men tried to kill me."

Chapter Fifteen

"NO," NIKOLAS SAID. "I don't accept that."

He still held her just as tightly, but his expression told her louder than his words that he rejected everything she had just said.

She knew he was going to react that way before she ever said anything. How could he not? He had known his men for far longer than she had been alive. They were his compatriots, his brothers and fellow soldiers, and he had already shown the depth of his commitment to them and to his people.

"Maybe it's a horrible misunderstanding," she said. "Maybe he didn't realize I'm on your side. Really, truly, I'm on your side. I'm helping you, and I want to help you. If we make that clear to them when they arrive, there won't be an issue, right?"

He stared at her almost as if he hated her, and that look in his eyes really hurt, but she had the smallest inkling of what he must be feeling, so she sucked it up and took it.

"You said, what are the vulnerabilities we have that we do not know?" he said through tight lips. "Right?"

She nodded.

"What did the man look like?"

"I don't know," she whispered.

His dark eyes snapped with anger. "What do you mean, you don't know?"

"I mean, I do not know. Someone came up to me from behind, and he started choking me. We were inside the manor house. The only ones inside were you and your men, me, and Robin."

"Robin," he growled, looking around with fresh rage.

His expression was frightening. She pulled out of his arms, rolled to her knees, and stood. As she turned to face him, she found that he had stood as well. "Why are you so angry at Robin?"

"He interfered with your vision somehow. I don't know what he did. He enhanced it, or he directed it. Maybe he twisted it." Nikolas snarled at the direction of the sitting room. "Come out here, you little bastard."

"Nikolas." She took hold of his wrists. "Stop. You're reacting emotionally, and why wouldn't you? My God, *I'm* reacting emotionally. I didn't want to say those words to you, and I can only imagine how you must be feeling."

"Can you, really?" He confronted her fiercely. "Those men are my family."

"Okay," she said in a gentle voice, her fingers tightening on him. "It was a mistake. The vision went wrong, that's all. We can let it go. I don't know what

Robin intended, but I do not believe he would intentionally hurt me." She raised her voice. "Would you, sweetheart?"

As if in reply, Robin crept into the kitchen. Giving Nikolas a wide berth, the monkey raced toward Sophie. When she held open her arms, he leaped into them. The puck buried his face into her chest, and she hugged him tightly.

Glaring at Robin, Nikolas started to pace like a caged, wild creature. "Tell me what you saw."

"No. It'll only make things worse."

He rounded on her, his face blazing. *"Tell me what you saw."*

She took a step back while she searched his face for any sign of understanding or belief. He was reacting like a wounded animal, and gods, she didn't blame him.

She told him, "I don't believe this is the right time to have this conversation."

Nikolas opened his arms wide. "When else, Sophie?" he snarled. "My men are going to be here soon. We're all alone, just you and I. Tell me, when else should we be talking about this?"

She looked down into Robin's eyes. He looked so sad. Stroking the puck's head, she said softly, "We were all in the manor house, and I knew we'd been looking for the answers to the broken pieces of crossover magic. It's just background to the vision, that knowledge. It puts everything in place, you know? Then I was on my own, somewhere in a big room, or maybe a long one. I was really excited about something, but someone came up from behind, put his hands around my throat, and started choking me. I fought, but he was really strong, as… as I'm sure you can imagine. He was tall too, maybe as tall as you are or even taller. A big man, with big hands, not someone as small as a puck." She kissed the monkey and whispered to him, "It wasn't you, was it?"

Ooh-ooh, the monkey mouthed, eyes wide and solemn. He shook his head.

Telepathically, she asked, *Robin, why did you interfere with the vision?*

She didn't expect a reply. By then, she had stopped expecting Robin to answer anything she said to him, so it was with a sense of immense surprise that she heard a voice, dry like the rustle of autumn leaves, say in her head, *Because you needed to know. Though he may not forgive Robin for it, he needs to know. Some of us are not who we seem, dear love.* The puck patted her throat with both hands. *Robin did not realize his interference might hurt you.*

Some of us are not who we seem. What did the puck mean by that?

It's okay, she whispered back. *But don't do it again.*

His response was fervent. *No, never again.*

Robin, did you interfere with my first vision of Nikolas? As the monkey hung his head, she said, *You did, didn't you? What were you hoping for?*

Help, the puck whispered. *A puck was hoping for help. The Queen made him do things he didn't want to do. Create fog, hide murders, dance like a monkey to her wicked whims.*

"Hoping for help…," she murmured aloud, staring at him. Once her mind started piecing things together, it wouldn't stop. "Robin, did you have anything to do with my car breaking down the night I found you on the road?"

Because it really was unusual for her technology curse to cause something as big as the car to stop working. And it was even more suspect that the car had started again perfectly, right afterward.

A puck was hoping for help, waiting for so long, Robin whispered. *Waiting for someone to notice he was gone, taken and lost, but no one ever came. So Robin helped himself. When you arrived, no matter how the terrible rope fought and bit him, he broke free and threw the last of his strength at a Sophie.*

He sounded so distressed she hugged him tightly. "Nobody understood where you had gone, but you have help now, I promise. You're not alone anymore."

On the other side of the table, Nikolas stood with his hands on his hips, staring at them. He carried so much bitter anger his Power felt like a volcano about to explode, all the more dangerous for that he had himself so contained.

"He's finally talking, isn't he?" Nikolas said abruptly. "He's talking to you."

"The Queen forced him to do things," Sophie said. "When he created the fog, he did something more that must have interfered with my vision like he did just now. He said he was looking for help. He also made my car break down when I first arrived, and he threw the last of his strength into escaping."

As she spoke, it took a concentrated effort to meet the dark, forceful blaze in his eyes. She could no longer tell if Nikolas was her ally, and it was astonishingly difficult to confront that reality. She had grown so quickly accustomed to the rapport that had been developing between them.

"Robin, did you help the Queen's Hounds find me that day?" Nikolas's fury seemed to reach its peak. *"Did you?"*

Robin seemed to shrink in Sophie's arms. Patting her throat again gently with his spidery hands, he whispered in her head, *Robin tried to show you. Things are not what they seem to be. A brother is not a brother. A house that is broken might still hold the key. The strongest force might still yet win the day, and holding true can create and heal all worlds, but dear love, beware the false one who betrays.* He looked sidelong at Nikolas. *He cannot hear these words. He loves too well in the wrong places.*

A brother is not a brother.

Beware the false one who betrays. Oh dear God.

As the heavy message in Robin's words sank in, her arms loosened. Robin said in Sophie's head, *Robin must go to create a storm.*

Just as Nikolas strode forward to try to grab at Robin, the puck leaped away and disappeared down the hall. "Stop," Sophie said to Nikolas. When he made as if to lunge down the hall after Robin, she threw herself in front of him and grabbed his arms. "Nikolas, stop it! Leave him alone! Robin didn't have anything to do with how the Hounds found you. All he did was create the fog."

"How can you still believe him after the way he hurt you?" Nikolas snapped. He glared at her. "By all the gods, Sophie. You. Stopped. Breathing. What would you have done if you'd been alone?"

"That didn't happen." Somehow she managed to say the words more or less steadily. "Nik, you may not believe Robin. That's your choice, but I believe him. He didn't mean to hurt me. It was a mistake, and he's sorry. Listen—*Listen!*" As he shrugged off her hold angrily, she caught at him again. "He tried to influence the vision, but he wasn't in control of it any more than I was. That's the whole point of divination magic, do you understand? I don't force my needs and desires to make up images. I open myself up to the images that come to me, based on the questions I ask, and the visions always carry some element of truth to them. Robin's interference that first time might have made us see each other, which is definitely not normal, but it wasn't false."

For a moment she thought she hadn't broken through to him. The violent emotions thrumming through his taut body felt like an arrow, notched and pulled to its most taut point before being loosed in a killing shot.

Then the tension pulled back, and he stopped

straining against her hold. In a low voice filled with reluctance, he muttered, "I hear you."

Relaxing slightly, she let her hands fall from his arms, and she realized for the first time that her neck actually felt sore. Clearing her throat, she said huskily, "I guess we accomplished something then."

But at what cost?

"I need some air," Nikolas said. Not looking at her, he turned and walked out.

The cottage felt strange after he had gone: bigger, colder, and emptier. At a momentary loss, Sophie looked around at the scattered stones, the magic-embroidered cloth on the table, and the brandy bottle still sitting on the counter.

She took a hit of brandy straight off the bottle and glanced out the window as, in the distance, Gawain walked a wheelbarrow full of firewood into the manor house. Then she swept up the stones and put them back in their velvet bag, folded the cloth, and went back to the bedroom.

Her nerves were shot, and a fine tremor ran through her hands. Unable to stay focused on anything complicated, she concentrated on the mechanics of the tasks in front of her.

Washing clothes. Packing. Stripping linens off the bed, she stuffed the bedding in the washer too. Checking up on her *what the fuck* list.

Just when she thought she was full up on crazy, something else happened. She was beginning to get a glimpse of something bigger than she had ever imagined. They were all caught up in a web of events, and none of them were in control.

What a terrible word, betrayal.

Robin was right. She couldn't say that word to Nikolas, and he couldn't hear it. He was too loyal. He had given everything he had to those men. It was admirable, really, and in this case tragic. How would she feel if she had found out Rodrigo had betrayed her and had tried to get her killed?

It was unthinkable. Her gut tightened, and tears filled her eyes as she remembered the urgent care Rodrigo had given her before the ambulance had arrived, his face raw with fear and concern.

Gah, she felt overwrought, wrung out. She was too tangled up in what was happening, too emotionally involved. How did she get here in just a couple of days? When did having (tremendous, mind-blowing, screaming, utterly fantastic, wildly pleasurable) sex with Nikolas somehow turn into making love in her head?

She knew better than to fall in love with him. She knew it before he had ever warned her, so why did she feel so twisted up inside? Was she really going to step into that manor house with a group of men, most of whom she didn't know, and one of whom would try to kill her, because of how she felt about Nikolas?

The Mini had enough gas to get her to Shrewsbury. She could grab Robin—if he wanted to go—and they could just leave and take the first plane she could book back to the States. How would she get a puck on a plane? Would they let him sit on her lap for the flight, like a baby?

Then she thought of the taut, furious anguish on Nikolas's face, and she knew she was squandering her imagination and energy in telling herself a story that simply wasn't true. She wasn't going anywhere, not as long as he needed her help. He might not like her for it—he might not thank her for it—and he might not trust her any longer, but she couldn't leave him.

Not until he asked her to.

In an act so gloriously dysfunctional she couldn't believe she was admitting it to herself, Stupid and Crazy™ had struck again. She knew better than to fall in love with Nikolas, but she had gone and done it anyway.

"Why are you built like this, you stupid woman?" she muttered as she stomped into the bathroom to collect her toiletries and fold the clothes in the dryer. "There is something wrong with your head. How did you know to zero in on the absolute very last man on the planet you should get involved with? There are so many men in the world, Sophie Ross. So. Many. Rodrigo, for example. Why couldn't you fall in love with your good, loyal, *available* buddy Rodrigo?"

While she was bitching to herself, she tried to make sense of the piece of black clothing she held in her hands. What was this? She didn't own anything like this.

Not only was it too big, it was inside out. As she finally got the cloth turned the right way, she made sense of what she was holding. It was one of Nikolas's black shirts. She had automatically put his clothes in the same load as her own.

For some reason that struck her terribly hard. It was funny, or awful, or something, she didn't know what. Crumpling the shirt in her fists, she started beating the heels of her hands against her forehead in time with the words running through her mind.

Sophie. Sophie. Sophie. Sophie.

This. Is why. You don't. Kiss assholes. He gives you an orgasm, and all of a sudden, you're washing his clothes.

She hadn't known him for very long. Maybe she was only a little bit in love with him, like catching a cold instead of the flu. That would mean she could get over him quickly, wouldn't it?

Something, some change in the air or some subtle noise, caused her to lift her head. In the corner of the bathroom mirror, she could see Nikolas standing in the doorway. She froze, watching his reflection sidelong. The expression on his face was raw and heartbreaking.

"You didn't see the man who was choking you," he said.

Wordlessly, she shook her head.

"You never questioned if it might have been me."

She blinked. "Of course not. I know it wasn't. You—you wouldn't do that to me."

"Because you trust me."

The emotion behind that was laced with complexity, unreadable. Was he thinking about how he had trusted his men for so long? In comparison, she had known him for such a short amount of time, but that didn't change her conviction.

Dropping her attention to his shirt that she still held, she nodded. "Yes. Because I trust you."

He walked forward, put his arms around her from behind, and buried his face in her hair. The blood was coursing through his body so fiercely she could feel his heart beating against her back. He was breathing hard, and he felt slightly damp with sweat as if he had been running.

"It isn't Gawain," he whispered. "It can't be Gawain. I don't believe it of him. He's not capable of that kind of betrayal. He would rather cut off his hands than hurt you."

Betrayal. Nikolas believed her. He trusted her, and he came to that word all on his own. Her chest squeezed tight with compassion.

Leaning against him, she reached to cup the back of his head. "I can't believe it of him either," she whispered back as gently as she knew how. "His heart is too good."

He lifted up his head to pull the long, curling length of her hair aside, then he put his face into the warmth of her neck, skin to skin. "When we go into the house, you stick with either Gawain or with me, you hear?

You don't go anywhere by yourself, not even to the privy."

This was no time to take a stand over free will and issuing unwanted orders. He needed reassurance, so she gave it to him. "I won't go anywhere alone, I promise."

He held her so tightly she felt the pressure of it in her bones, but she didn't protest or try to pull away. After a moment, he muttered, "I think I know who it could be, and it isn't just about what you saw they would do to you. It's more than that. I think it's about the Hounds' attack two weeks ago. It might even involve the Hounds' attack on the pub a few nights ago. The gods only know how far this goes."

She hadn't been expecting that, and surprise thudded through her. When she tried to twist around to face him, his hold loosened enough to allow her, then tightened again. "Oh no."

"I might be wrong," he said. "Thinking that any of them could do this is wrong, but for one of them, the timing of certain conversations and events would fit."

"You can't live with this doubt always playing in the back of your mind," she told him. "You can't trust someone to have your back in combat if you think they might have tried to have you killed."

"No," he agreed. His eyes were still reddened and raw, but the lines of his face had hardened. "So we'll set a trap, and we'll see if he takes the bait. You won't ever be alone, not for a moment, my Sophie. I swear to that, but—we can make him believe that you are. Will you help me?"

"Of course," she said instantly. "I'll do anything you need."

As her words hung in the air, she listened to what she had just said and inwardly winced. Well, shit. That had quite a ring of truth to it.

He stroked the back of his fingers down the side of her face, his gaze turned inward. "I'll have to tell Gawain so he understands why you can't be left alone when the others arrive, and so he can help to set the trap."

"That's going to be a hard talk," she whispered, rubbing his back. "Nik, I'm so sorry you're going through this."

He snapped into focus, and he looked at her as if he was seeing her fully for the first time. Cupping her face, he caressed her lips with both thumbs. "You have nothing to be sorry about. If it weren't for you, who knows what further damage this man might cause. It's hard to believe you came into our lives only a few days ago. Already you've helped to restore my hope, and now you're reshaping us. Walking away from you last night..." Suddenly he bent his head to cover her lips with his. He said almost soundlessly against the shape of her mouth, "Walking away from you last night was one of the hardest things I've ever done."

Then why did you do it?

The outcry of hurt feelings echoed in her head, but

she wasn't ready to hear the reason, so she didn't put voice to them. She didn't want to hear him weigh the relative worth of staying with her versus leaving. She felt too raw and exposed, and she already knew that she hadn't come out of that assessment on the winning side.

Instead, she flung all of it aside—hurt feelings, insecurities and all—and wound her arms around his neck to kiss him with all the strength of her pent-up feelings.

It was as if she had thrown a lit match into gasoline. He caught fire underneath her touch. Clenching her against his chest, he angled his mouth to kiss her with such raw, single-minded intensity, it brought another wave of dampness to her eyes.

His fire set her on fire. It ran down her nerve endings like lava, leaving her aching with hunger, yearning, and sheer roaring lust. Her thoughts splintered into singularities.

All she wanted to do was touch him. That was all. Yanking his shirt up, she ran greedy hands over his hot torso.

He hissed against her mouth, sinking both fists into her hair. It was a primitive, aggressive gesture, restricting her movements, holding her captive against his mouth while he kissed her with such raw, shaking intensity, her defenses crumbled. He walked her backward, his lean body trapping her against the wall.

Kissing him back, submitting to his aggression, inciting him for more, she fumbled at the waistline of his pants. Why couldn't she figure out how to get the fastening open? It was making her crazy. With a muttered curse against her lips, he brushed her fingers aside to help. Still kissing her, he pulled his pants open while she unzipped her jeans and wriggled out of them.

There was no finesse in what they were doing. It was all animal instinct. He yanked her gauzy top up, along with the camisole underneath, and she raised her arms over her head so that he could pull them off. As her breasts bounced free, he made a hungry noise at the back of his throat and cupped them.

Something coherent tried to worm into her brain. She broke away from his hardened lips to gasp, "What if Gawain walks in?"

Without looking, Nikolas shoved his hand out and slammed the bathroom door shut.

For some reason that struck her as funny. She started to laugh, drunkenly, but her laughter was cut short as he lifted her up against the wall and thrust his hips between her legs. His thick erection brushed against the sensitive skin high on her inner thigh, and she moistened for him in a liquid gush.

She was not a lightweight. While she might have lost some muscle tone since the shooting and subsequent injuries, she hadn't lost all of it. It took strength to haul her bodily around or lift and pin her against the wall, but he did it so effortlessly she relaxed into the experience and wrapped her legs around his hips.

"We have no business doing this," he muttered against her cheek.

Twisting to reach for his cock, she gasped, "You're not going to stop, are you?"

"Fuck, no." As her fingers wrapped around him, his head fell back, eyes closed in an expression that looked almost like anguish. He gritted, "You'd have to shoot me to get me to stop now."

"Come inside me," she whispered. Rubbing his broad head against her opening, she positioned him just right, and with a slow, relentless thrust up, he penetrated her. In this position, at this angle, he felt massive, and she heard herself making a high, whining noise as her inner muscles stretched to accommodate him.

She was especially sensitive after last night. His entry not only burned through her, it felt perfectly right, exquisitely good.

He paused, chest heaving, to ask roughly, "Am I hurting you?"

In answer, she tightened her legs around him, drawing him farther in. "Only in the best possible way," she breathed in his ear.

He angled his head to look at her. With one hand braced against the wall by her head, the other arm wrapped low around her hips, he began to pump into her.

She had always felt a shock of connection when she looked into his eyes, and now, coupled with the savage carnality of their coupling, it was almost too much. But she couldn't look away either. The hunger, the heat in his dark eyes, the intensity all fed her own. She couldn't take him in deep enough. Flexing, straining, she stretched to reach around the outside of her thigh to finger the place where they were joined.

A groan broke out of him, and she could tell that her caresses heightened his pleasure as well. "I can't get enough of you," he muttered. "This is making crazy."

"Me too," she whimpered. It shocked her. Did that whimper really come from her?

His heat and hardness, the rhythmic sensation, built up a pressure and a need inside her that had her clawing at his shoulders. "Come on." As he hissed in her ear, he gave her hips an insistent yank while he ground himself against her. *"Come on."*

It was such a demanding thing to do to order her to climax, so very Nikolas and quite entirely imperious. She didn't know whether to laugh or to be offended or shocked. Instead, she felt a primal response rise up from deep inside. Arching off the wall, she gripped him by the back of the neck as she slammed into an orgasm.

He watched every moment of it, fiercely, as he kept moving in short, fast jabs. The twisting pleasure wrung at her. She clenched on him, shaking, until the last of the waves subsided.

Still inside her, he sank to his knees. Sitting splayed on his muscular thighs, she wrapped her arms around his neck while he began to move again, harder and more urgently. Biting at his ear, she egged him on until he froze, muscles bunched, and suddenly the intolerable tension broke and she felt him spurting inside her. Rocking gently, she helped him as he had helped her, drawing out every last moment of pleasure.

Just when she thought his climax was subsiding, he gripped her by the hips so hard she felt the pressure from each individual finger, and he picked up the pace, to gasp in her ear a few moments later as he spurted again. His expression was taut, beautifully wrung out. Loving every sensation, every glimpse, she ran her fingernails down his back, only to have him arch up into her again, with another renewed wave of climax.

It was odd, addictive, delightful. She'd never experienced anything like it, but all her previous lovers had been human. Nikolas presented her with an entirely different, unknown landscape. Pulled out of her preoccupation with her own pleasure, she breathed every part of him in.

Finally he held her hips stationary as he gritted, "We have to stop."

We have to stop, he had said, not *I can't do any more*. He still felt as hard inside her as he had when they had first started. Did that mean he could actually go further, do more, climax again? She spiraled dizzily into wonder.

But he was right. They didn't have time for leisurely exploration. Still, her fingers wanted to cling to him, and her arms wanted to remain wound around his neck. It was physically and emotionally difficult to detach.

Did he feel the same?

Almost as if he had heard her thoughts, his arms tightened around her. "I don't want to let you go," he growled. "And I don't want to stop now, but the day is flying by and we must stop. This is why I don't have anything to offer a lover—there's no time to give you the attention you deserve."

Oh, that old thing.

That old understanding she had worked so hard to establish between them last night. This was just supposed to be sex, just an interlude. They weren't even supposed to like each other.

How had she put it? They had the opportunity to give each other some pleasure. There was nothing more to it than that. It certainly wasn't his fault that she had gone and changed the rules of the game in her head without him.

Don't be weird at him, Sophie, she admonished herself fiercely. In terms of pleasure, affection, and a transcendent experience, he's given you so much more than you had expected or asked for. Don't ruin it now.

He was studying her too closely, his expression brooding, so she gave him a quick smile and a kiss. "Thank you," she said. "That was more than I could have expected."

He scowled. "What the fuck does that mean?"

She blinked. "What do you mean, 'what the fuck does that mean'? Last night you said you couldn't give a lover time and attention. Today you repeated it. So okay, I said thank you. Was I supposed to beat my chest and say, oh my God, we had sex in the bathroom? Because if so, I didn't get the memo."

He took her head between his hands and said between his teeth, "You said thank you the same way you would thank someone for buying you lunch. You make me crazy."

She shouted, "I said it was more than I could have expected! What else was I supposed to say?"

In answer, he rose to his feet, grabbed his clothes off the floor, and stalked out. Utterly bewildered, she sat, legs sprawled on the bathroom floor, and watched him leave.

After a few minutes, she stirred to gather up her own clothes. She looked down at them, then started banging the heels of her hands on her forehead again.

Sophie. Sophie. Sophie. This. Is why. You don't. Kiss assholes. He gives you another orgasm, and all of a sudden you're in love with him. And somehow you both get naked, because that's a really bright idea that never goes wrong, and then you start shouting at each other for no comprehensible reason.

After a moment, she set her clothes carefully aside and turned on the shower. She washed away all the evidence of what they had done together, dressed, and got back to work.

Her excuse was, apparently she had no sense.

And his excuse remained exactly what it had always been, inexplicable.

Chapter Sixteen

A S EVENING FELL into darkness, clouds amassed on the horizon, and the air grew damp and electric with the energy of impending rain. The puck had disappeared some time ago. Now that Sophie knew what his magic felt like, she could recognize his touch on the wind.

They were going to get a fine storm that night. For someone who was only partially recovered, Robin was exerting a tremendous amount of effort.

At first Sophie thought she would start shouting at Nikolas the moment she laid eyes on him again, but they had no more time to waste on personal issues.

The three of them ate a quick, cold supper. Nikolas slapped meat between two slices of bread and wolfed it down. Gawain ate beans out of the can while he stood at the kitchen counter. Sophie followed Nikolas's example and ate as much of a sandwich as she could choke down past the nerves tightening her stomach.

"Robin might be able to wash away your scents with his storm," Sophie said worriedly, "but he's also exposing himself. If I can sense his magic on the wind, others will be able to as well."

"If they're still anywhere in the vicinity, they'll be out searching for him." Nikolas's expression had turned grim. "We have to plan on it and tell the others to hurry. This night could turn ugly."

Taking his warning to heart, she double-checked the spells she had painted on her arms earlier to make sure they were still viable, and she pulled the Glock out of the micro gun safe, inspected it quickly, and tucked it in the waistband of her jeans at the small of her back.

A gun tucked in the small of the back was not only uncomfortable, it was insecure. It could slip out her waistband in a struggle, and she would have preferred a proper holster, but she hadn't brought one with her from the States and they hadn't thought to give her one. She would just have to make do. Last, she slipped extra ammunition into each front pocket. She didn't want to risk running into one of those monstrous Hounds without being prepared.

Using the wheelbarrow Gawain had found in the shed behind the cottage, they transported things from the cottage to the manor house. They didn't bother to sort everything in the great hall but stacked things in haphazardly to organize later.

They emptied out the kitchen—all the food, the dishes, pots and pans, the table and chairs, and even the dishwashing liquid. Sophie dragged her luggage across the lawn, while Nikolas swung the settee onto his back and jogged it over. Gawain followed shortly afterward with the armchair balanced on his shoulder while he tucked the sitting room table under one arm.

While Sophie cleaned out the linen closet—sheets, blankets, bedspreads, towels and washcloths, laundry soap and toilet paper—and dumped everything into the wheelbarrow, the men insisted on moving all the bedroom furniture as well, even the bed frame.

"You're already giving up enough as it is," Nikolas said over her protests. "The least we can do is make sure you get a comfortable bed to sleep in."

Gawain even walked his Harley into the great hall. He said to Sophie, "The bike won't work in the land magic, but at least no one can vandalize or disable it while it's in the house, so we'll have it available just in case."

Straightening her aching back, she nodded. It was a good idea. "I only wish we could do the same with the Mini."

At that, the two men paused to assess the small car and then look at each other. "If we get both the oak doors open, it might fit," Nikolas said. "If we get enough momentum with the car, the engine will cut out when it gets close to the house, but it should coast close enough that we can push it the rest of the way."

"Really, guys?" Sophie didn't know whether to protest their effort or thank them.

"Yes, really," Nikolas told her. "It's a principle of siege warfare. You don't leave anything out for your enemy to use, dismantle, or destroy, if you can possibly avoid it. The Porsche is going to be toast. It's too big to fit through the doors, and sooner or later they'll find it, but we can at least hope to save the Mini. And you never know. We might need it."

His dark hair had fallen onto his brow with the expenditure of effort. He looked handsome, dangerous, and kissable all at once. Having sex in the bathroom might have turned into a debacle, but in spite of that, she had managed to fall even deeper in love with him. She was afraid she had gone well past the point of it being a bad, bad cold. This feeling was turning into a life-threatening, flu-strength illness.

Then she flipped over to a kind of cheerful, macabre train of thought. Oh, well, they probably weren't going to survive the siege anyway. Because none of them were talking about what might come next, after they had been in the manor house for so long their supplies had run out, while they could very well discover that the broken crossover passageway magic was just that—broken pieces that lead nowhere.

They were throwing everything they had at a mere possibility. They would be blockading themselves into a dead end with no proof of an emergency exit.

We're all insane, she thought. So I might as well enjoy loving him while I can, because it doesn't make any less sense than anything else we're doing.

In the meantime, she threw up her hands. "If you guys think you can fit it in through the doors, by all means. It's only a rental, but I didn't take out extra insurance for siege warfare and decimation caused by Hounds of the Light Court, so you'll be saving me some money."

Once they had cleared everything moveable out of the cottage, even the curtains, Sophie shooed the men outside.

She told them, "Don't step back inside now. We might be preparing for a siege, but we can also work on some misdirection. For whatever good it does, I'm going to clean everything with as many household chemicals as I can. Hopefully by the time Robin and I are done, nobody will be able to pick up yours or Robin's scents, either in the cottage or anywhere outside on the property. The storm might bring Hounds nosing around the property, but with any luck, if Morgan doesn't find anything, he should go away again, right?"

"We can hope," Nikolas said, giving her a dark look. "Unless Morgan gets information from another source."

By the mystified look on Gawain's face, Nikolas hadn't had a chance to tell the other man what they had learned from her most recent vision.

Her shoulders drooped. "Well," she said tiredly. "We'll do everything we can, and then we'll see how things play out."

Gawain patted her back. "That's all anyone ever can do."

Pulling out an extra burst of energy through sheer

will, she attacked the interior of the cottage. Through the kitchen window, she paused briefly to watch Nikolas and Gawain force the second oaken door open in the deepening twilight. Then Nikolas loped back across the lawn to start the Mini and drive it toward the open doorway.

Sure enough, within fifteen yards or so, the car's engine died. It rolled a little farther, but the thick turf and the broken flagstones must have provided too much of a barrier, because it stopped well back from the doorway.

Nikolas leaped out, and Gawain joined him at the rear of the car. Together they pushed the Mini, seemingly without effort, into the house.

Mmm-hmm, that show of masculine strength wasn't sexy in the slightest.

Sometimes she cracked herself up. She turned her attention back to cleaning the cottage. Basically, she threw bleach on everything that could take it and lemon floor polish on everything else. By the time she was finished, even she couldn't handle the smells inside. Stacking the cleaning supplies outside the door, she backed out of the cottage and locked it.

When she turned around, she found Gawain striding toward her. By the hard, tight expression on his face, she could tell that Nikolas had finally talked to him.

He put an arm around her and squeezed her against his side tightly enough to make her grunt. "You're going to be safe with us, lass," he told her. "I swear it."

Sighing, she let her head fall onto his shoulder as she slipped an arm around his waist. "I didn't believe anything otherwise," she told him.

"Good." Unexpectedly, he turned his head to press a kiss against her forehead. "We're all at sixes and sevens right now, but you should know—you matter to him. You matter a great deal. He has to work through some things, so he might not be able to tell you that himself. If it matters to you enough to do it, lass, try to give him some time, and hopefully he'll work his way through the heaviest of it."

At his words, the starch went out of her spine. She turned into him to give him a full-bodied hug. "Thank you for saying that, Gawain."

He returned the hug and patted her back. "You matter to me too, you know. Have faith, stay the course. We'll do right by you."

"It's okay," she told him. "I don't know the others, but I believe in you, and I believe in him. Whatever that means."

As he let her go, he smiled and touched the tip of her chin with his knuckles. As she looked up at his rugged, handsome features, she thought, oh Gawain, you're such a good man. You're not an asshole in the slightest. Of course I couldn't fall for you.

While Gawain helped her to load the last of the cleaning supplies into the wheelbarrow, the first fat splash of raindrops began to fall. She warned, "Your null spell is going to wash off in this rain."

He paused, considering. "Maybe it doesn't matter, as long as Nikolas works inside the house," he said. He narrowed his eyes at the manor house. "I can't sense anything with the null spell on my hand. Can you sense his presence?"

She tried and couldn't. "I can't sense anything but the land magic."

"That's good news, lass. Maybe it means the house will cover our presence like we'd hoped."

They jogged over to the manor house as the first few raindrops turned into a steady rain; then quickly it became a downpour.

They tossed everything through the front doors. As she peered inside, she saw that Nikolas had lit a small fire to one side of the massive fireplace, and he stood beside it, head angled as he peered up at the chimney.

"Is it running clear?" Gawain called out.

"There's some kind of obstruction," Nikolas shouted back. "I'm going to have to climb up to clear it."

As they watched, he reached up to grab hold of something high inside, and he levered himself up until he had completely disappeared.

"Go on inside now," Gawain told Sophie as he took the handles of the wheelbarrow. "No need for you to get any wetter."

She had to raise her voice to make herself heard over the rain. "What are you doing?"

"Gathering as much wood as I can," he replied. "I found a couple of deadfall trees earlier in the north copse. They're already down. They just need to be harvested."

"Are you crazy?" she said as lightning flashed overhead. "This is turning into a serious storm."

"It's not my first storm, lass," he said, giving her a wink. "Nor will it be my last. We need as much fuel as we can get. Wood will dry out, and so will I."

"Well, when you put it like that." She stepped back out into the deluge. "Let's go."

Within moments they were soaked to the skin. It had been another long day, and it wasn't long before exhaustion set it, narrowing her thinking down to the immediate.

Put one foot in front of the other. Stack the wood Gawain chopped. Push the wheelbarrow another yard. Strain built up in her back, shoulder, and arm muscles, and soon the sites of the old gunshot wounds radiated a hot fire. Consumed by misery, she gritted her teeth, ducked her head, and endured it.

Gawain soon stopped trying to chop the wood into neat logs. Instead, he hacked at the deadfall just enough to break it into transportable pieces.

While they worked, lights appeared, shining through the woods. Breathing hard, she paused to stare, and Gawain did too. It was a large vehicle, traveling down the road that led to the front gates.

"Is that good news or bad news?" Her voice had

gone hoarse.

He dug in his pocket to check the screen of his phone. "The men met up in Telford and got their hands on a lorry. They're here." In the faint light of the cell phone screen, he looked at her sharply. "We'll need everybody to get the truck unloaded, but your trick with the colloidal silver won't work in this downpour."

"No," she said, swiping at the water running off her nose. "But my trick with the nail polish will."

It would also use up the last of her supply. She had enough silver to make more shavings, but she would need more bottles of nail polish, damn it. She had never imagined she would use the bottle up so fast, and she hated to let go of it.

Put one step in front of the other. Fix one problem at a time.

Gawain said, "They took a risk, banding together. We're even more traceable in a group. They never would have done it if they hadn't been on the move."

As the lorry turned onto the drive and passed between the gateposts, Gawain ran toward it while she raced back to the manor house. Dashing inside, she paused to look at the piles of furniture and supplies they had stacked everywhere. The small fire Nikolas had started was a pitiful light source, and it was hard to make things out in the semidarkness.

"Nik, they're here!" she called out. "Where's my stuff?"

At first she thought he didn't hear her, but then in a

shower of debris and soot, he landed light as a cat in the huge hearth and scrubbed his face with the bottom of his shirt. "I don't know. Where did you last set it?"

"I thought I put it over here. We need the nail polish if we're going to use the null spell in this storm." She jumped onto the settee and rummaged blindly in the shadows behind it. Her questing fingers brushed a hard, pebbled surface she recognized as her suitcase. "Got it!"

While Nikolas stacked more logs on his small test fire, she hauled the suitcase over the back of the settee and wheeled it over to the hearth, where she knelt to open it to rummage through her things. A chill had set in the house with the storm, and fine tremors ran through her muscles. Soon her teeth were chattering. Her body was a mass of aches and pains.

Then Nikolas walked up. He squatted to wrap a blanket around her. For a moment his arms remained around her torso, then they loosened. "You look like a drowned cat," he said, his eyes both shadowed and lit by the nearby flames. "Stay by the fire and warm up. Gawain and I can spell the men."

She felt spent, and she wasn't going to argue with him. She located the bottle of nail polish and gave him a pointed look. "Have either you or Gawain ever used nail polish before?"

His eyes narrowed. "I think it's safe for me to speak for him when I say no."

Giving him an exhausted grin, she slapped the bottle in his hand. "Don't apply it to wet skin. It takes a few minutes to dry, then you're good to go. Nobody should go back out in the rain until their rune is dry to the touch. Gawain and I think the land magic is going to mask the group's presence when you're all in the house. I couldn't sense you in here."

"We'll double-check when we're all together, but that's good to know." He started to rise.

"Nik." She took hold of his wrist, and he paused. Her smile died. "Don't waste what's in that bottle. That's all I've got."

He frowned. "Understood."

Lightning flashed overhead, showing through the thick, archaic glass in the windows and briefly lighting the interior. Nikolas strode across the hall and disappeared outside. Left to herself, she pulled the blanket more tightly around herself and dragged one of the sitting room chairs over as close as she could to the growing fire. From that vantage point, she curled in a ball and watched as several men converged on the doorstep.

Between the distance and the deep shadows, she couldn't make out many details of the newcomers. They conversed quickly in the area just inside the doors, then one ran outside again. She heard a distant shout, "Can't sense a thing. We're good!"

Several of the men looked her way curiously. She could identify Nikolas easily enough. His tall form and catlike grace were indisputable, as he moved through the men, bending over their hands. She knew what he was doing—he was casting the null spell—and she hoped she would have a little of the nail polish left when he was finished.

It was a good thing the land magic didn't block magic as well as technology. Shifting to get more comfortable, she felt the Glock dig into the small of her back, but she didn't move to set it aside.

Even though the gun was useless in the house, she wasn't convinced that she was inside for the night. She was worried about Robin. He was expending so much energy on the storm, and even now, they had to be hunting for him.

After a lull of five to ten minutes, the men exploded into furious activity. They backed the lorry up to the house as close as they could without the engine cutting out. Then while it sat idling, they raced to unload the contents from the back, carrying heavy armloads of supplies into the front hall at a dead run.

Indirect light from the lorry's headlights lent a sharp, slanting illumination to the scene, bleaching everything into black and white. Out the front double doors, she could see the outlines of the men's figures working furiously in the driving rain. A couple of them gave her a nod in greeting as they came close, but nobody paused to talk. Talking could happen later.

She watched as stacks of supplies grew around her, everything from camping supplies to cases of bottled water, cans of food, boxes of pantry items, and stacks of weaponry. They even brought more fuel—cords of firewood, what looked like bottles of propane, and other things she couldn't identify from where she sat. As large as the great hall was, it was beginning to resemble an overcrowded warehouse, especially with the Mini and Gawain's Harley tucked against one wall.

When these men prepared for the possibility of a siege, they weren't fooling around. She didn't know if she was comforted by that or disturbed. The reality of their choices was beginning to hit home.

More quickly than she would have thought possible, they finished unloading the lorry. All told, she guessed it had taken them about forty minutes. The men converged again on the doorstep for a quick consult.

"I'll get rid of the lorry," Nikolas said. "Give me the keys. You all stay here and get dry."

"No need, man," one of the men said, holding up the keys to jingle them. "I got it."

Nikolas turned to him. "Gawain, why don't you take the bike and go with Ashe? You'll both get back here faster that way."

"You bet," Gawain said.

Ashe strode outside, and Gawain ran his Harley out the front door. A few moments later, the lorry's engine revved as it pulled away.

As she watched the exchange, her worry for Robin had grown. Where had the puck gone? How was he creating the storm, and why hadn't he shown up by now? Pushing out of the armchair, she approached the group of men still standing on the doorstep just as one of them lit an oil lantern and held it high. As one, they turned to look at her.

Nikolas stepped to her side. "Gawain and Ashe are getting rid of the lorry on the other side of town. It shouldn't take them more than an hour. We should be able to bar the doors well before midnight."

She nodded as she studied the five tall strangers who were studying her with the same amount of curiosity. Like her, they were all soaked to the skin. There was a high probability that one of them would try to kill her.

Nikolas introduced them quickly, and one by one, they stepped forward to shake her hand. She received an impression of each one along with a flurry of names. Braden, Cael, Gareth, Rhys, Thorne, and Rowan.

All of them were taller than she was. Since their Power was muted with the null spell, she couldn't get a sense of them magically, at least not yet, but every single one moved with the easy, predatory athleticism of an experienced warrior.

The last one, Rowan, was sex personified. His long dark hair fell in a wet tangle around a cynical, handsome face. He had a runner's build, a sensual mouth, intelligent, brooding eyes, and a rock star's innate charisma that she felt even through her exhaustion and the damp discomfort of her clothes.

His expression heated with interest as he lingered

over shaking her hand.

"Thank you," he said. "Seriously, for everything."

"You're welcome," she told him. Color her crazy, and she could end up being wrong, but somehow she just knew this scamp wasn't going to put his hands around her throat and try to choke her to death.

With a neat, decisive move, Nikolas cut between them. He slapped Rowan's shoulder with a flattened hand, knocking the other man back a step. His hard voice carrying a warning, Nikolas said, "No."

One corner of Rowan's sexy mouth lifted in a grin as he looked at her around Nikolas. *I could make you feel so damn good,* his bedroom eyes said, while aloud, he drawled, "What do you mean, no? All I was doing was thanking her."

This time using both hands, Nikolas knocked him back another step. *"I said no."*

"All right, all right!" Laughing, Rowan held up his hands.

Was this merely discipline, or was Nikolas... actually jealous? Sophie couldn't tell. All she knew was that she felt like smiling for the first time in hours. Hell, it felt like it had been days. She grinned at Rowan, who gave her a wink as Nikolas turned away from him.

When Nikolas glared at her, she tried to wipe the grin off her face, but she wasn't fast enough.

What the righteous fuck, Sophie—no! he snapped telepathically. He looked genuinely infuriated as he growled aloud, "I'm putting my old-timey foot down."

"Old-timey foot…?" one of the other men said blankly. Sophie hadn't gotten all the names and faces sorted out, but she thought it might be Braden.

It really, truly could be jealousy. She probably shouldn't feel so delighted since first of all that was insane. She and Rowan had barely exchanged five words together. And secondly, it was insulting.

What did Nikolas think, that she was going to instantly leap at one of his men for sex *without even talking first*, when they had just made love—*had sex*—themselves twice in the last twenty-four hours?

Rolling her eyes, she muttered under her breath at him, "You're crazy," and punctuated it with an emphatic nod.

For a moment Nikolas himself looked like he might be the one to choke her. Half amused, half angry, and totally exasperated, she stepped into his personal space and stood toe-to-toe with him, daring him silently with her eyebrows up to make good on the fierce warning stamped on his taut features. What are you going to do, Nik? Just, what?

Much to her shock, he snaked an arm around her, blanket and all, which trapped her hands and arms against his chest. Angling his head, he gave her a short, fierce, scorching-hot kiss that flatlined her thinking and wiped away both the anger and the amusement.

When he lifted his head again, his eyes were glittering. What a load of primitive crap. He had not just staked a claim on her, had he?

By God, he had.

She ogled Nikolas before she remembered to shut her mouth with a snap. A quick, sneaky glance around told her what she already knew—the other men were staring at them with varying degrees of surprise.

Rowan looked decidedly disappointed. She shrugged. Ah well, if the other man had persisted, she would have just had to turn him down anyway.

He shook his head at her. I would have made it so good for you, the sultry look in his eyes said.

I know, she blinked at him in resigned reply. It is all so very sad.

One of the other men—she thought it was Cael— had turned away from the exchange to look out into the night. "We might have gotten rid of the lorry, but the lawn is so soaked it still left some pretty definitive tracks."

They all gathered at the door to look. Nikolas hadn't removed his hold on Sophie. Instead, he just shifted his arm to circle her shoulders. While she wasn't sure what his actions implied other than he was behaving like a dog with a bone, she wasn't annoyed enough to shrug him away.

The weight of the lorry had torn through the turf, and it had left deep tracks with high ridges. "How much of a problem is that?" she asked. "All that the tracks reveal is that a truck has been here tonight. No one will be able to say why, only that some kind of activity took place here while the ground was wet."

While her tired mind tried to tease out if there were any further potential problems, Nikolas's arm dropped from her shoulders. He said, "It creates a question and leaves it unanswered, which points to more reason to scrutinize you. We want them to leave you alone if we can possibly manage it. Everyone else has a null spell painted on their hand, so I'll take care of it."

He strode out into the storm, a lean, pantherish, imperious man who carried as much Power as the lightning. Something about seeing him out in the elements brought a lump to her throat.

When he reached roughly the middle of the lawn, he went down on one knee by the tracks, placed his hands on the ground, and bowed his head. Something she didn't know how to define rippled out from him. The tracks melted back into place, and the torn turf knitted back together. By the time he stood, the sodden lawn looked unscarred again.

Sophie bent her head, hiding her mouth in a fistful of blanket as she watched. He could literally reshape the earth. This time she didn't even bother to run around in her own head to stamp out all the sneaky bits of awe.

As Nikolas turned back to the house, a creature appeared behind him, emerging out from under the nearby tree line, and raced toward him. It was a huge, werewolf-y looking monster, and it was followed by several more.

Many more.

Dread sucker punched her in the stomach as they kept pouring out of the woods.

The Hounds had arrived.

The men shouted a warning at Nikolas and lunged for weapons. Nikolas spun, saw the danger hurtling toward him, and sprinted toward the house.

He was fast, but the Hounds were too, lethally so. Other than his own inherent Power, Nikolas didn't carry a weapon. Along with the others, he had set his sword harness aside to work on moving furniture and supplies.

Sophie was still wearing all her weapons, both the magical ones painted on her arms and the Glock, which gave her precious seconds on the other men. Dropping the blanket, she lunged into a sprint, pulling the Glock out from the waistband of her jeans. How far away would she have to get before the gun worked?

She reached ten yards, eleven, twelve. Nikolas was roaring at her in fury, but she couldn't make out his words. That was okay; she probably didn't want to hear them anyway.

Watching the Hounds bounding forward while she raced toward Nikolas was one of the most terrifying things she had ever seen. Every moment stretched into an intolerable infinity. As she ran, she aimed at the nearest lycanthrope at the head of the pack, and she started pulling the trigger.

Click. Click. Click.

Not yet. Not yet. Not yet.

Chapter Seventeen

W HEN SOPHIE SPRINTED toward Nikolas and the Hounds, he couldn't believe it. It was every bit as insanely courageous as when she had run into the pub, and by gods, when he got his hands on her, he was going to *fucking murder* her for it.

"Go back!" he roared. "Go back, you crazy god-damn woman!"

But she didn't stop. Behind her, the other men exploded out of the double doors with weapons, and they raced toward him too. They would overtake Sophie within seconds, but Nikolas didn't know how close the Hounds were behind him, and in this instance, fractions of seconds mattered.

He spun to face the threat racing up to him. Just then, Sophie's Glock fired, and the lead Hound, the one closest to Nikolas, dropped like a stone.

Chest heaving, he stared at it. She was as good as she had said she was. She hit what she aimed at. Even at night, in the middle of a pounding storm.

More Hounds poured out of the woods. It was too late to formulate any kind of sophisticated strategy.

Gathering his Power, he flung a morningstar, straight and hard, at the second closest Hound.

Like a bolt of horizontal lightning, the morningstar split the darkness and exploded in the Hound's broad, furry chest. The force of it lifted the Hound and spun its body in the air before it slammed into the ground. It didn't rise again.

Not many warriors could cast a morningstar. Morningstars were one of the deadliest weapons he had at his disposal, but they were a hellish drain on his energy and they took seconds to amass. Whirling back around, he raced toward Sophie.

Now she strode forward. She didn't run. Sighting down the length of her arm, she held the Glock in a two-handed grip and fired repeatedly at the approaching Hounds. Even as he came up to her, he was counting her bullets, and he knew the exact moment she went out.

"You're out!" he shouted in her face. *"Go back to the house!"*

Unbelievably, she dug in her jeans pocket. She told him, "Just need to reload."

He cast a quick look around. Thanks to his morningstar and her marksmanship, there were four bodies lying on the lawn, but there were at least twenty or twenty-five more Hounds racing across the lawn while his men sprinted to meet them.

Gods damn it, he needed his sword.

"Nik!" The shout came from behind him. As he

looked over his shoulder, Braden tossed his sword harness at him.

Nikolas snatched it out of the air. "Get behind me," he snapped at Sophie. "Get down, low to the ground, and stay there!"

Miraculously, this time she did as he ordered, jumping to crouch low behind him. He pulled hard on his Power to amass another morningstar and flung it at the next closest Hound. It sizzled through the air and hit the Hound broadside.

Behind him and low to the ground, the Glock spat multiple times. Sophie had finished reloading, and he remembered what she had said when she had shown how she could assemble and load a gun without looking. *Because you should be able to do it in the dark, if need be.*

He was so furious at her for risking her life, but at the memory of that cocky, sexy little lift of her mouth, he felt a fierce grin break over his face.

At his best, he could amass four morningstars, perhaps five, before he was tapped out. And morningstars were no good at fighting in close quarters. Around him, Braden, Gareth and Rowan were armed with guns too, and the flat, erratic percussion of their firing punctuated the ominous roll of thunder from the storm. The rest of his men slammed into combat with the Hounds, so he drew his sword and dropped the harness to the ground.

He said to Sophie, "For the love of all the gods, do

as I said and get your ass back to the house. If you shut
the doors, the Hounds can't get inside. Nobody can get
inside unless you let them."

"You are such a sexist boor," she snapped. "Look
around—did any one of your men make that choice,
and are you bitching at them for it?"

I'm not in love with my men. The thought sprang,
sizzling and white-hot, like a morningstar in his head.

He shouted, "My men follow orders!"

"I'm a consultant!" she snapped. "Not your foot
soldier. I don't take orders from you."

"You're fired!" he growled.

He didn't have time to say any more or hear if she
argued. Not ten yards away, Cael was facing off against
two Hounds. Moving forward rapidly, Nikolas engaged
the closest Hound.

The battle turned into images he saw in microsec-
ond snapshots. The Hound turned its slavering jaws
toward him, and they feinted with each other, pacing in
a circle as the driving rain made every step a hazard.

Naturally, Sophie hadn't gone back to the house.
Instead, she calmly walked up behind the Hound while
its attention was fixed on him. As he watched in
incredulity, she tapped it on the haunch.

He thought he was beside himself before. This time
he nearly levitated out of his body.

"*What the fuck are you doing now!*" he roared.

The Hound spun to face her, then kept turning. It
looked skyward, then down at the ground, and turned

around the other way, head tilted.

"Confusion spell," Sophie told Nikolas breathlessly. "He'll do that for hours. I've got one left."

Even as he lifted his sword to behead the creature, Nikolas filled his lungs to lambast her with everything he had. Then he paused. "It'll be like this for hours?"

"Yep." Lifting the Glock, she shot one-handed at the second Hound that Cael was fighting. It was a headshot, clean and true. The Hound was dead before it hit the ground.

She was so limited and fragile. She wasn't nearly as fast as his men and not half as big or strong as the Hounds, yet in spite of that, she was one of the most dangerous fighters on the field that night, and he *adored* her for it.

"Keep an eye on it," he said, watching Cael salute her and race off to engage another Hound. "I want to question it if I can. If you have to, shoot it in the head."

"Got it," she said. While she kept her attention fixed on the incapacitated Hound, she quickly reloaded.

Abruptly, rage surged over him in a scalding wave again. He snarled, "Now you take my orders?"

She speared him with a brief, sparkling glance. "I accept your suggestions. You can stick your orders up your ass."

He would not laugh. Not while he was this furious. Spinning, he leaped into battle, amassing another morningstar to fling at a Hound that tried to flee the field.

It was a sloppy, ugly battle. Nikolas was able to amass two more morningstars before he tapped out. Aiming the last one strategically, he was able to take down two Hounds at once, and then he had to rely upon swordwork. Never moving too far away from Sophie, he kept on the defensive in a broad circle around her.

Within a half an hour, the battle was over. As Nikolas drew his sword from the throat of his last kill, he surveyed the field. A full thirty bodies littered the ground. When the Hounds had first appeared, the numbers had been decidedly against them, but now almost all of them lay dead, strewn across the clearing. Some of the bodies had already shifted back into human form.

They had gotten so damn lucky. If Sophie hadn't acted so quickly and been such a good shot, if Nikolas hadn't been able to amass the morningstars, if the other three men hadn't been armed with guns and silver bullets, this battle could have gone entirely the other way.

The sound of shouting had him spinning on his heel.

Sophie and Rhys confronted each other over the body of a dead Hound. She was swearing, sounding as furious as Nikolas had ever heard her. "What the hell is the matter with you? I told you to back off and leave it alone! I had it under control!"

Rhys advanced, moving his body like a weapon until they were face-to-face. He backhanded her in the chest, pushing her back as he shouted hoarsely over her, "You don't fucking tell me what to do, woman! He was an enemy! I cut him down like the murderous dog he was!"

Nikolas lunged over and slammed into Rhys so violently the other man skidded on the wet grass and went down on his ass. Breathing hard, Nikolas brought the tip of his sword to Rhys's throat.

"She was doing what I told her to do," he growled. "I wanted to question that Hound."

"I tried to tell him that, but he wouldn't listen!" Sophie exclaimed as she reached Nikolas's side.

Rhys's face distorted with rage. "You get a piece of tail, and now you're holding your fucking sword to my throat? Is that the kind of commander you really are?"

Ice took over Nikolas's molten rage.

"Yes." His voice turned stone cold. He pressed forward until the tip pressed against the skin at Rhys's throat. "That's the kind of commander I am. You touch her again like that, and I will cut your fucking hands off."

Beside him, Sophie had gone still. Nikolas grew aware that the other men had joined them and were bearing silent witness to the confrontation.

Nikolas bared his teeth in savage, naked aggression. "That goes for every one of you as well. This woman has risked her safety and her life for us. While you were scrambling for your weapons, she was the first one on the field tonight. We are guests in her house, and you will respect her expertise. And if I find out that one of you has verbally or physically threatened her in any way, I don't care how long we have fought together, I will end you. Is that clear?"

Rowan stepped forward to put his hand on Nikolas's taut forearm. "You're right, Nik," he said, his voice clear and calm. "That's not who we are. Rhys was just being an unbelievably massive ass, weren't you, Rhys? You didn't actually mean to strike our friend, host, and ally. And I'll bet you're counting the seconds until you can say you're sorry. Right?"

"Right," Rhys said, his wary attention trained on Nikolas. He made no move to try to stand or ease away from Nikolas's sword but instead remained sprawled half prone on the ground, his weight resting back on both hands. He looked at Sophie. "I apologize. I can't believe I hit you. I've never done anything like that before. It must have been the heat of the battle."

"Sure, it's okay," Sophie said easily. As Nikolas glanced at her, water dripped down her calm face. She smiled. "Battle fever can make the best of us do crazy things. No harm done this time. Just don't do it again, or you can forget about what Nik will do to you. I'll smack you into next week myself."

Expectedly, Braden started to chuckle. "I heard the truth in that statement."

Others started to laugh, and the tension eased. Rowan's grip tightened on Nikolas's arm until he forced his rigid muscles to relax. Taking a step back, he bent to clean the length of his bloody blade on the grass, then found his sword harness. Despite the discomfort of donning it while wet, he sheathed the sword and shrugged the harness into place.

He asked, "Did we get them all?"

"No way to tell," Cael replied. "Maybe. We got all the ones that charged, and you took out the one that tried to leave the field. There could have been others holding back, in the woods, but they would have charged too, unless they had other orders."

And Rhys killed the one that might have told us that, Nikolas thought. Out of the corner of his eye, he saw Sophie offer a hand to Rhys to help him up. After a second's hesitation, Rhys accepted it. It was a nice, diplomatic touch. A savage, barely controlled part of him wanted to knock their hands apart.

He watched closely until they stopped touching. Then he said, "I guess it doesn't matter. None of these Hounds will be returning, which is a message in itself." He told Sophie grimly, "I'm afraid all our hard work at misdirection has gone down the drain."

"Doesn't matter." Sounding tired, she swiped at her dripping nose. "Misdirection was a long shot anyway." She added telepathically, *They showed up here awfully quick after Robin's storm started though. Do you think Morgan knew I was lying after all?*

Nikolas said, *No. If Morgan believed you were lying, he*

would have come here himself, and he wouldn't have waited. Or he wouldn't have let you go in the first place.

She heaved a sigh, which turned into a cough. *It must have been Robin's storm that brought them then.*

Although he didn't say so, he disagreed. The puck might be a great many things, but he was neither naive nor stupid. A storm of this magnitude spanned miles, and Robin would never have made the manor house the center of it.

And Morgan hadn't witnessed the deep emotional bond Sophie and Robin had developed. He had believed Sophie when she had claimed the dog had disappeared, so he wouldn't have leaped immediately to searching for Robin here. He might have checked out the property as part of an overall search strategy, but there would have been no specific sense of urgency in doing so.

No, there was only one logical reason Nikolas could think of for a fighting force of thirty Hounds to show up on Sophie's doorstep not an hour after the men's arrival.

Betrayal. They were not supposed to live through this fight.

He watched Rhys closely for the next several minutes, but as the tension faded from the group, the other man appeared to relax gradually. He even stepped forward to mutter something at Sophie, which caused her to laugh.

Moving quickly, the men stacked the bodies of the

Hounds together close to the tree line. As they worked, a single headlight of a motorcycle appeared. Gawain and Ashe had returned.

Sophie and Rowan went to greet them and explain what happened, and within moments Ashe had joined the rest of the group to help, while Gawain ran his bike into the manor house.

Now that Gawain had returned and could help to keep an eye on Sophie, Nikolas felt a hypervigilant part of him relax slightly, and he could turn his full attention to the task at hand. Once all the bodies had been collected, the others stepped back several meters. While they kept watch, he knelt to put his hands on the ground once again.

It had been a long damn day with a hellish ending, and he was not only tired, he was still tapped out from amassing morningstars. But this one task had little to do with wielding his Power and more to do with asking the Earth to wield hers.

Reaching deep, he made the connection with the rich, abundant land magic all around him and asked it to take the bodies of the men. This type of asking never moved quickly, but after a few moments, the ground rippled gently and the bodies sank below the turf. When they had completely disappeared, he thanked the magic and let it go, then stood.

The first thing he did was look for Sophie. She stood by Gawain at the back of the group. At some point while Nikolas had been working, the puck had appeared, still wearing the form of a monkey. Robin sat on Sophie's hip like a toddler, his skinny, hairy arms around her neck.

No one offered to say any words at the Hounds' grave. They got the respect of a burial, but they would not get prayers from the Dark Court.

"That's it," Nikolas said, wiping his hands on his sodden pants. "We're done. Let's get inside."

The others didn't hesitate. They jogged to the house, and as soon as everybody was inside, Nikolas and Gawain closed the iron-bound oak doors while everyone else watched in the dim glow thrown from the fire across the hall and the single lit oil lantern someone had set on top of a case of canned beans.

The sound of the doors closing seemed very loud in the silence. Nikolas turned to find them all watching him. Sophie hugged the monkey. Everyone wore the same, sober expression he felt on his face.

Nikolas thought, none of us know if or when those doors will open again.

And one of us is a traitor.

"We've thrown the dice," he said. "Now we pray the gamble pays off."

Gawain clapped his hands. "In the meantime, we've got work to do. Let's dry off and get changed. Nikolas cleared the chimney so we can build up the fire to take the chill out of the hall. We can sort out the majority of this mess tomorrow, but let's at least get things shifted so we can have enough clear floor space to make bed pallets for the night. And I don't know about any of you, but I could use a late supper after all that work."

While Gawain issued orders, Nikolas turned his attention to Sophie. Dripping wet like the rest of them, she was visibly shivering, and her face was completely colorless. Searching the immediate area, he found the blanket she had left crumpled on the doorstep and enveloped both her and the puck in it.

His hands were reluctant to leave her. He clamped his fists in the blanket and drew her close. She didn't resist him. Neither did Robin, as the puck turned his face away and laid it on her shoulder.

"You looked spent hours ago, and a lot has happened since then," Nikolas muttered. "Let's get you out of these wet clothes. Then will you please sit by the fire and warm up?"

Her teeth chattered. "I would l-love nothing more than to fall asleep by the fire, but Nik, we haven't found the privies yet."

He told her, "The men can piss in a jar for one night."

She glowered at him. "I c-can't."

Unexpectedly, amusement welled up inside. Tucking the blanket higher around her neck, he said, "We'll set up a chamber pot for you and a blanket for privacy. We can locate the privies in the morning."

"Nikolas Sevigny, I am not going to pee in a chamber pot while I'm in the same room as the rest of you. Just wipe that concept out of your head." She sniffed and rubbed her nose on the blanket. "I'll feel better when I'm warm and dry. It's not going to hurt if we look around a little bit."

Heaving a sigh, he conceded. "All right, but only after we change into dry clothes."

They changed quickly. First Nikolas held up a blanket in one of the two corners closest to the fire so that she could strip out of her wet clothes in relative privacy. When she was freshly dressed in jeans, a sweater, and her black boots, he changed too. Thanks to Sophie washing his clothes, he had exactly four changes of clothes with him from his go-bag. In many ways, no matter how much or little time it took, this was going to be a long siege.

While he dragged on clean clothes and settled the damp sword harness into place between his shoulders, he said to Gawain, "We're going on a brief exploration, hopefully to find privies and a viable source of water without encountering a major shift between here and there." Switching to telepathy, he added, *When you set up pallets for tonight, be sure to put hers close by the fire, between yours and mine. She feels the cold more than we do, and we're not leaving her unguarded for a moment.*

You bet, Gawain said without a flicker in his expression. Aloud, he replied, "We'll have hot soup and bread waiting for you when you return."

"Thanks." Sophie was still shivering when Nikolas turned to her, and she had wrapped the blanket around her again, but there was more color in her face.

"Where's Robin?"

She shrugged. "Hiding in the shadows. Pilfering the food. Your guess is as good as mine. He took off when I changed clothes." She gave him the ghost of a tired grin. "He's a bit prudish, I think."

Nikolas dismissed Robin from his mind. The puck could look after himself, and he had a talent for disappearing when he wanted to. He took one of the nearby oil lanterns and lit it. "Ready?"

"Yeah." She looked at the chaos around them. "Wait, did we get chalk or paint?"

Gawain said, "I saw that box. Hold on a second." He rummaged between two stacks and lifted up a hand-labeled cardboard box. "Here it is—both chalk and paint and paper for drawing maps."

Sophie peered inside and pulled out a plastic package filled with white chalk. "This will do for tonight. If we find any shifts, we can mark them more permanently tomorrow."

Nikolas approved of that plan. He said, "Follow me."

As tired as she looked, her expression was alive with interest. She fell into step beside him as he led her toward the huge fireplace. "Why are we going into the corner—oh!"

Her exclamation came as he took her hand and led her into the deep shadow at the side of the huge hearth. Only when they came close did the light from the oil lantern reveal a dark, narrow hall, cleverly designed to remain hidden by the massive bulk of the fireplace.

He grinned at the look in her wide eyes. "I found it when I was clearing the chimney. It's not quite a hidden passageway, but it's close. Servants would have used this, probably to carry food and drink to the high table and important guests, so it should lead back to the kitchen, buttery, and pantry."

"And hopefully a water source," she said.

"Exactly. Also, this house is big enough, I have my fingers crossed for an inner courtyard."

The sounds of the men working faded as they went down the dark, narrow hall until black silence pressed at them on all sides. They could walk abreast of each other, but Nikolas's sleeve brushed the wall on his side, and he could see that Sophie didn't have much room on hers either.

She whispered gleefully, "This is creepy as hell."

"It is, a bit." Smiling slightly, he laced his fingers through hers. "Are you sensing any shifts?"

She shook her head. "Not at the moment. I'll be sure to tell you when I do." Her eyes gleamed as she glanced behind them. She shifted to telepathy. *The man who tries to strangle me. You suspect Rhys, don't you?*

His brief amusement faded. *He has pressed me for details at suspicious times. I look back at things he's said and how I've sensed a certain antipathy in him from time to time. He knew about Gawain scenting Robin and me going to investigate Old Friars Lane. And tonight, not an hour after the men arrived, we got attacked by a large pack of Hounds. When we might have gotten information from the one you had spelled, he killed it. It's all circumstantial, and none of it is definitive, but yes, I do suspect him.*

She squeezed his fingers. *I'm so sorry.*

The warmth of her hand in his was a comfort he hadn't expected to relish. He squeezed her fingers in reply. *Thank you.*

As they talked, they came to a heavy door, and he handed her the oil lantern before he set to pushing it open. The wood was swollen into place, and the hinges were rusty, so he had to throw his whole weight into the operation. The door screeched loudly as it finally gave and split into two pieces. The wood had rotted at the core.

He stumbled forward outside into the cool, wet night. Behind him, Sophie laughed and cheered. "You were right—there's an inner courtyard!"

As he righted himself, she held the oil lantern high. It was impossible to see everything in the insufficient illumination, but he got the impression of tangled, overgrown greenery, knee-high grass, benches, and even a few fruit trees, all bordered by stone colonnades. It wasn't by any means as grand as some courtyards he had seen, but still, it was a nice, spacious place.

His catlike eyes adjusted to the lighting, and he pointed across the courtyard. "There are your privy chambers, and in the opposite corner, there is my well. This house is part wealthy family home and part fortress. I suspected they would have wanted to keep their water supply guarded and to have privy chambers safe from outside interference. Nobody would want to get attacked while in such a vulnerable position. The kitchen, buttery, and pantry will be somewhere over there, by the well."

"This is fantastic." Her eyes shone.

He smiled. "If you need to relieve yourself, you'd better go behind one of the trees for now. Tomorrow we can make sure the structure of the privy chambers is safe and inspect the well."

"Actually, *erm*." She gave him a sidelong smile and slipped her hand out of his. She tossed her blanket into his arms. "I'll be right back."

"Take your time." He waited while she took care of her private business, content to study his surroundings.

The courtyard felt full of ghosts from the past. He could see the reason for everything they had done. The benches had been positioned so they would get the most shade from the fruit trees. The well had been covered before the household had left. It must have been an instinctive decision, in case they ever chose to return again.

The moon hung high overhead, lightly veiled in shadowed clouds. On the other side of the front doors, this night was the third night of the full moon cycle, but here, in this place, the moon was half-full. The sight was another reminder that they were not in alignment with the land outside the house, which was both comforting and disturbing at once.

She returned quickly, reclaimed her blanket, and pointed back the way she had gone. "There's a shift over there."

He looked in that direction. "You didn't cross it?"

"Oh, no." She shuddered. "The last thing anybody needs is for me to disappear for two weeks while I'm going to the bathroom."

"You're damn right." Setting aside the lantern, he drew her into his arms. She leaned into his embrace and tucked her face into his neck. Rubbing his cheek against her damp hair, he muttered, "You still make me crazy."

Crazy with desire. Crazy with a tangled mess of so many other emotions he didn't know how to track them all or sort through them. She flung him hurtling along a manic symphony of reaction. Interacting with Sophie was like trying to herd twenty cats at once.

"*I* make *you* crazy?" Dropping the blanket, she slipped her arms around his waist. She whispered, "I lost ten years of my life when I saw those Hounds racing after you. It was the most terrifying thing I've ever seen, Nik."

He felt her body shudder against his. Remembering his own rapid, violent array of emotions as he watched her run toward him, he pressed his mouth to the thin, fine skin at her temple and told her, "You're still fired. I mean it, Sophie. I won't work with someone who disregards my orders so blatantly."

"*Pfft,*" she said. "I don't need your stupid consulting job. You can keep your money and your high-handed, arrogant assumption that you get to order me around however you like. I'm going to still do what I want and act as I think best. I meant what I said too—I'm not one of your foot soldiers. Screw you."

As she told him off, she rubbed his back, the touch soothing and arousing at once.

"You are a truly horrible woman," he growled. He slid the tips of his fingers underneath the edges of her sweater, connecting with the warm skin at her torso. The need to kiss her, to feel her full mouth pliant and moving under his, was pounding in his head. "Screwing sounds better and better all the time."

"And I can't believe you're such an asshole." She crooned the words, almost as if they made her happy.

He tilted her face up. "Sophie," he whispered. "I'm no good for you. My life is desperate and violent all the time, not just tonight, and now you've gotten trapped in a conflict you can't leave."

"Oh Nik," she murmured, stroking his hair. "It really is impossible for you to grasp that I am fully capable of making all my own choices. I am fully autonomous in my own right. I'm not going to agree with you all the time, and I'm not going to take your orders. I am my own sovereign state, and I'm standing right here in front of you because I want to be here. I'm beyond being insulted by you. Right now I'm just weary. If you can't respect me enough to accept that, I don't know what the hell we're doing."

As she talked, she slipped out of his arms and turned away. He grabbed her wrist and pulled her back. "If I didn't respect you, I wouldn't be standing here right now," he growled. "Do you want to know the truth? You scared me tonight. I watched you running straight into danger, and I thought my heart was going to burst out of my chest. And when you don't take orders, and when you act like a loose cannon, I don't know how to plan my actions around you. That's what orders and acting like a cohesive fighting unit are for."

Her eyes flashed with shadowed fire. "All that would be true, and I could take it, except you ordered me back to the house like I was a delinquent child. Maybe I could accept your orders if you treated me like you treat your other men."

"You're not my other men!" he roared furiously. "I'm not in love with any of them!"

She froze, then whispered, "What?"

"I said I'm not in love with any of them!" he snapped. All but flinging her wrist away from him, he pivoted away to pace. "Everything about you drives me insane. We have been arguing and sniping at each other from the moment we met. But then I started to like you. You're courageous, funny and generous, and more beautiful than any woman has any right to be, and when we first made love…" He stopped pacing to run his hands through his hair as he tried to gather his thoughts.

"Made love?" she murmured.

"Made love," he repeated fiercely, turning to glare at her as if she might try to take the experience away from him. "When we first made love, I felt something I had never felt before. Instincts that I didn't even know I had. I'm part Wyr, and I felt the drive to mate with you. So I left because that's not what we said we were going to do that night. It was supposed to be an interlude of pleasure, nothing more. But then I couldn't keep my damn hands off you. I still can't."

In the golden slant of light shining from the oil lantern, he could see the shock in her face. Her lips parted as if she would say something, but he couldn't bear to hear it.

"Don't worry," he said bitterly. "I've thought it through. I'm not Wyr enough for the mating urge to kill me. You're under no obligation to be concerned about it."

She wrapped her arms around herself. "So you're not forced by the Wyr mating instinct to do something you're not willing to do. You sound as if you don't welcome it at all."

"Everything I first said to you is still true." Unable to look at her any longer and fight the pounding urge to take her back in his arms, he turned his back. "I'm in the middle of fighting a war, and I still don't have anything to offer a lover—no safety, no home, not even the promise of my time and attention."

Her breathing sounded harsh in the still of the courtyard. "Well, I guess we know where we stand now. You know what's funny? I fell in love with you too, you jackass. Your commitment, your bravery, even your imperious attitude. It hurt when you walked out so quickly after we barely finished making love, but I went with it. You asked me to trust you when you said you had good reasons for walking away, and I went with that too. In fact, I've gone with all of it—the danger, the uncertainty, the fighting, and just so you know, your finer sensibilities for why you shouldn't take a lover are outdated and delusional, because we're probably not getting out of this house again alive. But you know what I can't go with?"

He looked over his shoulder at her. "What?"

"I can't go with how unwelcome all this is to you. How unwelcome I am to you. I can accept everything about you, even your worst, most imperious, biggest asshole moments. But you can't accept me and who I am. You can't accept the fact of me in your life, for however long or short that life ends up being. You can't accept the fact that I might accept everything about your life, how restrictive it is and how danger-ous—that I have the power and the ability to make that choice rationally and accept the consequences, whatev-er they may be." Pausing, she dug the heels of her hands into her eyes before continuing raggedly, "So you may say you're in love with me, but you're not in love with me the same way that I am in love with you. We're using the same words, but we are not having the same experience, and I'm... I'm not going with this any longer."

As she said the last words, a footstep sounded in the hall behind her. Before Nikolas had consciously thought about it, he had drawn his sword and leaped to her side.

Gawain stepped out of the hall, into the light. The other man took in the scene at a quick glance—their tension, Nikolas's drawn sword. He cleared his throat. "Sorry to interrupt. I just wanted to let you know there's a hot supper when you're ready."

Sophie wiped her face as she turned to Gawain. "That sounds good."

"We're not done talking yet," Nikolas said harshly.

She didn't look in Nikolas's direction. "Yes, we are," she said. "We're done."

Bending to gather up her blanket, she stepped into the hall. After a brief hesitation, Gawain followed, leaving Nikolas standing alone in an overgrown courtyard filled with ghosts.

Chapter Eighteen

A S SOPHIE FOLLOWED Gawain back to the great hall, exhaustion set in, darker and heavier than ever. Not only did her whole body ache, but this time the exhaustion was emotional, and she knew she wouldn't be able to access a second (third? fourth?) wind.

Back in the great hall, light, warmth, and a certain amount of order greeted her, along with the appetizing smell of hot food. Either they had constructed torches, or they had brought some with them, for lit torches filled sconces at strategic intervals.

They had shifted the Mini and the Harley so that they lined the outside wall, under the windows. Supplies were coordinated and stacked along the inner walls. There were a lot of supplies, so it made the remaining space that much smaller, but there was still enough room to create a small sitting area in front of the fire with the settee and chair and a dining area with the kitchen table that was extended with a few crates added to one end. Sleeping pallets lined the stacked supplies along the sides.

Automatically she counted the pallets and came up one short, but before she could ask Gawain about it, he nudged her shoulder. "Come over here, lass. Look what we did for you."

Obediently she followed him to one of the two corners closest to the fireplace. He lifted a curtain stitched roughly together from the cottage curtains, and with one hand urged her to step inside. She complied and discovered they had created a tiny bedroom.

Two walls were the stone walls of the great hall, and the other two were built from crates and boxes of supplies. The double bed from the cottage was inside, and someone had even made it, complete with blankets and pillows. The bedside table held an oil lantern. Her luggage was stacked neatly at the foot of the bed, and the dresser was tucked in one corner.

The area was small and cramped, but it was private, and it offered a degree of comfort she hadn't been expecting. "This is amazing and incredibly thoughtful," she said. Her argument with Nikolas had left her feeling so raw she had to blink back tears. After giving herself a moment to recover by looking at everything, she faced him with a smile. "Thank you so much."

Gawain hadn't stepped inside. There wasn't enough floor space to accommodate his large bulk in addition to hers.

Smiling briefly at her pleasure, he told her telepathically, *Until we find out who the traitor is, Nikolas and I will be sleeping right outside. Nobody will get past us, lass.*

Aloud, he added, "Well, you have enough walls for now. Eventually those will disappear as we use up supplies, but hopefully by then, we'll either know if it's safe to use the bedchambers, or we'll have reached some other solution."

"It's wonderful. I love it." Impulsively she gave him a hug. Looking surprised and pleased, he hugged her back.

"Come get yourself some supper. There's oxtail soup and sandwiches."

Oxtail soup sounded decidedly odd, but she followed him to the dining table, where she was greeted with friendly looks and a few smiles. Nikolas hadn't returned yet, and abruptly she knew she couldn't face him again that night.

When one of the men—Gareth, she thought—made as if to shift over to make room for her, she told him, "Don't bother. I don't mean to be unfriendly, but I'm so tired I can hardly stand upright. I just want to grab one of these sandwiches and go to bed."

"No shame in being tired," Gareth said. "You fought well tonight."

"Thank you."

"Wait," Rowan said as he stood. He dug out a large mug, filled it with steaming soup from a camp stove, and offered it to her. "Take this."

She accepted it, along with a sandwich, and retired to a chorus of good nights. Setting her food on the bedside table, she pulled the privacy curtain down, and her bedroom fell into shadow.

She had the brief impulse to light the lantern but then realized she didn't know how, and suddenly the small task and her lack of knowledge became obstacles too big to overcome. Stripping out of her jeans and sweater, she crawled shivering between cold sheets. While she waited for the bed to warm up, she sipped at the soup, savoring the warmth and the rich, meaty flavor, and ate a few bites of the ham and cheese sandwich.

By then the worst of the chill had left the sheets, so she stretched out horizontally, and as she listened to the men's quiet conversation, she plummeted into a black pit.

For a while.

Then she was running through the warehouse while the gunman chased her. She rounded a corner, looking for a way out, but it was a dead end. As she whirled to run the other way, the gunman walked around the corner.

He brought up his gun. She stared down the barrel and heard the flat *tat-tat-tat* as he shot her, and she was falling.

Always falling.

Rodrigo, she tried to call. Help me.

She plunged awake as a hand settled over her mouth. The men had gone to bed, and the indirect light from the fire had died down, leaving the space in near total darkness.

A figure leaned over her, weight pressing down the edge of the mattress, but before she had time to panic, Nikolas whispered, "*Shh*, it's me. It's all right."

She gripped his wrist, shaking, and his hand shifted from her mouth to stroke the hair back off her forehead.

He said telepathically, *You were having a nightmare and whimpering.*

Unsurprised, she nodded. *Sorry I woke you.*

He exhaled, an impatient, nearly inaudible sound. *Move over, Sophie.*

She hesitated, torn between wanting to so badly she could practically taste it and remembering the bite of the last things they had said to each other. Her telepathic voice sounded small and uncertain to her own ears. *Maybe that's not such a good idea.*

He brought his forehead down to hers. *Let's take a time-out. You still meant everything you said, and so did I. Let this be its own thing. We can go back to fighting again tomorrow.*

Was that okay? Maybe that wasn't okay. Maybe she was supposed to stay strong on principle, but he was here and offering, and principle didn't have arms to put around her. Still trying to decide how she felt about it, she slid to one side of the bed.

Lifting the covers, he slid in beside her. Long, hair-sprinkled legs entwined with hers as he gathered her into his arms. The comfort was immediate and staggering.

She turned into him, burying her face in his chest

while he stroked her hair. He wore nothing but a pair of silk boxers, she discovered, as she fitted her body to his. He was longer, broader, and more muscular than she, and the sensation of his bare body against hers caused a tension that was coiled tight inside of her to ease.

Better? he asked.

She nodded.

Tell me about it, he said. *The nightmare. Maybe if you talk about what happened, it will make it go away.*

She sighed. *The nightmare doesn't bear much resemblance to reality. I'm in the same warehouse where the shooting occurred, but in the dream, I'm lost and the gunman is chasing me, and that didn't happen. I never make it out, and he always catches me. I see the barrel of his gun—that did happen—and he shoots me, and I fall. I always fall.*

As he listened, he ran his fingers through her hair. The rhythmic caress soothed her like nothing else ever had. Her muscles went pliable and boneless. *You called out a name*, he said. *I couldn't make it out.*

It took her a moment to think back, then she remembered.

Rodrigo, she replied. *He's a good friend on the police force. He and I are the only ones who survived. There were five of us— me and a team of four officers. We were going to take out a magic user who'd suffered some kind of psychotic break. We underestimated him. We thought he was relatively harmless. Everyone we talked to who knew him said so. We didn't know he'd been stockpiling guns and ammunition.*

Nikolas said quietly, *Oh no.*

We were talking him down—or so we thought—and then we went in to take him into custody, but he'd been playing with us and only pretending to go along with it. I was part of the team in case he decided to get slaphappy with magic spells, but instead, he opened fire on us the moment we stepped inside and came into range. He knew how to shoot. We were wearing bulletproof vests, and he still killed three of us with headshots. He'd been preparing.

Nikolas ran his hand along her torso, touching the scar high on her shoulder, and the other one in her abdomen. *He caught you along the edges of your vest.*

She nodded. *Rodrigo took him out. He did CPR on me until the ambulances arrived. He saved my life.*

As she told the last of her tale, he pressed his lips to her forehead and didn't move again for several moments. He murmured, *After what you've gone through, you still fling yourself at danger.*

No, she said tiredly. *I fling myself at situations that may or may not be dangerous. I help a dog at the side of the road. I give a bunch of homeless guys a roof over their heads.*

He brought fingers to her lips, stroking them lightly. *You run into a pub to save a screaming woman. You run straight toward thirty attacking Hounds.*

It's just a thing, she whispered. *It's no big deal. It's who I am. You ran into the pub too.*

I ran into the pub because you were there, he said.

She refused to let that divert her. She told him, *You would have done the same thing if I hadn't been. When those two*

Hounds were attacking Cael, you ran toward them, not away. It's the same thing, Nik. We're more alike than not, at least about that.

He rolled her onto her back, came on top of her, and put his elbows on either side of her shoulders, the fingers of his hands laced together at the top of her head. She felt enclosed, surrounded. Instead of feeling trapped, it felt comforting and good. The rightness of it hurt more than almost anything else she had ever experienced.

"I've lost so many people," he breathed against her lips. "So many people, my Sophie. I think of their names and their faces until sometimes I think I've become nothing more than a remembrance hall that bears witness to each of their stories and how they ended. That part of me is threadbare and worn to the bone, and until you showed up, I thought I didn't have it in me to care about anyone else again. But now I do, and yes, I'm struggling, because I don't think I could take losing you too."

Before, in the courtyard, pain had driven her side of the conversation, but now as she listened to him, compassion moved her to stroke his back. She murmured, "I thought we were taking a time-out."

"I lied," Nikolas said, and he kissed her.

She lost herself in the sensation of his mouth moving on hers, the weight of his body, the warmth radiating off his skin. Desire hit her low and hard. Her body felt empty and aching, and as she bent her knee, sliding her foot along his leg, his cock stiffened into a hard, thick length that pressed against her hip.

I'm going to walk away from you after this, she whispered in his head as she slipped her hand around his erection and squeezed him. Hissing against her mouth, he thrust his hips forward, sliding his cock against her palm. *This is the last time, Nik. I swear it.*

We'll walk away from each other, he promised. He slanted his mouth over hers, kissing her with such wild heat, a moan trembled on her lips. He swallowed it down, thrusting deep with his tongue while he ran his fingertips along the edge of her panties. The light touch left a trail of fiery sensation in its wake. *As soon as I get you out of my system, I'm gone.*

The bastard was telling the truth. Furiously she bit his lip, and a gasp shuddered through him. So he was going to leave as soon as he got her out of his system. Fine. Two could play at that game.

At least now she knew what this was, she thought. It was (tremendous, mind-blowing, screaming, utterly fantastic, wildly pleasurable, heartbreaking) sex.

She would cut him off before he did it to her. This was the very last time, so she grew determined to make the most of it. Pushing against his shoulder, she urged him to lie on his back, and he complied, pushing back the covers as he stretched out on the bed.

Rising on one elbow, she did what she had wanted to do ever since the first time they had been together. She ran her lips down his body, learning by feel each muscle and hollow, the whorl of hair around his flat, male nipples, the vein that ran down his bicep. She ran the tip of her tongue around the curve of his belly button while he tensed his long, flat stomach with a hiss.

By the time she reached the edge of his silk boxers, she didn't have a lot of teasing coyness left. Pulling aside the material, she grasped his penis at the root and took him into her mouth while his whole body went rigid.

His hands shook as he cupped her head.

They had to be quiet, so quiet. The others were just on the other side of the boxes and crates that made up her bedroom. It was torturously difficult to muffle the sound of pleasure she wanted to make as she suckled at the head of his cock.

He tasted earthy, delicious. Dizzy with enchantment, she licked down the side of his erection, relishing the velvet skin with the taut, hard flesh underneath. Cupping his sac, she molded and caressed him while she opened her throat to take him in all the way.

By then his whole body flowed like molten fire under her touch. He felt like he was burning up. She worked him, and worked him, drawing him in entirely before pulling back to the tip, while he swore an endless telepathic litany of profanities.

She had nowhere to put the noises she needed to make. It all had to go into his head. She crooned and sometimes laughed at his inventive swearing and told him how wonderful he felt and tasted, and how much she wanted to take him inside.

He reached down to circle her throat with one hand while he pumped, fiercely silent, between her parted lips. *Your mouth is like fire and silk.* He warned, *I don't think I can hold back.*

Delighted, hungry for him, she gasped. *Do it. I want you to come in my mouth.*

Gods damn—here. Here it is.

He slammed one fist into the mattress as he convulsed, and his cock began to pulse, jetting semen into her mouth. She milked at him and took all of it while she ran one flattened hand up the tense, shaking muscles of his abdomen. When his climax appeared to ease, she lifted her head and wiped her mouth.

Come here, he growled. *I'm not done yet.*

It was the Wyr mating urge. He gripped her hips and lifted her over his body until she straddled him. Then he took hold of his erection and rubbed it against her hypersensitive, private flesh, making sure she was ready for him before he pushed upward.

She was so empty she ached with it and shaking so hard she could barely keep herself propped up. He felt bigger and harder than ever as he entered her. As he pushed in, and in, she stretched to accommodate him, twisting at the piercing pleasure of his penetration.

Her breath came in quiet sobs. He put a shaking hand over her mouth. *Hush*, he said fiercely. *This is just ours. Just yours and mine.*

Blocking everyone else out. Nothing else mattered. Pride, hurt feelings, expectations, they all burned away until only they were left.

Male. Female.

Nikolas. Sophie.

He thrust into her until he reached a hard, driving rhythm, and she rode him as best she could. Reaching between their bodies, he stroked her gently at the place where they were joined. When he found her clitoris with the ball of his thumb, she was so primed to come it punched through her like a storm with gale force winds.

Shaking all over, she whimpered into his muffling hand as she climaxed until the peak came at such a height, she couldn't take any more of it, and she jerked his thumb away.

They held together, joined at the groin, in the great room's chill silence. The only sound she could hear was the quiet seesaw of their ragged breathing.

Then he sat up, wrapped his arms around her, and flipped their positions so that she lay underneath him again. He clamped tight around her, one arm around her hip, the other at the base of her neck, holding her clenched against the entire length of his body. It was a taut, uncomfortable pose. She could barely move. All she could do was grip him around the hips with her legs and wrap her arms around his torso.

He was still inside her, still hard and big, and now she was so sensitized every slight movement sent shock waves through her body.

Then he began to move again, hard, quick jabs that rocked her to the core. She really, truly didn't think she could take any more, but then she took it, still in that extreme silence until tears welled and flowed out the corners of her eyes.

She came again two more times before he was finally through. Toward the end, all she could do was hide her face in his neck and cling while the storm of his own making shuddered through them.

The Wyr mating urge might not force him to stay with her. He might still be able to walk away. But no matter how she tried to lie to herself, she was no longer certain she had that ability.

This isn't a cold, she thought. This isn't the flu. This is a soul-destroying illness that will tear me to pieces before it kills me.

Afterward, he gathered her against his chest, turning his head so that his cheek lay against the crown of her head. Resting against his shoulder, she fell into another black pit, only this one was without dreams. He had taken the scorched earth approach and blasted everything else out of her mind, leaving only him.

She slept long and hard, and when she woke up, she was alone in the bed. Her bladder was full and her stomach uncomfortably empty. Filtered sunlight from the iron-framed, antique glass windows at one end of the great hall cast an indirect, thin light over the top of the crates and boxes and created deep shadows in her tiny bedroom.

Sighing, she curled on her side and hugged a pillow to her chest. He could have stayed long enough to kiss her good-bye in the morning. They both might know what this is, but there were courtesies.

Finally her physical discomfort grew so much she was forced to dress. She dragged on the same jeans and sweater she had put on after the stormy battle last night and tried to fingercomb the tangles out of her hair. The curls sprang out everywhere in a mad, chaotic halo, but she felt too disheartened to dig for her comb and hair bands to force it into more order.

She had a feeling she looked like something a cat might have dragged down an alley before abandoning it, deeming it too pathetic for its attention.

There was an unfortunate metaphor in that.

As she sat on the bed to pull on her Doc Martens, she saw a bottle of nail polish sitting on the bedside table. Nikolas had returned what was left to her. Picking the bottle up, she shook it. As she had feared, very little remained in the bottle.

She still had the spells she had painted on her arms from yesterday afternoon, minus the one confusion spell she had used on the Hound, but those would peel off and degrade. After that, she might be able to cast one more spell, maybe two, and then her little made-up arsenal would be depleted.

Sighing, she tucked the bottle into the bedside table's shallow drawer, lifted the privacy curtain, and stepped out into the communal area. Several of the men sat at the table, drinking tea and talking. The smell of bacon hung in the air.

As she appeared, they turned to look at her. There was a moment of silence.

Then Rowan said, "I mean this in an entirely platonic way, but that crazy hair of yours has got to be one of the sexiest things I've ever seen."

"Do you have a death wish, mate?" Cael said to him.

Rowan lifted his hands. "I said I meant it platonically!"

Warmth washed over her cheeks. Nikolas stood with Braden and Ashe, over by the windows between the Mini and the Harley, looking out. He didn't turn at the exchange.

She said telepathically to Gawain, *I'm about to start tap dancing here. I know you've promised that either you or Nikolas would stay with me at all times, but you're all here in the great hall. I think I'm perfectly safe to go to the bathroom by myself.*

He frowned. *That will probably do for now.*

She told the group, "Privacy alert. I'm going to take a few necessary moments in the courtyard, so I'd appreciate it if everybody stayed here until I got back."

There. Now that she drew attention to it, everybody would be obligated to stay in the great hall.

Gawain told her, "There's soap and a bucket of water on the bench. It'll be cold, but you can have a bit of a wash too, if you like. We have a couple of solar showers—black bags with sprinkler nozzles that heat up in the sunlight—so later in the afternoon there'll be warmer water for showers."

"That sounds amazing," she said with such heartfelt fervency, a couple of the men grinned.

She slipped into the courtyard to take care of business and wash up, and she took a few minutes to wrestle her hair into a long, thick braid that fell down her back. When she returned, Cael slipped a plate of bacon and eggs in front of her, along with a cup of black coffee. He said, "The eggs will be good for a few days, so we should enjoy them while we can."

"Thank you so much." She glanced again at Nikolas and the other two men by the window, then turned her attention to the hot meal.

As she ate, Cael slipped a couple of pieces of toast on her plate. At first there was a lull in the conversation, but then, as the men grew used to her presence, the talk resumed.

They had a lot to say to one another after such a long, enforced solitude. From what she could glean, as she listened, they had only gathered at the solstices to raise the energies to contact home. Despite the danger of their situation and her own pessimistic outlook, they were relishing the chance to relax together, which made her smile.

As she finished the last of her breakfast, Nikolas stalked over. He was dressed in black again—she didn't think he wore any other color—and while she couldn't see his sword harness through the cloaking spell, she would bet good money he was wearing it. He looked leaner, darker, and harder than ever, and his dark eyes glittered with an expression she didn't want to try to interpret.

He said, "Ready to get to work?"

Her jaw tightened. "Good morning to you," she said. "How are you today, Sophie? I'm fine, thank you very much. I got a good night's sleep. How are you, Nik? Oh, I'm suffering from a severe case of rudeness this morning, but other than that, I'm okay."

Someone across the table made a strangled noise. She thought it might have been Gareth. Other than that, dead silence washed over the group. Nobody looked at Nikolas or at her although Rowan suddenly looked several shades redder than usual.

Nikolas gave her a dangerous smile. "Glad we have the pleasantries out of the way," he said in a silken voice. "Are you ready to get to work? I packed supplies for us."

Reaching close to the floor at one end of the table, he picked up two backpacks.

Oh God. She was going to have to spend the entire day with Mr. Sunshine. She glanced at Gawain for help, but he wasn't looking at her either. With obvious reluctance, she said, "I guess so."

"We've got a lot to do. Let's go."

She would not scowl. She would not give him the

satisfaction of letting him know he got to her. Pushing back from the table, she said to Cael, "Thank you for breakfast."

"You're welcome," he told her.

Nikolas said to the group, "We don't know what's going to happen when we encounter shifts. We'll try to keep you posted, but don't get too alarmed if we don't show up in sync with the day as you know it. And set up a schedule of round-the-clock watches, two men for each shift."

She joined him. "Watches?"

He told her grimly, "Morgan's here."

Her stomach clenched. "That's why you were watching out the window?"

"Yes."

She went over to the windows, murmuring, "Pardon me," to Ashe, who moved to let her look out. The thick square windowpanes were small and dirty, and the view through the antique glass was wavery and distorted, but she could still see the familiar tall, broad-shouldered figure who stood on the lawn, about twenty yards away.

Morgan had his arms crossed, and he studied the house with his chin tucked down. On either side of him, both men and Hounds stretched as far as she could see. She didn't have to see for herself to know they would have surrounded the entire house.

Ashe said, "He's been out there like that since dawn. Trying to figure out a way in, I expect."

Nikolas put a hand on her shoulder. Turning to him, she said, "I'm ready."

He handed her a backpack. "Lead the way. Where do you want to start?"

Immediately she turned to walk down the hall where she had found the first shift. "We know this one is here. And we know of the one in the courtyard. Let's get those marked first, then we'll move on." Telepathically she asked, *Why did you set watches?*

He said, *The house might not be in alignment with the land outside, but once those front doors are open, anybody can pass through. They can either go in—or out. And anybody from the inside can open the doors. I tested it myself yesterday.*

She frowned. *You're thinking the traitor might try to open them and let the enemy in—or get out?*

I'd say that was a distinct possibility. As soon as that thought occurred to me, I got up and kept watch until the others woke up.

The heaviness that had weighed her down since waking lifted somewhat. *I didn't hear you leave.*

Good. I didn't want to disturb you. You needed the rest.

She was so focused on him she almost forgot to watch for the place where she had felt the shift until they had almost stepped over it.

"Wait!" she said, grabbing his arm. "We're here."

The hall looked the same in both directions. Nikolas frowned. "I can't sense it."

"Maybe this one is a smaller shift, and you'll be able to sense a bigger one," she said. She frowned. "How are we going to measure what happens on either side of a shift? We can see the hall clearly—just like we can see the house from outside—but there will be a difference once we step to the other side."

"I think one of us needs to step over, while the other stays on this side," Nikolas told her. "Then we each count to ten. We can practice how fast we count so that we're keeping the same time. The first one who hit ten reaches for the other one. Since clocks don't work, it's not going to be an exact measurement, but it will give us an idea of what to expect."

"Okay, let's try it."

They practiced the beat of the count a few times, then Nikolas told her, "See you on the other side."

He stepped over the shift, and she started to count. When she hit seven, he reached for her hand and stepped to her side again. "That is so strange," she muttered.

"What number did you hit?" he asked.

"Seven, and we couldn't have been counting that far off from each other. So this means down the hall that way, time flows faster than it does over here and in the great hall." Kneeling, she opened her pack and pulled out a small can of white paint and a brush. "They didn't get colors."

"I don't think they understood what you wanted."

She gave him a sidelong grin. "Doesn't matter. We can just number the zones."

Nikolas pulled out a pad of paper and sketched as

she painted a line across the hall, then to one side by the wall, she painted 7:10. "The seven is on this side of the shift. The colon is the shift itself, and the ten is on the other side. Make sense?"

He nodded. "It does." He pointed down the hall. "One thing—we don't want to number that zone. We might go all the way around the house and come at this hall from the other side. If we label that 'zone two' right now and keep numbering zones as we find the shifts, this area might end up getting labeled 'zone nine' on the other side. To avoid confusion, I think the only zone we can label right now is the great hall."

"I hadn't thought of that." She sat back on her heels. "So the only things we should map right now are the floor plan and the shifts. We can label everything afterward."

"Right." He squatted beside her, leaned forward, and gave her a quick, hard kiss.

Hey. That wasn't playing by any of the rules either one of them had set up. She scowled, disturbed, maybe a little angry, and maybe more than a little delighted. "Stop that."

"I need to hear you say it." Nikolas's dark eyes were intense, heated, and far too close for her comfort. "Say, 'Nikolas, I want you to stop that.'"

He wanted to hear the truth or falsehood in what she said. "No. I'm not going to play your games."

"I'm not playing any games, remember?"

Tears pricked at the back of her eyes. Turning her

face away, she stood as she asked, "Then what the hell are you doing?"

"I can't leave you alone. I don't want to." He rose to stand beside her, still too close. "I heard the lie in your voice when you said last night was the last night."

"Screw you, Nik." She gave him a look filled with bitter hurt. "I heard the truth in yours, when you said as soon as you got me out of your system, you're gone."

His expression changed. As he reached out to her, a low rumbling noise started and rose in volume until Sophie could feel it vibrating through her feet.

Dread bolted through her. "What is that? It sounds like an earthquake."

"It's Morgan," Nikolas snarled. "He's calling up the land magic."

They raced back to the great hall and the front window, where the rest of the men had gathered, their expressions grim. Slowly the rumble died away. Nikolas shouldered his way to the window. There were too many men in the way for Sophie to follow him, so she climbed on the hood of the Mini to look out.

The low rumble began and rose in intensity. Rubbing a clear spot on the dirty window to peer through, she saw Morgan kneeling on the lawn, hands flattened, his pose similar to the one Nikolas had used when he had buried the Hounds. Morgan's head and shoulders were bowed, and even from that distance, she could see the strain in his body. Behind him, a tree toppled over and crashed into the roof of the cottage.

Rage and fear hit in equal measures. "He's destroying my property!"

Nikolas said harshly, "This must be how he broke the crossover passageways. He's using land magic to try to break through to the house. Can he do it?"

She sank both hands into the hair at her temples and squeezed her eyes shut as she tried to think. Could Morgan do it? *This* piece of land wasn't in alignment with *that* piece of land. Like Nikolas's morningstar, any kind of missile wouldn't make a direct hit.

But this wasn't a missile. This was a kind of magic she had never encountered before, and if Nikolas could call upon the land magic to bury thirty Hounds, what could Morgan do?

Somehow he could call upon the land magic Powerfully enough to break entire crossover passageways.

Opening her eyes again, she confronted nine sets of eyes watching her intently. Reluctantly she told them, "He doesn't carry Djinn magic, so he might not be able to get inside the house, but he might be able to bury the house with us in it."

Chapter Nineteen

NIKOLAS'S EYES NARROWED. "But the house isn't entirely in his dimension, right?"

"If his reach goes far enough and he causes enough damage, I don't think that's going to matter. What if he gets the land magic to swallow most of it up and we can't find a way to get out of the other parts? We'll still be trapped, and we'll still die." She shook her head. "I don't pretend to understand how all this works, but he is causing the earth to quake out there—and we're feeling it in here—so to a certain extent what he is doing will affect us. I've never encountered a magic user of his strength before."

Immediately Nikolas said, "We have to step up our game. Mapping the house and labeling the shifts just became a group effort. We've got to get this done so we can analyze our findings and figure out if there's a pattern we can use to reach Lyonesse."

He didn't say what they were going to do if they couldn't reach Lyonesse, Sophie noted, and nobody asked him. He went on to explain how they were going to map.

Sophie would locate the shifts and move on, leaving the men to work in pairs to paint the borders, test and catalog the time differences. When each pair finished, they would run to catch up. The process would be bumpy, and there would be some time lags as they moved through each shift, but it was still the quickest way to get the job done.

"And it's very important to make note of whatever we're seeing outside the windows," Sophie added. "We need to try to figure out if there's a pattern—or if anything seems familiar to you."

As she said it, she prayed, please let there be a pattern. Please let someone see something they recognize from home.

"Grab supplies and be quick," Nikolas told them. "Get food, water, lanterns, and tools. We might have to force our way into spaces. When we head out, we won't stop until we're done."

She and Nikolas stood in tense silence as they waited for the men to join them. The low rumble started again, shaking through their feet. It reached a peak, then subsided.

She couldn't imagine what kind of Power it took to cause that quake repeatedly. Morgan couldn't keep it up indefinitely. He would have to rest at some point. If he wasn't able to break through by evening, they might get a respite overnight.

That did little to make her feel better in this moment. Needing to feel the simple, animal comfort of

Nikolas's proximity, she moved to stand beside him, and in response, he rested a hand at the nape of her neck. She hooked her fingers in a belt loop of his pants. Neither one of them said anything, for which she was grateful. They had both shown themselves quite capable of ruining a moment, but this time they refrained.

Then the men returned, rounding the corner at a jog, and they began. They went down the hall, discovering a library and a chapel and stairs.

"Shift," she said, squatting to draw a quick line with the chalk near one corner of the chapel. Rhys and Cael paused to finish up, while the rest of the group moved on.

There were books in the library, she saw to her amazement, and manuscripts, and trunks, presumably filled with things. Apparently, Kathryn Shaw's ancestors not only didn't care to keep good records, they also didn't value reading very much either since they didn't bother to take the contents of the library with them when they left.

If we live through this, she vowed, this is the first place I'm coming back to.

At that point, Robin came bounding up to join Nikolas and Sophie. He climbed up Sophie's body and clung to her neck. She let him ride her back, drawing comfort from his presence.

They took the stairs two at a time until she stopped with a hitch. "Shift."

While they waited, she drew a line across the stairway. This time Ashe and Thorne stopped to finish up, while the rest moved on.

Upstairs, they found the family private chambers, six rooms all told. A scattering of items remained behind, along with a few moth-eaten tapestries. There was another stairwell that led back down to the courtyard that held the privy chambers, fruit trees, and the well across the way.

Then there was the kitchen, the buttery, the pantry, a smoke room and, down below the kitchen, a larder, which Sophie learned was a place to keep things cool.

"Shift," she said.

And again. "Shift."

"Shift."

Each time she drew a line, and she and Nikolas kept moving, while the others stayed behind in pairs to finish the job. They saw nothing out the windows that looked like it might be Lyonesse. All they saw were variations on the scenes around the house. From one window, they looked out at the courtyard in deep winter. Snow piled in great drifts across the open space.

There was an interior hall from the kitchens leading back to the great hall. Then, to the back of the courtyard, there were the servants' quarters and what looked to be a small barracks, a room with rotting racks that Gawain said was an armory, and even two cells at the end of a corridor.

"There's a shift nearby, I can feel it," she murmured, turning around in confusion near the cells at the end of the corridor. She felt like Pac-Man, stuck in a corner with no yellow dots to eat. "How many have we found so far?"

"Eleven," Nikolas said.

They had been combing the house for hours. She was tired, thirsty, and hungry, but nobody suggested they quit. The periodic quake that rose from the earth and shuddered through the house's ancient bones drove them onward.

They had lost two of their pairs, Rhys and Cael, and Rowan and Gareth. God only knew when the four would catch up with them.

As she turned around again, clenching her hands in frustration, Nikolas dug into his pack and pulled out a bottle of water. He thrust it into her hands. "Take a minute. Drink."

Accepting the need for at least a brief break, she moved down the hall a few yards, away from the others, while she tried to think. Robin jumped to the ground and ran through the rooms in the corridor. The puck appeared to be searching too.

Sophie dropped her pack and eased into a sitting position, with her back against the wall. Sticking her knees up, she propped her elbows on them and buried her head in her hands.

Nobody said anything, but she felt like such a failure. It was her fault they were all trapped inside the house. She shot off her big mouth and speculated on things that she didn't know enough about, and because of her, all their lives were now in danger.

Well, and hers too, but by this point, she felt like she deserved whatever she got. She couldn't even find the stupid shift nearby even though it felt massive, like all the other shifts put together.

Another low rumble began, shaking through the house. It vibrated through the stone. She felt it in her ass and through her ankles, coming up from below.

Coming up from below, in the earth, just like the massive shift.

Robin caught her attention. The monkey was loping in circles, inside one of the cells. As she stared at him, he slapped the floor with both hands.

Excitement lifted away the dread. She leaped to her feet. "I've got it! The shift is below us!"

Quick footsteps came up from behind. At first she thought it was Nikolas, but then hard hands like manacles circled her neck, choking her. Her attacker spun her around so that they faced the other men, clamping her back against his chest with a hand around her throat while out of the corner of her eye, she saw him reach for the knife in his belt. He drew it and held the tip to her jugular.

They were all so much faster than she was. It happened so quickly she barely had time to grab hold of his forearm.

Several feet away, she caught a glimpse of the others—Gawain, Braden, Thorne, and Nikolas. That meant Ashe was the one who had taken her hostage.

The men lunged down the hall toward them. Nikolas's expression turned savage.

"Back up," Ashe barked. "Back up, or I'll break her neck! I mean it, Nik—I'll snap her like a twig. Back the fuck up!"

The men jerked to a halt.

"I'm going to murder you," Nikolas whispered.

His eyes blazed, and his features seemed to… shift?

She blinked. He looked wrong somehow, monstrous, with talons instead of fingers. She had heard sometimes Wyr partially shifted when they were under extreme emotional stress. Was that what was happening?

"We're going to walk to the front door, you and me," Ashe growled in her ear. "And then we're going to walk out of this godsforsaken place. I don't have to hurt you if you cooperate and they keep their distance, understand? What happens to you is your choice."

Oh sure, except for the knife to her throat, and by the way, what would happen to her once Ashe got to the front door? He couldn't let her go and still hope to escape Nikolas, and she had a feeling Morgan would no longer be quite so friendly and nonthreatening if and when they came face-to-face again.

Which spell should she use, telekinesis or confusion? The tip of that knife pressing into her flesh was awfully pesky. Even if he got confused by the spell, he might still retain enough presence of mind to press it home.

Oh man, this was going to suck.

She had to do both actions simultaneously. Bracing herself back against his chest, she pushed as hard as she could against his forearm, lifting the tip of the knife momentarily from her throat—just an inch, but hopefully it would be enough. With her other hand, she reached back and smacked him upside the head.

The blow lifted them in the air and sent them flying back several feet. As Ashe crashed into the wall, his hold on her loosened. She crashed into Ashe, which wasn't quite as bad as stone, but it was still bad enough. A line of burning pain flared along her collarbone as the edge of his knife ran across her upper body. They fell in a sprawling tangle of arms and legs.

She didn't have to win this fight. All she had to do was get out of the way. Kicking free of him, she rolled and kept rolling.

A heavy weight slammed down on her. *Ugh!*

She got ready to smack Ashe with the other telekinesis spell, but then she realized the man was covering her body with his.

"Easy, lass," Gawain muttered in her ear as he sheltered the back of her head with both hands. "I've got you."

Overhead, there was a cyclone of savage movement and breathless cursing. She tried to turn her head to see what was going on, but Gawain's hands were in the way. She gasped, "I can't see."

"Hold on."

As the fight shifted down the corridor, Gawain lifted off her. Hooking one arm around her waist, he picked her up and ran several feet away. Only then did he set her on her feet, and together they turned to the confrontation.

Nikolas was the cyclone, but she knew that before she ever laid eyes on him. He had drawn his sword and was slashing with vicious, brutal accuracy at Ashe, who gave way down the hall and parried as well as he could with his knife.

"Did you tell the Light Court where I was going to be on the road to the solstice gathering?" Nikolas asked. "When I showed up that night, you asked me if I had taken the M6."

"I'm sorry I grabbed her! Look, let's stop to talk about this." Ashe backed down the hall. "I lost my head, Nik. That's all it was. I swear it."

Even Sophie heard the lie in that. Ashe's face twisted, and he swore under his breath.

Nikolas lunged so fast he turned into a blur. Suddenly a line of red appeared down the side of Ashe's face. "Did you tell them about the puck? How Gawain and I met in the pub in Westmarch? *Did you, you son of a bitch?*"

Pressing relentlessly forward, he lunged again and pierced Ashe high in one shoulder. Ashe reeled back, then in a liquid twist, advanced to slash at Nikolas's abdomen. With a catlike grace, Nikolas leaped back, and the attempted blow went wide.

"How many people, Ashe?" he asked. "How many of our people did you kill with small betrayals? What did they pay you? How much were our lives worth to you?"

Suddenly Ashe roared, "It wasn't about how much your lives were worth! It was about saving mine! They were killing us—they've been killing us *for centuries!*— with no way home, no way out."

Nikolas paused, chest heaving. "You could have deserted."

Bitterly Ashe snapped, "With what money? How far could I have gotten? I struck a deal for amnesty and enough cash to start a new life and get out from under this godsforsaken doom the Dark Court has been under *for centuries.* All I had to do was feed them information until I could deliver you to them. Once the commander of the Dark Court force had fallen, I would be free. Then *she* showed up and found her way into this pile of shit, and you decided it would be a bright idea to make this your last fucking stand."

"The Hounds waited to attack until you and Gawain had left with the lorry, didn't they? That's why you insisted on going." After such an extremity of rage and movement, Nikolas held still and sounded eerily calm. "You told them we had come here. You turned this into our last fucking stand, Ashe. You did this."

Down the hall, the other four men had appeared. They walked forward, staring, their expressions stricken and shocked. The pain and rage emanating from every one of the men was so raw and palpable Sophie could hardly bear it.

She felt like she shouldn't be watching the confrontation. This was their betrayal and their pain, and they had the right to deal with it in privacy, but there was nowhere she could go to escape it. They blocked the way to the courtyard. All she could do was retreat into the cell with Robin. Sitting on the floor, she scooped him into her arms.

An odd, incongruent sound filled the hall as Ashe began to laugh. He staggered, shoulders shaking. The blood from his shoulder wound had spread down his side.

"I guess you're right, Nik. I was too goddamn stupid to make a break then. The deal did hinge on your life, after all."

"Why didn't they attack the group at summer solstice?"

"Because they thought they were going to get you before then. I'd already met up with the others by the time we found out what had happened, and besides, you might have gotten away. I thought I might still meet the bargain if I could only let them into the house when everyone was sleeping—but everybody had so much to say to one another, some of you talked through the night, and then this morning, you got the bright idea to set watches. What a clusterfuck, hey?" He looked around at the circle of stony faces surrounding them. "None of it was personal."

"Well, it felt pretty fucking personal to me," Nikolas said. He sprang forward, and his sword flashed again.

This time it was a direct hit to Ashe's heart. Ashe didn't try to dodge or parry. Instead, he let his arms fall to his side and accepted the blow. Sophie covered her head with a hand. The body fell to the floor with an audible thump.

Afterward, heavy silence descended in the hall.

Rhys said thickly, "I suspected someone was working with the Light Court. Nik, I'm sorry, I thought it was you."

"And I thought it was you. You asked enough questions, I thought you were pumping me for information, and you killed the Hound I wanted to interrogate. I didn't connect that the only one besides Gawain who wasn't present for the attack was Ashe until he grabbed Sophie." Nikolas sounded so soul weary Sophie's eyes dampened. "He was right about one thing. Gods, what a clusterfuck."

While the men talked, Robin tugged on Sophie's sweater. Wiping her eyes, she looked at the puck. *Ooh-ooh*, he mouthed. He slapped the floor by her thigh. Then he slapped it again, and again, so insistently it caught her attention.

Here, Robin said telepathically. *Down here.*

Frowning, she concentrated. Robin was right. The massive shift was directly down below. This close, it felt bigger than ever.

For the first time, she focused on the floor of the cell. Part of it was wooden. She ran her fingers along one side while she studied the square. There were hinges.

A pair of boots appeared in the corner of her vision. She looked up as Nikolas knelt beside her. His expression was bitter but composed, until he looked down at her sweater.

Then his eyes blazed, and he grabbed hold of her with tense care. "Goddamn it, Sophie! Why didn't you say something?"

"About what?"

Her gaze followed the direction of his, down to her shirtfront. Okay, that looked pretty bad. Blood had soaked into her sweater, and it had run down her side. She looked as awful as Ashe had.

Making a face, she told him, "I forgot about it. It looks worse than it is. He caught me on the collarbone. Nik, there's a trapdoor."

"Who the fuck cares?" he said. His touch was much more gentle than his tone, as he eased the collar of her sweater aside so he could inspect the wound. He pressed lightly against her skin near the long cut.

"Ouch! Stop that!" She tried to shrink away from him.

"Goddammit," he growled. *"Hold still."*

Something about the way he said that told her he was barely holding on to his self-control. She forced herself to sit still, although she couldn't help from bitching about it.

"You will never learn how to ask politely, will you?" she muttered. "How hard is it to say, 'Will you please hold still a moment, Sophie?' Well, let me tell you, it's not hard, because I just said it."

"He cut you to the bone, you stupid woman," Nikolas snapped.

She opened her eyes wide. "Why are you calling me stupid, like that was *my* fault?"

She had seen Nikolas angry before, but this time his rage seemed transcendent. "You *hit him* with a telekinesis spell *while he held a knife to your throat!*"

His taut expression was so full of rage and pain and residual fear she paused and tried to swallow the snarky response that rose to her lips.

Setting her hand gently to the side of his furious, dangerous face, she said in a soft voice, "Well, yes. Yes, I did. I'm so sorry I did something to get myself out of a bad situation instead of waiting for you or one of the other menfolk to rescue me. Next time I'll go sit in a tower and learn how to knit, mm-kay?"

So… swallowing the snark hadn't exactly been a success. As they stared at each other, she watched a muscle tic in the side of his jaw, and she almost, very nearly, yes indeed came so close to feeling bad about that.

Cupping her hand to his cheek, he placed the flat of his palm over her injured collarbone, gathered his

Power, and spoke in his Celtic-sounding language. Warmth spread over the area, and she could feel the torn flesh knitting together. It was not an altogether comfortable sensation, but that was such a small price to pay for the healing, she gritted her teeth and stuck with it.

When he had finished, he pressed a kiss to her fingers and whispered, "You still make me. So. Crazy."

She loved him so much it twisted her up inside. Stroking his lips with her thumb, she smiled as she whispered back, "And you're still very much an asshole." She shifted to lean her forehead against his. *I'm so sorry about Ashe.*

He took in a deep breath. *It had to be one of them. I'm glad I killed him.*

Another shock wave rose from the earth. This time the rumble was so long and sustained the structure over their heads groaned from strain. Nikolas's face tightened. He said calmly, "Maybe we should step out into the courtyard."

"No," she told him. She patted the floor. "We need to go down."

Gawain and Rowan shouldered their way into the cell. Coming down on one knee beside them, Gawain said, "Lass, this is most likely an oubliette. There won't be anything but a pit down there and no way to get out if the building comes down around our ears."

She twisted to look at Robin, who hovered at her elbow.

Down, the puck said. She had never seen him look so desperate. *Robin needs to go down.*

Robin isn't going by himself, she told him. Turning to Nikolas, she said, "Going out to the courtyard is just a way to prolong death. While this isn't a guarantee of anything, there's a massive shift down there. Let's at least take a look."

Instantly Nikolas scooped her into his arms and rose to his feet. Striding to one side of the cell, he ordered, "You heard her. Get the trapdoor open."

Once he stepped off the wooden section, he set her on her feet. Gawain and Rowan threw themselves at the task, while Rhys slid into the cell to help. The others crowded around outside, looking in. Not one of them, Sophie noted, left to go to the courtyard.

The hinges had rusted, and it took the combined strength of all three men to pry the floor up. As it creaked open, it revealed a lightless black of unknown depth. The monkey leaped into the oubliette.

"Robin!" Sophie flung herself forward, hand outstretched, but she was too late to stop the puck.

Rowan rubbed his face and swore. Nikolas said, "Get one of the lanterns down there."

The group had two lanterns with them. Cael lit one of them, tore the edge of his T-shirt into a strip to tie around the handle, and passed it forward. Accepting it, Nikolas lowered it into the blackness.

The light touched rough-hewn rock along the sides and what looked like it might be the bottom. Sophie leaned farther to get a better look. At the very edge of the light, she caught sight of the puck. While she couldn't tell for sure, he appeared to be digging.

"Massive shift, you say." Nikolas rubbed his chin.

She repeated, "Massive."

He looked around at his men. "We're going to go down. If the shift is that big, there's no telling how long it will take. If any of you want to go to the courtyard, go ahead and do it."

"Sod off," Cael said, mildly enough. "The sooner you get down there, the sooner we can follow."

Sophie held out her hands. "Lower me down."

She half expected Nikolas to start an argument about who got to go first, but instead, he took hold of her hands. They locked their fingers around each other's wrists, and when she nodded that she was ready, he swung her down into the darkness. When he had lowered her as far as he could, he released her wrists and she dropped, landing in a crouch to save her ankles.

As soon as she hit bottom, she scrambled to the side, and Nikolas leaped in after her. They took hold of the lantern and moved deeper into the pit, as one by one, the men jumped down to join them. Cael and Gareth lit the second lantern.

The pit was larger than Sophie had expected. Followed by Nikolas, she scrambled over the uneven, rocky terrain to reach Robin.

As she reached the monkey's side, he looked at her,

eyes huge and frantic. He said out loud, "*Home.*"

It was as if Robin had doused the men with gasoline and lit a match. They blazed with so much hope it was almost unbearable to look at them.

"He's a nature sprite," Nikolas said. "He knows home when he senses it." He twisted. "Get anything you can dig with!"

"Out of the way, lass." Without asking, Gawain picked her up and passed her back to the men behind him.

Braden took hold of her and passed her back to Rowan. She didn't protest being manhandled. In this case, it was clear she was outclassed, and there wasn't enough room to take up space just because she was curious.

They attacked the earth with hand axes and crowbars. Watching from the rear, she caught only glimpses now and then of Nikolas. When the men at the forefront paused, at first she didn't see what was going on, but then she felt a ripple up ahead, and she knew Nikolas was working with the land magic.

Gawain said, "That got us a good six meters. Do it again."

There was a pause, and another wave rippled out. The men moved forward and started digging again.

Left to her own devices for the moment, Sophie found an outcrop of rock and went to sit down. Something crunched under her feet. Looking down, she realized she had stepped on a long bone, perhaps a femur. A bare skull lay nearby.

She picked it up to study it. Someone had died down here, alone in the blackness. Maybe they had been a criminal, but maybe they had just been an enemy. It was even possible the victim had been one of Nikolas's people.

Kathryn Shaw might be wonderful, and her father sounded like he'd been a miracle to many, but those earlier Shaws...

They didn't like to read, she thought. They didn't like to write. They threw people into black pits. They sided with the Light Court. Those earlier Shaws had been terrible people.

Sighing, she sat, set the skull in her lap, and wrapped her arms around it while she waited.

Another wave rippled through the land magic, and a sharp, cold wind blew into the pit. A thin, pale illumination followed. Someone roared—she thought it was Braden—and then others joined in. They hacked and slashed at the ground in a frenzy until suddenly they surged forward.

Still holding the skull, Sophie stood and picked her way forward through the short tunnel they had created. Details came clearer, as one by one, they climbed out of the hole. Outside, despite the biting chill of a winter wind, they hugged one another while someone laughed. Another one sobbed.

Sophie was the last one out, staring at the heavy snowfall that weighted the limbs of nearby pine trees.

Pine trees that grew in Lyonesse. It was twilight, and the thin illumination came from a moon wreathed in storm clouds.

As she climbed awkwardly up, Nikolas's head and shoulders suddenly filled the opening. He offered a hand, and she took it. When he helped her out of the hole, the fierce exhilaration in his expression hitched as he caught sight of the skull she had tucked under one arm.

"What on earth are you doing now, my Sophie?" he asked.

"I promised him I wouldn't leave him alone in the black pit," she explained. "Even though I might be centuries too late."

In the middle of the other men's jubilation, he stood still. Then he stepped forward to put his arms around her. He said from the back of his throat, "Thank you for bringing us all home."

In answer, she rested against the hard length of his body and put her head on his shoulder.

Then his arms loosened, and he pivoted. He said to the others, "We can't relax. We're not done. This is the only way we have right now to get back to Earth, and time here moves so much more slowly than it does there. We've got to get word to Annwyn at Raven's Craig as quickly as we can, muster troops, and climb back through to stop Morgan before he closes this passageway for good."

"Shit," Gawain swore. "Raven's Craig is a good ten

leagues from here. Even running as fast as we can, it will take us at least two days in this weather."

Nikolas said, "It might take us two days, but it wouldn't take Robin that long."

Shivering as the wind bit through her clothes, Sophie turned to look in the same direction as the others. Several yards away, the monkey played and rolled gleefully in the snow, flinging handfuls into the air.

What did Nikolas mean, it wouldn't take Robin that long to travel ten leagues? How long was a league? Assuming the men could run for two days, that would make it thirty miles? Forty?

And even assuming they could run that long, she couldn't.

Gawain said, "Even if he would agree to take a message, we can't send Robin by himself. He's been absent for too long. Annwyn would never trust him."

"Someone would have to go with him." Nikolas raised his voice. "Robin, we have a favor we need to ask of you! Will you carry one of us to Raven's Craig?"

As she listened, her questions kept coming. How would a monkey carry one of them thirty or forty miles?

But Robin wasn't really a monkey.

As Nikolas called out his question, the puck's head lifted, and he turned to look back at the group.

The puck said, "No."

Nikolas strode toward the puck. "I wouldn't ask it of you, except our need is so urgent. You can bargain for anything you like, and if it's in my Power to give it to you, I will."

Lifting one hairy arm, the monkey pointed around the group. "Not a single one of you looked for Robin. Not a single one of you asked if a puck might be all right, what might have happened to him, or how you might help."

"Robin," Gawain said, stepping forward too. "We didn't know any better, and I, for one, am so sorry."

"I'm sorry too," Nikolas said. "Deeply sorry. You deserved to have someone ask those things."

Sophie could hear the sincerity in both men's voices. She held her breath. Could Robin?

The monkey shook his head. "Still, I say no. What I would have bargained for, what I would have given my entire soul for, you already refused to give. I will consent to carry only one of you—for she is the only one who carried me and asked nothing in return."

Sophie was so wrapped up in the conversation, and also so tired, it was only when everyone turned to look at her that she realized who the puck was talking about. "Who, me?" she said. "I can't go to that place and talk to your people. They won't trust me any more than they would Robin."

Nikolas strode rapidly over to her.

He said, "Sophie, you have to. You're dressed in Earth clothes. You speak in a strange accent. Annwyn will listen to what you say, especially if you take her this." He twisted his signet ring off and offered it to her. "The only way you could be carrying the ring of the Dark Court commander is if you had traveled from Earth. Trust me—she will believe you."

Every taut line of his body was an intense plea. It was impossible to come this far only to refuse him.

She sighed. "Oh God, fine. I'll go."

She held out her hand, and he slipped the ring on her thumb. In return, she handed him the skull. Power shimmered in the air. When she looked in the puck's direction, the monkey had disappeared and a tall black stallion stood in its place.

He was magnificent, with fiery eyes and a mane and tail that flowed with magic. The pale moonlight shone on the muscled bulk of his shoulders and haunches. With a regal toss of his head, the puck sidestepped over to her.

She put a hand on his velvet nose and murmured, "I've never ridden a horse before."

"I will not let you fall," the puck told her.

When she turned back to Nikolas, he pulled her into his arms and kissed her hard. "None of us will be able to thank you enough for everything you've done."

"Shut up," she said. Of everything she might want to hear from him, gratitude didn't play any part of it. This is why you don't kiss assholes, Soph—yet still you keep kissing him and kissing him. The wind gusted, and she shivered harder. "Help me get up on his back before I change my mind."

Setting the skull on the ground, Nikolas put his

hands around her waist and lifted her effortlessly onto the stallion's wide back. Thankfully, the puck radiated heat, so she had some hope of not freezing solid within the first ten yards.

As she glanced around at the men, they all looked so solemn it was beginning to scare her.

She sank her hands into the stallion's mane. "Run your heart out, Robin."

The stallion reared. When he came down, his huge hooves struck fiery sparks.

Robin said, "We will run our hearts out together, dear love."

Chapter Twenty

AFTERWARD, SHE WAS never able to fully describe the experience of that ride.

There was a wild speed and so much magic, and the land sped past impossibly fast. Sparks from the stallion's hooves lit up the night, and something in the wind laughed in response.

Terrified and freezing, she lay along the stallion's back and clung with her knees while clenching her hands so tightly in his mane she couldn't feel her fingers. She tried to look out at the landscape, but the air was too frigid, and tears streamed down her face. Eventually she gave up and hid her face in the puck's mane while he raced along precipices and leaped over ravines.

Just when she thought she couldn't hold on any longer and she might fall off despite Robin's help, he surged up a long incline, past torchlit sentries, tents, campfires, and makeshift houses. Shouts rose behind them, far too late to stop the puck's forward movement.

Finally Robin galloped up to a stone building at the

top of a bluff. As guards ran up, one made as if to put his hand on Robin, and the stallion screamed a warning and reared in response, kicking out so violently the guards scrambled back.

Someone ran into the building, while Robin whirled to threaten off the guards that circled them.

"Stop doing that or I might be sick!" Sophie called out hoarsely as the world spun.

Baring his teeth at the guards, Robin stopped spinning.

Soon several more guards poured out of the building, along with a tall, auburn-haired woman in armor. "What is going on? Robin! Where have you been?"

"Away," said Robin. "I have been away and trapped by evil."

"I need to speak to Annwyn." Sophie's teeth chattered. "We came from Earth, and it's urgent."

"I'm Annwyn," the woman said, crossing her arms. "Get down and say what you've come to say."

That was easier said than done. The ground was so far away, and her fists had stiffened in Robin's mane. "Robin," she muttered. "Help me."

Bowing his head, the stallion went down on his front knees. Sophie slid off his back in an ungainly sprawl. When she yanked her hands free, she tore long black strands out of his mane, but he didn't complain.

She didn't trust herself to get to her feet. Instead, she turned on her knees to face Annwyn and the circle of suspicious guards staring down at her. Holding out her shaking hand, she showed them the gold commander's ring on her thumb. For the first time, she noticed the lion rampant on the head of the ring.

"Nikolas," Annwyn whispered. Lunging forward, she knelt in front of Sophie. "Bring a cloak and a hot drink!" Annwyn turned back to Sophie. "Are you wounded? You have blood all over you. You're insane to ride out in this weather dressed like that. How did you come here—and where is Nikolas?"

"I was wounded, but I'm healed now. We don't have time for niceties. Listen." Sophie grabbed her hands, and while Annwyn froze at her presumptuous touch, the other woman did not shake her off.

Words tumbled out of Sophie. Earth. A stray dog. The house. Broken passageway. Nikolas and the other men. The pub attack. Lycanthropes. Morgan.

She didn't mention Ashe. That matter felt too private and raw, and it deserved its own telling, by someone other than she.

"*Wait!*" This time it was Annwyn who grabbed hold of her. "They're *here*, in Lyonesse? You're saying you found a way through?"

"Yes, but we might l-l-lose it," she stuttered. Someone settled a fur-lined cloak around her shoulders, and someone else thrust a tankard of mulled wine into her hands. It was too hot for her frigid skin, and the tankard slipped through her clumsy, cold-numbed fingers to spill on the frozen ground. "Time moves faster on Earth than it does here, and when we left,

Morgan was trying to tear down the house. He might destroy the way back if we don't stop him."

Annwyn swore, then said behind her shoulder, "Muster a force of five hundred. We ride within the next half hour." As guards raced to do her bidding, she said sharply, "Puck! Your master is in an enchanted sleep, and we need to search for help from Earth. If we don't get Oberon the medical attention he needs, he'll die, and the idea of Lyonesse will die with him. Will you let us ride in your wind? I fear if we ride on our own, we will be too slow—and we will arrive too late again."

The puck stood protectively at Sophie's back. He blew in her hair. *Robin owes them nothing*, he said in her head. *Because nothing is what they did for him.*

She looked over her shoulder, into the stallion's fiery eyes. *Robin, you were hurt in your heart as well as in your body, and I understand how terrible that was. But sweetheart, not everybody could have known to look for you or send help. Not everybody abandoned you. The people in Lyonesse have been as caged as you were. Don't let your hurt blind you to what is true and right, because if you do, Isabeau will have destroyed you. She will have won. Please don't give that victory to her. You don't belong in the cage of your abuser any longer. Choose to be stronger than that. Choose to be free.*

The fire in the stallion's eyes grew hotter, brighter. He said, *And if we cannot get back to Earth, we can't defeat her.*

"Yes," she said out loud.

The puck said to Annwyn, "You may ride in my wind, this once."

Annwyn told him, "Thank you." The other woman turned her attention to Sophie. "You should stay here, rest, eat, and warm up. You are in no shape for another ride with the puck."

"No," Sophie said so fiercely the other woman looked taken aback. "Tie me to Robin's back if you must, but I have to go back."

"If you insist," Annwyn said.

AFTER SOPHIE AND Robin disappeared, the night felt even more cold and bleak with emptiness.

Finally Nikolas forced himself to stop looking after them. As he turned back to the other men, he found Braden standing at his elbow.

"Vicansha and the children are so close," Braden whispered.

Nikolas's chest tightened. As difficult as the last decades had been for him and the other men, they had been even harder for Braden.

He gripped Braden's shoulder. "When we get reinforcements, I'm releasing you from duty. You can go to your wife and children."

Tears spilled down the other man's taut face. "Thank you, sir."

Nikolas paused. "How do you do it?" he asked. "How do you make that kind of commitment, when we live such dangerous lives?"

Braden shrugged and wiped his face. "The love has to be bigger than everything else. The isolation, the separation, the danger. When the love is bigger than all that—you just do it. You pay the price in uncertainty and sometimes bereavement, because every moment you're together is worth the cost. If the love is big enough, yet you don't take that chance... man, it doesn't matter what you're fighting for. You've lost."

Nikolas tightened his fingers, then let his hand drop and bent to pick up the skull again.

Watching him with a grim expression, Gawain said, "We might have known that poor bloke well. He could have been a friend."

"Whoever he was, we need to give him a proper burial," Nikolas said. "Sophie promised." He tucked the skull aside carefully so that it could be attended to later, and he told the others, "We need to get a fire going and build a wind barrier."

They set to work. After some quick effort, they had a large lean-to built and propped against the hillside to cover the hole that led to the oubliette. It was constructed of pine branches heavy with needles so that it blocked the worst of the wind.

While some worked on building the lean-to, others sourced deadfall wood, and soon they had a fire going. It didn't feel like it warmed the area so much as eased a little of the bitter chill, but at least they could heat some of the water and the food they carried in their packs for calories and warmth, which helped.

Nikolas thought of Sophie, riding the puck in the elements, and clamped down on a surge of worry. None of them were dressed for deep winter, but they were hardier than her, and they had the advantage of some rudimentary shelter.

Time passed, and the moon traveled across the sky. Most of the others huddled close to share body warmth while they napped, but Nikolas couldn't rest. He fed the fire and kept watch.

Sophie and Robin had to have reached Raven's Craig by now. He imagined them talking to Annwyn. What would happen next? She would muster a fighting force, and while they would have the advantage of horses, the route would be treacherous with snow and ice. It might be another thirty-six to forty-eight hours before anyone arrived.

He sat on a log, at one end of the lean-to, his head in his hands. Two days in Lyonesse would be weeks on Earth. Morgan might have weeks to do as much damage as he could. After so much effort, they might not make it back across in time after all.

Thunder sounded in the distance and grew louder. It approached too quickly to be a thunderstorm.

It sounded like many galloping horses.

Cael stirred and murmured, "What's that?"

Nikolas stood, looking out as the first of an army of five hundred appeared over a rise, with a fiery black stallion racing at their head. Annwyn had made the two-day journey within a few hours.

Robin plunged to a halt in front of Nikolas, followed by Annwyn astride a dappled gelding, along with Hershel, Rogier, Dihanna, and many others Nikolas recognized.

But he had eyes only for the cloaked figure lying prone along the stallion's back. Running over to Robin, he lifted back the hood to stare at Sophie's white face. As he touched her cold cheek, she whispered through bloodless lips, "I'm okay. Just super cold and tired. They tied me on so I wouldn't fall off."

"Oh, for fuck's sake," he swore. He felt along her arms to discover the rope tied around her wrists and worked to get the knots undone.

Her mouth trembled. "Don't yell at me right now."

"I'm not going to yell at you, my Sophie," he whispered. "I'm going to yell at them."

Annwyn approached. She clasped Nikolas's arm in a tight hold and gave him a look that sparkled with unshed tears. Then she moved to untie Sophie's other wrist.

"I tried to talk her into staying behind at Raven's Craig, but she insisted," Annwyn told him.

"I take it back," Nikolas said to Sophie. "I am going to yell at you."

As her hands came free, he lifted her off the stallion's back and cradled her in his arms. Bowing his head over hers, he hugged her tight.

"Fine," she gritted, shivering. "But I get to have a

cup of coffee first."

He looked up at the puck, who stared back, ferocious and unfriendly. Telepathically he said to Robin, *Thank you for carrying her safely. And for bringing the others. We owe you—I owe you so much.*

Some of the starch seemed to go out of the stallion's black mane, even as Robin said fiercely, "You will not forget a puck again."

"Never," Nikolas said. "I swear it." He looked at Annwyn. "Much as I would love to have a leisurely reunion, we don't have time."

"We will take time on the other side." She clapped him on the shoulder, then turned to start issuing orders.

Some of the troops would stay behind to set up a winter camp and care for the horses. Annwyn had laid plans based on hope. Temporary shelters would need to be erected, while wagonloads of supplies and more troops would arrive over the next two days. The troops that remained behind would then work on erecting more permanent structures.

In the meantime, Nikolas and Annwyn would be able to take as many as four hundred and fifty troops across to Earth—assuming they could get through.

He looked down at Sophie, who had revived enough to stare at him pointedly. Eyes flashing in the moonlight, she told him, "Shush. Don't you start yelling. My coffee is in the great hall."

Laughter bolted up from his belly. He clenched her

tighter so that he could bury his face in her hair. "We'd better go get it then."

If there was a great hall to get back to. Neither one of them said it.

"Put me down," she told him.

"Are you sure you can stand?" Gingerly he set her on her feet.

She wobbled but stayed upright. Beside them, in a shimmer of magic, the stallion vanished and a monkey took its place.

The monkey leaped onto Sophie's back, and she staggered. "I can stand. I can't run, and I don't have another fight in me, but I can stand."

"You've had your fight. This next one is ours." Exasperated, Nikolas said, "Robin, can't you go under your own steam?"

"We go together," the monkey said, wrapping its arms around Sophie's neck. "We go at the same *time*."

The emphasis he put on the last word was a good reminder of how much time slippage there would be on the way back. Nikolas told Sophie, "You and I are going at the same time too, and I'm in the forefront."

She looked upward briefly, as if to ask for help from the heavens. "I will deign to agree, but only because I dislike winter so much and my coffee is back on Earth. The fact that my decision coincides with your orders is purely coincidental."

He took a deep, bracing breath and reached for patience. "I'm well aware of that."

He led the way back to the hole, where he found all his men except Braden waiting. He told all of them, "You're relieved of duty too."

Gawain shook his head. "Not happening, mate."

"Me neither," Rowan said.

The rest of them shook their heads as well.

He was so damn proud of them. So damn proud.

Giving them a curt nod, he said, "Let's go."

After that, things appeared to happen quickly. The first wave of troops, including Nikolas, Sophie, the puck, and the rest of his team, went through the cramped tunnel to the oubliette.

"I did the math," Rowan said almost cheerfully. "A fortnight in Lyonesse roughly equals six months on Earth. It took four hours or so for Sophie to contact Annwyn and to bring the troops. That means it's been two and a half days on Earth. Not counting all the time slippages from when we ran around in the house, of course."

Gawain growled, "If you mean to be encouraging, you're not helping."

Together they hoisted Cael up, then Rhys, who took a rope ladder with them. After a long, long— long—moment, they tossed one end of the ladder back down. The next man up carried another rope ladder, and the fourth man carried another, and then there wasn't any room for more.

Nikolas went up before Sophie, and when she climbed up with Robin on her back, he was waiting to lift her the rest of the way out. They strode down the corridor. Someone who had come before them had moved Ashe's body. Nikolas caught a glimpse of a still form lying in the armory, covered with a tapestry.

Cael met them in the courtyard. "Watch yourself," Cael warned. "There's damage, and the bastard hasn't stopped."

"Of course he hasn't," Nikolas growled. He exchanged a look with Sophie, then they both hurried down the passage that connected the courtyard to the great hall.

Once there, they turned in a circle, taking in the scene. It had changed drastically. Giant cracks marred the hall. The iron-bordered windows had warped, and the chimney over the large fireplace had broken in two. Stones had fallen out of the balcony floors, and timbers from the roof crisscrossed the open floor.

The monkey jumped off her shoulders and ran to the window. Sophie rested both hands on top of her head, her expression dismayed.

"My beautiful, spooky house." Her mouth drooped. "I don't have chimney or roof insurance for a house built on a broken crossover passageway."

"Don't think about that right now," Nikolas told her. "We're here, and we're not blocked off from Earth yet."

"I know that's the most important thing," she said bitterly. "But I loved this place, and he's tearing it to pieces. If he's broken my jar of instant coffee, I'm going to have a meltdown."

As she went rummaging in the grocery supplies, Nikolas joined Robin at the window to look through fractured panes of glass. A rumble began low in the distance and grew to vibrate through the building. He could feel the strain in the flagstones underneath his feet.

The interior of the house had taken serious damage, but outside, the scene looked downright apocalyptic. Trees had been downed, and wide, deep cracks ran in the earth across the clearing. Most of the gatekeeper's cottage had crumbled to rubble. The gate pillars themselves, at the border of the road, had toppled over.

Morgan knelt outside, hands planted flat on the ground, while Hounds kept watch in a circle around the house. Nikolas checked the sun's position. He guessed it was late morning. It looked like the bastard hadn't taken a break in three days.

Nikolas said over his shoulder to Sophie, "You're not going to like what he's done to the rest of your property either."

"Goddammit! I haven't even gotten the title documents yet!" she wailed around a mouthful of food.

She joined him at the window, carrying a half-eaten protein bar in one hand and a bottle of black water in the other. She had changed her blood-soaked sweater for a clean, long-sleeved, gray cotton shirt. As he watched, she shook the bottle of water, uncapped it, and took a long swig while she glared out the window.

Distracted by the sight, he curled a lip in disgust. "You're drinking cold, instant black coffee."

"It's caffeine and hydration," she muttered. "I'm still on my feet, aren't I? Besides, I didn't feel comfortable lighting one of the propane stoves."

"Good point." Squeezing her arm, he turned to face the great hall.

Soldiers poured in.

"Archers to the front," he said. Four women and three men stepped forward. He told them, "We're not going to make the same mistake we made the last time we fought on this land. We concentrate everything we have on bringing Morgan down. The Hounds might be dangerous, but they're incidental."

Cramming the last of the protein bar into her mouth, Sophie turned to listen. When he paused, she said telepathically, *Every good magic user I've ever known has some version of an avert spell for defense. And clearly Morgan is one hell of a magic user.*

He raised an eyebrow. *Your point?*

Well, you don't want to just shoot at him, right? She drank the last of her coffee. *You want to take out his magic too.*

He said out loud, "The null spell. We need the null spell on as many arrows as we can get. How much magic-sensitive silver do you have?"

"Not enough to spell all their arrows," she said grimly, gesturing to the group. "I was on *vacation*. Choose your best archers, and we'll go from there."

While Nikolas prioritized the group, Sophie retrieved her luggage and pulled out a small package. She called out to the gathering crowd, "Gawain?"

"Right here, lass." Gawain shouldered through to her.

"Did you get metal-making tools for me?"

"We didn't have time."

Her shoulders drooped. "Okay. Doesn't matter. This doesn't have to be pretty. We're going to need to light a propane stove after all and use one of the cooking pots. All we have to do is get the silver melted enough to dip the tips of the arrows in it, and then we can cast the spell."

"Got it."

As they set to work, Nikolas organized others to shift the supplies, along with the fallen timbers and stones, into the side halls to make more room for arriving troops. They weren't going to get all four hundred and fifty into the great hall, but if the troops stood shoulder to shoulder, they could get most of them in. The rest would have to line up back in the courtyard.

"Watch out for the painted lines!" he called out to the workers. "They mark time-space shifts. There's a shift along one side of the courtyard too—Rhys, go back there and make sure people know to avoid it."

"I'm on it." Rhys worked his way to the back.

Annwyn appeared at Nikolas's side. She stared at the Mini and the Harley for a long moment and took a breath as if she meant to ask a question. But then, in the next moment, she seemed to think better of it, for she shook her head and let it go.

"How many have come through?" he asked.

"Close to three hundred," she told him.

Nodding, he strode to Gawain and Sophie, where they bent over a small propane stove set on the dining table. He asked, "What do you have?"

As he spoke, another low rumble started. This time it rose and rose, and a sharp *crack* sounded overhead. Immediately Gawain doused the flame while Nikolas lunged forward to cover Sophie's head and shoulders with his, and people swore and crowded as close as they could to the walls.

For a long moment everyone in the great hall held tense and still as they waited, but nothing fell. Then Sophie said in a cranky, muffled voice from underneath him, "We'll get you ten spelled arrows as soon as you get off me. Any minute now."

With a growl, he expelled a sharp breath and rubbed his face in her hair.

Crazy. She made him crazy. Somehow in spite of that, he was more in love with her than ever.

Straightening, he said to everybody, "Get back to work."

Activity resumed. Gawain lit the propane stove again, and he and Sophie went back to spelling arrows. Annwyn joined them and said, "I don't think this old place can take much more."

"I don't either," Nikolas told her. "Soon as Gawain and Sophie are done, we'll make our move."

"We're done," Gawain said. He doused the flame again, and he and Sophie sat back. She handed Nikolas two fistfuls of arrows.

He strode over to the archers and handed the strongest ones two arrows each. "These are only to be used on Morgan," he said. "This is your only job."

"Understood," the lead archer said, her expression direct and clear.

As Sophie joined them, Nikolas said, "Morgan doesn't know we've broken through to Lyonesse. He doesn't know about any of you. Let's keep it that way until we strike. I'm going to hide you with a cloaking spell. We'll open the doors, and then you'll hit him with everything you've got."

"Yes, sir."

They strode over to the doors. Annwyn said to the troops, "Get ready."

The troops drew their swords and readied shields, then silence fell in the great hall.

When Nikolas, Gawain, and Sophie reached the doors, Nikolas cast a massive cloaking spell over the five archers who took their places behind them. Then Nikolas fixed Sophie with a stern look. "You'll stay out of it."

She widened her eyes. "Oh, believe me, this is not my fight."

They pulled open the doors. Morgan lifted his

head.

Sophie surveyed the wreckage of landscape with tightened lips. She called out, "I don't know if you're a monster or if you're massively misunderstood. But I do know one thing."

Morgan stood. Even from the distance of twenty meters, Nikolas could sense him amassing Power, as Morgan asked, "What is that, Sophie Ross?"

"You need to get off my lawn," Sophie said. She stepped to one side.

Nikolas whispered, "Now."

Five arrows flew through the air. Morgan dodged, moving so fast he turned into a blur. Most of the arrows missed.

One didn't.

It struck him in the arm. The Hounds to either side of Morgan broke into a run, hurtling toward the house.

Even as Morgan reeled back, he flung his hand out in the direction of the open doors. Nothing happened. Behind Nikolas came the distinctive sound of the archers drawing their bows. Raising his hand, he kept his eyes trained on Morgan and the approaching Hounds.

Morgan tore the arrow out of his arm. The archers loosened their arrows, and he blurred again as he dodged. Another arrow hit, this time in his side. He stumbled and fell to his knees.

Nikolas dropped his hand and roared, "Go! Go!"

Soldiers sprinted out the open doors and collided

with Hounds. More and more poured past Nikolas while he drew his own sword. He lunged onto the field eagerly, looking for Morgan.

This time, centuries later, the Daoine Sidhe had not come too late.

Chapter Twenty-One

THE BATTLE WAS a complete rout.

Sophie climbed onto the Mini to get out of the way as troops streamed past. The sound of shouts, growls, and screams rocketed back through the open doors, echoing in the shattered great hall.

Robin had disappeared. Nikolas, she knew, would be in the thickest of the fight. He had lived for the eventuality of this battle. When the last of the troops had sprinted out of the manor house, she limped to the front doors to look out.

She'd been telling the truth earlier—she didn't have another fight left in her. After running through every one of the shifts in the house, digging through to Lyonesse, and then coming back again, she couldn't even imagine how to calculate how long ago it was that she might have slept.

She had jet lag on steroids. She had only eaten a protein bar in a very long time, probably in at least a day. The fight with Ashe had been short, but it had wounded her and knocked her around, and the wild ride to Raven's Craig and back again had made every joint in her body ache.

Still, adrenaline coursed in her blood so strongly her hands shook. Just in case, she retrieved her gun from the micro vault and loaded it so she had some kind of physical weapon with her. The runes on her hands and arms were itching and beginning to crack and peel, but for now, she still had one telekinesis spell and one confusion spell left—she always counted her spells, just as she counted her bullets—and she watched from the doorway as the last of the Hounds was killed.

She could see no sign of Morgan, no sign of Nikolas. She saw Rhys and Rowan in the distance, and Annwyn strode across the clearing with two swords bloodied, looking fierce and magnificent. Finally, when the fighting died down and it looked calm enough to walk out, Sophie stepped outside and surveyed the full extent of the devastation.

Bodies littered the area as far as she could see. The nearby clumps of forest had been all but leveled. The small lake behind the house had drained into a huge crack in the ground. The cottage was rubble. One man had done this. One man had torn the earth apart, trying to get to them.

Her hands wouldn't stop shaking.

Fight or flight. Fight or flight.

She hadn't seen Robin since they had returned to the manor house, but she wasn't worried. When they had broken through to Lyonesse, the puck had been revitalized, and he had shone with a kind of Power that had been nonexistent when she had first found him.

She walked to the cottage ruins and checked for the scent of gas. She didn't smell anything, so she shrugged, found a likely piece of wall to perch on, and watched the aftermath. The Hounds had been decimated, but there had been injuries and casualties on the other side as well.

After some time, Nikolas, Gawain, and Cael walked out of the woods. Sophie sagged in relief. They moved slowly like they'd been running hard and were tired. Even from where she sat, she could see Annwyn lift a hand in inquiry, and Nikolas shake his head in reply.

Shading his eyes, he paused to survey the scene. He looked in her direction and strode across the field to her. She stood as he neared, running her gaze hungrily over him. He was streaked in blood. Her hands clenched.

She managed to ask without a quaver in her voice, "Are you hurt?"

"It's not mine."

Relief made her lightheaded. "And Morgan? I saw you signal Annwyn. You didn't find him?"

"He got away." He shook his head grimly. "I don't know how he moved that fast, because he was wounded badly, and with silver arrows, no less. He must have had a vehicle parked nearby. We were hoping we would catch him before he reached it."

"If he was wounded that badly with silver, that

means he'll be out of commission for a while, right?" She forced the tense muscles between her shoulder blades to relax. "So at least that's something."

"Yes. Healing spells and potions won't help him. The bastard is going to be in a lot of pain over the next couple of months," he said with savage satisfaction. He glanced back at the battlefield, and she did too.

"I had the impulse to help," she said quietly. "But most of them don't know who I am."

"You've done more than enough already," he told her. "I'll have a couple of soldiers set up a tent for you, and you can go to bed."

"Please don't," she said. "There's too many wounded, not enough shelter, and you all have enough on your plate as it is. I'll go to a hotel."

At that, he turned his full attention onto her. "No, you're not. You're staying right here where I can keep an eye on you. Just wait here. I'll send someone to get you when they have a tent set up."

She coughed out an angry laugh. He was *forbidding* her to check into a hotel. Was there any point in having an argument over this? She was beyond her limit on patience and energy, and everything else.

After a moment, she said dryly, "Sure, Nik. Whatever you say."

"What?" he snapped. "I don't have time for this." As he spoke, Annwyn called out his name from the direction of the house, and he raised a hand in answer.

"Of course you don't, and I'm not arguing with

you," Sophie told him. She took a step back. "Go do what you need to do."

He frowned at her. "We'll talk about this later."

She gave him a grim smile. "If you say so."

She watched him lope across the lawn and join Annwyn. After a few moments, they both walked around to the back of the house.

Rubbing her tired face, Sophie assessed the gap between the fallen gate pillars. It looked like there would be room enough for a small car to pass through.

She limped over to Rowan, who was the nearest familiar face.

"I hate to bother you," she told him. "But can you get someone to help you push the Mini out?"

With a frown, Rowan said, "Sure, if you want. Are you leaving?"

"There's too many people here and not enough shelter," she told him. "You—all of you—need time for a reunion, and with so many people you're going to stretch the town's resources too." She paused. "I'm going to drive into Shrewsbury and check into a hotel."

Rowan's frown deepened. "Have you told Nikolas?"

"Yes, I did, and he forbade me to go," she told him with such grim emphasis, his eyes widened.

"I'm sure he didn't mean to actually forbid you," Rowan said uncertainly.

"It doesn't matter what he actually meant to do. What matters is what he said." She gave him a tight smile. "So I'm drawing a line in the sand that he can't cross. About that Mini."

Rowan tapped two strapping men on the shoulder. Between the three of them, they pushed the Mini out the open double doors and over the rocky ground until they reached a section of the gravel drive that was still more or less level. She went back into the house one last time to make sure she had collected all her things, and Rowan helped her to carry her luggage to the car.

As she closed the boot, Rowan turned to her. "Are you sure I can't talk you into staying?"

"No, you cannot," she said steadily. "Morgan has been badly injured. The Hounds have been thoroughly crushed. This is the perfect time for me to go, and it's not just a good decision for you—it's the right decision for me. I'm going to shower and sleep in a clean bed. Check my email. Connect with my own life." Then, remembering, she pulled the commander's ring off her thumb and handed it to him. "Go be with your people. Mourn, celebrate, visit. Hug the friends you haven't seen in decades. If anybody needs to reach me, my solicitor in Shrewsbury is Paul Shipman." She gave him a small smile. "Take care of yourself."

He pulled her into an awkward hug. "Get some rest."

She patted his back. "You too."

Now if only the damn car would start.

The engine purred to life on the first try. Carefully she drove between the gate pillars and pulled onto the road, and she didn't quit driving until she reached Shrewsbury. Once there, she stopped at the first hotel she saw.

No, they didn't have any available single rooms, the polite attendant told her when she stepped inside to ask. They did have a small, two-room suite if she was interested.

It was a splurge, but why the hell not? she thought. You only live once.

She signed where he asked her to sign, showed her passport and credit card, and tipped someone to bring up her luggage. Then, as dirty as she was, she fell fully clothed onto the clean double bed and plummeted into sleep.

There was shouting, a roar of Hounds, and a clash of swords.

She plunged awake in a clench. Disoriented, staring around the strange bedroom, she listened hard for any sound of battle, but there was none. She glanced out the window. It was gray, wet, and foggy outside, but it was definitely daylight. It appeared she had slept quite a while, and the battle had happened yesterday.

At least she hadn't dreamed about staring down the barrel of a gun for once. Her nightmares were changing.

Dragging herself off the bed, she dug out her toiletries bag, underwear, flannel pants, and T-shirt, and hobbled into the bathroom. Her muscles had stiffened even more overnight. A hot shower loosened things up quite a bit, and after wrapping her hair and torso in towels, she brushed her teeth with reverence and gratitude.

The hot shower had caused the runes on her arms to degrade. She scratched the last of the nail polish off. She was still exhausted. Somehow she had collected quite an array of bruises again, and she felt as hollow as a reed, but by God, at least she was clean. Huzzah.

As soon as I get you out of my system.

From nowhere, the tears welled up. Sitting on the toilet, she buried her face in her hands and sobbed.

The tortured little dog with his tongue torn out. *A puck was hoping for help. Waiting for someone to notice he was gone, taken and lost, but no one ever came.*

The oubliette. The skull. The torn bodies, in the pub, strewn across the field. Nikolas's raw voice and distorted features as he confronted Ashe.

The wreckage of the gatekeeper's cottage and the manor house. She had barely gotten the chance to fall in love with the property. Now it lay in ruins.

Nikolas's mouth, his hands, the sensation of taking him into her body. The passionate clench he had held her in as he had moved, and moved, and moved inside her.

As soon as I get you out of my system, I'm gone.

The storm of tears wracked her body. She was as helpless to stop it as a woman giving birth.

It's okay, she thought. I'm just wrung out. I'm overwrought.

I'm heartbroken.

I'll get some food. I'll pull it together. Food and maybe a nap, and I'll feel like a new person.

From nearby came a shimmer of familiar, wild magic. She lifted her head as the door to her suite opened and closed. Pulling off the towels, she tore into her clothes and burst out of the bathroom and into the tiny sitting area.

An inhumanly slim figure stood at the windows, looking out. He was perhaps as tall as a thirteen-year-old boy and wore skinny jeans, boots, a brown leather jacket, and a navy blue scarf with gold buttons. He had spiky, nut-brown hair and pointed ears.

Wiping her cheeks, she asked, "Robin?"

The figure turned. The puck had a thin, triangular old/young face, fiery, wild eyes, and when he smiled, he showed too many teeth. "Robin brought you cake, dear love."

As the puck stepped forward, she plunged blindly across the room and threw her arms around him. More stupid tears fell. He pulled back to wipe them from her face, and she saw that he had too many fingers as well.

"I'm sorry, I've sprung a leak this morning," she muttered. "You look—you look—"

"Healed," the puck said. "Whole."

Her attention fell to his scarf. The material and the gold buttons were familiar. She fingered one of the buttons. "You made this out of the jacket?"

"I wear a kindness around my neck," Robin told

her. "When the cage threatens to take over my mind, I touch my scarf and remember I am free."

"I'm so glad," she whispered. She straightened the scarf around his neck unnecessarily and smoothed it over his narrow chest.

"I've come to say good-bye." Robin laid his hands over hers.

"Oh no, not good-bye," she echoed in dismay. Just as she fell in love with things, she seemed doomed to lose them. "Are you going back to Lyonesse?"

"No home for Robin," he said. "Not yet. I go to create mischief for a Queen and her cruel Court. I aim to strike a blow at the very heart of her strength. It will be tricky. There are strings to pull, while I am just a puck. I have no true power over what rules the hearts of others, but I do know what power will bring about her downfall. We old ones play our games of war and dominance, and we forget, you see. We forget how much strength is in the heart, and how much can be transformed and defeated by love. Lord, we're fools."

"It sounds dangerous," she whispered. "I don't want you to go."

He kissed her cheeks. "Don't worry, dear love. They tricked me once; they won't capture me again. I will come to visit when I can."

"Promise?"

"Always, Sophie." He smiled, looking both gentle and feral at once. "Enjoy your cake."

He slipped out of the suite like a shadow. Sophie

stood, listening to the emptiness in the room. Then she noticed the cardboard box on the coffee table. Sitting on the edge of the sofa, she opened the lid.

Inside, there were tiny cakes, iced and decorated with impossible colors and fantastic shapes of spun sugar and fondant. Delicate magic rose with the aroma of sugary goodness. Her mouth watered. Selecting a lavender confection, she popped it in her mouth. It was utterly delicious and melted with a tinkle of magic that spread through her body, smoothing away aches and pains, and leaving behind a feeling of refreshment and well-being.

Holy cow. What a rare, delightful gift. Briefly she struggled to hold back and not eat them all at once, but she had grown too hungry and she couldn't help herself. She fell on the cakes and consumed every last one.

When she had finished, she felt like she could face the world again. First things first. She checked her phone, and it was completely dead. Of course it was. The fucking fucker.

She needed to buy a new phone. She should also call Paul to give him an update on what had happened to the property. She needed to find out what might happen to the entailment if the house collapsed. Maybe she should just swing by his office to talk to him in person.

Digging out his card, she used the suite phone to call the office. When Paul's secretary Trevor answered, she said, "Hi, this is Sophie Ross. Is Paul available?"

"Sophie!" Trevor exclaimed. "Paul has been trying to ring you. Where are you?"

"I'm in Shrewsbury," she told him. "I... actually, I'm not entirely sure where I am. I was pretty out of it when I checked in yesterday. I'm in a hotel near one of the bridges."

"As there's nine bridges here, that narrows it down to many," Trevor said, humor evident in his voice. "Hold on, I'm transferring you now."

She waited for the heartbeat it took to transfer, then Paul answered, exclaiming with every bit as much fervency as Trevor had, "Sophie! I'm so glad you rang. I've emailed and tried to ring you. Are you all right?"

"Sure, of course," she said, bemused. "Listen, I need to talk to you."

"I need to talk to you too. Between last night and this morning, I've taken about a dozen phone calls from the Dark Court. One of them is an absolute madman. And—are you sitting down?" he asked. "Because if you're not, you might want to."

An absolute madman. Oh dear. She felt behind her for the edge of the chair and lowered herself into it. "I am now."

"The King's cousin Annwyn—who, I guess, is now the regent since he's fallen ill—has made quite an offer to buy the property. Sophie, she offered ten million pounds."

"I—She *what?*" The world wobbled around her,

and she couldn't believe what she'd just heard.

"You're probably wondering if you heard me right," Paul told her, laughing. "Forgive me for cackling like a lunatic, because I am, in fact, quite serious. The Dark Court wants to pay you ten million pounds for the Shaw family albatross, lock, stock, and barrel."

"But Paul, the house is unlivable. It has cracks in its foundation, and it's barely standing upright."

"Prices for country estates in the UK are astronomical. Just the land alone is worth a great deal of money. To be honest, if you wanted to bargain with them, I think you could probably get them up to fifteen million."

Fifteen. Million. Her mind refused to take that number in.

"Lock, stock, and barrel means the contents of the library too, right?" she replied faintly. "I had wanted to go through that."

"Yes, they want the library too. At this point, it's sight unseen, of course, but they feel there is some possibility they might find some useful information there. Apparently, the Shaws had worked in opposition to them in the past. Annwyn said they feel it's worth the gamble financially. Between that, acquiring the annuity that goes with the house, and gaining control over a viable crossover passageway, she believes they're offering fair market value."

"I-I don't know what to say," she muttered.

On the one hand, she felt an inexplicable reluctance, but on the other, the property was now so damaged it bore none of the charms she had first enjoyed about it. Instead of having a viable living space, if she didn't sell, she would be facing renovation bills she didn't have the liquid resources to pay. And besides, the Dark Court had a legitimate claim and a very real need.

"You don't have to say a thing," Paul told her. "Just take a few hours to absorb the news and come on into the office. We can go over the details. I'll take you to lunch and buy you champagne."

"Well... Okay, thank you. Of course I'll listen to the details," she told him. "For ten million pounds, how can I not?"

"Exactly. See you soon."

In a daze, she set the receiver on the cradle.

What did the madman have to say? Did he want to yell at her, now that she'd had some coffee? Was he trying to close the deal?

After dressing in jeans, the Doc Martens, a black, long-sleeved sweater, and a denim jacket, she braided her hair, checked her Glock and tucked it into her purse. Then she opened the door.

Nikolas stood outside, dressed in black, carrying so much Power he felt like a bolt of lightning barely sheathed in the form of a man. The planes and angles of his face, so sharp they appeared cut from an immortal blade, were clenched, and his dark eyes glittered.

The impact of his forceful presence hit her so hard

she fell back a step.

He advanced. She retreated more. She only realized they had stepped fully back into the suite when he shot out a hand to slam the door shut.

"What are you doing here?" she asked.

He said between his teeth, "Chasing after you."

She stared at him, breathing hard. After a moment, she said, "I'm not going to fight with you."

"I'm not here to fight." He turned away and ran his fingers through his hair. Then with quick, vicious movements, he shrugged out of his sword harness and threw it across the room. In a quiet, raw voice, he said, "You left. You just left."

"Yes, I did," she said softly.

"You left without a goddamn word. You just drove off."

"Not true," she said. "I had a word with Rowan."

She could hear his breath sawing in his throat, a ragged, telltale sound. "You left without a goddamn word to *me*."

She whispered, "Maybe I'm done talking to you."

"Well, I'm not done talking to you." He turned to face her. "I'm sorry."

She was so braced for a fight anyway at first the words didn't make sense. "What?"

"I said I'm sorry." He strode over and took her by the shoulders. "Rowan told me what you said, about drawing a line in the sand. I didn't realize I had pushed you so far."

"You had a lot on your plate yesterday. Anyway, it doesn't matter anymore." She pulled away from him, shrugged out of her jacket, set her purse aside, and went to sit on the sofa. Leaning forward, she rested her elbows on her knees. "We accomplished what you needed. You're reunited with your people, and you have access to your home. I'm done."

"You can't be done." Striding over, he crouched in front of her. "Come back."

"No," she said.

He braced one hand on the edge of the couch by her thigh and leaned closer. "Sophie, come back."

"No, Nikolas." She had cried so long and hard her well was dry, but her chest felt like a giant bruise. She focused on the floor between her feet to avoid looking at him.

There was a long silence. Then he asked, "Why not?"

Staring at the floor didn't give her enough distance from him. She buried her face in her hands. "What do you mean, why not? You know why not. There's no point to any of this fighting or apologizing, because we're not partners. We're not in this together—we're not in anything together. I'm not coming back, because as soon as you get me out of your system, you're gone, and I'm not going to hang around for that experience. Because I love too much and too hard, for too long. If I go back with you, I'll invest even more of myself in you, when you have told me repeatedly you don't have anything to give a lover, and you will break me even harder—"

Realizing where she was headed with the last of that sentence, she stopped abruptly, but the unsaid words still hung in the room.

You will break me even harder than you have already.

Gently he curled fingers around one of her hands and coaxed it down. Then he took hold of her other hand and coaxed that down too. He held her hands to his lips and said quietly against her fingers, "We've said some pretty awful things to each other at times, haven't we?"

Her throat closed. She nodded.

He kissed her fingers. "There are different levels of truth, my Sophie. On the one hand, there is this—as soon as I get you out of my system, I'm gone. That was a defense mechanism, said in the heat of the moment when you told me you were making love to me for the last time. But on the other hand, there is also this—I will never get you out of my system. Never. Can you hear the truth in that?"

She could, and her heart started to pound.

"Then," he said, even more quietly, "there are truths that change. Before I met you, I was adamant about not investing in a relationship. I was constantly on the run, my life in danger, and that is a terrible thing to take to a woman's bed. And I met you. You're stubborn, infuriating, courageous, inventive, generous, and kind. You make me laugh. You make me crazy. You make me rediscover things inside myself that I thought were dead forever. You make me hard as a rock until all I can think about is tearing off your clothes. How long have we known each other?"

"Maybe four days, or maybe seventeen." At a loss, she shook her head. "Who the hell knows anymore?"

He gave her a crooked smile. "No matter how you calculate it, or how many time slippages we've gone through, it hasn't been very long."

"No," she whispered. "It hasn't."

He paused. "Tell me you don't love me."

"I don't love you," she told him.

The falsehood lingered in the air between them. He smiled. "Tell me you don't want me."

She looked him in the eyes and said, "I don't want you."

Oh, that one. That was laughably false.

His smile died. "When you went to Raven's Craig, I asked Braden how he and his wife made the kind of commitment they had, when we live such dangerous lives. He said, the love has got to be bigger than everything else. The isolation, the separation, the danger. When the love is bigger than all that—you just do it. You pay the price in uncertainty and sometimes bereavement, because every moment you're together is worth the cost."

"What a beautiful thing to say," she whispered.

His grip tightened on her hands. "I can't lie. Part of

me is still struggling, because if I let you into my life I feel like I'm putting you in danger. Also over the last week, my life has changed somewhat. We have reinforcements now, which means we can create pockets of safety, but there'll still be violence and danger. We didn't kill Morgan. Isabeau still hates us. Oberon is still unconscious. Yet in spite of all that, I need to ask you. Can we make love bigger than everything else?"

With all his responsibilities, he had still left old friends and comrades, and the command of his army, to come this morning and ask her this. Well, and to bitch at her a little bit too, but she would get over that.

Leaning forward, she wrapped her arms around his neck, and he pulled her down on the floor to hold her. It felt so good to be back in his arms. Closing her eyes, she concentrated fiercely on soaking every moment of it in.

She told him, "Yes, we can. I can handle everything, as long as you don't push me away—and Nik, I mean it. You've got to fight that instinct, because rejection hurts almost more than anything else in the world, and I won't put up with it. You've got to go all in."

"I'm all in," he whispered.

"Oh God, we're going to fight, aren't we?" She turned her face into his hair.

"It's going to be ugly." He rocked her. "You make me so crazy."

She laughed unsteadily. "Your autocratic nonsense

drives me batty." She lowered her voice and said gruffly, "I'm going to issue orders now, because it never occurs to me that somebody might have a mind of her own."

"Shut up." He sank his fists into her hair. "Shut up."

She opened her eyes very wide. "*See?* You just issued an ord—"

Growling, he covered her mouth with his. He told her telepathically, *There's really only one way I know of to shut you up.*

Well, sure, she said sarcastically. "*OUT LOUD. There's really only one way to truly, truly shut me up.*

He lifted his head. His expression had caught fire. He growled, "Orgasms."

Caught by surprise, her mouth hung open. She said, "I was about to say, you'd have to knock me out, but your idea sounds much more fun."

"I think so too." Standing, he scooped her into his arms and walked with her into the bedroom.

Oh dear *Lord*, he *carried* her into the *bedroom*. It was such a quintessentially Nikolas thing to do, she was nearly beside herself with exasperated glee. She stuck out one leg and regarded with bemusement the sturdy Doc Martens boot at the end of it.

He was never going to learn.

Never.

Chapter Twenty-Two

IN THE SHADOWED bedroom, Nikolas set Sophie down. Before her feet touched the floor, he was kissing her, plundering that soft, generous mouth. He yanked the tie out of her hair and pulled the braid out, sinking his fists into the fragrant, curling mass.

It had been such a long, difficult night, he had no patience. Dealing with the needs of his army, talking strategy with Annwyn in bursts as they found time. Looking for Sophie whenever he had a moment until he finally ran into Rowan, who had given him his ring, told him what she had said, and that she had left for Shrewsbury.

The news had been a kick to the gut. She had gone, just gone. No word of explanation. No information about where she was staying.

This is how people die, he thought. You expect them to be there, and then suddenly they aren't.

Well after midnight, when he felt like he could finally leave, he had taken Gawain's Harley to go look for her. She didn't answer her phone. Her stupid solicitor didn't know a goddamn thing. He had to resort to going from hotel to hotel until finally he recognized the Mini parked in the street.

The experience had scared him and made him angry. Not that he had truly believed she might die. She had been right when she had said to Rowan that it was the perfect time for her to go.

It had scared him and made him angry, because she had left him.

Facing that possibility burned everything else away, and he understood what Braden had been saying. While they collected the bodies of their fallen troops and prepared them to be transported back across the passageway for burial at home, he confronted what his life would be like if Sophie was truly out of his life, and he realized he would have done anything to spend as much time with her as he possibly could.

Pushing the night into the past where it belonged, he focused on the here and now. Sophie stood in front of him, healthy and whole. She spread her hands over his chest, and her touch soothed the last of the rawness away.

Need took control of his actions. He yanked her shirt over her head, and as her arms came free, she scrambled out of her bra. His skin was on fire, and the restriction of his clothes felt intolerable. He tore them off while she wriggled out of the rest of her things.

Then they came together, flesh to flesh, with nothing between them. It felt so necessary and right he paused with his mouth resting on the pulse at the base of her neck, breathing her in, taking her into every darkened, solitary corner in his soul so she could light him up with her presence.

She seemed to understand he needed that moment; as she rubbed his arms, her head tilted back to expose the slender curve of her vulnerable throat.

"I'm still going to try to protect you," he whispered.

She stroked his hair. "I'm still going to try to protect you too, and I'm never going to sit in a tower and learn how to knit."

"We have so much war ahead of us."

"I know, Nik," she said, gently steady. "I accept all that. I will try to learn how to be the best partner I can be, for you."

"As I will, for you." He kissed her while he let his fingers stroke along the underside of her breasts. With the last of his rational thought, he murmured, "We work well together, even when we're fighting and driving each other insane."

"We do, don't we?" She nuzzled him. "We work well in other ways too."

The fire in his veins took over, and he pulled her onto the bed. Time broke apart as they traversed their own crossover passage, passing from uncertainty, fear, and anger into acceptance, optimism, and passion. Her taste drove him wild. He licked and bit her everywhere, leaving marks, while she twisted and gasped underneath him.

She incited him to more, scraping her fingernails along his sensitized skin, sinking her teeth into his lower lip, rubbing herself along the length of his body with such evident pleasure, he almost spurted against her hip.

Finally he couldn't tease her any longer. As she lay back against the pillows, he rose and pushed between her legs. She welcomed him, her expression flushed and sensual, reaching between them to caress his cock and guide him to her entrance.

Thrusting in, he rocked gently, working his way into her with care while she made the most delicious sound, a shaking, needy moan, and arched her torso up to him.

Then he slipped all the way in, pushed as hard against her flesh as he could while he kissed her with the force of all the fierce emotions raging inside. He drank in the sight of her, the velvet, excruciating sensation of her inner muscles gripping him as tight as a fist. He drank all of her up.

When he saw tears glittering in her eyes, he paused, breathing hard. "My Sophie," he whispered. He loved saying that every chance he could, biting into the possessiveness like eating a ripe, succulent peach. "Are you okay?"

"Yeah, I am." She stroked his back, and then a mischievous smile broke over her face. She said with genuine delight, "Thanks for asking, asshole."

He burst out laughing and kissed her extra hard as

punishment. He was almost certain it was punishment. To be sure, he kissed her again and again as he started to move inside her. She caught the rhythm and moved with him.

"I love you," she whispered against his mouth.

Pleasure spiraled high on brilliant wings. He thrust harder, deeper, watching as her lips parted in a gasp. "I love you too," he gritted. "You're mine now, Sophie. Do you understand that?"

She nodded, touching his hair, his face. "You're mine too. I don't know what on earth I'm going to do with you—what we're going to do with each other— but you are mine."

"We're going to make love bigger than anything else," he said.

Words fell away as he lost himself in movement and fire. He took her with him, working her with just the right caress until she gasped and shuddered under-neath him. Her inner muscles pulsed with her climax, which hurtled him over the edge.

Then he took her there again, and again, playing her body like a musician while he found his home inside, until the only thing left in the room was some-thing shining, new, and pure.

Afterward, he wrapped her in his arms, and she rested her head on his chest. They dozed for a while, then suddenly Sophie swore and sat up. "Damn it, I forgot. I was going to meet Paul for lunch. I'd better give him a call."

Nikolas settled back against the pillows, enjoying the shapely lines of her back. "Clearly something came up," he drawled, letting his fingers walk down her spine.

She gave him a laughing glance over her shoulder. "Oh, snicker."

He grinned. "You'd better make that call quick while you can. I think something is coming up again."

AFTER SPENDING THE night in Shrewsbury and meeting Paul for breakfast, they headed back to Westmarch and the manor house.

Their battle over who would drive the Mini was brief and idiotic. Finally he accused, "You don't even want to drive. You said yourself you don't like driving on the wrong side of the road."

"Well… yeah." She scowled. "You just held out your hand for my keys in that preemptory way, and then I had to argue on principle."

He sighed. He was truly mystified by how happy she made him. "Get in the car, Sophie."

She gave him an arch look. "I'm getting in the car because I choose to get into the car. Not because you told me to."

He barked out a laugh.

Happiness. The emotion felt foreign, breakable. On the way back he reached over and laced his fingers through hers and drove one-handed.

Turning onto the property, he saw the troops had started to clear away the cottage rubble and the downed trees. When he switched off the engine, they looked over the land. An army camp had been erected. The doors to the manor house had been taken down, and there were two visible cracks in the outer structure.

"Ten million pounds is so much money," she said doubtfully.

"You are the world's worst negotiator," he told her. "As serious as our problems are, Lyonesse's treasury is rich. Now that we have a viable crossover passage, we need to have access to it. Take the deal."

"Well, I don't really have a choice." She waved a hand at the mess in front of them. "I don't have the means to fix this, and you deserve to have the property. I'm just a little sad about it. I had been planning on living here."

"The land can be healed," he said. "It'll be green again. We'll plant trees and restore the lake. We want to make this our permanent headquarters so you and I can build a house here. We'll need to build several structures to house a permanent fighting force to protect this place. That tunnel is our only viable crossover passageway, at least for now. I think even the manor house can be repaired, at least enough to make the structure safe again, although Annwyn wants to tear it down. She says the very fact of it is offensive to her."

Sophie made a face and sighed. "When I think of why the house was built in the first place, and the Dark

Court perspective on what happened here, I can't blame her. What would happen to the annuity?"

"That's a question we can ask Paul."

As they climbed out of the car, Annwyn stepped out of the manor house and strode to meet them. She touched Nikolas's shoulder in greeting and turned to study Sophie in frank assessment. Having grown so accustomed to the clothing fashions on Earth, Nikolas found Annwyn's boots, leggings, and tunic a disturbing combination of the familiar and the strange.

She was just as he had remembered her—sleek and racy as a cheetah, and just as dangerous. The sunlight touched on the strands of white at the temples of her auburn hair.

"I'm glad you've decided to return," Annwyn said to Sophie, offering her hand. "I've been hearing stories about you from Gawain, Rowan, and the others."

Color touched Sophie's cheeks as she shook Annwyn's hand. "I deny all the bad bits."

Annwyn laughed. "There are no bad bits. Do you accept my offer to buy this land?"

"Yes, on one condition. I want to explore the contents of the library with you. If there's anything relevant that pertains to the Dark Court, it's yours, but I want everything else." Sophie shrugged. "I don't even know if it will be interesting or if I'll want to keep it. I just don't want to give the whole thing away sight unseen."

Annwyn cocked her head as she considered. "That's acceptable. It's a deal." She paused. "I want you to consider something else as well. There are other broken crossover passageways. With some exploration, we might be able to make one or two of them viable as well. Will you help us?"

"I'll do what I can," Sophie said. "I'm not as Powerful as a full Djinn though. If we find I'm not able to help, you can always see what they might be able to do for you. If you go that route, just please be careful when you bargain with them."

"I have a condition of my own about that," Nikolas said. Both women turned to look at him, eyebrows raised. He said to Annwyn, "She doesn't go to any of the other broken passageways without me."

"Done." Annwyn smiled. She strode off.

Sophie watched the other woman walk across the torn lawn. "What about the crossover passageways Morgan has hidden?"

"We haven't figured out yet how to dissipate his spells." Nikolas crossed his arms. "He's also hidden the passageways that lead to Avalon, the Light Court land, so if we can figure out how to reveal our passageways, we can uncover theirs again too. That reminds me, have you seen Robin? Somehow he escaped from Isabeau, so he might have found a way to use their passageways."

The corners of her mouth turned down. "He stopped by yesterday morning to say good-bye. He said he's going to strike a blow at the heart of her strength. I'm worried he might have meant he's going to attack

Morgan."

Nikolas pinched the bridge of his nose. "We're going to have to trust he knows what he's doing—or at the very least that he can keep from getting captured again."

"He promised to come back when he could. I hope he returns soon." She squared her shoulders and turned to face him. "We need to get back to something you said earlier."

She looked like she was ready to go into battle again. He crossed his arms and readied himself. "What's that?"

"You said we'll build a house together, but Nik, I'm not going to move in with you."

His impulse to smile died away. He scowled. "Of course you are."

"No," she said, "no, I'm not. We've known each other for four days."

"Seventeen," he reminded her.

A not-quite-smile trembled on her lips. "Seventeen," she agreed. "But no matter how you do the math, like we said, it hasn't been very long. So we've both agreed we're together, but that doesn't mean we need to live together. In fact, I think that would be disastrous. You go ahead and build your own house, and I'll find some place to rent in town."

"Unacceptable," he snapped.

She cocked her head and planted her feet in a sturdy, immoveable stance. "I'm sorry you're going to have a difficult time with my decision."

"No, Sophie—I'm serious. It's not acceptable. If you move to town, I'm going to have to assign a security detail to you twenty-four/seven. That's going to cost me fifteen to twenty men."

Her eyes flew wide. She gave him a look filled with horror. "Oh no. You're not doing that. No security."

"Yes, security," he growled. "Put aside our personal relationship for the moment. You've become a major asset to us, and that means you've become a major target. If Isabeau got her hands on you, she would have you disemboweled for half the things you've done."

"Ugh!" She dug the heels of her hands into her eyes and turned her back to him.

She was so clearly upset his frustration with her intransigence evaporated. Walking up behind her, he slipped his arms around her and rested his cheek on top of her head.

"I do hear what you're saying," he said after a moment. "There are five acres here, and Annwyn is looking to see if she can buy more." He pointed in the direction of the lake, or at least where the lake had been and where it would be again. "When we restore the lake, we'll build you a place there. How would you like that?"

She sniffed and leaned back against him. "I'd like that a lot."

He swiveled her around to face the opposite direction. "And we'll build a house for me over there. We'll be as far apart as we can possibly be from each other, all right?"

"Oh for God's sake," she exclaimed. "That wasn't the point. I didn't mean for us to be *as far apart as we can possibly be from each other*, I just think it would be healthy to keep our own spaces so we don't kill each other while we work on developing our relat—"

He slipped a hand over her mouth, cutting off the flow of words, and said in her ear, "You need more orgasms, don't you?"

She froze. Then nodded.

"I thought so," he whispered. He bit lightly at her neck. "I might need a few more myself."

But where do we go? she asked.

He lifted his head. Urgency roughened his voice. "They'll have a tent set up for me."

He was correct. They did have a tent set up for him. As befitting a commander, it was a spacious and comfortable two-room affair, with a bed in one area and a sitting room with table and chairs for meetings in the other.

Tearing off their clothes, they fell into the bed, and together they made again that pure, shining creation.

A love bigger than anything else.

That was their respite. Their refuge.

In the following weeks, Nikolas's duties took long, demanding hours. He coordinated an intensive search for Morgan and the Hounds that had escaped the battle, which ultimately turned frustrating.

"Morgan was wounded twice with silver-tipped arrows," Nikolas said one night, burning off his frustration by pacing in the sitting area of his tent. "I saw it. He won't be able to heal those wounds magically. He's at his weakest right now, yet we can't find him."

"Are you saying Morgan is a lycanthrope?" Sophie set aside the book she was reading.

"He's not just the Captain of Isabeau's Hounds," Nikolas told her. "He is a Hound himself. That's how he's survived all these centuries. If he had remained a human, he would have died a very long time ago. He must have reached Avalon to disappear so completely."

She uncurled from her position on the settee and approached to rub his back. "Don't get discouraged," she said. "We've still made so many strides."

We, she'd said.

That small, simple word warmed him.

Turning, he pulled her into his arms and soaked in the comfort she offered. Not that long ago, he had lived a barren existence where there had been no comfort to be found. "Yes, we have made huge strides."

As the summer turned heavy, ripe and golden, the sale of the manor house went through, and Sophie became a wealthy woman. They celebrated by having a picnic on the floor of her new, four-room cottage. When the needs of the Dark Court became less urgent, she talked about searching for what happened to her family, but it was never with any sense of personal urgency. She knew her parents must be dead. She just wanted, someday, to discover their story.

Sophie and three Dark Court scholars began to inspect the contents of the library. It would take a while to get through everything. Many of the documents had been half eaten by mice, and none of it was organized. There were estate records, correspondence, bills of sale, and a hodgepodge of illustrated books that looked to be in the best shape, as they had been stored in trunks and apparently never handled or read.

The army engineers got scaffolding erected throughout the manor house to support the areas that had been weakened. Knowing they needed to complete many of the new buildings by winter, the barracks, communal halls, and small, individual houses were built quickly.

Those who had an affinity for land magic worked on healing the scars Morgan had created. They trucked in mature trees to replace copses and hired workers from town to handle electrical wiring, gas pipelines, and other modern Earth techniques that were foreign to the Dark Court engineers.

Nikolas had been concerned about how the townspeople in Westmarch would react to having such a strong Dark Court force on their doorstep, but they were such an economic boon to the area, everyone he talked to professed themselves delighted, especially when he coordinated with the local constabulary to increase security in the area.

Annwyn began to search for physicians who might be able to help with the malady that held Oberon in its icy grip. After talking with Sophie, Annwyn researched Kathryn Shaw's background and made an initial approach to hire her for a consultation on Oberon's condition.

Kathryn turned Annwyn down. While, Kathryn replied, she was sympathetic to the Dark Court's plight, as the official doctor for the sentinels who governed the Wyr demesne in New York, she had her own duty to attend to, and the time slippage between Lyonesse and Earth was too extreme.

Nikolas moved into his house and got a new car since his Porsche had disappeared. Sophie moved into hers. In theory, separate dwellings were a good idea, but the reality was, either he slept at her place, or she slept at his.

Unless they fought. Then five acres didn't seem like nearly enough space to put between them.

We, she had said.

Nikolas couldn't let it go.

One morning in her cottage, Sophie announced, "My visa is going to expire in a few weeks. According to Paul, I'm going to have to leave the UK and come back in. It shouldn't be that big of a deal. I'll show proof that I have an income and apply for residency."

"You don't have to go through all that." Nikolas gathered his clothing off the floor where they had dropped it the night before. "Apply for Dark Court citizenship. Annwyn will grant it in two seconds."

"Not going to happen." She shook her head.

He pulled his shirt over his head and frowned at her. "Why on earth not? You can still keep your American citizenship. You'll have more legal protections, and you won't have to leave and come back again."

"No, Nik. I'm not going to become a citizen of your demesne." She sat on the edge of the bed to tie her shoes.

"Of *my* demesne." What happened to *we*? "You need to think about this rationally."

"Oh, believe me," she said. "I have."

He planted his fists on his hips and glared at her. "Prove it."

"If I become a citizen of your demesne, I become subject to your laws. And because you're high up in the governance of the Dark Court, and you're the commander of the military, I become subject to your authority. That's not going to happen. You're overpowering enough as it is. Remember, I am my own sovereign state."

"That's ridiculous," he snapped. "Nobody is their own sovereign state. You're subject to all kinds of laws. Besides, when you marry me, you'll become a Dark Court citizen anyway."

She wagged a finger. "Nope. Nopers. Noperooni."

"Those aren't even words!" he shouted.

She fixed him with a glare. "First of all, nobody has *asked me* to marry him, and I don't randomly marry people because they order me to. Secondly, Sophie don't do nothing Sophie don't want. I'm not your employee, I'm not a soldier in your army, and I'm not going to become your subject. I am a *consultant* on *vacation*."

He strode around the bed to take her by the arms. "You're not on vacation! This—you—me—you made a commitment. Why wouldn't we get married?"

"Wait a minute. Maybe this will bring it home to you." She pulled out her phone. Holding on to his patience, he waited while she did some incomprehensible search. She stuck the screen of her phone into his face. "Here. This is me."

He watched a clip of an octopus running away along the ocean floor. The words, "Nope. *Nope. NOPE.*" appeared at the bottom of the screen.

"What the hell am I looking at?" he barked.

"It's a *nope* GIF. You've never seen a *nope* GIF? There are hundreds on the Internet." She smiled. "We literally never have to have this conversation again. You'll bring it up again, and I'll just send you a GIF. Subject closed."

But she didn't wait for the topic to come up again. She started sending him *nope* GIFs anyway. In one, a gorilla stood on his hind legs and walked off into a forest. In another, a cartoon character built a rocket, climbed inside, and shot to the moon. In yet another, a dog wearing a Christmas sweater ran under a sofa.

For some reason the dog was the last straw. When Nikolas's phone pinged and he saw that she had sent him yet another email, he stormed out of his office, which was located on the ground floor of his own house.

Sophie was supposed to be cooking dinner instead of harassing him. As he rounded the corner to the kitchen, he thundered, "Stop sending *nope* GIFs to my work email, or I'm going to plant my old-timey foot in your ass."

There was silence in the kitchen. Sophie had opened the back door, and Annwyn and Gawain stood just outside. All three of them stared at him as if he had lost his mind.

He understood why Annwyn and Gawain looked at him that way. It was Sophie's utterly unjust expression that sent him ballistic.

Gawain did that thing he did when he was trying to cover up a laugh by coughing into his hand.

Amusement gleamed in Annwyn's eyes. She said, "I understood only three words in that sentence."

Nikolas angled out his jaw and rubbed the edge of it. "I'd explain, but it's a long, exasperating story."

Sophie twirled a curl around her finger. "I'll leave you three alone to talk."

She slipped out the door before Nikolas could stop her. After he, Gawain, and Annwyn had settled their business, Nikolas went to hunt Sophie down.

He found her sprawled on her stomach, on the sofa in her living room. She had kicked off her shoes.

"I thought you were going to cook dinner," he said.

"I lost my impetus." When he sat on the floor and leaned his back against the sofa, she said, "I won't send any more *nope* GIFs to your work email."

"Thank you." He leaned his head back, and she slipped her fingers through his hair. No matter how much they argued, or how angry he got, her touch always soothed him. "Marry me."

"No."

He reached behind his head to capture her hand and brought it around to press a kiss to her palm. "Marry me."

"No, Nikolas."

She had dug her feet in. He would have to go at this from another angle. He said, "Tell me you don't want to marry me."

She sighed and turned on her side, curling around his shoulders. "I don't want to marry you."

As falsehoods went, that one was a whopper. It had neon lights all over it, blinking *LIE*. He began to smile.

Thinking through all her objections, he asked, "Will you marry me sometime in the future when we're both ready for it, if I get a special dispensation from Annwyn exempting you from my military and/or governance authority so you can remain a consultant on vacation and your own sovereign state?"

Because he was pretty sure she wasn't really objecting to dual citizenship.

Rising on her elbow, she said in his ear, "That was awfully wordy."

"You had an awful lot of objections," he told her.

"Do you know what I heard?" She pressed a kiss to his jaw.

He turned his face toward her, relishing the caress. "What's that?"

"I heard you ask me," she whispered. She slipped an arm over his shoulder and hugged him.

His voice turned husky. "I haven't heard you answer yet."

"Yes."

He twisted around to cup her face, kissing her lingeringly as he stroked her cheek. "That's my Sophie."

She nuzzled into him. "Now that we've got that settled, what do you think about having some orgasms to celebrate?"

He smiled. "Best idea I've heard all day."

Thank you!

Dear Readers,

Thank you for reading *Moonshadow*! I hope you enjoyed reading about Sophie and Nikolas—they've become one of my very favorite couples.

Would you like to stay in touch and hear about new releases? You can:

- Sign up for my monthly email at: www.theaharrison.com
- Follow me on Twitter at @TheaHarrison
- Like my Facebook page at facebook.com/TheaHarrison

Reviews help other readers find the books they like to read. I appreciate each and every review, whether positive or negative.

Happy reading!
~Thea

Coming Soon:

Spellbound
Available Summer 2017

Look for these titles from Thea Harrison

GAME OF SHADOWS SERIES
Published by Berkley

Rising Darkness
Falling Light

ROMANCES UNDER THE NAME AMANDA CARPENTER

E-published by Samhain Publishing
(original publication by Harlequin Mills & Boon)

A Deeper Dimension
The Wall
A Damaged Trust
The Great Escape
Flashback
Rage
Waking Up
Rose-Coloured Love
Reckless
The Gift of Happiness
Caprice
Passage of the Night
Cry Wolf
A Solitary Heart
The Winter King

CPSIA information can be obtained
at www.ICGtesting.com
Printed in the USA
LVOW13s2302080817
544321LV00009B/112/P